GEORGE ELIOT AND ITALY

George Eliot and Italy

Literary, Cultural and Political Influences from Dante to the *Risorgimento*

Andrew Thompson
University of Genoa, Italy

First published in Great Britain 1998 by
MACMILLAN PRESS LTD
Houndmills, Basingstoke, Hampshire RG21 6XS and London
Companies and representatives throughout the world

A catalogue record for this book is available from the British Library.

ISBN 0–333–69456–2

First published in the United States of America 1998 by
ST. MARTIN'S PRESS, INC.,
Scholarly and Reference Division,
175 Fifth Avenue, New York, N.Y. 10010

ISBN 0–312–17651–1

Library of Congress Cataloging-in-Publication Data
Thompson, Andrew, 1962–
George Eliot and Italy : literary, cultural, and political
influences from Dante to the Risorgimento / Andrew Thompson.
p.   cm.
Includes bibliographical references and index.
ISBN 0–312–17651–1 (cloth)
1. Eliot, George, 1819–1880—Knowledge—Italy.   2. Eliot, George,
1819–1880—Political and social views.   3. Political fiction,
English—History and criticism.   4. Eliot, George, 1819–1880.
Daniel Deronda.   5. Dante Alighieri, 1265–1321—Influence.
6. English fiction—Italian influences.   7. Eliot, George,
1819–1880.   Romola.   8. Italy—In literature.
PR4692.I82T47   1997
823'.8—dc21
                                                                97–16082
                                                                     CIP

© Andrew Thompson 1998

This book is printed on paper suitable for recycling and made from fully managed and sustained forest sources.

10   9   8   7   6   5   4   3   2   1
07   06   05   04   03   02   01   00   99   98

Printed and bound in Great Britain by
Antony Rowe Ltd, Chippenham, Wiltshire

This book, *che m'ha fatto per più anni macro,* is for my parents

Contents

List of Abbreviations

Biography	Haight, G.S., *George Eliot: a Biography*, Penguin, Harmondsworth 1985 (1968)
Cross	*George Eliot's Life as Related in Her Letters and Journals*. Arranged and Edited by Her Husband, J.W. Cross, (3 vols), Edinburgh and London: Blackwood & Sons 1885
Extracts	'Interesting Extracts' manuscript 14, The Folger Shakespeare Library, Washington 3, DC
GE	George Eliot
GE Diary	MS diary for 1879 (Berg Collection, New York Public Library) MS diary for 1880 (Yale)
GE Journal	MS Journal, 'Recollections of Italy' 1860 (Yale MS 2)
GHL	George Henry Lewes
GHL Journal	MS journal, number XI, April 1st, 1859 – January 1st, 1866 (Yale)
Letters	*The George Eliot Letters*, G.S. Haight (ed.), 9 vols, New Haven and London 1954–78
Notebook 1854–79	*George Eliot: A Writer's Notebook 1854–1879, and Uncollected Writings* edited by J. Wiesenfarth (Charlottesville, Virginia: University of Virginia, 1981)
Theophrastus	*Theophrastus Such; Essays and Leaves from a Notebook* Blackwood, Edinburgh and London 1901
WR	*The Westminster Review*

Acknowledgements

The best guide to the many debts I owe in the writing of this book will be found in the Bibliography, though there were many other influences, of some of which I am probably not even aware. I would, however, like to single out a number of works as being of particular importance and without which the task facing me would have been far more daunting. I am particularly indebted to Romana Cortese's unpublished Ph.D. thesis *George Eliot and Dante* and to the invaluable painstaking work of Joseph Wiesenfarth, William Baker, J.C. Pratt and V.A. Neufeld in producing annotated editions of George Eliot's notebooks. I hope my debt to these scholars has been sufficiently acknowledged. I would like to thank my father, Professor Doug Thompson of the Italian Department of the University of Hull UK, for his comments and suggestions concerning Dante and the nineteenth-century Italian context and for the many discussions which helped stimulate and focus some of the ideas in the book, as well as for much help and advice of a practical nature. I am grateful to both my parents for being patient, supportive and critical readers of the various drafts of the manuscript. I would also like to thank Dr Graham Handley for his valuable comments on the later drafts of some chapters and Professor Giuseppe Sertoli of the University of Genoa for his interest and encouragement throughout the project. Thanks, too, to Charmian Hearne, Sheila Chatten and the staff at Macmillan for seeing the work smoothly through the press. Special thanks are due to Patrizia Vadalà and to Nadia Santini. Any faults and shortcomings in the book are of course entirely my own.

ANDREW THOMPSON

*... the pathos of his country's lot pierced the youthful soul
of Mazzini, because, like Dante's, his blood was fraught
with the kinship of Italian greatness, his imagination filled
with a majestic past that wrought itself into a majestic future.*
(George Eliot, *Impressions of Theophrastus Such*)

Italy was little more to her than a vast museum, ...
(Lord Acton, *Nineteenth Century Fiction* 17 (1885))

Introduction

Several years ago the critic W.J. Harvey noted how, although the novels of George Eliot embody a total response, only a small part of her intellectual range is actually represented in any single work: 'one has, very often, the feeling that she is working well within the limits of her mind and that what is left, as it were, unwritten in the margin affects that which is there on the printed page'.[1] This comment is as true for the Italian elements in her work as it is for any other influences. This book is about the ways in which Eliot's contact with Italy and its culture affects that which appears on the page.

George Eliot went to Italy on six occasions, spending a total of over six months on Italian soil and travelling widely in the country at a time of national regeneration. She learned Italian in order to be able to read in the language and wrote about the country, first in her journalism and then in her fiction. Our reading of Eliot's fiction can, I believe, be enriched by an awareness of this Italian dimension, and especially by a close focus on the work of Dante Alighieri and on the *Risorgimento*. This study takes particularly these two loci as its two broad areas of inquiry and argues that Dante and the nineteenth-century cultural and political revival were highly productive for Eliot's *oeuvre*.

The first chapter of this book establishes the broad background for Eliot's engagement with Italy. It deals with the years of the Italian national revival, with British attitudes to Italy in the years leading up to the Unification of the country in 1861, and with the importance of Dante in Italy and Britain in the first half of the nineteenth century. George Eliot's contact with Italy and its culture in the years before the completion of *Romola* is then examined in Chapter 2. In dealing with Eliot's trips to Italy, my treatment has been deliberately selective, and I have preferred to concentrate on the earlier journeys which, to my mind, better establish the Italian context for her work, rather than attempt to give an exhaustive account of her Italian travel or reading. Thus, I have tended not to give detailed descriptions of Eliot's movements within Italy or of the works of art and the monuments she stopped to admire with Lewes and Cross: the 1864 and 1869 trips, for example, are mentioned only in passing. This is not, then, primarily a book about George Eliot *in* Italy.

1

Much of the evidence for Eliot's contact with Italian life and culture comes from her notebooks and letters. Eliot took down well over a hundred quotations from Dante in her notebooks, and many of these are identifiable as direct influences in her fiction. Often these jottings draw attention to a particular image or phrase, but sometimes they also serve a mnemonic function as reminders of whole episodes from the *Divine Comedy*. Eliot came to know the Florentine poet well, and four of the chapters in this book deal specifically with Eliot's engagement with Dante and the ways in which she assimilates him into her own work. Dante is all but absent in the early work, though in the later fiction, from *Romola* onwards, he becomes an increasingly important presence (Chapter 5). In her Italian novel, Dante's function is to provide an historical perspective from which to view the Florence of Savonarola's Republic and he is also present as a moral touchstone against which to measure character, and as a lodestone to help readers keep their moral bearings in the treacherous world of fifteenth-century Florence. There are too, I argue, a number of broad parallels to be drawn between Dante's epic journey in the *Comedy* and that of Eliot's heroine in *Romola*. There is however a sense that Eliot was experimenting: she is occasionally insecure in her handling of Dante, who was still being written in or out of the text at quite a late stage, and there is also, I think, some slight forcing in the uses to which he is put.

In her next novel, *Felix Holt, the Radical*, Eliot incorporates allusion – in imagery, echoes and scenes which transform episodes from the *Comedy* – and direct quotation to create a 'moral landscape' which sometimes closely parallels Dante's (Chapter 6). In Eliot's moral universe, growth through suffering requires a Dantean balance between judgement and compassion, though Dante is again also present as a moral touchstone to guide readers' responses to the text. In *Middlemarch*, by contrast, Eliot allows one of her important characters consistently to *misread* through Dante: Will Ladislaw, I suggest in Chapter 7, indulges in a literary form of courtly worship of Dorothea in which Eliot structures his emotions upon Dante's narrative scheme in the *Vita Nuova* and the Earthly Paradise of the *Divine Comedy*. Indeed, by the end of the novel, Dorothea becomes transfigured and takes on some of the attributes of a secularized Victorian Beatrice.

In her last novel, Eliot's assimilation of the *Divine Comedy* is similar in many ways to that in *Felix Holt*. Again she uses the

Comedy as a means both of creating and of bringing into focus her moral landscape, and to illustrate her great theme of moral growth through suffering (Chapter 8). *Daniel Deronda* draws on the Florentine poet more systematically than any of her earlier fiction, consciously paralleling Dante in the Gwendolen narrative of infernal then purgatorial experience to the extent that the heroine becomes a Dante-pilgrim guided by the Virgil-like Daniel. The *Comedy*, I argue, becomes a central metaphor for Gwendolen's moral growth in *Daniel Deronda*, though there are also significant departures from Dante where Eliot, on occasion, deliberately writes against the expectations aroused by Dante's text, thereby destabilizing her own Dantean metaphor and undermining the linear reading of the heroine's progress which it appears to offer.

Dante was also an essential part of nineteenth-century Italian nationalist mythology, as the 'prophet' and 'father' through whom the country first found a voice and an identity, so that my discussion of Dante overlaps to some extent with the other area of inquiry in this study, namely the impact which Eliot's contact with a culture infused with the struggle for national identity and liberation from foreign oppression made on her work. Eliot's taste for mythmaking is well known, and she drew on classical, biblical and folk myths extensively, pressing them into the service of her own vision. Another rich source of myths is present in the powerful mythology of the Italian *Risorgimento*, which drew on a matrix of references to Italian culture, from Roman times to the recent past, to create an overarching myth of the slow but inevitable growth of 'Italia' to achieve independence and full identity. Five chapters in this study look at Eliot's fiction in relation to the mythology of the national revival.

In Chapter 3, I argue that in 'Mr Gilfil's Love Story' from *Scenes of Clerical Life*, Eliot makes the story of her Italian exile (the orphaned Caterina) a metaphor for the position of women in British patriarchal society. However, unlike the heroines of Mme de Staël's *Corinne* and Elizabeth Barrett Browning's *Aurora Leigh*, who are empowered as artists in an Italy imaged as a feminine realm of 'romance', Eliot's Caterina is denied this empowerment through her art, and in England her singing voice is marginalized and finally silenced altogether. By the time she had finished *Romola*, however, the Unification of Italy had already taken place. In Chapter 4 I argue that evidence of this momentous historical change in the seven years since 'Mr Gilfil's Love Story' is seen in the way Eliot situates the six years of the turbulent history of Savonarola's Florence within the wider context of the great arc of *Risorgimento* history leading to the fulfilment of the Italian 'prophecy'. The novel's title, for example, is a reminder of the foundation of Rome by the mythical Romulus (Romolo) and, after her struggles, Romola herself is allowed to emerge as an 'Italia' figure, a *Risorgimento* icon symbolizing maturity, achieved independence and fully realized identity. A clear division emerges in Eliot's allusion to Italian literature in *Romola* between those authors who are interpreted as 'moral' agents (Dante, Petrarch, Savonarola and Machiavelli) placed within and contributing to the 'great tradition' leading to the birth of Italy, and the 'immoral' or at best 'amoral' writers (Lorenzo de'Medici and Luigi Pulci) whose voices Eliot eventually silences.

In the England of 1829–32 in *Middlemarch*, however, Italian history could not be interpreted according to any 'binding theory' such as that of the *Risorgimento*. Dorothea is unable to interpret Rome which, in its 'stupendous fragmentariness', remains alien, vast and illegible and can only be related negatively to her own experience, as a correlative for her ignorance and for Casaubon's life's work, his dead 'Key to all Mythologies'. Dorothea's response may be set against those of Ladislaw, the painter Naumann, and those of the Italian *Risorgimento*, all of which bring the past into vital, living relation to the present. British opinions of Italians in the 1820s and 1830s were often far from flattering, and indeed, Eliot's Middlemarchers mobilize a range of anti-Italian prejudices to 'place' Ladislaw, the outsider challenging established socio-cultural codes, to defuse the threat this implies and to bring him within known frames of reference (Chapter 7). By contrast with Dorothea's failure to do so in *Middlemarch*, I argue that Italian cultural artefacts are assimilated as living knowledge speaking forcefully to the present in *Daniel Deronda* (Chapters 9 and 10). Eliot sketches out the course of Italian history, from a pre-*Risorgimento* state of statuesque passivity and subjection to the moment when the Italian prophecy of independence was about to be fulfilled, incorporates musical settings of texts by Dante and Leopardi charged with significance within a *Risorgimento* context, and alludes to the contemporary mythologization of the 'prophet of modern Italy', Mazzini. The myths and artefacts of nineteenth-century Italian nationalism are also part of a hermeneutic strategy aimed at familiarizing a little known Jewish culture, and also constitute an analogue with predictive force for Jewish national aspirations within the novel. The

Italian experience of national regeneration is also allowed to stand as paradigmatic and prescriptive of Eliot's humanist vision of nationalism, one which she opposes to the aggressive nationalism and arrogant imperialism she saw emerging in Britain and Europe in the 1870s.

Eliot went back both to Italy and to Dante in the last years of her life. She reread the *Inferno* and *Purgatorio* with her husband John Cross and Dante is present in her letters and in *Theophrastus Such*. In the final chapter of this study I consider the mythmaking surrounding Eliot herself in which friends and admirers, and later critics and biographers, likened her to 'il divino poèta'. Eliot did not resist, and occasionally courted, this comparison with Dante and seems herself to have identified with various aspects of the Romantic and Victorian Dante, with the sage and world-weary exile. Dante also played a role in bringing Eliot and Cross together and in shaping their relationship, with the pilgrim Cross being guided by the wise Eliot on their Italian honeymoon.

George Eliot kept returning to Italy and to its literature, both for renovation and for new inspiration. This book is written in the conviction that the country, its culture, and its fate as an emerging nation mattered a great deal to her. Today the literature and the events of the *Risorgimento* no longer have the same power to move and sway readers as they did in the heady days of the struggle for freedom, for the energies they contain have gradually diminished and been lost as the period has faded further into history. Yet Italy stirred George Eliot – sometimes passionately – both emotionally and intellectually, and this sustained engagement with the life of that country must be taken into account in reading her work.

1

Dante, the *Risorgimento* and the British: the Italian Background

The first part of this chapter traces historical events in Italy during the *Risorgimento*, considers what Italy had meant to the British before 1815 and examines their reactions to the events of the *Risorgimento* in order to provide a broad historical framework within which George Eliot's engagement with Italy and with Italian culture may be discussed. The second part deals in particular with the figure of Dante Alighieri, with his significance for Italians in this period and with the creation of a *Risorgimento* Dante 'mythology'. I then consider some of the ways in which readings of Dante influenced British culture in the first half of the nineteenth century and try to give some idea of the kind of knowledge of Dante with which the educated reader might have come to George Eliot's fiction in the 1860s and 1870s. Without claiming to give an exhaustive account of the Italian *Risorgimento* or of Italian and British intellectual engagement with Dante, the present chapter aims to provide a framework and to offer some coordinates to help orient the reader in the discussion which follows. This being the case, a number of themes and ideas which are merely sketched out here will be given fuller treatment later on when examining Eliot's work. This chapter, then, is not specifically about George Eliot. Those who are already familiar with the Italian history of this period and with Dante's works may wish to move on directly to the second chapter.

The term 'Risorgimento', which can be translated as a 'rising again', 'resurgence', 'revival', or as Eliot herself translated it 'regeneration',[1] was coined by the poet-patriot Vittorio Alfieri (1749–1803). It refers to that moment in Italian history when Italy became a 'nation' and a part of the 'modern' world. The period of the *Risorgimento*, the years from the Congress of Vienna (1815) to Italian Unification in 1860–1, but which in this study includes the decade up to 1870 and the final inclusion of Rome as the capital of Italy, saw the collapse of the *Ancien Régime* and the replacement of local or regional identities by a single national culture. In addition, the process of transformation from a rural to a modern urban society, from a feudal to a capitalist economy, got under way. These were also the years in which the three 'founders' of modern Italy, Giuseppe Mazzini, Giuseppe Garibaldi and Count Camillo Benso di Cavour emerged, along with the defining political ideas, liberalism, nationalism and republicanism.

The word *Risorgimento* also refers back to a common Italian past, which came to be idealized by those who believed that Italy could be liberated from its present subjection through resistance. We can talk of the creation of a *Risorgimento* mythology[2] made up of a series of interrelated myths, often built upon or including certain significant historical individuals (Pope Gregory VII, Arnold of Brescia, Dante Alighieri, Cola di Rienzo, Machiavelli, Savonarola and Alfieri for example), particular texts like Dante's *Monarchia* and the *Divina Commedia*, or important historical events like the 'Sicilian Vespers' of 1272. Those seeking to make Italians conscious of their past during the *Risorgimento* period looked to history and made heroes of those who in some way had nurtured Italian greatness, conceived Italy as a single unified territory or had resisted foreign oppression through their words and deeds. Many of the myths created or revived by *Risorgimento* apologists were variously pressed into the service of nationalist ideologies: myths of the Roman Republic, the Holy Roman Empire, of the medieval free City-states (communes), the Renaissance and the myth of the papacy. In addition to its importance for the Italian *Risorgimento*, this latter myth was of great significance for millions outside Italy as well as to the great European powers. The Pope's territory was claimed by the whole of Christianity, and the Papal States, lying in the middle of the Italian peninsula, were inhabited by a population which racially, culturally and linguistically (though not socially or economically) was one of the most homogeneous in Europe.

The Unification of Italy has long been seen as a natural and inevitable consequence of the *Risorgimento* by Italian historians.[3] Recent British historians, however, have attempted to deconstruct this Italian interpretation, arguing that the exact relationship between the *Risorgimento* and Unification is very difficult to determine. Mack Smith's view, which 'demystif[ies] the "legends" of Risorgimento historiography' is one shared by many historians and the centrality of the *Risorgimento* has been questioned by revisionist historiography, so much so indeed, that 'the Risorgimento may well be an outmoded historical concept'.[4] Nevertheless, as Lucy Riall recognizes, it remains true that 'some belief or claim to embody a "resurgent" Italy motivated Italian liberals and was used to demoralize Restoration usurpers'.[5] What is important for the purposes of this study, however, is not the truth or otherwise of the *Risorgimento* 'myth' of a national revival leading inevitably to unification, but its potency: it provided a rallying cry for Italian patriots and their supporters and entered into the currency of informed opinion on Italian affairs in Britain. The persistence and impassioned defence of the idea of a *Risorgimento* by historians in the twentieth century is further evidence of its life and energy and of its appeal as an explanatory principle. For a writer of fiction like George Eliot, who was drawn to myths and herself given to myth-making,[6] the Italian *Risorgimento* provided a rich source of material (events, figures, images and key texts) which could be incorporated into her own fictions to generate precise meanings locally within her texts, but which also resonate outwards suggestively towards the larger body of myth with which they are connected. An appreciation of this generalized myth (or group of myths) of the *Risorgimento*, tracing the origins of a national consciousness struggling to express itself from the earliest times of Roman and medieval history, developing as a literary and cultural process of a spiritual nature and as an affirmation of collective and individual autonomy from the beginning of the nineteenth century until 1859, and ultimately leading to the 'birth' of Italy in 1860, is central to an understanding of that engagement with Italian life and culture which became so productive for Eliot's fiction. Only rarely do we find anything approaching 'political' analysis of the Italian situation in her writings, this being an activity largely alien to her own cast of mind, and one which is (sometimes notoriously) eschewed in her fiction. Politics, both for Eliot and for those historians and publicists who had assimilated the teleological assumptions underlying *Risorgimento* mythology, were only one factor among many, only one part of the 'invisible motion' leading to 'visible birth' as Eliot was herself to put it in her poem 'How Lisa Loved the King' (see Chapter 7), and the myths of history which the *Risorgimento* offered were therefore congenial to her and could be made to serve her own meliorism. Besides, any detached assessment, any questioning of the myths the *Risorgimento* offered, any probing of the social, political and economic realities behind the nationalist rhetorics in this far off southern European country, was hampered by a simple lack of reliable information. George Eliot, whose view of Italy was formed through engaging with the cultural productions of the *Risorgimento* and nourished by the highly charged climate in Britain surrounding the 'Italian Question' in the 1850s and beyond, did not feel the need to probe the myths of the Italian *Risorgimento* too deeply, but rather allowed them to stand in a causal relation to that most 'miraculous' event in European history, the Unification of Italy.[7]

THE ITALIAN *RISORGIMENTO*

After the fall of Napoleon, the Congress of Vienna (September 1814– 1815) largely restored the Italian states of the eighteenth century. Absolutist regimes were established in the Kingdom of Sardinia-Piedmont, in the independent duchies of Tuscany, Modena and Parma, in the Papal States and in the Kingdom of the Two Sicilies. The ancient republics of Genoa and Venice were not restored, however, the former being given to Piedmont and the latter to the Hapsburg kingdom of Lombardo-Venetia. The settlement brought Austrian sovereignty into the richest area of Italy (Lombardo-Venetia) and Austrian influence into much of the rest of Italy. Relatives of the Hapsburgs were recognized as the rulers of Tuscany and Modena, Metternich placed an Austrian garrison in Ferrara and protective alliances were signed with the Papal States and the Kingdom of the Two Sicilies.

The achievements of the Napoleonic regimes in Italy were appreciated by the educated professional classes who were already familiar with the ideas of the Enlightenment and the reforms of Grand Duke Leopold (1765–90) and Joseph II (1765–90) in Tuscany and the Austrian provinces. The comparatively enlightened administrations of the Napoleonic era were swept away everywhere except in Tuscany, and the restoration was accepted as inevitable by most of the politically conscious. The only real resistance to the new regimes came from those ready to join secret societies like the *Carbonari*. Insurrections planned by the Carbonari in Naples and Piedmont, aimed at securing the constitutions which had been denied, broke out in 1820 and 1821 but were suppressed with the aid of the Austrian army. Ten years later there were risings in central Italy in the duchies of Modena and Parma, and in Bologna and the towns of the Papal Legations, the latter sparked off by intolerable clerical misgovernment and the corrupt judicial system of Popes Pius VIII and Gregory XVI. These were likewise crushed by Austrian and French armies. One of the Carbonari members involved in the 1831 insurrections, for which he was briefly imprisoned, was the young Giuseppe Mazzini (1805–72). After his release he founded a new secret society, 'Young Italy', from exile in Marseilles (1831), with the aim of replacing the older groups which had been largely discredited by the failures of 1831. The immediate aim of 'Young Italy' was to build up a network of followers of Mazzini who would prepare the ground and be ready for revolution. A series of Mazzinian uprisings were also doomed to failure in 1832 and 1834, while the infiltration of 'Young Italy' by police spies and its subsequent repression forced Mazzini to seek refuge in London in 1837. Nevertheless, the growing support for 'Young Italy' during the 1830s and 1840s is evidence of the immense importance of Mazzini as an educator of young, mainly middle class Italians towards a national consciousness.

Alongside an anti-clerical Mazzinian nationalism, there arose in the 1840s a more moderate nationalist movement. Among its main figures were Cesare Balbo and Massimo D'Azeglio whose works were highly successful in Italy. While Balbo advocated a federal solution to the organization of Italy, D'Azeglio emphasized the need for continued non-violent agitation for reform. Both, however, recognized that force would probably be necessary to drive the Austrians out of Italy. Others looked to the Pope to lead a regeneration of Italy. Foremost among the figures of the neo-Guelph movement (named after the pro-papal party in the Italy of the Middle Ages) was Vincenzo Gioberti, who suggested that the princes should unite into a confederacy under the presidency of the Pope as a means of reversing the present political subjection and restoring the past historical and cultural greatness of Italy. The election of the liberal-minded Pope Pius IX in 1846 seemed to augur well for neo-Guelphism. He immediately granted a political amnesty, reformed the judiciary and granted freedom to the press. By 1848, Pius IX had become identified with the cause of nationalism in the eyes of many Italians, but speedy disillusionment followed, on his refusal to be drawn into a war against Austria.

The year 1848 saw a series of risings within the Italian peninsula. The January revolution in Sicily and the liberal movement in Naples forced Ferdinand II to grant a constitution. In Tuscany a constitution was granted in February and a *Statuto* was introduced by King Charles Albert in Piedmont. Agitation in Milan culminated in the 'Five Days' with a civilian revolutionary army forcing the Austrians to withdraw to the defensive fortresses guarding the entry to Austria. In Venice a successful revolution led to the restoration of the Republic, and a republic was established in Florence after the flight of Grand Duke Leopold. Piedmont declared war on Austria, but the failure of Pius IX to lend his support, the re-establishment of Ferdinand II in Naples, and a crushing defeat at Custozza obliged Piedmont to withdraw its claims to the Austrian provinces. Meanwhile, Pius IX fled from Rome to Gaeta in January 1849. A democratic Roman Republic with an executive (the Triumvir) which included Mazzini was established and, in the six months it lasted, carried out a number of genuine reforms. Though defended by Giuseppe Garibaldi, it was defeated in July 1849 by Louis-Napoleon, who was determined to restore the Pope. Grand Duke Leopold was restored in Florence, while the Venetian Republic eventually succumbed to the Austrians at the end of August. Meanwhile in Piedmont a second declaration of war against Austria had led to overwhelming defeat at Novara, leaving Lombardy and Venice to Austria, and eventually leading to the abdication of Charles Albert in favour of his son Victor Emmanuel II.

The failures of 1848–9 did not signify a wholesale return to the past, however. Garibaldi's epic exploits had fuelled the growing nationalist mythology and the short-lived republics had provided a taste for a return to the past glory of the medieval communes. In Piedmont the *Statuto* survived, and under the guidance of Camillo Benso di Cavour (1810–61), a series of domestic reforms was introduced to reduce Church influence on the State, strengthen the economy and turn the *Statuto* into a more parliamentary constitution. The important part played by Piedmont in the Crimea and Cavour's presence at the Congress of Paris (1856) ensured that the 'Italian Question' was debated by the European powers and confirmed Piedmont as an important player in European diplomacy. The immediate effect of the debate was merely the withdrawal of British and French recognition from Ferdinand II of Naples, but Cavour also obtained closer diplomatic links with Napoleon who had already decided to take up the Italian Question, and whose resolve was only strengthened by an assassination attempt by an Italian patriot in 1858.[8]

Although until 1859 Cavour did not believe that a fully united Italy was politically possible, he negotiated with Napoleon to try to gain Lombardy and Venice in return for ceding Nice and Savoy to France. The alliance was formalized at Plombières (1859) and Austria was provoked into a war in which Victor Emmanuel, aided by Napoleon III, gained Lombardy but not Venice, after the bloody battles of Magenta and Solferino. Cavour himself resigned in protest at Napoleon's failure to continue the war. During this 'Second War of Independence' risings organized by the 'Italian National Society' peacefully removed the rulers of Tuscany, Parma and Modena and, upon Cavour's return to office in 1860, Napoleon agreed to the Piedmontese annexation of the Papal Legations in return for the cession of Nice and Savoy.

In April of that year, the famous 'Journey of the Thousand' led by Garibaldi took place. The 'Thousand' landed at Marsala and by the end of May Garibaldi was in control of Sicily. Moving northwards, and after initial defeat at Volturno, they effectively destroyed the Kingdom of Naples. Garibaldi's men then marched towards Rome, a move which in Cavour's opinion would only provoke intervention from the French Emperor as Catholic defender of the Pope. To forestall Garibaldi, Cavour organized a Piedmontese invasion of Rome (September 1860) and when Victor Emmanuel and Garibaldi met at Teano on October 26th the revolutionary general handed over the conquered territories to Piedmont. The Piedmontese Constitution was extended to the whole of the territory and the new kingdom was proclaimed in March 1861 under Victor Emmanuel II with Turin as its capital. Cavour briefly became Prime Minister, but died suddenly at the age of 51. In the south, however, a five-year guerrilla war was waged against the new rulers of the Kingdom of Italy and in any case unification was incomplete. Rome was still occupied by French troops and Venice was in the hands of the Austrians. Garibaldi again attempted to take Rome in 1862, but was halted by Victor Emmanuel's army at Aspromonte. The French did withdraw their garrison in 1864, however, when Italy agreed to protect Rome and to move its capital from Turin to Florence.

After Aspromonte, Mazzinians concentrated their efforts on agitating for the annexation of Venice, which was finally gained after the Austro–Prussian War in which Italy sided with Prussia. The alliance with Bismarck, diplomatic negotiations with Napoleon and the Prussian victory over the Austrians at Sadowa proved enough to ensure the Austrian withdrawal from Venice. Garibaldi's further attempt upon Rome provoked the return of the French who were to hold the city until 1870, when troops were withdrawn to fight in the Franco–Prussian war. After the French surrender at Sedan, an Italian army defeated papal forces and took possession of the 'eternal city', leaving the Pope in possession of the Vatican. With the restoration of Rome to its rightful status as the country's capital, the Unification of Italy, 'the most striking of the successes of nineteenth-century nationalism,' was complete.[9]

ITALY AND THE BRITISH

During the second half of the seventeenth century, once the Renaissance had been absorbed in Britain, Italian influence lessened in literature and Italian authors began to be replaced by French. In some areas though, and in spite of the widespread condemnation in Puritan England of Italian morals and behaviour and of a corrupt Church, Italian influences remained, so that to the cultured Englishman in the mid eighteenth century, Italy had become the country of Palladian architecture, opera, and of the Grand Tour. Italian opera became well established in England after 1711, when Händel arrived in London. The works of Porpora, Vinci, Veracini and Scarlatti were popular and were later followed by those of Paesiello, Cimarosa and Cherubini. The popularity of Italian opera also encouraged the study of the Italian language, in particular of the *libretti* of Pietro Metastasio (1698–1782), who was usually the first, and often the only, Italian poet tackled by the British learners. From 1818 until the early 1830s Rossini dominated Italian opera in England, where his music achieved an unrivalled popularity and influenced other composers of both operatic and instrumental music. Bellini, Donizetti, Mercadante and Pacini were also popular. In the 1830s, the British began to turn to the Germans and to French and British composers and the Italian opera fell from fashion, although Verdi made some impact. The fortunes of the Italian singers (Catalani, Camporesi, Grisi and La Blanche for example) who dominated the opera in these years, attracting large audiences and large fees, reflected those of the Italian opera itself, though until at least mid-century the Italian opera still had a sizeable following. The activities of the numerous teachers of Italian likewise suffered with the decline in the fashion for Italian opera. British travellers in Italy both before and after 1815 were usually appalled by the poor state of the Italian theatres, the poor standards of performance and the fact that Italians treated the opera as primarily a social occasion. The presence of Italian opera is felt both in Eliot's early fiction 'Mr Gilfil's Love Story' from *Scenes of Clerical Life*, where the heroine is only able to express her emotions through Italian arias, and in *Daniel Deronda*, where a number of Italian composers are specifically mentioned and musical settings of Italian texts play an important role.

The Grand Tour, an important part of the education of well-bred Englishmen in the eighteenth century, usually had Italy as its farthest destination. Travellers admired the wild, untamed prospects of the Italian countryside and its sublime and mysterious landscapes were worked into numberless gothic novels. The Grand Tour often included the study of painting, sculpture and architecture from Classical, Medieval and Renaissance Italy, and many works by Italians were brought back to England to furnish the numerous country houses built in the Palladian style during the eighteenth century. In Eliot's 'Mr Gilfil's Love Story', for example, Sir Christopher returns from Italy with various art treasures and begins remodelling Cheverel Manor in the Palladian style. During the Napoleonic Wars (1793–1815), it was no longer possible to travel on the continent and contacts between England and Italy were consequently weakened. A number of important works on Italy were published in Britain, however, and in these years there was a large influx of works of art removed from Italy to escape the ravages of war. After 1815, and until about 1830, the British went to Italy in large numbers and the Italianate fashion became 'Italomania'.

There seem to have been two prevailing views of contemporary Italians voiced by British travellers in the period, though the initial sentimental 'romantic' cast of mind gave way after 1815 to a more realistic approach which is reflected in accounts of the practical difficulties of travel. Expressions were often either of strong sympathy or strong antipathy. Visitors were struck by the contrasts to be found in the 'land of gigantic ruins overgrown by verdure and crawled under by monks, beggars and *dilettanti*'[10] and a comment by Beolchi, summarizes popular belief well: 'The Italian was considered capable of great excellence in the fine arts, and especially in music and singing, but cowardly and liable to knife you in the back'.[11] There was little real contact between the British and Italians in Italy, and the wide social and cultural differences opened up space for the exercise of prejudices. English observers often found the Italians ignorant, superstitious, licentious, dirty and dishonest.[12] The Italian character was found to be impassioned, impulsive and bloodthirsty. The already strong anti-Catholic bias among English travellers was frequently confirmed when they saw Rome and witnessed the superstition and misery of the Italian peasantry. Many political exiles in Britain, including Foscolo, Rossetti and Panizzi, had flown from papal oppression, and many more, including Mazzini, were strongly anti-Catholic. Catholicism, then, being strongly associated with the present decadence of Italy, probably helped to reinforce the negative view of Italians held by the English, though the revival of Catholicism itself in England after 1829 did something to counter this. A writer in the *Edinburgh Review* in 1840 gives voice to both cultural differences and current prejudices:

> ... the Italians are Papists – they spit on the floor – the peasantry draw their knives when they quarrel – the gentlemen do not give dinners; in all classes of society there prevail, as in every other nation in the south, certain habits and forms of speech which offend our Teutonic delicacy – the ladies have loud voices – the lower orders are subject to gross superstitions – the upper ranks are destitute of that dignified reserve which we think both becoming and necessary, ...[13]

This view of Italians crystallized into a strongly negative national stereotype (one to which we shall return in Chapter 3 on 'Mr Gilfil's Love Story' and Chapter 7 on *Middlemarch*), which it took many years and the events of the *Risorgimento* itself to break. A very different view was expressed by others who felt it necessary to defend the Italians from the exaggerated charges levelled against them by their detractors. Their emotional temperaments and the artistic abilities elicited sympathy from Lord Byron, one of the few Englishmen to know Italians well, who praised 'the fire of their genius'. The political situation and the widespread poverty and degradation caused by oppression and misgovernment drew both sympathy for Italy and condemnation of the Austrians.

There was also travel in the other direction, from Italy to England, as Italians came either to work or to escape oppressive regimes. Most of the political exiles who found refuge in England arrived after the failure of Neapolitan and Piedmontese *Carbonaro* uprisings of 1820–1. By the mid 1820s there were several hundred political exiles in England, some of whom had come via France or via

Switzerland, where the government was soon under pressure from
Austria to stop harbouring exiles. Others came after the failure of
later risings in the early 1830s and Mazzini came in 1837. Although
there were a relatively small number of Italians in Britain their
influence was considerable. Among them were a number of distinguished literary figures. Ugo Foscolo, who arrived in 1816, published critical works on Italian literature; the poet Giovanni Berchet
came in the early 1820s; Antonio Panizzi, who arrived in 1823,
wrote on Boiardo, Ariosto and Dante, became Keeper of Printed
Books at the British Museum and even gained some political influence through his friendship with William Gladstone, whose enthusiasm for Italy has been attributed in part to Panizzi by Gladstone's
biographer John Morley; Gabriele Rossetti came in 1824. Many of
the Italians lived by giving lessons in the Italian language to those
intending to travel, read literature or sing the popular arias from
Italian operas, the latter activity being a necessary and fashionable
accomplishment for young singers both professional and amateur.

Among the British who lived for a time in Italy were the poets
Byron, Shelley and Landor who, along with the many attractions of
the country, appreciated the difference in the cost of living. Scott,
Coleridge, Wordsworth, Keats, Hunt, Rogers, Hazlitt and Macaulay
all travelled in Italy and the influence of Italian history and literature on their works is considerable. Prominent statesmen and poli-
ticians were also familiar with Italy and some were well versed in
its literature, language and culture. Lord Liverpool, Brougham,
Robert Peel and Palmerston had all been in the country and the
latter knew Italian; Lord John Russell knew Italy and its literature
well and was friendly with a Genoese family; Gladstone too visited
Italy in 1849, and studied Italian literature (especially Dante, Leopardi and Manzoni) extensively.[14] It was this kind of contact which
inspired sympathy with the Italians in these men and left them well
disposed towards Italy over the Italian Question in the crucial
decade of the 1850s.

The renewed interest in Italian literature found in many quarters
dates from the mid eighteenth century. Giuseppe Baretti moved to
London in 1751 where he published critical works on Dante,
Ariosto, Pulci, Boiardo and Boccaccio. Translations of Italian
authors also began to appear. The increased interest in Dante is
evident from the fact that in the first half of the eighteenth century
only three translations were published compared with nine in the
second. Cary's important translation of the *Comedy* appeared in

1814, was popularized by Coleridge, and exerted considerable influence on English literature in the first half of the century.[15] Italian history had been rendered more accessible and comprehensible through the publication of a number of historical studies including Edward Gibbon's *Decline and Fall of the Roman Empire* (1776–88), William Roscoe's *Lives* of *Leo X* (1806) and *Lorenzo de'Medici* (1822) and Sismondi's *Histoire des républiques italiennes du moyen âge* (Paris, 1809–18). Historical enquiry tended to concentrate on the late Middle Ages and the early Renaissance and it was here that historians found evidence of the survival of the social and cultural elements from which a new Italian civilization might arise. British poets and novelists repeatedly explored the theme of the struggle for freedom against tyrants and exploited the unrestrained passion and violence and the deeds of figures from Italian history in their works.

Sympathy for the Italians, the victims of French oppression in particular, was common both before and during the Napoleonic wars and travel books, accounts in journals and letters denounced French behaviour in Italy. At the beginning of the nineteenth century, Sicily, of great strategic importance for shipping in the Mediterranean, was occupied by the British and a short-lived constitution modelled on the British one was granted the Sicilians. The British commander in Sicily, Lord William Bentinck, encouraged the Tuscans to liberate themselves and restored the 1797 republican constitution to Genoa. Official British policy, however, was to perpetuate Austrian influence in Italy, and Bentinck was soon withdrawn. The effect of his action, though, was to encourage Italian patriots and set an example for the future to those British liberals who deplored the regressive Restoration settlement of 1815.

Often, pro-Italian sentiments took the form of a merely general goodwill and when coupled with the rather negative view of Italians, the conclusion was inevitably drawn that, although they were oppressed by French and Austrian tyrants, they were not yet ready for the type of representative government enjoyed by the British, or even that 'the people deserve their fate, because they are timid, degraded and very wretched'.[16] There were also good reasons for entertaining strong pro-Italian sentiments, for Catholicism was hated by most people in Britain, so that religious interest in Italy was more widespread, fervent and closely related to the political question than literary and artistic interest. The British found it easy to sympathize with Italians against a Pope who, as a temporal power, appeared to be obstructing the path of freedom for Italy. For some, a cultural interest in Italy extended into a strong sympathy with political aspirations. The classical education of the well-educated Englishman (through which Italy became synonymous with Imperial Rome) was of great importance in inspiring interest in Italy. Moreover, 'the idealized English patriotism was in some measure the outcome of countless generations of English school-boys studying the models of Roman antiquity', and British school-boys 'imbibing patriotism from the history of Rome' could become men like Russell or Gladstone for whom 'the ruins of the Forum were as familiar, sacred, and moving...as to Mazzini and Garibaldi themselves'.[17] Many of the poets and writers living in or visiting Italy were among this group and political events in Italy inspired a substantial number of works.[18]

In Britain, then, sympathy with the Italian cause increased in the light of the injustices of the Vienna Settlement and with increasing knowledge of Italy's past greatness. After 1815, the public was kept well up to date with events through newspapers, returning travel-lers and contact with the Italian exiles whose opinions were some-times published in periodicals. The British government and a large section of public opinion did not, however, wish to see the balance of power in Europe disturbed and viewed the prospect of revolu-tions and secret societies with alarm. The repeated failure of the risings in Italy contributed to reinforce the unfavourable opinion of Italians. The failures were seen as the inevitable outcome of their undisciplined and unstable characters and this opinion was fre-quently aired in the 1820s and 1830s when the British were either disappointed by the political inertia in Italy or indifferent to its affairs. A widespread indifference to foreign affairs generally extended well into the 1840s until the Revolutions of 1848. From then on though 'the focus of interest is overseas; the soldier, the emigrant, the plots of Napoleon III and the red shirts of Garibaldi, take and fill the imagination'.[19] This renewed interest had much to do with British perceptions of the changes in Europe in the late 1840s. Until 1848, France had been a liberal country, and a liberal Pope, Pius IX, had been elected in 1846, but the victory of absolut-ism, especially the seizure of power by Napoleon III and the 'papal aggression' which linked the Pope to the absolutists, left the British feeling themselves to be the only defenders of constitutionalism and civil and religious liberty in Europe. Consequently, as Beales points out, the British became 'much more self-consciously active propagandists for their own ideology'[20] and, given the prevailing mood, it was much more likely that they would sympathize with a national constitutionalist movement against despots. Protestant opinion supported the anti-clerical policies of Cavour's Piedmont in the early 1850s, and its *Constitution* was seen as a welcome step towards representative government following the British model. Cavour's espousal of free trade was also popular and Piedmont was rapidly becoming a safe and lucrative market for investment. In strong contrast was British contempt for Ferdinand II of Naples, known in the press as 'Re Bomba' for his action in bombing his own cities in 1849. This loathing was strengthened after Gladstone described the horrors of a tyrannical regime which was 'the negation of God erected into a system of government' in his *Two Letters to the Earl of Aberdeen* (1850). The need for sweeping reforms in Naples and in the Papal States was obvious, but an oversimplified view of the Italian situation was held by most people as a result of their reasoning, from the myths of their own history, that Italy could achieve freedom and prosperity if only liberal reform and constitutional government were peacefully brought in.

Giuseppe Garibaldi was already well known in Britain before 1860. His activities as a guerrilla leader in South America and in the defence of Rome in 1849 had received attention in the newspapers and he visited England in 1854. In 1860, Garibaldi was a hero for the British, who followed his exploits with great interest. The other great revolutionary leader, Giuseppe Mazzini, was a respected figure espousing the Italian republican cause, attracting many friends, establishing fund-raising societies and, through tireless journalism, helping to promote an understanding of the Italian situation and overcome British insularity in the face of events in Europe. Mazzini's views amounted to a system of beliefs about the nature of nationality, and indeed humanity as a whole, and about Italy's mission within this broad context. His appeal was intellectual and esoteric by comparison with Garibaldi's, and therefore somewhat alien to a great number of Englishmen whose own beliefs could not easily be reconciled with Mazzini's. His achievements in the Roman Republic of 1849 were widely recognized and some of the substantial support for the Italian exile came from influential quarters. There was a public outcry in 1844 when the Home Office was accused of opening Mazzini's correspondence, and Thomas Carlyle wrote to *The Times* in support of his friend. Acceptance of Mazzini's ideas in Britain was usually rather short lived. Some were

committed early on but the Italian gained only a few disciples.
Unlike Garibaldi, Mazzini made very little impact upon the working classes so that the influence of his ideas on the ordinary English
attitude to the Italian Question was negligible. George Eliot had
great admiration for Mazzini who figures in her journalism and
again in her last novel. Her support for him was not unqualified,
however, and she shared the view that Mazzini's hopes for a general rising in the whole of Italy were unrealistic and that lives were
being lost in plots which seemed to be deliberately obstructing the
progress of a liberal Piedmont. During the 1850s, British support
swung strongly behind Piedmont and by 1859 Mazzini was an
isolated figure. Overall, and in spite of the fact that 'Italy was the
only country in Europe or America about which we English in
the middle of the nineteenth century were really well informed',[21]
the British understanding of the political and social realities in Italy
remained rather superficial and simplistic, so that the majority of
those interested could be pro-Italian without being either committed Mazzinians or Cavourians.

After this survey of the main historical events of the *Risorgimento*
and of British social, political and economic relations with Italy both
before and after 1815, we consider the figure of Dante Alighieri and
the revival of interest in the poet and his works in Italy and in
Britain.

DANTE AND THE ITALIAN *RISORGIMENTO*

During the eighteenth century comparatively little critical attention
was focused on the work of Dante, indeed discussion of his work is
almost incidental, often subsumed into the broader discussion of
'the primitive'. Readers' interest is limited to a few passages of the
Divine Comedy and to certain aspects of Dante's art. The strongly
contrasting features of the text, the 'Gothic' elements for instance,
could not easily be integrated with the rest and the work was
perceived as being very uneven in quality, to the extent that some
critics thought it possible to reduce the *Comedy* to a few hundred
lines of good poetry while discarding the remainder. The work of
Dante, then, was somehow at odds with the poetic tastes of the
eighteenth century which, largely ignoring the poet's classicism,
focused on the 'primitive' and 'Gothic'. It was not until the last
years of the century that Dante began to be recognized as a poet

of great originality and power, and the classicism of the great follower of Virgil, the great sculptor of statues and groups in the *Comedy*, came to be fully appreciated.

Dante, who had chosen to write the *Divine Comedy* in the vernacular rather than Latin and who had defended his choice in *De vulgari eloquentia*, was celebrated as the creator of a modern language which, through the power of his genius, he had mastered and shaped to his will so that 'he seems at times like a despot, dragging the language into freedom'.[22] Cesarotti's political simile, the paradox of the despot as liberator, already gives a hint of some of the themes which Dante criticism was later to address. The poet-patriot Vittorio Alfieri (1749–1803) recognized the great power of Dante's language and acknowledged him as the father of Italian literature and of Italy, though both terms (Italian 'literature' and 'Italy' itself) were still as yet without fixed referents. Alfieri emphasizes Dante's complete freedom and originality and argues that the fact that he was independent of the patronage and protection of a prince enabled him to write with such power.[23] Dante's greatness is linked explicitly with the ideals of civil and individual liberty against a dynastic organization of Italian territories which only shackles individual genius.

It was increasingly recognized that the *Comedy* was closely bound up with the history of the fourteenth century. Sismondi's *De la littérature du midi de l'Europe* and Hallam's *View of the State of Europe* were important in bridging a gap between the poetry and the political and institutional history of Dante's day. In Foscolo's essays the historical setting is examined as an element inseparable from the poet's work as a whole. In Foscolo's view, Dante takes as the material of the *Comedy* the ordinary events and incidents of his day and translates them onto a plane on which they take on a universal interest in the context of the history of his age. Foscolo's Dante, the creator of 'the Language and the Poetry of a nation' is also 'a reformer of morals, an avenger of crimes (particularly of political crimes) and an asserter of orthodoxy in religion',[24] one who tried to help shape the course of events for the future. Given the strength of nineteenth-century teleological views of history, in which changes are seen in relation to some ultimate goal or inherent purpose towards which history is moving, much of the attention devoted to Dante by this 'historical' vein of criticism concerns the importance for later history of the 'father of Italian poetry'.

From the late 1820s until at least 1848, the year of revolutions, the figure of Dante the father gives way to that of Dante the prophet. The poet is seen as a religious reformer foretelling the Reformation or, alternatively, as the patriot with a vision of the future unity of Italy. And in this second view, which was insistently and eloquently expressed by proponents of the *Risorgimento*, Dante embodied the *idea* of an Italian national and cultural identity and was seen as 'the most Italian Italian there has ever been', a true 'spirito magno'.[25] The historical events in the *Comedy* – those of the period of the communes and of the struggle between the Empire and the popes – now become a central focus, so much so that from the 1840s to the late 1860s historical, or often semi-historical, material was sought out and used both to reconstruct accounts of Dante's life and to support readings of the *Comedy* as a transposition of Dante's own experiences onto a universal level. In his *Dante et la philosophie catholique au treizième siècle*, Antoine Frédéric Ozanam universalizes Dante's experience, making him representative of the 'spirit of the age' and traces both the general process of transition from the thirteenth to the fourteenth century which, says the author, required that the scholastic philosophy of the time should be popularized and eternalized in poetry, and the way in which the events and experiences of Dante's life fitted him for this task.[26] In Ozanam's treatment, we have a double movement then, 'the historicization of the writer and the mythicization of the man'.[27] George Eliot possessed copies of both Balbo and Ozanam and would have been familiar with their views of Dante.

Italian Romanticism, particularly after 1815, was highly charged politically, and discussions of Dante took on a political colouring. In Italy a conscious attempt was made to transpose the Romantic insight that poetry is great when it is also popular onto the patriotic sentiment. And it was in Dante that the two romanticisms of *poetry* and *patria* met.[28] Dante had conceived of Europe as a Christian community under the guidance of the divinely appointed authorities of the *imperium* and the *sacerdotium*, the Holy Roman Empire and the Church. Dante's belief was that the only hope for peace lay in the Empire united under the authority of the Emperor. He saw papal policy and the mediations of France in favour of either Pope or Emperor as a source of perpetual dissension and discord. In the *Monarchia* (1310–13), Dante argued that temporal monarchy is necessary to the well-being of the world and that the Empire, achieving the greatest degree of unity by embracing all men under its rule, is the most perfect form of government. The Roman people were justified in 'assuming the dignity of empire' by the fact that 'putting aside all greed, which is always contrary to the public interest, and choosing universal peace with liberty, this holy people pious and renowned, is seen to have neglected its own advantage to care for the public safety of the human race'.[29] Divine providence had clearly intended Rome to rule the world. Dante further asserts that imperial authority is derived directly from God and not through the Pope and concludes that possession of temporal power is in principle contrary to the nature of the Church, whose kingdom is not of this world. Thus, in the *Monarchia*, there was ample material – in the myth of the primacy of Rome, in Dante's insistence on unification under one ruler and in his opposition to the papacy – to inspire generations of Italian patriots prepared to adapt his arguments and appropriate his authority, however anachronistically, to their own ends.

By Catholic 'neo-Guelphs' Dante's work was seen as supporting orthodox Catholicism, portraying the universalism of the faith and advocating a balance between the political authority and the ideological leadership of the Church. In a slightly different reading by liberal Catholics like Silvio Pellico, Dante appeared a Savonarola, who had never been irreverent to Church or dogma, but was the 'poet of Catholicism'. Both Cesare Balbo and Vincenzo Gioberti were orthodox Catholics advocating a non-revolutionary nationalism. They saw Dante as the father of the nation and the harbinger of federalism in Italy. Both men largely ignored the 'dissident Dante' of, for example, *Purgatorio* XVI in which Marco Lombardo's words appear to refute the papal supremacy and praise the valour and courtesy which were once to be found in Italy.[30] What Balbo and Gioberti projected onto Dante was of course both a distortion of history and highly anachronistic, but it was a role which was to be influential in the course of the *Risorgimento*.

The 'lay-Ghibelline' or anti-papal interpretation, on the other hand, took up the Promethean Dante of Alfieri, exalting him as the father of Italy and the prophet of future unity and reading him as the political intransigent and martyr who denounced the moral corruption of his own day and of Italy in later centuries.[31] The real creator of the *Risorgimento* cult of Dante was Giuseppe Mazzini, drawn by the irresistible temptation to transform Dante from the prophet of medieval Empire to the prophet of the unified nation.[32] Mazzini linked Dante with Arnold of Brescia and Savonarola as

political revolutionaries and put a political theory alongside the
Divine Comedy: Italian unity, for Mazzini, was the dominating
thought in the soul of Dante. Mazzini built upon the work of
Foscolo, arming himself with Foscolo's authority to encourage belief
in the myth of Dante as father of the nation independent of papal
authority. It may be doubted whether Mazzini himself fully
believed Foscolo's interpretation of Dante, but he undoubtedly
recognized its importance in propaganda terms. Mazzini's Dante
was 'the father of his country', 'the genius of national freedom
which groans over the overturned statue [of Italia]... [who] was
filled with rage against those who had hurled it into the mud'.[33]
Dante had discerned a true country in Italy and gone far towards
uniting it linguistically. Finally, Dante was the noble spirit who
refused to compromise his own principles: 'though forced to beg a
crust of that bread *which tastes of salt* from the Italian rulers, he did
not bend before their power, he did not prostitute his genius and his
muse in the hope of reward from the princes'.[34] Mazzini's Dante
entered *Risorgimento* mythology as the exiled prophet, the guardian
of a national culture and language. Mazzinians saw the *Divine
Comedy* as bodying forth an irresistible spirit of 'Italianness' which
required no further explanations. In particular, the sudden appear-
ances of the character 'Italia' seemed to be an incarnate criticism of
imperialism in the *Divine Comedy*. 'Italia', like the exiled Dante who
had refused to compromise with despots, was exhorted by Mazzinians to stand alone, to 'make a party by [her]self'.[35] These myths
appealed to Eliot and, I shall argue, their influence can be felt in her
later work.

The Mazzinian or 'lay-Ghibelline' reading of Dante seems to be
the stronger in the period of the *Risorgimento*, particularly from 1816
to the 1830s, because of the intensive and sustained exploitation of
Dante for the practical purposes of education or propaganda by
Italian patriots. Dante's work lent itself to this type of treatment,
with passages being extracted and used as patriotic hymns denouncing the state to which Italy had been reduced. Particularly popular
passages were those mentioning 'Italia' or 'Roma', for example the
lines 'Ah, Italy enslaved, hostel of misery, ship without pilot in
great tempest, no princess among the provinces but a brothel!'[36]
Dante's influence could be felt in all areas of the *Risorgimento* struggle for freedom, whatever the particular form it took and, as one
critic puts it, 'there is hardly a corner of patriotic folklore where you
do not come across the poem or the name of Dante'.[37]

Cesare Balbo begins the second part of his *Life* (entitled *Dante in Exile*) with a list of illustrious Italian exiles including Tarquin, Coriolanus, Camillus, Cicero, Ovid, Tiberius, Germanicus, Dante and Alfieri. Of these, says Balbo, Dante was the greatest. For contemporary exiles persecuted by the foreign oppressor, Dante provided a role model and the historical perspective of a common struggle for a cause far greater than that of any one historical moment. Guido Mazzoni's account gives an idea of the powerful sentiments involved in the patriots' close relationship with 'il divino poèta':

> Our exiles went wandering through Europe and the Americas and it was a comfort for them to know that they were of the same mind as ... Dante, who went begging his bread crust by crust. [...] They were imprisoned in secret places by the Bourbons and Austrians, and groaned from the new Inferno of tyranny: – Abandon every hope, ye that enter! – but were soon heartened between one prison and the next, exchanging fraternal greetings through snatches of Dante ... The Germans were all the more gluttonous for them because Dante had branded them so; Italy was all the more beautiful because Dante had said it was; the foreigner had to be pushed back to the other side of the Alps also because Dante had so defined Italian territory;[38]

The strong temptation among nineteenth-century exiles was to see parallels between their own condition and Dante's exile from Florence, when he was to learn 'how salt is the taste of another man's bread and how hard is the way up and down another man's stairs' (*Paradiso* XVII, 58–60). Francesco Guerazzi, the exiled radical wrote in 1859: 'Should I beg them to grant me a pardon in the name of the provisional government...? Rather than return home dishonourably Dante remained in exile, and I shall do the same if no other way can be found.'[39] Ten years later, in 1870, the most famous Italian exile of the *Risorgimento*, Giuseppe Mazzini, was to write of a prospective return to his homeland: 'I shall not accept, *oblivion, grace, or pardon* for thirty-five years of work in the service of the fatherland. This is not the way to return home! said Dante. I am not Dante, but I have a duty, however insignificant I may be, towards the father of exiles. And I will die an exile.'[40] Contemporaries were also drawn by the temptation to make the comparison between Dante and Mazzini himself. Goffredo Mameli, for example, in his poem *Dante and Italy* (1846) affirms that Mazzini, that 'Sublime apostle / Of the word of life' had united 'the new spirit now abroad with the idea of Dante'.[41] This habit of drawing parallels across the centuries, this way of discerning 'likeness amidst diversity' (as George Eliot was to put it in a different context in 'The Modern Hep! Hep! Hep!'),[42] and uniting past with present in a common cause, is a characterizing feature of the Italian *Risorgimento*, and one which tended towards a mythicizing of the present or recent past. The *Divine Comedy* lent itself well to this kind of treatment and, as Mazzoni says, 'no other people...possesses a work of art which is either similar to or as great as the *Comedy*, which is personal, national and universal at the same time. This being the case, it was inevitable that the Italians should make profitable use or sometimes (if we prefer) misuse, of it during the Risorgimento.'[43] George Eliot, then, was markedly sensitive to this Italian version of romantic mythmaking and its influence can be felt in her later fiction.

DANTE AND THE BRITISH

By the 1820s, Italian literature was being widely discussed and reviewed in Britain and attention was closely focused on Dante who was becoming the most important Italian literary influence on British writers. The revival of interest in Dante was due in part to the multifaceted nature of his appeal to the Romantics. Through the work of German idealist philosophers and critics it became possible to see the *Comedy* as a whole, rather than as the fragmented and uneven work portrayed by much eighteenth-century criticism. Schelling made links between the present and the Middle Ages and, with Schlegel, emphasized the shaping genius of the poet while placing him in a vital, creative relationship with his age and its ideas. Thus, Dante was to become emblematic of medieval civilization and his great poem, the expression of the fusion of the individual and collective consciousness, was seen as embodying the 'spirit of the age'.

The great interest in Dante in England after the Napoleonic wars is in part a consequence of German interest. In 1818 alone, in addition to the two essays by Foscolo published in the *Edinburgh Review*, Hazlitt and Coleridge both lectured on Dante, Henry Hallam published his *View of the State of Europe during the Middle Ages* and the Revd Francis Cary's translation of the *Comedy*, which was to become the most widely read translation of Dante, was relaunched after

Coleridge's commendation of it. To some extent continuing the German Romantic readings of Dante based on sentiment, on human feelings for the plight of Francesca da Rimini and Ugolino for example, the enthusiasm of British readers of Dante concentrated on the immediacy of the reader's rapport with the poet based largely on his ability to interest by exciting sympathy through the power and passion of his writing, and on the vividness and accessibility of his imagery with its tremendous communicative power.

Though in the early years of enthusiasm for Dante, the late 1810s and early 1820s, much criticism was not based on any extensive reading or scholarship, historical research into the Middle Ages and into Dante's life allowed Byron and to a lesser extent Shelley,[44] following Alfieri's picture of the poet, to elaborate the 'personal' image of the Promethean Dante, the melancholy, gloomy poet of liberty. Byron, who came to identify his own condition as an exile with that of Dante, admired the moral courage of the exiled Florentine: 'I don't wonder at the enthusiasm of the Italians about Dante. He is the poet of liberty. Persecution, exile, the dread of a foreign grave, could not shake his principles.'[45] Byron called upon the Italians to unite in the name of Dante to liberate themselves from oppression in *The Prophecy of Dante* (1819), a poem which was destined to be highly influential both in Italy and in Britain, where Carlyle's treatment of Dante in his 1840 lecture 'The Hero as Poet' was the apotheosis of Byronism.

The Romantics shared Dante's concern with language, eschewing the overuse of classical images and rhetorical formulae. Where critics had before seen a lack of polish and taste in style in Dante's language in parts of the *Comedy*, they now regarded his style as a means of allowing a greater depth and range of expression. In Britain, too, one of the most important aspects of readers' appreciation of Dante was his use of the vernacular in the *Comedy* which provided a strong basis for the future development of a common language spoken by Italians and thus also a strong foundation for the rise of Italian nineteenth-century 'language nationalism', deriving from Herder and strongly present in the writings of Mazzini and others.[46] Carlyle too stressed this point at the close of 'The Hero as Poet': 'poor Italy lies dismembered, scattered asunder, not appearing in any protocol or treaty as a unity at all; yet the noble Italy is actually *one*: Italy produced its Dante; Italy can speak! ... The nation that has a Dante is bound together as no dumb Russia can be.' In the same lecture Carlyle also attributes a mystic quality of *song* to the *Comedy*:

> I said, Dante's Poem was a Song: it is Tieck who calls it 'a mystic unfathomable Song;' and such is literally the character of it. Coleridge remarks very pertinently somewhere, that wherever you find a sentence musically worded, of true rhythm and melody in the words, there is something deep and good in the meaning too. For body and soul, word and idea, go strangely together here as everywhere. Song: we said before, it was the Heroic of Speech! All *old* Poems, Homer's and the rest, are authentically Songs.[47]

This concern with the power of the song and its singer is one which is shared by George Eliot. The singer and the finding of a voice are central metaphors for the creative woman artist, who is usually a singer (Lisa in 'How Lisa Loved the King', Armgart and Alchirisi and Mirah Lapidoth in *Daniel Deronda*) or who fails to sing (Gwendolen).[48] The theme of song, and particularly the poetry of Dante and Leopardi as song, will need to be explored within the Italian contexts of Eliot's fiction during the course of this study.

Most of the Romantics had read at least some parts of Dante. While Wordsworth and Coleridge knew the poet well, it is in the younger generation of Romantics that Dante's appeal is more strongly felt. A small number of passages from *Inferno* and *Purgatorio* were worked and reworked by the younger Romantics, for whom Dante was the poet of love in the *Paolo and Francesca* episode of *Inferno* V, of terror in his attempts to excite emotions in exploring the darkest, deepest recesses of the human soul in the *Ugolino* episode (*Inferno* XXXIII), and of Nature in the beauty and calm of the peaceful scene of Matilda gathering flowers (*Purgatorio* XXVIII, 1–51). Numerous translations of selected passages had already been made in the eighteenth century, and the *Ugolino* story with its potentially Gothic terrors proved very popular also in the nineteenth.[49] George Eliot was able to refer directly or through allusion to each of the passages mentioned above in the knowledge that they would be familiar to educated British readers. Indeed it is no accident that these *all* appear, some more than once, in Eliot's later fiction. There was a decline in the popularity of Dante in the 15-year period from 1815 to 1830 it is true, but a substantial body of works, including new translations, studies of Dante and literary works, as well as many paintings and sculptures, continued to be produced.[50] Browning's *Sordello*, drawn from Dante's character in *Purgatorio* VII, was published in 1840; Tennyson's *Ulysses* (*Inferno* XXVI) came out in 1842 and *In Memoriam* in 1850. From the late 1830s onwards, there was a growing tendency to concentrate on the figure of Beatrice and on Dante's relationship with her. Among the artistic advantages of this type of treatment were those of divorcing Dante from political contexts and concentrating discussion on the personal and intimate. The closing cantos of *Purgatorio* thus took on a heightened significance and a central position in the drama of Dante and Beatrice, as they are the fulfillment of the 'promise' of the *Vita nuova*, and the beginning of the 'hymn of love' of the *Paradiso*.[51] Dante Gabriel Rossetti, whose work will be discussed in Chapter 7 on Eliot's *Middlemarch*, eulogizes the Beatrice of the *Vita nuova* (who was to become a particular Victorian favourite)[52] rather than the Beatrice of the *Comedy*, seeing her as the idealization of his conception of womanhood, and I shall argue that the influence of this Rossettian Beatrice can be felt in Eliot's novel.

Our reading of George Eliot's later novels can be enriched by an awareness of the various readings of Dante in circulation. Part of the purpose of this book is to examine the ways in which George Eliot drew upon the various Dantes constructed by the nineteenth century and created her own Dante in her work. This will involve both close focus on her texts and a wider view, placing Eliot's work in relation to currents of *Risorgimento* thought and Victorian sensibility towards Dante. Another closely related aim is to explore the nature and extent of the influence of the *Risorgimento* on George Eliot's work and to examine some of the ways in which she selectively draws upon a combination of personal experience of Italy and a wider knowledge of Italian life and culture in her fiction.

2

George Eliot's Contact with Italian Life and Culture 1840–61

Having examined the Italian background, we now look at George Eliot's own contact with Italian life and culture as revealed through her reading, letters and journals, her journalism and her trips to Italy in the 20 years or so until Unification. The treatment given is roughly chronological, though I have not attempted to give an exhaustive survey of Eliot's contact with Italian life. Rather I have concentrated on those elements which seem to me to be of significance for her fiction or which convey a sense of Eliot's sometimes passionate engagement with Italy in the period up until 1861.

There is evidence that Eliot was well aware of the political situation in Italy early on. In May 1840, she was rereading Byron's *Childe Harold*, and paraphrases the opening stanzas of canto IV, the particularly 'Italian' canto in which 'Byron...checks reflection on individual and personal sorrows by reminding himself of the revolutions and woes beneath which the shores of the Mediterranean have groaned'. She also writes: 'I fear I am laboriously doing nothing, for I am beguiled by the fascination that the study of languages has for my capricious mind...'.[1] George Eliot had already begun to study Italian by May 1840 with the intention of reading the literature in that language. She took lessons once a week from an Italian teacher, a Joseph Brezzi from Coventry, and soon afterwards began German, finding after six months that 'there seems a greater affinity between German and my mind than Italian, though less new to me, possesses'.[2] Among the first books she read were Carlo Botta's *Storia d'Italia* (*History of Italy during the Consulate and Empire of Napoleon I*) (1828) and *Le mie Prigioni* (*My Imprisonments*) by Silvio Pellico, 'that I might have something containing familiar Italian'.[3] The latter, often recommended to students of Italian, holds a place of particular importance in *Risorgimento* history. Pellico, a patriot and writer, joined and became one of the leaders of the *Carbonari* in Lombardy in 1820, was arrested and condemned to death by the Austrians following the uprisings of 1820–1. His sentence was then commuted to 15 years' imprisonment in the infamous Spielberg castle. *My Imprisonments* (1832, trans. 1833), which was immediately banned by the Austrian authorities, is an account of his experiences in prison until his pardon in 1830. It is comparatively restrained in tone, and instead of inciting to revolt is rather intimate and pious, and thus well suited to touch the Romantic sensibility. It had not been intended as propaganda, yet it became a powerful weapon in the hands of the Italian nationalist movement. The book was quickly translated into several languages and reached a vast audience in Europe and beyond. Pellico's account aroused strong sympathy for his suffering, for he was perceived as personifying the fate of Italy itself. The imprisonment of an intellectual in the land which had been the home of intellectual inquiry during the Renaissance grated particularly with the British. After the harsh suppression and trials (1821–4) following the 1820–1 risings and the suppression of the 1831 insurrection, the publication of Pellico's book led to widespread condemnation of Austrian policy in Italy, so much so that Metternich pronounced that its publication was 'worse than a battle lost'. Pellico, whose book had become a locus of *Risorgimento* mythology, may not have made much impact on Eliot at the time, however, for when reviewing a similar work, *The Austrian Dungeons in Italy* by Felice Orsini[4] in the *Leader* in 1856, she commented that it 'has not the literary charm belonging to Silvio Pellico's narrative which we have known a young student of Italian, in blissful ignorance of Austrian policy, to take for a romance, and devour it with a culpable reliance on "guessing" instead of the dictionary'. A wry comment perhaps on her own earlier reading of Pellico? She does however implicitly recognize *My Imprisonments* as the archetype of this kind of work and acknowledges the influence of Pellico in the same review: 'Since the publication of Silvio Pellico's narrative, Austria has somewhat alleviated the treatment of her political prisoners. The bastinado is rarely administered, and is disavowed by the officials, and the *carcere durissimo* is abolished.' While at one level Eliot in her review was merely voicing the widespread indignation against the Austrian treatment of political prisoners, on another, the plight of Pellico, Orsini and others seems to have taken hold of her literary imagination:

If De Foe were alive again and had to rewrite his *History of the Devil*, he could hardly add a more striking supplementary chapter than one on Austrian prisons and Austrian tribunals in Italy, [...] there are frightful hardships to be endured in most cases, though the worst features of the Austrian system at present seem to lie less in physical cruelty than in the unscrupulous devices and slow tortures of the judicial process, which has no other object than to prove the prisoner guilty in the end, and in the meantime to entrap him into avowals that will compromise as many of his friends as possible.

The same 'diabolic' ingredients which Eliot describes in the Austrian dungeons and the same highly charged themes of despotism, torture, guilt, betrayal and punishment recur in Italian contexts in Eliot's early fiction and again in her last novel.

There is earlier evidence of Eliot's anti-Austrian feeling and of her contempt for the French monarch Louis-Philippe in a well-known letter to John Sibree (March 8th) discussing events in Europe on the outbreak of the French Revolution of 1848. In the heady atmosphere of revolution, Eliot declares that Louis-Philippe, his moustachioed sons and other decayed monarchs should be pensioned off, though 'our little humbug of a queen is more endurable than the rest of her race', and that the eminently inferior British working classes are only fit for the slow progress of *political* reform. She continues: 'I should not be sorry to hear that the Italians had risen en masse and chased the odious Austrians out of beautiful Lombardy. But this they could hardly do without help, and that involves another European war.'[5] Ten days later the Italians did indeed rise en masse in Milan in the movement known as the *Five Days* (March 17th – 22nd), pushing the Austrians back to the defensive forts of the Quadrilateral. This action was eventually unsuccessful largely through the failure to press the advantage and indecision of the 'decayed monarch' of Piedmont, Charles Albert, who later abdicated. Interestingly, Eliot's mention of 'beautiful Lombardy' reveals the strength of her romantic attachment, common among the English, to a country which she had not yet had occasion to visit, and which was only really known to her through literature and the accounts of recent events in papers and journals.

The first time Eliot travelled on the Italian peninsula was in 1849. Her father had been buried on June 6th and Charles and Mary Bray planned the trip to distract Eliot from her grief. They set off from

London on June 12th, travelling via Paris, Lyons, Avignon and Marseilles, then along the Grande Corniche to Genoa, where they stayed a week. Unfortunately there is no written record of Eliot's stay in the city, though it is clear from her later writings that Genoa made a strong impression on her.[6] On leaving Genoa, they went up into 'beautiful Lombardy' to Milan and then on via Como to Geneva. Here the Brays left Eliot in the Campagne Plongeon and started back for England. Other guests in the pension included, for the first month, the Marquis and Marquise de St Germain who had fled Piedmont accused of hiding the proscribed Duc de Visconti. Eliot was very favourably impressed by the family: 'The good Marquis goes with his family and servants all nicely drest to the Catholic church. They are a most orderly set of people – there is nothing but their language and their geniality and politeness to distinguish them from one of the best of our English aristocratic families.'[7] Her comment in her letter to the Brays seems intended to refute the common prejudices regarding Italians and Eliot, characteristically, works her comparison to the advantage of the Italians. Eliot was befriended by the Marquise who invited her to visit the family in Italy, where they returned at the end of August after the declaration of a general amnesty in Piedmont. Eliot moved into lodgings in the house of the painter François d'Albert Durade in October 1849 and stayed in Geneva until March of the following year.

In 1851, after her return to England, Eliot became assistant editor of the *Westminster Review* which had been acquired by John Chapman. From 1852 to 1854 she advised on the choice of authors and subjects, which included a wide range of political, literary, philosophical and moral topics, edited the contributions by cutting and reorganizing as she felt necessary, read the proofs and supervised the setting. She also made a number of contributions to the 'Contemporary Literature' section. Either in her editorial role or through the weekly parties given by the Chapmans, she came into contact with a great many writers and thinkers, including refugees of the 1848 revolutions. Along with Pierre Leroux and Louis Blanc, Eliot probably met Mazzini in one of his visits to the Strand with his friend and sponsor Peter Alfred Taylor.[8]

Mention should be made here of another radical journal, the *Leader*, which helped to shape a part of political opinion in the 1850s and contributed to the mythologizing of the Italian *Risorgimento* in Britain. It was founded by Thornton Hunt, who became its political editor, and G.H. Lewes, who was already well known in

London in the second half of the 1840s and who had a large cosmopolitan group of acquaintances which included Mazzini. The *Leader* first came out on February 4th, 1850. The revolutions of 1848 had given the editors a sense of mission, and the journal functioned as an important mouthpiece in England for several European revolutionaries, including the French Socialist Louis Blanc and the Italian Joseph Mazzini.[9] A politically radical journal published weekly, the *Leader* reported the activities and sayings of Mazzini, of international associations and other revolutionists abroad and in London. Interest in Italian liberty was further evident in the notices and editorials dealing with the Neapolitan prison scandals sparked off by Gladstone's *Two Letters to the Earl of Aberdeen*. The *Leader* called on the politician to go even further in his criticism of the Neapolitan government and to state that *absolutism* itself was responsible for the Neapolitan miseries. A review of Gladstone's *Letters* was carried in the same number of the journal. In February 1852, the *Leader* called for a subscription of one shilling to be paid into the bank for J. Mazzini and L. Kossuth and for use by the European Democratic Committee. In 1850, then, Lewes was 'at his busiest and most radical'.[10] From about 1852, we need to recognize the increasing importance of Lewes himself as an 'Italian' influence on Eliot. Already well established in London before Eliot arrived, he had a strong interest in the Italian struggles, knew Italian well and had contributed important articles on Italian literary figures to British journals.[11]

In 1851, Giuseppe Mazzini was back in London after failure of the short-lived Roman Republic of 1849. The insurrections spreading from Sicily through to Lombardy in 1848–9 had all been successfully repressed and many activists driven into exile. On February 25th, Mazzini wrote to Emile Ashurst (one of his sponsors in England) announcing his intention to 'start up an Italian agitation; and a Society of the Friends of Italy', and two days later he reported: 'Within a few days the Society of the Friends of Italy will be established. All exiles are concentrating here to a frightful extent: driven from France and Switzerland where persecution is now shameful.'[12] The *Society of the Friends of Italy* included some of the leading Liberals of the day: David Masson (the Milton scholar), William Ashurst, Professor F.W. Newman, Arthur Trevelyan, Walter Savage Landor, Peter Taylor (later MP for Leicester) and G.H. Lewes and Thornton Hunt of the *Leader*. The society aimed to promote their view of the Italian Question through propaganda and the holding of public meetings, to further the cause of Italian independence in the English Parliament and to aid efforts towards independence and religious and political liberty through the raising of funds.

In this highly charged political climate of an apparent return to despotism in Europe, and after the publication of Gladstone's *Letters* in July 1851, Eliot at the *Westminster* realized the importance of the Italian opponents of despotism and the strength of public interest in the Italian Question. In January 1852, she wrote to Sarah Hennell: 'We are trying out Mazzini to write on Freedom v. Despotism. Don't tell of course'.[13] The commissioned article 'Europe: Its Condition and Prospects' came out in the April number of the *Westminster* and contains a number of Mazzini's most important ideas.[14] He attacks the English prejudice that it is only the French who have provided models for political development. The initiative, says Mazzini, passes from one nation to another and he fully expected that Italy, 'a predestined nation', would take the initiative in a common struggle amounting to 'an up-rising...of the whole human race' in which the revolutionary leaders embodied in their own persons 'a new unity' arising out of the collapse of belief in the old European order. The struggles of these years are 'sacred as liberty, sacred as the human soul. It is a struggle which has for its symbol [...] the great type of Prometheus'. Mazzini further proclaims 'the unity of God, and, therefore, of the human race...We believe no more in that narrow dualism which established an absurd antagonism between heaven and earth, between God and his creation.' In the *Westminster* article, Mazzini expounds his belief in life as a duty and mission: 'Europe is now agitated and unconsciously led by the...eminently religious definition of life as a mission: a series of duties, of sacrifices to be accomplished for others, in view of an ulterior moral progress.' Duty consisted in 'the individual submitting himself to the idea of the collective aim to be attained'.

Progress is the consciousness of progress. Man must attain it step by step, by the sweat of his brow. The transformation of the *medium* in which he lives only takes place in proportion as he merits it; and he can only merit it by struggle; by devoting himself and purifying himself by good works and holy sorrow. He must not be taught to enjoy but rather to suffer for others; to combat for the salvation of the world.

While George Eliot might well concur with some of the abstract ideas advanced by Mazzini, here the argument turns of course on the definition of 'struggle' and 'combat' and the forms these should take in practice.[15]

Mazzini also opposes two conceptions of nationality, a 'princely nationality of aristocracies or royal races', of despotism and empire, and a 'nationality of the peoples', which he defines as 'a human group called by its geographical position, its traditions, and its language, to fulfil a special function in the European work of civilisation'. Mazzini presented a simple, unambiguous theory of nationalism. The State, representing the general will, and the Nation, representing a homogeneous people, should be coextensive. Physical and ethnological boundaries were seen as the 'natural' boundaries of states, in place of the traditional historical unit of the state of the old regimes. This 'continental' nationalism conflicted both with continental notions of empire and with a version of nationalism in which the nation was only one of a number of elements making up the state. The most perfect states, according to the latter theory, were those which included different races and nationalities without oppression. In practice, however, this theory could easily be pressed into the service of expansionism and colonialism. At the end of his *Westminster* article, Mazzini consciously plays upon the growing English fears of 'an attempt at universal restoration in Europe' after 1848 by raising the spectre of 'Prussian, Austrian, or French despotism... employ[ing] its brute force on each isolated people;... The menace of the foreigner weighs upon the smaller States; the last sparks of European liberty are extinguished under the dictatorial veto of the retrograde powers.' Eliot followed the critical reception of the articles in this issue of the *Westminster*, noting the 'ridiculously various' opinions expressed on the review articles, and noting in particular that 'Greg... calls Mazzini's sad stuff – mere verbiage'.[16]

Many of the ideas expressed in this article were not new, nor were many of them original to Mazzini, but one can see various points of contact which might make his thought attractive to Eliot: the emphasis on the duties rather than on the rights of the individual; the slow transformation of society (as abstractly stated by Mazzini); the belief that the individual and society are linked to a wider humanity in the realization of a 'divine' idea; Mazzini's idea of the nation set against an aggressive nationalism such as was to resurface in the later 1860s and 1870s; the role of the individual leader; and finally a common belief in the *Risorgimento* myth, that the Italian *Risorgimento* was itself part of the progress of a wider humanity. Mazzini's promotion of Dante as the 'prophet of Italy' has already been mentioned (Chapter 1), but a further aspect of his thought should be considered briefly here: his advocacy of a European literature, an idea taken from German thought, in particular Goethe, and one with which Eliot was familiar.[17] Literature should take the initiative by going beyond merely isolated nationalisms and reach towards a Europeanism, the next stage in the progress of man on the way to a universal humanity. In the Romantic credo of Mazzini, the expression of a universal human nature, a collective soul of the people, could be greatly aided through the increasingly efficient diffusion of literature by the press. In George Eliot's later fiction, and particularly in her last novel, there is a strong sense that Eliot, though in a different context in which she sometimes appears to be fighting a rearguard action against the advance of bellicose isolationism, is using other literatures, European and non-, to move beyond merely national identities, to communicate across, and break down, national divisions which reveal themselves to be radically unstable in her work.

In February 1852 Eliot had dined at the house of Peter Taylor, a personal friend of Mazzini's and the Secretary of the 'Friends of Italy' and the friendship she established with the Taylors was to last a lifetime. In March of the same year Eliot wrote to Mrs Taylor: 'I did go to the *conversazione*; but have less to regret than you think. Mazzini's speeches are better read than heard.'[18] The *conversazione*, which Eliot attended at the Freemason's Tavern on March 24th, was one of a number of such events organized by the 'Friends of Italy'. On this occasion F.W. Newman presided and Mazzini expressed his view of the papacy as the curse of Italy and his belief that if the Austrian and French troops were withdrawn, the Pope would also flee and that his withdrawal as a spiritual and temporal power would thus remove an important obstacle to the creation of a republican Italy. Despite Eliot's lack of enthusiasm for Mazzini's delivery, the meeting appears to have been highly successful, and the *Examiner* reports the enthusiastic reception given to Mazzini.[19]

Eliot's strong anti-Austrian bias is clear in her other journalism in the 1850s. Among the foreign literature she reviewed for the *Westminster* and the *Leader*, there were a number of books dealing specifically, or in part, with Italy. In her review article entitled 'Memoirs of the Court of Austria' (1855) on Vehse's multivolume *History of the Austrian Court and Aristocracy, and of the Austrian Diplomacy*, Eliot is particularly scathing about the Austrian emperors in an Italian context:

> The two years of his feeble and dissolute brother Leopold's reign, [...] were followed by the long reign of Francis II, who, in that notable shuffling of the cards known as the congress of Vienna...became 'Emperor of Austria'. Francis's affectation of the Viennese dialect, his professed interest in the private affairs of his citizens, his ostentatious observation of trivial laws, and his will, in which he bequeathed his love to his people, and promised to 'pray for them at the throne of God', prevailed on some of his credulous subjects to believe that the virtual gaoler of Spielberg, the man who imprisoned Pellico and Gonfalonieri, and who betrayed Hofer, was a kind soul – a people's emperor. Civil crimes...he often pardoned, but towards political crimes he was implacable;...[20]

The volumes by Vehse relating to the Austrian Court had been banned by the authorities there and the book had gained a certain notoriety in Germany where 'its influence is said to be highly democratic' though, says Eliot, 'Vehse himself is no hot democrat but a moderate Liberal' and 'so far as we are acquainted with his volumes, we trace in them no spirit of partisanship'. A year later in July 1856, in the *Belles Lettres* section of the *Westminster*, Eliot found 'the first in ability and interest' to be a novel '*Doctor Antonio. A Tale* by the Author of *Lorenzo Benoni*', which she singled out not for its hackneyed plot and incidents, but for its picture of Italian comradeship and solidarity during the Neapolitan insurrection of 1821 at the end of which the enslaved 'Doctor Antonio still suffers, prays, and hopes for his country'.[21]

> The culminating point of interest in the book is where the writer, forsaking the function of a novelist, and sternly taking up that of historian, presents us with a picture of the Neapolitan revolution, and the ghastly iniquity of Neapolitan trials. Here is truth that towers above the mere fiction of the novel, as the battle of Drumclog and the trial of the Covenanters tower above the sorrows of Henry Morton and Edith Bellenden in 'Old Mortality'.[22]

This same 'towering truth' was praised a month later in Felice Orsini's *Austrian Dungeons*, which otherwise, she thought, was 'thrown together with little art' so that 'it reads like hasty notes':

> But it has one grave source of superior influence on the reader, namely, that it recounts *recent* facts – that it sets before us Austrian prisons and tribunals as they are in the present day, and it does not allow us to get rid of any painful sympathy by conjecturing that 'things are different now'.[23]

Again, in the *Westminster* in January 1857, in reviewing T.A. Trollope's *The Girlhood of Catherine de'Medici*, Eliot mentions that 'the noble Palazzo Riccardi and the Via Larga of Florence, for many years the residence of illustrious families', are 'now the stabling of Austrian dragoons'. In the same review, in discussing Mrs Browning's *Aurora Leigh* Eliot singles out a passage ('Italy from the Sea') in which the narrator watches day break over Genoa from a boat anchored off shore.[24] Eliot had by this time seen Genoa herself, and the passage must have been particularly vivid to her imagination. In *Daniel Deronda*, Eliot locates the dramatic scenes of Gwendolen's captivity on the yacht and the drowning of the despotic Grandcourt just off Genoa.

Less than a year before the publication of 'Mr Gilfil's Love Story', which treats themes of anti-Italian prejudice among the English, Eliot discusses the same topic in a review of Margaret Fuller's *Letters from Italy. At Home and Abroad; or, Things and Thoughts in America and Europe* in which, says the reviewer, the author's 'wide sympathies had found a grand definite object in the struggles of the Italian people'.[25] For Margaret Fuller 'the English in Rome [in 1847–9] were anything but admirable . . .; she often bursts into indignant description of their coldness and selfishness'. Eliot then quotes from Fuller:

> It is droll to remember our reading in the class-book,
>   'Ay, down to the dust with them, slaves as they are;' –
> to think how bitter the English were on the Italians who succumbed, and see how they hate those who resist. And their cowardice here in Italy is ludicrous. It is they who run away at the least intimation of danger, – it is they who invent all the 'fe, fo, fum' stories about Italy, – it is they who write to the *Times* and elsewhere that they dare not for their lives stay in Rome, where I,

a woman, walk everywhere alone, and all the little children do
the same, with their nurses.

Eliot notes that Fuller was also 'caustic on the weaknesses of her
own countrymen', and that

> in her remonstrances with her countrymen for their want of
> sympathy for the struggling Italians, she mentions an appeal
> which ought to go home to the English conscience as well as the
> American: 'Some of the lowest of the people', she says, 'have
> asked me, "Is it not true that your country had a war to become
> free?" "Yes". "Then why do they not feel for us?" '

To illustrate Fuller's descriptions Eliot chooses the departure of
Garibaldi and his soldiers after the French had taken Rome in
1849, which she considers to be 'a fine mixture of the pathetic and
the picturesque'. Margaret Fuller was an ardent follower of Mazzini, and as such, says Eliot, 'had from the first no faith in the
permanence of such paradoxes as a liberal pope and a reforming
Romanism' of Pius IX. Eliot reviewed the same volume in the
Westminster in July 1856. She draws attention to Fuller's Letters
from Italy as being of historical interest for the period 1847–9, and
pays tribute to Mazzini along with the author:

> It is very interesting to read the warm testimony which a close
> observer like Margaret Fuller bears to the noble conduct of Maz-
> zini, both in the days of revolutionary triumph and of revolu-
> tionary tribulation. In closing her very last letter to the *Tribune*,
> she says, 'Mazzini I know, the man and his acts, great, pure, and
> constant – a man to whom only the next age can do justice, as it
> reaps the harvest of deeds he has sown in this.'[26]

The choice of books to review and the particular focus when
writing were a question of the reviewer's personal preference. Taking the Italian reviews (which appeared anonymously in the *Westminster* and the *Leader*) as a whole, Eliot was clearly well informed
on Italy, and brought her knowledge to bear in her journalism,
whether simply to inform or to denounce the iniquity and injustice
of the existing situation. She puts forward a consistently liberal
viewpoint and as an admirer of Mazzini and Garibaldi in the
1850s, is indignant against the French and Austrian oppressors

and the papacy, intolerant of those who persisted in negative attitudes towards Italians and, like so many educated British people,
romantically attached to Italy.

The earliest example of Eliot's use of Dante is also to be found in
her journalism, in her review of A.F. Rio's *Léonard de Vinci et son
École* in the July 1856 *Westminster Review*:

> M. Rio tells us, that [...] the artist was continually absorbed in the
> contemplation of the Divinity, and his hand trembled whenever
> he began to paint this supreme object of art – a detail noticed by
> Dante in the devout painters of his time:-
> > 'Similmente operando all'artista
> > Ch'ha l'abito dell'arte *e man che trema*.'[27]

George Eliot's second trip to Italy took place in 1860.[28] There is a
much fuller record of this trip than of the others, with letters and
journals written by both Eliot and Lewes during the journey, as well
as a journal, 'Recollections of Italy', which Eliot wrote after their
return. The importance of this Italian trip for Eliot is immediately
apparent from the 'Recollections', which fulfils the need to fix and
clarify the impressions from three months' travel: 'We have finished
our journey to Italy – the journey I had looked forward to for years,
rather with the hope of the new elements it would bring to my
culture than with the hope of immediate pleasure.'[29] Much of this
journal is a record of the great art which the couple saw.[30] I shall not
concentrate on these here, but on those parts of her correspondence
which give some insight into Eliot's engagement with other aspects
of Italian life and culture.

There can be no doubt that Eliot, the writer of fiction with
three books behind her, was aware of a compelling need to add
'new elements' to her culture but also of turning these elements
to good use in her writing. Eliot realized that she had exhausted
a particular seam with the completion of *The Mill on the Floss*:
'I am grateful and yet rather sad to have finished – sad that
I shall live with my people on the banks of the Floss no
longer. But it is time that I should go and absorb some new life
and gather fresh ideas.'[31] From 1860 onwards, then, it is interesting
to watch Eliot selecting and registering her impressions of
Italy, as a number of these appear in her fiction in some form
or another. The letters of both Eliot and Lewes radiate
enthusiasm for the land to which they had both felt intellectually,

culturally and sentimentally attached for so long without ever having visited.

They set off for Paris on March 24th, coming into Italy via the Mon Cenis Pass by night in a sledge. After breakfasting at Susa they went on by train to Turin, which was celebrating the union of Tuscany and Emilia with Piedmont-Lombardy which had recently been negotiated between Cavour and the Emperor Napoleon III. Eliot later commented on Turin in her journal:

> A handsome street, well broken by architectural details, with a glimpse of snowy mountains at the end of the vista, collonades on each side, and flags waving their bright colors (*sic*) in sign of political joy, is the image that usually rises before me at the mention of Turin. [...] This is the place that Alfieri lived in through many of his young follies, getting tired of it at last for the Piedmontese pettiness of which it was the centre. And now, eighty years later, it is the centre of a widening life which may at last become the life of resuscitated Italy.[32]

At Turin station they 'had a sight of the man whose name will always be connected with the story of that widening life – Count Cavour' who was waiting to receive the new Viceroy of Tuscany, the Prince de Carignan.[33] For Eliot this was 'a really pleasant sight – [...] Count Cavour, in plainest dress, with a head full of power, mingled with bonhomie'.[34] Eliot's comment and sketch of Cavour indicates the extent to which British support, including that of liberal intellectuals like herself and Lewes, had swung behind Piedmont by this time, even though the diplomatic solution which had been arrived at was far from satisfactory, and 'several fellow-travellers who belonged to Savoy...were full of chagrin at the prospect of the French annexation'[35] under the terms of the peace settlement of March 24th, by which Nice and Savoy were assigned to France. During the five hour rail journey down to Genoa, they met a Baron de Magliano, a Neapolitan who had been living in France but was now returning to enlist in the Sardinian army with the intention of helping to remove the Neapolitan Bourbons.

On arriving in Genoa they 'slept the sleep of – travellers'.[36] Eliot wrote to John Blackwood from Rome that Lewes' 'rapturous delight in those streets of palaces and the amphitheatre of softly shadowed hills gave [Genoa] the best sort of novelty to me'.[37] The Journal entry is still more enthusiastic and more detailed in its account:

George was enchanted with the aspect of the place, as we drove or walked along the streets. It was his first vision of anything corresponding to his preconception of Italy. After the Adlergasse, in Nürnberg, surely no streets can be more impressive than the Strada Nuova and Strada Nuovissima, at Genoa. [...] And all this architectural splendor [sic] is accompanied with the signs of actual prosperity. Genova la Superba is not a name of the past merely.[38]

In Genoa they went out sightseeing, and heard a performance of Verdi's *Rigoletto* and, like so many British travellers before them, were struck by the poor performance of the singers. After resting two days in Genoa they left on the steam packet for Leghorn, stopping to look at the Jewish synagogue, then on to Pisa, before returning to Leghorn where they reboarded the steam packet to Civitavecchia, arriving in Rome at noon on Palm Sunday.

Their arrival in Rome was uninspiring and 'there was nothing imposing to be seen'. After some difficulty finding somewhere to stay in Holy Week, they started their tour of Rome through 'a weary length of dirty, uninteresting streets' to St Peter's, 'which was not impressive', with 'a rather heavy load of disappointment on [their] minds' at having seen nothing 'that corresponded with [their] preconceptions'.[39] The next day, having found better lodgings with 'a good little landlady, who can speak nothing but Italian, so that she serves as a *parlatrice* for us, and awakens our memory of Italian dialogue – a memory which consists chiefly of recollecting Italian words without knowing their meaning, and English words without knowing the Italian for them',[40] the couple ventured out, and Eliot did find scenes which 'resembled strongly that mixture of ruined grandeur with modern life which I had always had in my imagination at the mention of Rome',[41] so that by April 4th, she could write that 'since our arrival, in the middle of Sunday, I have been gradually rising from the depth of disappointment to an intoxication of delight'.[42] Lewes, however, remained unimpressed by Rome, writing in his diary on April 18th:

The disappointment, & almost dislike, created by the city has not worn off: it is ugly, colourless, dirty, incommodious, with none of the advantages of a capital.... The antiquities are deeply interesting, & make Roman History & Literature living things for one. The art is of a 'mingled woof' – immense quantities of bad & detestable, & some few supreme works.... Papal Rome is very odious; built on shams. But the Roman people, like the Italians generally, seem remarkably good natured, easy, happy & unintellectual.[43]

By the end of their stay, though, he too was 'intoxicated' by Rome. Eliot revised her opinion of St Peter's, though she thought the exterior 'even ugly'. Her first impression of the interior was 'at a higher pitch than any subsequent impression, either of its beauty or vastness', and she was disturbed by the fact that on later visits 'the lovely marble, ... was half-covered with hideous red drapery'.[44] On the whole, the couple regretted that they had timed their visit to coincide with Holy Week: Eliot found the ceremonies 'a melancholy, hollow business' and Lewes was 'wearied with the hollow sham of shams in the shape of Papal Ceremonies, washing the feet of the Apostles &c. Thoroughly disgusted with the whole business'.[45] On coming out of St Peter's on Maundy Thursday, Eliot and Lewes became separated – she came out and knelt down to receive the blessing of the Pope as he passed the crowd but later wrote: 'I have a cold and headache this morning, and in other ways am not conscious of improvement from the Pope's blessing. I may comfort myself with thinking that the King of Sardinia is none the worse for the Pope's curse.'[46] Pius IX had excommunicated Victor Emmanuel II for his part in Garibaldi's coup and for accepting the annexation of the Papal Legations. Eliot continues: 'It is farcical enough that the excommunication is posted up at the Church of St John Lateran, out of everybody's way, and yet there are police to guard it'. Her anger and indignation are then directed at the Roman authorities and Napoleon, whose soldiers were there to protect the Pope: 'I feel some stirrings of the insurrectionary spirit myself when I see the red pantaloons at every turn in the streets of Rome'.

> I suppose Mrs Browning could explain to me that this is part of the great idea nourished in the soul of the modern saviour Louis Napoleon, and that for the French to impose a hateful government on the Romans is the only proper sequence to the story of the French Revolution.[47]

Both Eliot and Lewes were, of course, fully aware that their first trip to Italy coincided with the momentous moment of the rebirth of the nation. Indeed, Eliot felt the need to explain to Blackwood why their own personal affairs figure more prominently in her letters than the conquests of Garibaldi's 'Thousand' in Sicily. Lewes' and her own good health were

> more important to us than the politics of Sicily, and so I am apt to write of it to our friends, rather than of Garibaldi and the Tuscan filibusters; [...] Tuscany is in the highest political spirits for the moment, and of course Victor Emanuel [sic] stares at us at every turn here, with the most loyal exaggeration of moustache and intelligent meaning. But we are selfishly careless about dynasties just now, caring more for the doings of Giotto and Brunelleschi, than for those of Count Cavour. On a first journey to the greatest centres of art, one must be excused for letting one's public spirit go to sleep a little.[48]

The couple moved down to Naples and on to Salerno, Paestum, Amalfi and Sorrento, before returning to Naples to catch the steamer for Leghorn on May 15th. Only a few days later, Eliot wrote from Florence that '...things really look so threatening in the Neapolitan kingdom that we began to think ourselves fortunate in having got our visit done'.[49] The 'recollections' of Florence are again for the most part of the monuments and works of art of interest which they visited. Among the descriptions is one of the visit to Santa Croce to visit the tombs of Michelangelo, Dante, Alfieri and Macchiavelli: 'I used to feel my heart swell a little at the sight of the inscription of Dante's tomb – "onorate l'altissima poeta"'.[50] Those artists Eliot names were, of course, a living part of *Risorgimento* mythology, and Eliot's reaction before Dante's tomb is a further sign of her emotional engagement with the myths and of a growing interest in Dante, who had figured, albeit very briefly, in the novel she had just finished.[51] It was in Florence, too, that Lewes made the suggestion that Savonarola's 'life and times afford fine material for an historical romance'.[52] Eliot was enthusiastic about the project and wrote to Blackwood that 'there has been a crescendo of enjoyment in our travels, for Florence...has roused a keener interest in us even than Rome, and has stimulated me to entertain rather an ambitious project,...'.[53] This was the germ of her next novel, *Romola*, and by the time she had reached Berne in Switzerland, she was 'athirst to begin'.[54]

Eliot and Lewes left for Bologna (June 1st) and then went on to Ferrara (Savonarola's birthplace) on the 3rd and Padua on the 4th, where they saw the Giotto frescoes in the Arena Chapel. Eliot notes in her Journal that 'while [Giotto] was at work on it, Dante lodged with him at Padua'.[55] Eliot was captivated by Venice on her arrival, finding it 'more beautiful than the romances had feigned'.[56] This impression was to remain and deepen during their stay. The architecture of Venice gave her the sense of being in 'an entirely novel scene, but one where the ideas of a foreign race have poured themselves in without yet mingling indistinguishably with the pre-existent Italian life'.[57] Among the catalogue of the art seen and places visited in the Journal is a 'recollection' of the Bridge of Sighs and the prisons where, Eliot comments, 'the horrible, dark, damp cells, ... would make the saddest life in the free light and air seem bright and desirable'.[58] By contrast, she felt that 'Of all the dreamy delights that of floating on a gondola along the canals and out on the Lagoon is surely the greatest'.[59] They were 'so enchanted with Venice, that [they] were seduced into staying there a whole week instead of three or four days'.[60] From Venice, they moved 'across the green plains of Lombardy' to Verona for a short stay which Eliot greatly enjoyed, and then on to Milan, where they stayed at the Albergo Reale, the same hotel where Eliot had stayed with the Brays in 1849. Eliot particularly enjoyed her visit to the Brera Gallery and the Ambrosian Library, where they 'saw MMS. surpassing in interest any even of those we had seen ... in Florence – illuminated books, sacred and secular, ... private letters of Tasso, Galileo, Lucrezia Borgia, etc'.[61] They then went up to Como and over the Splügen Pass where 'the mighty wall of the Valtelline Alps shut [them] out from Italy on the 21st of June'.[62] Eliot felt that this journey, and especially the Italian part of it ('after Venice we considered ourselves merely on our way home'[63]) had been of immense importance for her. Once back in London she wrote: 'We have had an unspeakably delightful journey – one of those journeys that seem to divide one's life in two by the new ideas they suggest and the new veins of interest they open up'.[64] The resurgence of Italy in 1860 was also the occasion of an imaginative rebirth for George Eliot.

Having hatched the project for a book set in fifteenth-century Florence, Eliot felt the need for another journey to research it.[65] Eliot's third trip to Italy, her second with Lewes, lasted almost two months between April 19th and June 14th, 1861. Travelling down through France then along the Grande Corniche, they stayed two days in Genoa, reading in the Doria Gardens and sightseeing. Lewes wrote to his son Charles: 'We were so enraptured with Genoa last year that I feared lest a second visit should be a disappointment. But "a thing of beauty is a joy forever, its loveliness increaseth"... and our stay at Genoa was again intoxicating...'.[66] They heard Verdi's *Attila* 'bawled with great vigour' at the Opera, and Eliot 'sternly resisted Genoese velvets and Genoese bracelets', though they did buy a few volumes of Italian literature and history.[67]

While in Genoa, Lewes wrote, 'At the table d'hôte we were much struck by the fine massive energetic head of an Englishman with a huge iron grey beard'.[68] On May 5th, Lewes wrote again to his son: 'At the hotel where we stayed there was Garibaldi's Col. Peard – his "Englishman" of whom you doubtless often heard. We had been very much struck by his appearance before we learned who he was, and *after* learning it we saw him no more.'[69] Garibaldi's Englishman was John Whitehead Peard (1811–80), who had achieved European celebrity with the Italian *Cacciatori delle Alpi* (1859). He was made commander of the British Legion (the British volunteer force), accompanied Garibaldi on the Sicilian expedition of 1860 and was made a colonel. He later commanded the English Legion in the advance upon Naples and was decorated by Victor Emmanuel. It is very much in the *Risorgimento* spirit that Eliot and Lewes should have been struck by the 'fine massive' countenance, which seemed to figure energy, resolution and strength, before learning that he was in fact an authentic piece of (British) *Risorgimento* mythology.[70] Trevelyan gives a romantic portrayal of this 'gentleman adventurer' and of the *Cacciatori* who 'were mostly men of education and ideals',[71] and quotes Peard's Journal (1859) describing how the soldiers would entertain each other in the evenings by reciting Tasso, Ariosto or the tragedies of Alfieri, a detail which further points up the close connection between Italian literature and the struggles to achieve a national identity in *Risorgimento* Italy.[72] Eliot and Lewes had occasion to meet Peard himself in Florence only a few weeks later, when he was a visitor at Villino Trollope during the celebrations of Italian liberation on June 2nd, 1861. The strong tendency to mythologize the events and figures of these years is perhaps highlighted by more recent assessments of the role played by Garibaldi's Englishman. Peard, says Andrea Viotti, was not a good commander and was himself 'chiefly responsible for the bad reputation of the British Legion'.[73]

After Genoa the Lewes moved down the Ligurian coast to Pisa, and then on to Florence (May 4th), where Eliot spent the next month 'drinking in' the city and researching *Romola*.[74] They were not wholly absorbed in this project, however, and followed the course of events in Italy with great concern. Eliot wrote from Florence on May 19th: 'I look forward with keen anxiety to the next outbreak of war – longing for some turn of affairs that will save poor Venice from being bombarded by those terrible Austrian forts'.[75] They had planned to leave Florence earlier than they did, but 'Mr Trollope has returned and seduced us into prolonging our stay for another week, in order that we may witness the great national festival of regenerated Italy on Sunday'.[76] The Lewes, then, were actually in Italy at this important moment in the history of the country, and observed the celebrations at close quarters. A few days earlier, on May 29th, they had been given tickets for a ceremony held in Santa Croce, in honour of the Tuscan heroes of 1848, the 'devoted youths who fell in 1848 fighting for Liberty': 'Padre Angelico... preached a politico-religious sermon with affecting eloquence and most impressive oratory. He is old and blind, and it was intensely interesting to the Mutter, as you may imagine, to sit and look at his face and hear him uttering brave, wise words to the Florentines.'[77] After the 'Papal shams' of Rome the year before, Lewes concluded that 'Altogether this is *the* religious ceremony which I have most thoroughly enjoyed; generally they have been wearisome and rather exasperating, but this was grand throughout and had a real feeling in it'.[78] Lewes' attitude no doubt reflects the fact that it was a *politico-religious* celebration, and of a cause which both he and Eliot had actively espoused for many years. Eliot's intense interest in the ceremony can be seen, says Haight, in her transposition of the scene into *Romola* as Savonarola's sermon (Chapter 24).[79] Eliot, then, creates a direct link across the centuries between the political struggles of fifteenth-century Florence and the *Risorgimento* struggles for the Unification of Italy.

Thomas Trollope accompanied the Lewes on expeditions to see the monasteries at Camaldoli and La Vernia (June 3rd – 6th). Lewes' account of their trip is contained in his journal, where he notes that both Wordsworth and Sismondi had signed the visitors' book before them at Camaldoli.[80] Trollope too reported the Camaldoli excursion and provides an insight into Eliot's knowledge of Dante:

> The path as it descends to the town, winds round the ruin of an ancient castle, beneath the walls of which is still existent that Fontebranda fountain which Adam the forger in the *Inferno* longed for a drop of, and which almost all Dantescan scholars

and critics mistake for a larger and nowadays better known fountain of the same name at Siena. On pointing it out to George Eliot, I found, of course, that the name and the whole of Adam the forger's history was familiar to her; but she had little expected to find his local habitation among these wild hills; and she was unaware of the current mistake between the Siena Fontebranda, and the little rippling streamlet before us.[81]

On the morning of June 7th as they were leaving Florence, they heard the news of Cavour's untimely death. The return journey to England took them via Genoa and Berne, and they reached London on June 14th. Mrs Trollope sent them a copy of the account of Cavour in the *Athaeneum* (June 29th, 1861), a piece 'which stirred me strongly', wrote Eliot.[82]

George Eliot *was* strongly stirred by Italy, by her contact with Italian life and culture, and by the *Risorgimento* and its heroes. The letters and journals of both Eliot and Lewes reveal strong sympathy and emotional engagement with the country and convey a sense of excitement at witnessing what they realized was a great moment in the country's history. From well before the 1860 trip, Eliot had consciously been 'absorb[ing]...new life and gather[ing] fresh ideas' from Italy and when these were added to her extensive reading about the country, they furnished a rich and potent source which could feed into her writings. Much of this book is concerned with tracing ways in which the fiction is 'immensely enriched with [the] new ideas and new veins of interest' which Italy opened up.

3

Eliot's Italian Exile in 'Mr Gilfil's Love Story' (*Scenes of Clerical Life*)

George Eliot's first fiction was written in 1856–7, with 'Amos Barton' being published in *Blackwood's Magazine* in January 1857, 'Mr Gilfil's Love Story' between March and June and 'Janet's Repentance' from July to November. The second of these three, 'Mr Gilfil's Love Story', presents a historically accurate picture of British attitudes towards Italy and the Italians in the period preceding the French Revolution and reflects Eliot's interest in and engagement with Italy. The main character is not in fact Maynard Gilfil but an orphaned Italian girl, Caterina Sarti, brought back to England by Sir Christopher and Lady Cheverel in 1773. The story deals with the meeting of English and Italian cultures both in Italy and England, and registers a range of anglocentric attitudes towards foreigners in general and Italians in particular, attitudes which Eliot's narrator at times appears to resist, and at others to embrace. Whereas in her fiction until *Romola*, Eliot is mainly concerned with English provincial life, in 'Mr Gilfil' we observe a concern to incorporate a European perspective which takes the form of an exploration of cultural relationships. This concern with Italy was in itself the continuation of an interest already present in her journalism. There is also a further, more precise continuity with Eliot's journalism in the period immediately prior to 'Mr Gilfil' in the influence of Elizabeth Barrett Browning's *Aurora Leigh,* which Eliot had reviewed in the *Westminster Review* in January 1857, when her own story was taking shape in her mind. It is clear that Eliot had read the long poem carefully and that it had made a great impact upon her: '...no poem embraces so wide a range of thought and emotion, or takes such possession of our nature'. In the review Eliot employs what, in her fiction, was to become her favourite and most potent metaphor for female empowerment – the woman artist as singer – to characterize Barrett Browning's achievement, praising 'the beautiful feeling, the large thought, the rich melodious song of this rare poem', and paying tribute to 'a full mind pouring itself out in song as its natural and easiest medium'.[1] The 'song', 'a work which exhibits all the peculiar powers without the negations of her sex' becomes an eminently empowering and liberating medium, and Barrett Browning embodies the genius of the woman artist channelled through song. Soon after reading *Aurora Leigh*, George Eliot created the first of her women singers. Caterina, who is neither strikingly gifted or beautiful nor a poetess like Aurora, is temporarily empowered in *Scenes of Clerical Life* through the beauty of her voice.

That Eliot had *Aurora Leigh* in mind when she wrote 'Mr Gilfil's Love Story' may also be deduced from the many similarities in plot between the two works. Both heroines have Italian origins; Aurora is half Italian but brought up in Italy until the age of 13, while Caterina is orphaned and brought back to England when only two. In the space opened up by the transplantation of these heroines from Italian to English soil, their authors perceived potential for exploring contrasts between the two cultures and for gaining a critical vantage point from which to survey their own societies. Eliot, like Barrett Browning, perceived the possibilities for heightening and intensification in the many correspondences between the situation of women in Britain and the plight of Italy and the Italians in the mid nineteenth century. She explores the themes of exclusion and exile, imprisonment and liberation, silence and the finding of a voice. This chapter explores the ways in which 'Mr Gilfil' relies on fictional models and on British stereotypes and prejudices concerning Italians, and argues that in Caterina's story there is also present an allegory of the silencing of the 'nation' of Italy.

'Mr Gilfil' has often been regarded as the weakest of the *Scenes of Clerical Life*. David Lodge notes how the 'infinitely more effective' understatement of 'Amos Barton' is missing in Eliot's 'over-anxious appeals to the reader to appreciate the intensity of the heroine's emotions' and concludes that 'Caterina is all too obviously a character deriving from "fiction" rather than "actual life"'.[2] Eliot does indeed draw heavily on fictional models in her depiction of Caterina, but from the point of view of this study at least, the story is of interest precisely because of this intertextual aspect.

Behind *Aurora Leigh*, too, there is the strong influence of fictional models, and particularly of Mme de Staël's *Corinne or Italy* (1807), in which the heroine is likewise culturally displaced while still young. *Corinne* had a tremendous influence, particularly on female readers, and Eliot too knew the novel well.[3] While she has Mme de Staël and Elizabeth Barrett Browning strongly in mind, Eliot essentially writes *against* the models of the heroine which they offer: Caterina is denied any lasting form of empowerment, nor will she be allowed to escape the constraints of the society and culture in which she finds herself. Before looking at 'Mr Gilfil's Love Story', we shall briefly examine *Corinne* and *Aurora Leigh* to establish the kinds of fictional models which presented themselves to Eliot.

The gifted poetess Corinne is able to preserve her independence from both Italian and English cultures to a large degree. The novel is highly critical of the strongly patriarchal and puritanical culture of England, obsessed as it is with hierarchies and history. England becomes a prison for women. Confined in mind, body and spirit, female talent is repressed by hostile social forces. Too unsubmissive to accept a husband, Corinne is an insubordinate heroine, free of ties and answerable to no one but herself. She embodies and perpetuates antidomestic revolt, fleeing the ties of home and family and exulting in the liberating air of Italy[4] where, after hearing Monti's song *Bella Italia*[5] she falls into a sort of 'drunken state', confessing 'everything that love makes one feel I felt for Italy; desire, enthusiasm, regret; I was no longer mistress of myself' (*Corinne*, XIV, ii). As Gutwirth comments, 'In a nearly mystic ecstasy, she marries herself to her own fate – as poetess of Italy – instead of to that of a man'.[6] Corinne's art thrives in Italy and she achieves success and fame. In *Corinne*, Mme De Staël espouses 'a counter-patriarchal feminine cult of transcendence through art', of immanence in which art is lying just below the surface of life ready to be transformed, and in which the heroine lives life as art in emulation of Dante, 'at [whose] voice all the earth is turned to poetry; objects, ideas, laws, phenomena become a new Olympus of divinities'.[7]

Within *Corinne*, Italy takes on precise and powerful significance. In the incoherence and muddle of antiquity, its continual rise and fall from power and the greatness of its science and arts, Italy represents the coexistence of past and present. Its non-linear temporal quality is associated with Corinne's genius, and stands for a Romantic fullness which includes the mystery of the unknown and points up the inexplicable complexity of life itself. In this more 'natural' and accepting environment, Corinne grows freely, unconstrained by rigid social and cultural mores. This 'feminine' Italy is set against the 'masculine' linearity of Enlightenment England. Italy comes to stand not only for art but for individualism and for woman herself. This latter affinity can be taken still further, for there is a strong parallel to be drawn between the fate of Italy and the fate of women. Corinne's defence of Italy might equally be applied to the fate of women: 'I am not sure whether I err in this, but the faults of the Italians inspire in me only a feeling of pity for their lot. Foreigners have laid waste this beautiful country, the object of their eternal ambitions in every age'.[8] The 'faults of the Italians' – who were often stereotyped as childlike, indolent, frivolous and volatile – are often applied to women too. Mme de Staël, like others of her contemporaries, attributes these traits to the habit of dissimulation which the defeated culture (or sex) internalizes.[9] Italy is bereft of all power except that of its artistic and spiritual traditions, but it is these which Corinne claims and turns into instruments of her own poetic powers, and through which she aims to transcend the constraints of patriarchy. She becomes, indeed, an 'Italia' figure, exulting in her hard-won freedom. The presence of Italy, with her restorative liberating influence, was a strong component in the creation of the Corinne myth in which the heroine claims equal access for women to culture and the right to self-definition and self-realization in ways other than those legitimized by (English) patriarchy. It is *Corinne* which establishes the broad terms for the romantic engagement with Italian culture, and tenets which Barrett Browning and George Eliot could either follow or write against.

Both the eponymous heroines of *Corinne* and *Aurora Leigh* are strongly independent and highly gifted, the former with precocious talent, the latter with a fine intelligence, a combination of character and talent which allows them to transcend the roles which patriarchy prescribes for women. However, whereas in *Corinne* there is a radical opposition between a feminine, poetic Italy and a masculine England, in *Aurora Leigh* this is modified so that England nurtures the mind and spirit and Italy the passions. The strong sexual stereotyping in *Aurora Leigh* is drawn straight from *Corinne*: 'Comparing England, where her mind and spirit mature, to Italy which represents the body and passion, [Aurora] describes England as a series of negations of the sexualized Italian panorama' in a 'subversive assertion of female sexuality'.[10] She does find the success and recognition there as poetess which was denied Corinne, whose gifts, regarded in Italy as celestial endowments, are merely a deformation in England. Nevertheless, Italy 'remains the "magic circle" where love can be expressed and experienced', where Aurora accepts her cousin Romney Leigh's love after refusing to marry him in England.[11] As Cora Kaplan points out, in *Aurora Leigh*, 'as in *Corinne*, and in so much other Protestant writing about Italy, classical architecture, Catholicism and warm weather come to represent a blurred sensuality missing in England, which opens itself to its permitted corollary, love'.[12] For both Mme de Staël and Barrett Browning, then, 'Italy / Is one thing, England one'.[13]

Eliot too presents Italy as a 'feminine realm' of romance in 'Mr Gilfil's Love Story'. Caterina is associated with 'taper-lit shrines' (p.147) and with 'a symbol of divine mercy and protection', 'a little tinsel madonna', before whom Sarti leaves his daughter in Milan Cathedral (p.150). As she grows up, Caterina takes on Madonna-like qualities, with her 'large dark eyes' which 'spoke of sadness' (p.130). Significantly, however, in the patriarchal culture of Cheverel Manor, the feminine symbol of comfort, mercy and protection is replaced by the image of a face above the main door which 'looming out of blackness, might, by a great synthetic effort, be pronounced a Magdalen' (p.153). Moreover, the 'shrine' at which Gilfil reveres Caterina after her death, seems singularly devoid of rejuvenating power, suggesting instead only stagnation, old age and sterility.[14] In spite of this contrast, so strongly felt in *Corinne* and *Aurora Leigh*, the whole of Eliot's story takes place in the 'masculine' realm of England, and Caterina is denied the return to Italy granted to Corinne and Aurora.

The text presents us with a historically accurate picture of pre-revolutionary anglocentric attitudes towards foreigners in general and Italians in particular. Voiced by a number of characters, these range from the blind prejudice of the lower orders, aired by Gilfil's parishioners and the servants at Cheverel Manor, to the comments of aristocratic and well-to-do but uninformed English tourists. Caterina, is first introduced as a 'furriner': 'I've no opinion o' furriners,' says Mrs Patten, 'for I've travelld in their country with my lady in my time, an' seen enough o' their victuals an' their nasty ways' (p.131). Mrs Sharp, the Cheverels' servant in Italy 'had the smallest possible admiration for fair Ausonia and its natives' (p.148). Caterina's identity can only be established (and her character partly redeemed) by recourse to another aspect of the Italian stereotype: ' "Mrs Gilfil come from It'ly, didn't she?" "I reckon she did, but I niver could rightly hear about that. [...]. It's the Italians as has such fine voices, an' Mrs Gilfil sung, you never heard the like." '

(p.131). 'Furriner' and 'Italian' are run together so as to become synonyms among the servants. Even the well-to-do Mrs Assher, in conversation with Caterina, airs the vacuous platitudes of national stereotypes of so many fashionable travellers on the continent:

> 'I hear you are the most beautiful singer,' was of course the opening remark. 'All Italians sing so beautifully. I travelled in Italy with Sir John when we were first married, and we went to Venice, where they go about in gondolas, you know.' (p.172)

Much of Eliot's portrayal of her heroine draws heavily on the stock characteristics attributed to the Italian character. Although Caterina is taken to England when very young, and might therefore be expected to become fully integrated into English society, Eliot's text insists upon difference, and difference which excludes her as much because of her foreignness as because she is female and without independent means. The Cheverels mean to 'train this little Papist into a good Protestant, and graft as much English fruit as possible onto the Italian stem' (p.152) and the process begins almost immediately, with Caterina being initiated into 'Mrs Sharp's new dispensation of soap and water' washing away Italian dirt and ignorance. Eliot's narrator assures us that the young Caterina soon 'breaks down all prejudices against her foreign blood' and becomes 'the pet of the household' (p.157). Yet, as the plethora of animal imagery (often coupled with diminutives – 'Tina' not Caterina is used throughout) employed by the household to describe her repeatedly demonstrates ('clever black-eyed monkey', 'little singing bird' or 'linnet' when she sings before Sir Christopher; Blenheim spaniel, grasshopper, or references to her 'mouse-like ways'), feelings and wishes, indeed full humanity, are effectively denied Caterina by means of a variety of signifiers through which language erects a strong barrier between her and the rest of the household. She is classed along with the other pets who 'ask no questions, pass no criticisms' (p.181). The prejudice against foreign blood is deflected, submerged in a reconstitution of the identity of the child as a 'household pet', an identity which of course implies an owner. Unlike the untamed Italian girl of *Corinne*, Caterina is tamed by the text's insistent imagery. Significantly, this imagery changes in the moment of her rebellion, when she becomes a 'tigress' and a 'mad little thing' (p.146). While George Eliot resists the temptation to give any foreign inflection to Caterina's speech (the child has after all been brought up to 'speak summat better nor gibberish' (p.155)),[15] Caterina herself is apparently complicit in the role imposed upon her, calling Sir Christopher 'Padroncello' (an affectionate epithet, but one stemming from 'padrone' – master or owner) which, when set alongside his 'little monkey', exposes the underlying basis of the relationship between them.

Descriptions of Caterina's physical appearance also register a series of anglocentric attitudes and emphasize racial differences. 'This tiny, dark-eyed child of the south, whose face was immediately suggestive of olive-covered hills and taper-lit shrines' could not be looked upon with a wholly approving eye, for the evocation of the natural beauties of the landscape is marred by the suggestions of papism. The 'childishness' of Sarti's faith in the *'little tinsel madonna'* (my italics) with which he leaves his daughter may be intended to play upon the contemporary reader's disapproval of Catholic superstition. We need also to keep in mind here the wider context of the story as one of a series of 'Scenes of Clerical Life' concerned with the 'drama of Evangelism'.[16] With the 'pale southern-looking complexion', in the miniature portrait of the adult Caterina, there are 'large dark eyes' and 'a coquettish head-dress', hinting obliquely perhaps at the licentiousness and moral laxity so often associated with Italian passion.[17] The incongruity of Caterina's appearance in the setting of Cheverel Manor, the strangely *pale* complexion, is conveyed yet again through animal imagery: it is 'almost as if a humming bird were found perched on one of the elm-trees in the park, by the side of her ladyship's handsomest pouter pigeon' (p.147). Caterina's pallor and diminutive stature, suggesting physical fragility, image her as some exotic plant displaced from its native soil in which it would thrive to be deposited in a strange and harsh environment.[18]

Fictional models and popular Italian stereotypes are likewise employed in the delineation of character. Caterina has a 'loving, sensitive nature', indeed 'her only talent lay in loving' (p.160). As a child, however, she had fiercely resisted 'any discipline that had a harsh or unloving aspect (p.158) and she displays 'a certain ingenuity in vindictiveness', revenging herself for unpleasant prohibitions imposed upon her. When it becomes clear that Wybrow is to marry Beatrice, Caterina's suffering is that of fierce jealousy, even though 'the peace of the whole family depends on [Caterina's] power of governing [herself]' (p.191). Although she makes repeated efforts to do so, her ultimate failure to control her passions stands as an indictment of an impetuosity, a volatility, which contrasts strongly with the character of Lady Cheverel, 'a proud woman who [had] learned to submit' (p.194). Wybrow, although a 'Jackanapes'[19] intent on hiding his own poor conduct, resorts to the stereotype in explaining Caterina's behaviour: 'With that Italian blood of hers, there's no knowing how she may take what one says. She's a fierce little thing, though she seems so quiet generally' (p.200). Though his duplicity is immediately exposed in this statement, and his 'explanation' is seen to be hollow in the moment of its utterance, the pressure of the text's insistence on Caterina's supposed difference weighs heavily against her.

The plot appears to support Wybrow's facile explanation and to reinforce the stereotypes. What Caterina intends to be the defining action of her life (that of taking the dagger to revenge herself on Wybrow) is essentially a *crime passionnel* issuing from jealousy and the desire for revenge, all of which have been foreshadowed in the text. Caterina's character, then, ultimately evinces all those traits, the strong ungovernable passions which formed 'the keystone of the English conception of the Italian character'[20] and proves to be an example of the kind of restrictive stereotyping which the following passage on the Italian character presents:

> Unhappily the energy and violence which marked their national character was often directed to evil purposes by such dark and vindictive passions as, in these more temperate times, we find it difficult to account for or excuse. It is hard for us to credit the strength of the stormy passions in southern climes... The emotions of hatred and jealousy which in colder climes occasionally ruffle our bosoms, and are mastered by steady principle and placid temperament, there burn with an intensity which makes their unhappy victims the objects of our pity no less than reproach.[21]

At one point, indeed, Eliot's text degenerates into the cloak-and-dagger stuff of melodrama based on medieval and Renaissance Italian history, with Caterina rushing noiselessly along passages and up gallery stairs with gleaming eyes and bloodless lips and clenching a half-drawn dagger (pp.211–12). The melodrama and theatricality of Gothic romance is undeniable, and this of course can hardly be associated with 'life', but rather with fictional models. The text points up the fact that Caterina is not playing a 'woman's role', but one more akin to that of the Gothic villain, often of course male and Italian. Blackwood asked whether it would not be more decorous for Caterina to dream of stabbing Wybrow instead of actually intending to do so. Eliot's reply that 'dreams usually play an important part in fiction, but rarely, I think, in real life' betrays an apparent unwillingness to acknowledge the fact that her 'realism' here relies all too heavily on models from fiction and on her faith in the reader's willingness to go along with the Italian stereotype with its hot-blooded passions.

The contrast between the heated passions of the Italian character and the coldness of the English, by comparison, is also present. A spontaneous gesture of affection by Caterina towards Sir Christopher jars on Lady Cheverel ('Caterina, that is foolish,' [...] 'I wish you would leave off those stage-player's antics' (p.143)) who 'looks down with severity on all feminine assumption as "unbecoming"' (p.194), and Caterina's action is mistrusted as an example of Italian theatricality and hyperbole. This reaction hides a fear of a subversive assertion of female sexuality which, according to English mores, ought to remain unacknowledged by young ladies in England. Lady Cheverel is 'cast in a very different mould of womanhood' (p.133), with 'an expression of hauteur which is not contradicted by the cold grey eye'. Shunning the direct sunlight, she looks like 'one of Sir Joshua Reynold's stately ladies who had just stepped from her frame to enjoy the evening cool'. The same concentration on duty above feelings, so prominent in Book I of *Aurora Leigh* in the figure of Aurora's aunt who 'did / Her duty to me ... Her duty, in large measure, well pressed out / But measured always' is also registered.[22] Captain Wybrow appeals to duty ('You know I have duties – we both have duties – before which feeling must be sacrificed') in justifying his poor treatment of Caterina (p.145).[23]

The other Italian in the story, Sarti, is also associated with moments of melodrama ('Will the Eccelentissima, for the love of God, have pity on a dying man, and come to him?' (p.150), 'Holy mother! He is dead!' (p.151)), but he gathers to himself many of the characteristic British images of Italy and Italians current in pre-revolutionary Europe. A 'primo tenore' for a season before losing his voice completely and being condemned to silence, he is now 'little better than a cracked fiddle, which is good for nothing but firewood' and 'like many Italian singers, ... too ignorant to teach' (p.149). After an illness, which leaves him enfeebled in body and brain, he becomes, in fact, the 'poveraccio' (contrasting with the other Italian term, 'padroncello', used of Sir Christopher) thrown upon the goodwill of Lady Cheverel.[24] The descriptions of Sarti as he approaches Lady Cheverel – 'the frowsiest, shabbiest man you ever saw', 'fleas and worse', a 'sallow and dingy' beggar 'with a restless wandering look in his dull eyes, and an excessive timidity about his deep reverences, which gave him the look of a man who had been long a solitary prisoner' (p.148) – is a distillation of common British perceptions of Italians before and after the French Revolution. Dwelling on dirt, ignorance and abject poverty, the text also hints at the curtailment of a natural talent and Sarti's reduction, through no fault of his own, to a condition of bodily and mental suffering which has left him without memory or wits. The 'restless look' suggests the wanderings of an exile, and his suffering evokes the image of the tortured prisoner and turns Sarti, whose decline is concomitant with his loss of voice, into a symbol of the Italian people reduced to poverty and subjection yet exculpated for being seemingly without historical memory or the ability to change their lot.

Caterina inherits her father's natural talent, and 'this rare gift of song' endears her to Lady Cheverel and makes possible her promotion from being merely Mrs Sharp's helper in the house to the station of lady (p.161). Though she cannot speak or write like Corinne or Aurora, Caterina pours out her feelings through song, in her renderings of Gluck's '*Che farò senza Eurydice?*' ('What am I to do without Eurydice?') and Paesiello's '*Ho perduto il bel sembiante*' ('I have lost the fair face'), which are clearly indirect expressions of her own suffering in losing her beloved Wybrow. Caterina's deep feeling for, and engagement with, her art are in stark contrast to its reception by the Cheverels, for whom it remains merely entertainment without real communication. Its expressive force is lost on the listeners, for whom the performer, never credited with real human feelings anyway, remains a 'clever black-eyed [performing?] monkey'. When Lady and Beatrice Assher pay their visit during which it becomes clear that Caterina is to be excluded by Beatrice, the existing relations at Cheverel Manor are temporarily reversed, 'for while [Caterina] was singing she was queen of the room' and her music is 'animated by a little triumphant contempt', by 'the fierce palpitations of triumph and hatred' (pp.174–5). Her suffering as a result of Wybrow's indifference is relieved temporarily by the cathartic experience of singing, 'the one thing in which she ceased to be passive, and became prominent', her only means of articulating her misery and the personal and social injustices perpetrated against her (p.195). Caterina's artistic expression, through the language and cultural production of her native country, gives voice to extreme emotions of loss and incompleteness which resonate at both the personal and the wider social and national levels. The critique of English society, implicit in the story, lies in its failure or inability to listen to those voices from the 'feminine realm', to acknowledge the importance and place of passion and feeling, which are marginalized and relegated to being mere pastimes. As DeCuir points out, the implication in the story 'is that without the nourishment of Italy, the feminine realm, [Caterina's] talent will wither away and die' (p.70).[25] This process of the loss of voice, and of the inability to listen attentively is already evident in Lady Cheverel, who had cultivated her own fine soprano voice 15 years earlier in Italy but who no longer sings. After learning to suppress her own voice, she now appears unable to hear Caterina's as expressing anything other than the song as a product valued by English culture in and for itself. Having been tortured and repressed by this culture to the point at which she rebels and then goes into exile from it, Caterina is restored to herself (her 'soul floating in its true familiar element of delicious sound as a water plant that lies shrunken on the ground expands into freedom and beauty when once more bathed in its native flood' (p.240)) through the power of music when it is no longer being appropriated as entertainment. Gilfil, who has not imposed his will upon Caterina and does not have access to the powers of patriarchy, becomes the answer to the question in Caterina's rendering of Gluck's '*Che farò*...?' ['What shall I do...?']: 'the soul that was born anew to music was born anew to love' (p.241) in what, we are asked to feel, will be a more inclusive, accepting union than any of the others offered in the story.[26] Nevertheless, there are no references to Caterina singing or continuing her art after her marriage to Gilfil. She is herself subsumed into that dominant patriarchal English culture, within a cultural matrix which imposes childbirth and motherhood as the only wholly legitimate role for women. And it is that imposed role, along with the culture which has drained her vitality, which finally kills Caterina. George Eliot, like de Staël and Barrett Browning before her, exposes the constrictive character of English patriarchal culture in stifling Caterina as a woman artist, but – and here Eliot's realism comes into its own – allows her heroine no escape, no 'magic circle' in which identity can be realized. Eliot's story plays out the consequences of the marginalization and exclusion of the 'feminine realm' to the end. Her story is at once the stifling and the suppression of the single voice and that of a whole culture, drained of its potency and resonance through insensitive, imperialist appropriation of it as decoration and entertainment.

Themes of conquest, as well as of subjection and repression are central to this story and generate possibilities for readings at several different levels. William Myers argues that in Caterina's singing, which includes both the aesthetic complexity of the eighteenth-century drawing room and the immediate, intense emotions which relate it to the spontaneity and warmth of common life, Eliot identified a principle in art through which the class division and the suppression of feelings upon which it depends can be transcended. In this sense, then, 'Caterina embodies unique, even revolutionary possibilities of integration in the world of the novel'. The story becomes a symbolic representation of major social divisions and historical collisions.[27] Within the story itself, though, these possibilities remain largely unrealized – the servants at Cheverel Manor still prefer 'a good old song ... [to] all the fine Italian toodlin'' of their masters (p.156). Despite the fact that part of the 'urgent meaning' of singing for Eliot is 'the channelling of utterance, and of outrage, for her heroines who would otherwise be doomed to silence',[28] silence is precisely the fate awaiting Caterina when she is finally subsumed into the social matrix of patriarchy.

One of the 'historical collisions' which has not been investigated extensively in 'Mr Gilfil's Love Story', though like the social divisions of class conflict and the 'Woman Question' it was highly topical in the 1850s, is the 'Italian Question'. The analogies and intersections between this and the Woman Question have already been reviewed briefly and the way in which these two strands in the story complement and reinforce each other will, I hope, be further illuminated in the remainder of this chapter. At one point, Eliot quotes directly from a sonnet, *Italia*, by Vincenzo da Filicaia (1642–1707). As the handsome Captain Wybrow is lamenting the responsibilities imposed upon him by the fact that two women (Caterina and Beatrice) are in love with him, the narrator comments, 'clearly it was the "dono infelice della bellezza" that laid these onerous duties upon him' (p.193).[29] In Filicaia's analysis of his country's troubles in this sonnet, the 'unlucky gift of beauty' was the reason why Italy, 'the slave of friend and foe', had repeatedly been conquered, sacked and exploited throughout history. Filicaia's sonnet was well known, along with Petrarch's *Italia mia*, as one of the great Italian patriotic lyrics. It appeared in Sismondi's *De la littérature du midi* (where it is praised as 'the most celebrated specimen which the Italian literature of the seventeenth century affords') and was frequently translated into English. Filicaia's theme and his sentiments and expressions of outrage at the despoliation of Italy by the barbarian hordes were borrowed by de Staël in *Corinne* (the extemporized *chanson* in I, iii) and by Byron.[30] Just as Filicaia's sonnet is generated by a patriot's despair and misery, so Caterina channels her misery into song. Her voice parallels the suppressed voice of Filicaia, and Eliot's narrator underscores this by expanding the misery of the individual outwards towards the weak and defeated generally:

> . . . all the passion that made her misery was hurled by a convulsive effort into her music, just as pain gives new force to the clutch of the sinking wrestler, and as terror gives far-sounding intensity to the shriek of the feeble. (p.210)

There is heavy irony in the fact that the quotation from Filicaia is associated with Wybrow, undoubtedly one of the conquerors, who has exploited Caterina and played with her feelings for his own amusement. The despair of the conquered which generated the revolutionary impulse in the first part of the nineteenth century is ironically reversed in Wybrow's version, to become a conqueror's lament. The true 'dono infelice della bellezza' is Caterina's. She, like Italy, must accept things as they are arranged for her by powers beyond her control, while her art is plundered and sacked. The Italian context of Eliot's quotation and the heavy irony in the reference to 'the fatal gift of beauty' would not have been lost on readers in the late 1850s who might well recognize the allusions to the travails of Italy in Caterina's suffering.[31] As the voice of Filicaia's sonnet, born of despair and misery and pain, had 'a far soundingintensity' for Italian nationalism, so Caterina, though 'sinking' and 'feeble', draws strength from pain. Eliot, then, taps into the discourse of Italian nationalism directly in her story. In Filicaia's text (also known in Britain through Byron's translation in *Childe Harold*), we find a sub-text offering close parallels between the plight of Italy and that of Caterina.

In 'Mr Gilfil's Love Story', an allegory of the subjection and oppression of Italy is being played out on the domestic stage of

Cheverel Manor. This allegory is framed by the events leading up to and after the French Revolution. We are first introduced to Sir Christopher reading of 'the last portentous proceedings of the French parliaments' (p.135) just a year before the outbreak of the Revolution. A deliberate parallel is created between 'the great nation of France...agitated by conflicting thoughts and passions' and the 'terrible struggles' in Caterina's breast (p.147), in the 'hasty summer' of 1788 which seemed to be 'hurrying on the moment when the shadow of dread [would] be followed up by the moment of despair' (p.165), culminating in a 'counter-revolution' in which Caterina's place with Wybrow would be usurped by Beatrice Assher. By contrast with events on the continent, the inertia of England is highlighted by the fact that division and hierarchy are merely reinforced by the changes taking place at Cheverel Manor: the daughter of the 'poveraccio' is supplanted by a lady of aristocratic origins. Again, there is heavy irony in the juxtaposition of the two sets of events, for the apparent egalitarianism of Cheverel Manor in which Caterina had been afforded a place, gives way to a reinforcing of the *Ancien Régime* of the Cheverel family through a marriage contract. Caterina's 'rebellion against her destiny' (p.143) is of course intended to mirror the violent overthrow of the *Ancien Régime* in France. The events occur in England, however, and the threat of violence is deflected by the plot, which bears out Eliot's 1848 opinion on the improbability of any such rising occurring in England.[32] Sir Christopher himself comes from a line of conquerors: his house bears all the signs of his illustrious lineage and supports the stereotyping of the English, obsessed with hierarchy and history, presented in *Corinne*. In the drawing-room at Cheverel Manor, for example,

> hung the portrait of Sir Anthony Cheverel, who in the reign of Charles II was the renovator of the family splendour, which had suffered some declension from the early brilliancy of that Chevreuil who came over with the Conqueror. A very imposing personage was this Sir Anthony, ... and he had known how to choose a wife too, for his lady, hanging opposite him, ... was a fit mother of 'large-acred' heirs. (p.142)

Sir Christopher, descendant of men who had helped establish and then restore monarchy, creates a domestic empire in which he holds absolute power. It is he who decides that Wybrow, the heir to his estate, is to marry the daughter of a neighbouring landed family, that Gilfil is to have a living in his gift and that Caterina is to have Gilfil: 'I never in my life laid a plan, and failed to carry it out. I lay my plans well and I never swerve from them – that's it. A strong will is the only magic' (p.212).[33] The long gallery in Cheverel Manor contains the spoils of the Cheverel family plunder:

> Greek statues and busts of Roman emperors; low cabinets filled with curiosities, natural and antiquarian; tropical birds and huge horns of beasts; Hindoo gods and strange shells; swords and daggers, and bits of chain-armour; Roman lamps and tiny models of Greek temples; and, above all these, queer old family portraits... (p.144)

The family portraits, placed *above* the miscellaneous objects of conquest, and the family's occasional visits of inspection underpin the Cheverels' status as conquerors who have appropriated history as trophaic and decorative.

Nevertheless, it is in the Gothic setting of the long gallery, where 'the bright moonlight... throw[s] into strange light and shadow the heterogeneous objects' and she herself appears 'like the ghost of some former Lady Cheverel come to revisit the glimpses of the moon' (p.144), that Caterina's repressed self is released. Here, in a place separated from the culture which imprisons her, she experiences both sexual desire (when Wybrow's arm steals round her waist) and violent rebellious impulses. The objects in the long gallery ('swords and daggers and bits of chain-armour', the Cheverel children in the portraits *'imprisoned* in stiff ruffs' [my italics]), reflect the unacted desires of Caterina's repressed self. In the unworldliness of the Gothic moonlight, these artefacts and symbols of power from past civilizations appear merely part of a dead world, but in the light of the midday sun the chain-armour glitters brightly, rousing Caterina to rebellion, and the seemingly random objects take on a more suggestive role, hinting perhaps at the resurgence of Greece in the 1820s leading to independence in 1830, at the current unrest in India which was to culminate in the Indian Mutiny of May 1857 (as 'Gilfil' was being serialized in *Blackwood's*) and, of course, at the Italian struggles. Thus, the long gallery becomes momentarily a locus of rebellion and resistance to oppression. Caterina, 'the incarnation of a fierce purpose' (p.211), is no longer a *woman* yet becomes the quintessential stereotyped *Italian* in her passion, and can directly challenge imperialism and the culture of oppression in the name of her sex and of those suppressed cultures with which she is strongly associated in the story. Eliot's text here continues a long Gothic tradition of drawing on fears of the disturbance of the established order, the transgressing of boundaries and the breakdown of national and sexual identities. One commentator, writing in 1796, noticed how 'our *unsexed* female writers now instruct, or confuse, us and themselves in the labyrinths of politics, or turn us wild with Gallic frenzy'.[34] Then in *Jane Eyre*, and Eliot may consciously have paralleled Charlotte Brontë here, as Jane wanders through the third storey of Thornfield Hall, (also 'a shrine to memory'), observing the relics 'by the pallid gleam of moonlight', her woman's restlessness and 'silent revolt' are explicitly linked to political rebellion: 'Nobody knows how many rebellions beside political rebellions ferment in the masses of life which people earth'.[35] This connection is made more mutedly in 'Mr Gilfil', but Caterina, neither woman, nor English, nor fully Italian in *her* 'frenzy', likewise destabilizes the accepted categories.

Caterina's history has been prefigured in Sarti's, which suggests both imprisonment and the wanderings of exile. Caterina's imprisonment at Cheverel Manor forces mental tortures on her which are continually repressed until they explode into rebellion. Immediately though, as Wybrow's body is being carried back to the house, 'she forgot the interval of wrong and jealousy and hatred – all his cruelty, and all her thoughts of revenge – as the exile forgets the stormy passage that lay between home and happiness and the dreary land in which he finds himself desolate' (p.217). This image (continuing the Italian associations of repression, rebellion and exile) foreshadows Caterina's own self-exile from Cheverel Manor. Her physical removal merely renders objective her condition throughout: an exile from both cultures, unable to realize any fully independent identity, she moves uneasily between a liberating, feminine Italian and a constraining male-centred English culture. Exile is no empowering experience as it had been for the great Italian exiles Dante or Mazzini, however. It marks her complete loss of voice and her reduction to the inferior status of a child, a condition of utter powerlessness without the strength even to rebel. Caterina's personal history follows a similar course to that of her homeland and like 'Italia' in the Filicaia sonnet, she is reduced to abject dependence.

Eliot's story addresses the question of women's place in a strongly patriarchal society and both challenges and urges revision of cultural codes concerning women whose voices are suppressed.[36] The dual themes of repression of women and of whole cultures merely because they are in a weaker position interpenetrate each other in the story and are, indeed, fused in Caterina. That same fusion between the individual woman and a cultural and national identity runs through the mythology of the Italian *Risorgimento*, in the personification of 'Italia', the weeping woman in chains,[37] and Eliot, like de Staël and Barrett Browning before her, draws on Italy and its culture to provide the metaphors of silence and suppression, submission and rebellion, imprisonment and exile. Caterina bears the triple burden of being foreign, a woman, and of low social extraction. By contrast with *Corinne* and *Aurora Leigh*, Eliot's heroine is never really empowered either by her art or by direct rebellion. When she finds Wybrow dead of heart failure, she can only return to the place of her repression to be overcome by feelings of guilt and weakness. Her exile is no more than a prostration before forces too powerful for her, and though it may be possible to read the story as a triumph of the power of love,[38] it is also a triumph of the 'masculine' over the 'feminine realm', with Caterina losing her voice and ultimately her life (during childbirth) in the process of being assimilated into English patriarchy. Like Caterina, suspended between song and silence, rebellion and submission, life and death, the Italian cultural artefacts in the story tremble between silence or being merely faint ghostly voices powerless to claim individuals or channel energies, and forceful eruption into the present to attempt a radical modification of existing relations. Paradoxically, our first sight of Caterina is after her death, in the miniature painting contained in Gilfil's shut-up shrine to her memory. Like the objects in the long gallery, she too becomes a silent artefact: her voice vanishes and she belongs to the ghostly Italy of dead history. Our last tantalizing glimpse of 'the bright Italian plains, with the sweet *Addio* of their beckoning maidens' which the narrator associates with 'rich brown locks, passionate love, and deep...sorrow' (p. 243), identifies Italy as ever the place of romance, still 'the magic circle'. It is an inaccessible realm 'on the other side of the mountain', 'far back in time' from which Gilfil, now 'worn and grey', is shut out by the 'sombre rocky walls and...guttural voices' which indicate the borders of the realm of limited, ordinary experience. Eliot's narrator is recounting the events 60 years after they occur, yet the apparently 'bright' image of Italy is a deeply negative one in terms of Eliot's mode of symbolic representation. It is still de Staël's land of romance existing outside and apart from the harsh realities of the time-bound world.[39] As an allegory of Italian nationalism, then, 'Mr Gilfil' ends in stalemate. In spite of the struggles to be heard, the angry impulse to rebellion, the exile and ultimate sacrifice which 'Mr Gilfil' enacts, the Italy of 1857 seems no nearer to becoming a political reality than it had been in Caterina's time and can only exist as romance which must ultimately be expended.[40]

As a narrative of the lives of Caterina and of Italy, 'Mr Gilfil' ends in defeat and stasis. It is in many ways the least successful of George Eliot's experiments in *Scenes of Clerical Life*. Caterina's Italian origins, while helping to create the conditions under which the tensions and shortcomings of patriarchal English society may be exposed, if anything confuse the issue of woman's place within the story. The force of Caterina's rebellious anger is undermined and deflected by the implication of a causal link between her character and actions and her 'hot-blooded' Italian origins and by the text's insistence upon Italian fictional models and stereotypes. Eliot's use of this mode of representation seems to pull in two opposing directions at the same time. She signals a gap between her own view of Caterina and those of her characters through her use of textual irony: our interest and sympathies are engaged for this seemingly insignificant, weaker, foreign sister as a fitting subject for a story, but Eliot then proceeds to erect strong barriers between the English and the Italians where relationships (in which power is all on the side of the English) are mediated through layers of prejudice so thick as to be recognizable immediately by the 1850s as the product of outdated ignorance. If, however, part of the story's project is to 'explore the possibilities of integration within the novel', then it is undermined by a plot which relies heavily on divisive Italian stereotypes, on the very mental automata which Eliot ostensibly eschews.

4

Italian Mythmaking
in *Romola*

In 1863 Robert Browning called *Romola* 'the noblest and most heroic prose-poem'.[1] It is indeed a novel with epic pretensions which tries to unite the particular historic moment with myth in 'an attempt to explore the present in the context of the past, and to probe, at the same time, the external human condition'.[2] Felicia Bonaparte argues cogently that Eliot's novel deals with nothing less than the development and future of the whole of western civilization.[3] George Eliot herself defined her novel of *Romola* as a 'historical romance' and in the work she unites the two great shaping traditions in European literature, of realism and romance, in a wider examination of history in an 'orphaned' age, to determine whether the past could provide a creed for the present. History, no longer merely the context of the novel, becomes its subject. Eliot here speaks through mythology, particularly the myths of the Graeco–Roman and Christian worlds, to create her own mythopoesis in the service of her overall vision. The great quest myths of Homer and Virgil were for Eliot a symbolic expression of the collective human consciousness, and the concrete facts of history were, she believed, the continuing embodiment of the great universal myths. In *Romola*, Eliot places her realistic narrative in an epic perspective. On a symbolic level, her characters Tito and Savonarola become the embodiments of Bacchus and Christ, and the 'ideal' heroine Romola[4] moves symbolically from the pagan to the Christian world, through a knowledge of joy to one of pain and sorrow, and ultimately emerges as the embodiment of Eliot's positivist vision for the future of civilization. *Romola*, then must be read as a prophetic book, a prospectus for the progress of western civilization. This epic design is present in germ from the very beginning: a 'night-student' questions 'the stars or the sages, or his own soul, for that hidden knowledge which would break through the barrier of man's brief life, and show its dark path, that seemed to bend no whither, to be an arc in an immeasurable circle of light and glory' (p.43). The imagery in which this teleologically-based vision of human history is expressed, with its 'dark path' becoming 'an arc in an immeasurable circle of light and glory' is suggestive of the great Christian poet of the medieval world, Dante, and Eliot wishes to place *her* work in the epic tradition of Homer, Virgil and Dante, who had given expression to visions which had then become the dominant cultures of the western world. In the same way that Virgil had 'invented' a hero to embody the spirit of the Roman world by rescuing Aeneas from relative obscurity in Homer and Dante had reinvented himself as Dante-pilgrim, so Eliot invented her own heroine as the symbol of her vision of the modern world that she might speak for the modern era as earlier poets had for theirs and in a form characteristic of the age.

Eliot's epic is also a specifically *Italian* one. The six years of turbulent history in Renaissance Florence were highly significant in the historiography of the Italian *Risorgimento*. The myths of the *Italian* resurgence, the 'dark path' which becomes an arc in a 'circle of light and glory', could be contained within the overarching myth of Eliot's wider epic design, and can be read as a substantive metaphor for her vision of the progress of western civilization. The title of the novel is itself a reminder of the great arc of Italian history for it leads back to the founding of Rome, which to the Victorian imagination was the concrete embodiment of 'the past of a whole hemisphere', by the mythical 'Romolo' (Romulus).[5]

In *Risorgimento* mythology, the years of Savonarola's Republic are a high point in the epic journey of Italy towards an independent identity. From within the microcosm of Florence, Eliot looks backwards to Dante and Petrarch; the turbulent present of her novel includes the figures of Savonarola, Lorenzo the Magnificent and Luigi Pulci and anticipates the immediate future with the appearance of Machiavelli. The historical present of *Romola* must also be set alongside the moment of its publication when the Italian epic journey was almost complete and the prophecy fulfilled, and when the themes of the search for and growth to maturity and a full identity had an urgent relevance. Through a wealth of allusion to Italian literature and in her choice of texts which were often highly charged positively or negatively within the framework of the *Risorgimento* epic, Eliot both traces the moral progress of 'Italia' and helps readers keep their bearings in the turbulent years of *Romola*.

When G.H. Lewes suggested Savonarola's story as an excellent subject for a novel, he already knew something of the historical period and of Savonarola's importance within Italian history. The comment in his journal gives a hint of the direction in which Lewes imagined such a project developing: 'it occurred to me that [Savonarola's] life and times afford fine material for an historical romance. Polly at once caught at the idea with enthusiasm. It is a subject which will fall in with much of her studies and *sympathies;*' (my italics).[6] Savonarola came to power on the death of Lorenzo, and substituted a Republic for the (albeit enlightened) despotism of the Medici. He was of the Church but 'antipapal' in resisting the authority of Rome and he revealed himself to be a great leader of men. To write about *this* particular period of Italian history in 1861–3 was necessarily to engage with some of the main issues of the *Risorgimento*: the kind of government (despotism, monarchy or democracy) which was best for Italy; the role of the Church and the Pope; and the role of great leaders of men as prophets and visionaries. The years of Savonarola's ascendancy in Florence were singled out as highly significant in Italian *Risorgimento* mythology precisely because of the clear analogies between past and present and the way in which these years, which saw a last manifestation of an Italian spirit of independence before 'Italia' was enslaved by the foreign oppressor, could instruct and admonish the present. Eliot would have been well aware of the *Risorgimento* Savonarola before she embarked on her novel, and she would almost certainly have discussed this with Lewes as one of the many possible lines of development once the project began fermenting in her mind.[7] She would also have become aware while reading that the figure of Savonarola was a problematic one[8] and, although Eliot is broadly in sympathy with the Savonarola of *Risorgimento* historiography, in her own text she resisted much of the mythologization and mystification associated with him.

If the blind Bardo represents the pagan world of marble statues and shattered fragments of the past greatness of Italy, the visionary Savonarola stands for the Christian world. He is repeatedly portrayed as the chief civilizing agent and moralizing influence on Florentine society at the end of the fifteenth century in general and in particular on Romola, for whom he acts as guide and mentor. Savonarola represents the second stage of Romola's journey in which she places her faith in the precepts of the Church. The Frate stands in clear opposition to the pagan world as it manifests itself in Florence, both in the scholarly endeavours of Bardo to recover it, and in the paganism of the court of Lorenzo de'Medici. It was important for Eliot to preserve a clear distinction between the pagan and Christian worlds in *Romola,* and herein may lie a part of the reason why Eliot was unsure as to how much prominence to give to Dante in the novel.[9] 'Il divino poèta' straddled both these worlds, not rejecting but incorporating the pagan into the Christian vision. Too much Dante, then, would have clouded the distinction and been detrimental to the dialectical movement of *Romola* towards a Positive world vision. Clearly though, Savonarola is heir to those 'grim Florentines' who included Dante's Cacciaguida and Dante himself, and becomes the torch-bearer of morality for his age. Nevertheless, Dante is an important presence in the novel and his influence will be discussed in the next chapter.

Eliot's reading on Savonarola in preparation for *Romola* was of course extensive, but two works were particularly influential. The first of these, Iacopo Nardi's *Istorie della Città di Firenze* (1582), is a detailed account of Florentine history from 1494 to 1538. Eliot's copy (read between August and October 1861) is heavily marked. Certain passages concerned with the historical background were lifted almost verbatim from the *Istoria* and she acknowledges Nardi's influence by having him appear towards the end of the novel to witness the execution of Savonarola.[10] The other author upon whom Eliot relied heavily was Pasquale Villari, Italy's outstanding historian of the nineteenth century, whose books *Savonarola* and *Machiavelli* are masterpieces of modern historiography.[11] Villari places Savonarola within the grand narrative of *Risorgimento* history as an agent of a great truth struggling for expression in the face of an existing external order and the Frate's life is read as the embodiment of this conflict:

> ... he had the spirit of an innovator, ... Savonarola was the first to raise the standard announcing the uprisal of the truly original thought of the Renaissance at the close of the great epoch of humanist learning. He was the first man of the fifteenth century to realise that the human race was palpitating with the throes of a new life, and his words were loudly echoed by that portion of the Italian people still left untainted by the prevalent corruption. He accordingly merits the title of the prophet of the new civilisation.[12]

In Villari's account, Savonarola endeavoured to conciliate reason with faith and religion with liberty, and the desire to reform

Christianity and Catholicism is one he shared with the greatest
minds of Italy, with Dante and Arnold of Brescia. Villari claims
that the people had listened to Savonarola's religious teaching
only for as long as it had lent weight to popular government, but
that as soon as they began to see in him a danger for the Republic
they had abandoned him to the Pope. Religious enthusiasm had
been contingent upon a greater design and the love of liberty alone
had fired their enthusiasm.[13] In Villari's accounts, Savonarola's
influence becomes more explicitly secular and the religious element
is further decentred to portray the years of the Florentine Republic
as an expression of an emerging 'national' consciousness. Villari's
Savonarola, then, is assimilated into the great *Risorgimento* narrative
of the march towards freedom from oppression by Church or despots either from within or outside Italy.

Though she would have been aware of this as one of the possible
interpretations of Savonarola, Eliot resists the grand *Risorgimento*
narratives in her Savonarola. She includes a political analysis of the
Frate's actions but resists any notion that the people are motivated
by anything but short-term promises of good or driven by anything
other than private motivations and grudges (pp.471–3). In the complex political milieu of Florence, says Eliot's Machiavelli, Savonarola is accumulating the hatred of average mankind for wishing to
'lay on them a strict yoke of virtue', of the stronger powers in Italy
who want to farm Florence for their own ends, and 'of the people, to
whom he has ventured to promise good in this world, instead of
confining his promises to the next' (p.472). Machiavelli, of course, is
disposed to judge Savonarola's character 'by a key which presup-
posed no loftiness' (p.522) and sees him as a political leader *manqué*:
'with the times so much on his side as they are about Church affairs,
he might have done something great' if only his falsehoods had
been 'all of a wise sort' (p.627). Machiavelli's *political* analysis of
Savonarola, which takes no account of any genuine religious spirit
as a force for change in society, can only be partial in *Romola*.
Ironically perhaps, Eliot uses Machiavelli as a means of underlining
the central Eliotian truth that the power of smallmindedness and
egoism in resisting the forces of change can only be combated by
slow degrees. Social relations are as multifaceted and complex
in fifteenth-century Florence as they are in nineteenth-century
Middlemarch and Eliot eschews the *Risorgimento* mystifications of
Savonarola's ascendancy as an expression of a collective desire for
liberty.

Savonarola's Christianity is ultimately revealed as inadequate and it is Romola who carries forward those aspects of it which are of enduring universal value for humanity. Savonarola, who mixes religion and politics, is prepared to sacrifice Bernardo del Nero, and confuses his own party with 'the cause of God's kingdom' (p.578). Romola transcends Savonarola's by now compromised doctrine in her impassioned reply that 'God's kingdom is something wider – else, let me stand outside it with the beings that I love'. Eliot, however, is at pains to underline the genuineness of Savonarola's beliefs. Romola heard only the ring of egoism in the Frate's declaration, yet Savonarola's words 'are the implicit formula of all energetic belief', although 'tender fellow feeling ... is apt to be timid and sceptical towards the larger aims without which life cannot rise into religion' (p.587).

There is though a marked tendency in *Romola* to associate Catholicism with Gothic, and with all the detrimental connotations of superstition and barbarism with which that genre is freighted: in the Masque of Time at the end of Book II for example, or in Romola's anti-Catholicism which is evident when she visits her dying brother Dino and sees in his 'monkish aspect' only 'grovelling superstition' (p.209).[14] Alongside these vague anti-Catholic gestures, Savonarola's is the voice of a more pronounced anti-papalism, shared by British readers and many Italian *Risorgimento* reformers alike, which denounces corruption and the betrayal of Italy by the papacy. While preaching in the duomo he says: 'And thou, O Italy, art the chosen land; has not god placed his sanctuary within thee, and thou hast polluted it?' (p.292). Later he tells Romola that she ought to be in the city 'helping in the great work by which God will purify Florence, and raise it to be the guide of the nations' (p.433). Again, 'the death of five men ... is a light matter weighed against the withstanding of the vicious tyrannies which stifle the life of Italy, and foster the corruption of the Church; ...'(pp.577–8). Eliot also quotes Savonarola's final 'Confession': 'I had it in my mind to do great things in Italy and beyond Italy'. In each of these passages anti-papalism is closely associated with strong tones of nationalism. The linguistic intersections between Savonarola's words and *Risorgimento* rhetoric mask the anachronism inherent in identifying Savonarola's Italy with nineteenth-century Italy. Some slippage between the specific historical context of the novel and modern *Risorgimento* rhetoric of nationality is inevitable so that, like those proponents of the *Risorgimento* who

anachronistically read the modern idea of the nation into Dante's
'Italia', Eliot is able to draw Savonarola into a national cause easily
recognizable by British readers in the 1860s while (like *Risorgimento*
propagandists) avoiding questions of historical accuracy. There is
also an element of evasion in Eliot's treatment of Savonarola's
religion. Myers points to a serious misuse of religious vocabulary
in *Romola*. The specificity of Savonarola's Catholic faith is 'conveni-
ently blurred' as when he talks of 'the believer who worships that
image of the Supreme Offering, and feels the glow of a common
life': *a* common life meant historically *the* common life of the Catholic Church. As Myers points out, this deliberate evasion was
intended to establish a common ground between Catholicism and
Positivism, and to avoid any danger of annoying English Protestant
readers who would have taken exception to Savonarola's views.[15]

Eliot was sensitive to the epic dimension of Villari's account, and
occasionally her text echoes his. Eliot mentions Christopher Columbus twice in the Proem to *Romola*, 'waiting and arguing for the three
poor vessels in which he was to set sail' (pp.43–4). Columbus does
not then figure in the novel. In Villari, Columbus is coupled with his
fellow Italian Savonarola ('the prophet of the new civilisation') as
one of 'the champions of Thought', an innovator 'who foresaw the
progress of civilisation towards a vaster synthesis of the human
race. [...] two Italians were the first to initiate [the true Renais-
sance]. Columbus discovered the paths of the sea, Savonarola
those of the soul'. The two men are numbered among 'a handful
of oppressed and persecuted men' who 'disperse the darkness, and
cleave a passage for the new road'. Theirs is 'the prophetic mind,
the hero's heart, the martyr's fate'. In Villari's narrative, society is
renewed and redeemed through the courage, sacrifice and martyrdom of these men whose 'blood generates thousands of followers;
their ideas become the accepted creed of the human race, and are
the main promoters of modern civilisation'.[16] While resisting much
of this mythologizing, Eliot accepts that the Frate was a visionary
who had '[seen] the true light' of freedom from oppression religious
or secular, internal or external, in which God's kingdom on earth
might be realized by his chosen people. Though there was no
evidence of any wish for martyrdom in Savonarola says Eliot, '*therefore he may the more fitly be called a martyr by his fellow-men to all time*'.
Eliot italicized this sentence in the Cabinet Edition of 1878, though it
was not italicized in earlier editions, perhaps wishing to pay further
tribute to Savonarola as part of the great epic of western and Italian

history.[17] Eliot's Columbus helps establish that epic perspective, though within that broad canvas is contained the much more closely focused epic of Romola's individual history. Ultimately, Eliot's Savonarola is a great moralizing and civilizing agent, but one whose influence extends to the few like Romola and is most effective at the personal level. Eliot seems to wish to play down the importance of Savonarola's role in this epic. So much so indeed that he fades out of the novel towards the end. The Florentine people themselves appear largely untouched by Savonarola, and are fired by neither true religious fervour, by love of liberty nor freedom from the corruption of the Church. Thus Savonarola's actual achievements, including the establishment of a Republic in fifteenth-century Florence, seem lacking in substance in *Romola* and his vision remains strangely blurred and unfocused. Eliot's final evaluation of Savonarola's achievement decontextualizes it and his influence is perceived wholly in abstract moral terms: '*he* had the greatness which belongs to a life spent in struggling against powerful wrong, and in trying to raise men to the highest deeds they are capable of' (p.675). Eliot was content to tap into the spirit and the *epic* dimensions of *Risorgimento* narratives as they concern Savonarola, but her overall design of showing the slow progress of civilization and her eschewal of the simplifications and mystifications of *Risorgimento* mythology led her to rewrite the myth so as to be able to integrate Savonarola into her own meliorist vision in which Romola's religion of humanity becomes the underlying civilizing force.

The court of Lorenzo de'Medici was strongly associated with a revival of interest in Greek learning and philosophy, with the neo-platonism of Marsilio Ficino being elevated into almost a state religion and the Court of Florence becoming a new Athens. Lorenzo himself was a poet and patron and supported other poets including Luigi Pulci and Poliziano. During the nineteenth century, Lorenzo was often portrayed as a scheming tyrant who indulged the populace in poetry and merrymaking in order to deflect their attention from his tyranny and this image is reinforced by prints made during Lorenzo's life of the poet among the crowd singing his poetry. Some of George Eliot's Florentines are clearly victims of this Laurentian propaganda. For Nello the barber, Lorenzo is 'the Pericles of our Athens' (p.74) and 'the very pivot of Italy'. Lorenzo's most famous poem 'Quant'è bella giovinezza' ['How beauteous is youth'] was interpreted as the 'hedonistic *carpe diem* of an Epicurean dabbler in verse' and the dominant idea in *Canti carnascialeschi* [Carnival Songs], to which this poem belongs, was seen as being 'enjoy life today, give yourself over to pleasures, don't think about tomorrow'.[18] Eliot's Tito Melema fits easily into this intellectual climate. An element of moral degeneracy, which Savonarola was to attack, could also be seen in much of the new poetry encouraged by Lorenzo, particularly in the burlesquing spirit of comedy, farce and parody of Luigi Pulci and Matteo Franco, 'an untainted sceptic' with whom Pulci had exchanged a series of mutually abusive sonnets (*Romola*, pp.411–12). The reactionary Bardo blames Lorenzo for encouraging Pulci's 'dabbling, lawless productions', which he sees as 'the delusive prelude' to an 'age of tinsel and gossamer in which no thought has substance enough to be moulded into consistent and lasting form' (p.109). In *Romola*, the poetry of both Lorenzo and Pulci is associated mainly with Tito Melema and is juxtaposed with the great ideals of Dante and his predecessors, to Savonarola, and to that great tradition of thought which *was* 'moulded into consistent and lasting form' to be taken up by the *Risorgimento*.

Tito sings the first lines of Lorenzo's most famous Carnival song in Italian to the accompaniment of the lute; 'Beauteous is life in blossom! / And it fleeteth – fleeteth ever; / Whoso would be joyful – let him! / There's no surety for the morrow.'[19] These four lines however include both a careless spirit of assertive merrymaking and the haunting refrain that no one can predict the future. The next lines of this poem (also known as the 'Song to Bacchus') are 'Here are Bacchus and Ariadne, / Both beautiful, and each yearning for the other; / Since time flies by and deceives / They are always together in happiness.'[20] Lorenzo's poem anticipates and ties in with the imagery through which Tito conceives his relationship with Romola, for he of course commissions the triptych in which he is figured as Bacchus and she as Ariadne, 'images of youth and joy' (p.261) which '[lock] all sadness away' (p.263). Their wedding takes place during Carnival, but almost as soon as they emerge from the ceremony, time reasserts itself in the Masque of Time which passes before Santa Croce. The masque, a Dantesque presage of Tito's own infernal future, belies the whole message of Lorenzo's *canzona*. Character is destiny for George Eliot, and never more so than in Tito Melema, who relentlessly creates his own future today. There is heavy irony intended then in Eliot's use of Lorenzo's *canzona*, for time does indeed fly and deceive Tito.

Luigi Pulci, a thoroughgoing sceptic, 'suspected of not believing anything from the roof upward (*dal tetto in su*)' (p.48) is also associated with Tito, though rather to provide a critical commentary on his character than to reinforce the suggestion of the immorality associated with Laurentian paganism. Nello the barber quotes from Pulci's *Morgante* (II, 68) early in the novel to allude to Romola's moral influence over Tito: 'Da quel giorno in quà ch'amor m'accese / Per lei son fatto e gentil e cortese' (p.143) [From the day that love enflamed me I have become through her both noble and courteous]. The commentary is ironic here too, for Tito is capable of 'becoming' all things to all men, a characteristic which leads him into treachery, and the idea of 'amor' offered is a far cry from those of Dante for Beatrice and Petrarch for Laura. Later on, Eliot's narrator uses Pulci again to illustrate the attitude of powerful Florentines towards Tito: 'as their own bright poet Pulci has said for them, it is one thing to love the fruits of treachery, and another thing to love traitors – "Il tradimento a molti piace assai, / Ma il traditore a gnun non piacque mai"' [Many people greatly love treason, / But nobody has ever loved the traitor (*Morgante*, XVII, 69)] (p.560). The first of two unused epigraphs from Pulci, 'Roses wither away, and only the thorns remain: / Judge nothing before the end' (*Morgante*, XIX, 26) for Chapter IV entitled 'First Impressions', was to have warned the reader to be wary of Tito, and foreshadowed the development of his character, as well as continuing the Dantean theme of a beautiful exterior masking an evil nature. With hindsight, Eliot was perhaps wise to have discarded this particular epigraph, as it is rather too direct an address to the reader which gives away too much too early. The gradual revelation of Tito's true nature is the more effective for being subtly managed. Pulci's practical scepticism is also turned to account in a discussion of the source of the power which the preaching of Savonarola currently had over the people: 'For what says Luigi Pulci? "Dombruno's sharp-cutting scimitar had the fame of being enchanted; but," says Luigi, "I am rather of the opinion that it cut sharp because it was of strongly-tempered steel"' (p.225), and Pulci's own sceptical mind is likewise characterized as being 'like sharpest steel which can touch nothing without cutting' (p.412). He is also briefly associated with Romola, whose hair 'raggia come stella per sereno' ['...shines like a star in the clear sky' (*Morgante*, III, 17)] (p.85).[21] Eliot chooses to emphasize Pulci's scepticism, rather than the frivolity and licentiousness of which he was accused by Bardo. However, though associated

with a burlesquing spirit of scepticism rather than the moral seriousness of Dante and Savonarola, his work is made to serve on
occasion as a reliable guide to character.[22]

Pulci is also of interest to Eliot in portraying the dual nature of the
Florentines, characterized by the adjectives 'grave' and 'grim' but
also by the burlesquing spirit which she found in Lorenzo and
Pulci. Eliot commented that:

> The general ignorance of old Florentine literature, and the false
> conceptions of Italy bred by idle travelling (with the sort of
> culture which combines Shakespeare and the musical glasses),
> have caused many parts of 'Romola' to be entirely misunderstood
> – the scene of the quack doctor and the monkey, for example,
> which is a specimen, not of humour as I relish it, but of the
> practical joking which was the amusement of the gravest old
> Florentines, and without which no conception of them would be
> historical. The whole piquancy of the scene in question was
> intended to lie in the antithesis between the puerility which
> stood for wit and humour in the old Republic, and the majesty
> of its front in graver matters.[23]

Lorenzo himself is denounced for this dual character by Ser Cioni in
Romola: 'he'll play the chamberer and philosopher by turns – listen
to bawdy songs at Carnival and cry "Bellissimi!" – and listen to
sacred lauds and cry again "Bellissimi!"' (p.61). Eliot may have had
in mind Machiavelli's famous comment that Lorenzo was 'two
different people, joined together as if by an impossible union'.[24]
This same characteristic is reflected too in Eliot's Boccaccio. Romola
has read him many times, and 'there are some things...[she] do[es]
not want ever to forget' but, on the other hand, 'a great many of
those stories are only about low deceit for the lowest ends. Men do
not want books to make them think lightly of vice, as if life were a
vulgar joke' (p.501). George Eliot puts Boccaccio on the Pyramid of
Vanities, and has Romola pass a mixed judgement on him. Yet
Romola's own flight is both a deliberate echo of Boccaccio's framing
narrative in the *Decameron* (Florence is morally plague-stricken and
flight becomes imperative) and an inversion of it, for Romola is only
able to re-establish the human bonds and ties which have been
systematically broken in Florence by contact with physical suffering
and by attending the victims of bodily plague in the village. Indeed
Eliot draws attention to the fact that Romola's 'drifting away' in the

boat which carries her to the village is directly inspired by Boccaccio's story of Gonzaga.[25]

Eliot uses Machiavelli rather differently from the ways in which she employs Lorenzo and Pulci. Strong prejudices attached to the name of Machiavelli in Britain as abroad. Macaulay points out that 'out of his surname they have coined an epithet for a knave, and out of his Christian name a synonyme for the Devil'[26] and Eliot herself hints at this view in an exchange between Cennini and Machiavelli in Chapter 60 of *Romola*: ' "there is a clever wickedness in thy talk sometimes that makes me mistrust thy pleasant young face as if it were a mask of Satan." ' Satan, replies Machiavelli ' "was a blunderer, an introducer of *novità*, who made a stupendous failure" ' (p.581). This exchange undoubtedly reinforces the associations between 'pleasant faces' (those of Machiavelli and Tito) and wickedness and treachery. Indeed, Machiavelli is repeatedly associated with Tito Melema in the novel, but although 'his name is, at the present day, allied to every thing false and perfidious in politics'[27] it is in fact Tito who is the true 'Machiavellian' involved in the diplomacy, spying, political squabbling and treachery of the political milieu of Florence and who embodies Machiavelli's idea of human nature. Eliot's character is a dispassionate observer, not so much immoral as non-moral, who finds ample material for his own later writings and his nascent theories of statecraft in Tito and in the events surrounding Savonarola. The young Machiavelli 'had penetrated all the small secrets of egoism' (p.469) and is well aware that Melema is 'a pestiferously clever fellow' involved in political double dealings. Eliot conveys the partiality of Machiavelli's vision in his exclusive concentration on the game of politics to the exclusion of social, economic and religious factors except insofar as these impinge upon the political. His cold analyses are diametrically opposed to the religious fervour of Savonarola and the fellow-feeling of Romola, and his inability to understand Savonarola's nobility and greatness bears out a common nineteenth-century criticism that he was dead to all enthusiasm. Savonarola and Romola counterbalance Machiavelli's opinions and reveal the shortcomings of his philosophy. In *Romola* though, Eliot carefully reproduces the amused irony with which Machiavelli discusses Savonarola in his writings, and the clarity of thought which cuts through the indecisions and equivocations of the contemporary political milieu.[28]

Given the strong negative connotations attached to Machiavelli, the question arises as to why Eliot, who strove so hard for historical accuracy, should have wished to introduce Machiavelli, who was as yet invisible on the political scene in Florence, into the life of her novel. One reason, I think, is that he was regarded as another prophet by the Italian *Risorgimento,* and a greater one than Savonarola. Foscolo saw in him a hero in the secular struggle against the priests and usurping princes. Mazzini promoted the myth of Machiavelli as patriot and prophet of independence, and Vincenzo Gioberti emphasized the message of independence contained in the last chapter of *The Prince.* Villari saw in Machiavelli the last great and original manifestation of the Italian national spirit before it was suffocated by foreign invasions and the Renaissance 'with all its uncertainties and contradictions was as it were turned to stone before our very eyes'.[29] Machiavelli was one of the most widely read Italian authors in nineteenth-century Italy. Like Dante, he was subjected to the most widely differing interpretations for propaganda purposes and became one of the great legends of the *Risorgimento.* Eliot's Machiavelli needs to be seen in this wider context and as the writer reinstated by Sismondi in Europe and Macaulay in Britain.[30] At the end of his long essay arguing that Machiavelli's work needs to be interpreted in its Renaissance context, Macaulay draws Machiavelli into the great narrative of the struggle for freedom. The greatest statesman of Florence will be properly recognized and revered

> when the object to which his public life was devoted shall be attained, when the foreign yoke shall be broken, when a second Procida shall avenge the wrongs of Naples, when a happier Rienzi shall restore the good estate of Rome, when the streets of Florence and Bologna shall again resound with their ancient war-cry, *Popolo; popolo; muoiano i tiranni!*[31]

By his very presence then Eliot's Machiavelli prophesies the future and foreshadows the next stage in the great *Risorgimento* narrative of the journey towards freedom and independence. Implicit in his final words in *Romola* ('It is a pity [Savonarola's] falsehoods were not all of a wise sort. ... With the times so much on his side as they are about Church affairs, he might have done something great' (p.627)) is his belief that a 'hero' was needed to found the State. Explaining Machiavelli's thought in 1862 one historian wrote '... it therefore falls to a Romulus, to a Theseus to found the third Italy. Nor could the new Romulus be a Republican, in Machiavelli's view, as he judged that the Italians had reached the lowest levels of corruption.'[32] At the end of *The Prince*, Machiavelli calls upon the younger Lorenzo de'Medici, Duke of Urbino, to become the defender and liberator of Italy and closes with a quotation from Petrarch's celebrated political poem 'Italia mia', in which the poet addresses himself to Italian rulers and exhorts them to cease the fratricidal struggles which were devastating Italy.[33] Petrarch's poem manifests a profound spirit of love for the *patria*, pity for its misfortunes and a deep desire for peace. Machiavelli himself was expressing a sentiment rather than any well-defined plan for unification on a national scale in drawing upon Petrarch, but the text became an important one in *Risorgimento* mythology.

George Eliot consigns Petrarch to the flames of the Pyramid of Vanities in *Romola*, which included 'copies of Ovid, Boccaccio, Petrarca, Pulci, and other books of a vain or impure sort' (p.498). Eliot relied heavily on Nardi's *Istorie* for the details of this scene, where 'the works of Boccaccio and Morgante [by Pulci] and similar books' are placed on the Pyramid and where Petrarch is *not* specifically mentioned.[34] Her modification of Nardi allows Eliot to draw attention specifically to the 'heavenly Laura', in Romola's presence, in the painter Piero di Cosimo's comment: 'Look at that Petrarca sticking up beside a rouge-pot: do the idiots pretend that the heavenly Laura was a painted harridan?' (p.501).[35] Petrarch then reappears in the Epilogue where Lillo is learning 'Spirito gentil'. Another celebrated political poem, this one is addressed to a statesman (perhaps Cola di Rienzo) exhorting him to restore peace to Rome. Petrarch contrasts the glory of ancient Rome with the present decadence throughout Italy, exalts the greatness of Roman civilization which has been obscured but not eliminated for a thousand years, and finds the inspiration and the model for the resurgence of Italian civilization in ancient Rome rather than in the Papal city. Along with 'Italia mia', 'Spirito gentil' stands at the beginning of a long tradition and is perhaps the greatest expression of the myth of Rome as it converges with that of Italy and the spirit of an Italian nation. Although Eliot merely alludes to Petrarch's poem, it is a powerful and relevant subtext at the end of *Romola*, for it draws together the threads both of the *Risorgimento* narrative and of Eliot's own mythmaking:

Noble spirit, you who govern those members within which dwells pilgrim a valorous, knowing, and wise lord: now that

you have gained the honoured staff wherewith you correct Rome
and her erring citizens and call her back to her ancient path,

I speak to you because I do not see elsewhere a ray of virtue,
which is extinguised in the world, nor do I find anyone who is
ashamed of doing ill. (ll.1–9)[36]

The poem is apt at this point as it leads into Romola's discussion of
the nature of true greatness, and also because it would have been
taken as prophetic of the leaders of the *Risorgimento* by many
Victorian readers.[37] In the Epilogue, it is Romola herself who
emerges as the symbol of hope for Italy. Like the statuesque 'Italia',
she has endured political treachery, feuding and the influence of a
corrupt Church in Florence, and been drawn to the brink of despairing self-destruction. Finally, though, she stands independent,
mature and serene. In Eliot's myth of resurgence, Romola herself
is the 'spirito gentil' hailed by Petrarch, the new Romulus sought
by Machiavelli. At the beginning of the novel, the statuesque
Romola had herself moved among broken images of arrested
energy, loss of identity and broken power ('a beautiful feminine
torso', 'an uplifted muscular arm wielding a bladeless sword')
suggestive of a petrified 'Italia'. In her final tableau of Romola set
against the arch of the loggia in the Epilogue, however, Eliot writes
her own prophecy for the future of Italy which encompasses the
whole of its past history, in the Petrarchan image of the heavenly
Laura, Dante's Beatrice, the Madonna and 'Italia' nurturing and
protecting her children. By end of the novel, Romola is firmly
aligned with the gravity, majesty and moral seriousness of Dante,
Petrarch and Savonarola. Eliot's final icon resonates with echoes
from the great *Risorgimento* tradition which has been traced in
Romola and which has formed the life of Italy. The voices of burlesque and scepticism (of Lorenzo and Pulci) have now been
silenced and their absence reveals them not as feeding the great
moral tradition, but as merely false trails on the epic journey of
resurgence in *Romola*, as leading not to maturity and full identity
but to dissolution and destruction. A clear message for modern Italy
is contained in *Romola* which, although it ends at a historical
moment of negation (the burning of Savonarola and the breakdown
of the Republic), is finally suffused with optimism. The novel both
points up the fragility of national unity and of peace and contains a
prophecy of completion and fulfilment. And *Romola*, of course, is

endstopped. By 1863, 'knowing' readers were already looking back on a story the outcome of which they knew.

In another sense, however, all the Italian writers Eliot uses in *Romola* were important in creating the life of Italy, in that they contributed to the creation of the Italian language itself through the gradual development of the vernacular as the language of literature, at the expense of Latin. A line can be traced from Dante's *De vulgari eloquentia* through the development of Tuscan in the fifteenth century to form the basis of the Italian language. This development, important in terms of the rise of a *Risorgimento* language nationalism (in which the language itself was deemed to embody the whole culture of a people), also provided Eliot with a paradigm for her own vision of slow meliorism. She presents the struggle for dominance between Latin and the vernacular through paraphrase and a wide range of quotations (street cries, invectives, exclamations, proverbs and poetry) to render the variety and richness of the emerging idiom. Though Eliot's Florence remains a very literary affair, the range of 'literary' language from Dante to the deliberately non-intellectual popularizing burlesque of Pulci and Antonio Pucci shows her concern to incorporate the language question into her novel and trace the development of the vernacular as a unifying and liberating influence.[38]

5

Dante in *Romola*

Early in *Romola*, Dante is established as a strong part of the cultural milieu of fifteenth-century Florence, familiar to scholars and barbers alike.[1] After some early references self-consciously drawing attention to the poet, however, he seems to be strangely absent from much of the rest of the novel, so that it would be easy to see the presence of 'il divino poèta' as providing little more than local colour. The influence of Dante can however be felt over the whole novel, though some of the references are oblique and require a good knowledge of the poet to be appreciated fully.

We can identify two main areas in which the Dante material functions in *Romola*. Firstly, it provides a historical perspective, whereby the Florence of Dante's time is compared and contrasted with the years of the Florentine Republic in which the novel is set to give a perspective on the present of *Romola*. Secondly, Dante helps establish and maintain a moral perspective, for he is often present locally in the novel as a touchstone against which characters, and particularly Tito Melema, can be measured. Over the whole arc of the novel, there are broad parallels between the moral vision of Dante's epic journey in the *Comedy* and Eliot's in *Romola*, and these parallels are in part a structural device to help the reader maintain a clear moral focus and steer a course in the treacherous world of fifteenth-century Florence. During the writing of *Romola* Eliot experiments with a variety of ways of incorporating Dante into her own text, making use of scenes mirroring those in the *Comedy*, of echoes and paraphrase (which may be serious or comic in its intent) and of direct quotation, often as epigraphs (or 'mottoes'). Eliot occasionally follows Dante's narrative scheme closely or employs Dantesque imagery, sometimes assimilating this into her text without acknowledging Dante as a source. A small number of scenes and images from Dante which she drew on first in *Romola* and then again in her later novels appear to have been particularly significant for her. Overall, Eliot's experiments with Dante in her Florentine novel set the pattern for those which come after, and some of the techniques first used in *Romola* are refined in the later works.

Eliot makes comparisons across the centuries in *Romola* and these involve Dante from the outset. The novel opens in a moment of uncharacteristic calm, with the streets which rang with the clash of fierce battle between rival families now only noisy with unhistorical quarrels. Dante helps establish political instability and petty rivalries as a theme in *Romola* in a way which bodes ill for the immediate future. Dante is recalled again when Bernardo del Nero mentions the name of Farinata degli Uberti in the context of Florentine party rivalries: 'if any man asks me what is meant by siding with a party, I say as he did, "To wish ill or well, for the sake of past wrongs or kindnesses"' (p.121). Farinata, mentioned twice by Dante in *Inferno* cantos VI and X, stands as a symbol of party strife in Florence, and his words to Dante in *Inferno* X ('Who were thy ancestors?' and 'They were fierce enemies to me...' [42; 46–7]) place him as head of the Florentine Ghibellines in opposition to the Guelphs which included the Alighieri family in the generation before Dante.[2] Farinata adds historical authenticity to Eliot's text by introducing a great Florentine familiar to Dante readers, and reiterates factional strife as a constant theme in Florentine history. A further allusion to the *Comedy* continues the same theme when Eliot quotes in passing the exiled Dante's own nostalgic reference to Florence as a 'beautiful sheepfold' from which he has been exiled (p.140).[3] In Chapter 39, 'The Supper in the Rucellai Gardens', Eliot characterizes the Florentines as 'a sober and frugal people' and contrasts this mentality with that of the few wealthy aristocratic families 'who kept a great table and lived splendidly' (p.409). Amid the luxury and excess of the Supper Dante's own great great grandfather, a noble representative of an older order, is mentioned (p.410). 'Dante's pattern old Florentine', Cacciaguida, lived when Florence was 'a community so loyal,... so sweet a dwelling-place' and its inhabitants 'abode in peace, sober and chaste'.[4] In Cacciaguida's comparison of the Florence of his own day with that of Dante's, the former greatness of the city is contrasted with its decadence in Dante's day. By recalling Cacciaguida here, Eliot gains a vantage point from which the continued decline of Florence is highlighted. The excessive luxury, decadence and ostentation of the Medici feast in which 'peacock was served up in a remarkable manner' (p.413) is thrown into relief, and the present crusader, Savonarola, who 'was teaching the disturbing doctrine that it was not the duty of the rich to be luxurious for the sake of the poor' (p.413) is placed in the sober tradition of the

moral scourges of corruption and luxury of which Cacciaguida and
Dante himself were illustrious representatives.[5]

Eliot places the great Florentine poet alongside Savonarola and
points up both similarities and contrasts between the periods in
which the two lived. Dante, the champion of God and Empire, is
the ideal figure for comparison with Savonarola within the great
moral and historical quest in which 'men still yearn for the reign of
peace and righteousness' (p.50). Part of this quest took the form of
looking to external help to right the wrongs of Italy. As the French
king Charles VIII descends into Italy in 1494 Eliot's narrator in
Romola comments on the tendency 'of the Italian populations, accus-
tomed, since Italy had ceased to be the heart of the Roman Empire,
to look for an arbitrator from afar,... as a means of avenging their
wrongs and redressing their grievances' (p.273) thus placing this
particular historical event in a wider context. The sentence above,
however, is all that remains from a longer passage present in the
manuscript copy but excised from the novel:

> To judge fairly of [Savonarola's] preaching which may shock
> minds nurtured in the strong feeling of national independence,
> we must remember... the long habit of Italy, since it had ceased
> to be the heart of the Roman Empire, to look for an arbitrator from
> afar. The greatest of Italian poets recorded in his vitriolic verse his
> hope of a deliverer for Italy, and the deliverer was the German
> Emperor, Henry VII. How could it be otherwise? A nation of
> divided and jealous interests must always want an empire with
> an army at its back.[6]

The above passage shows Eliot's mind stretching backwards and
forwards from the present of the novel over the course of Italian
history, ancient and modern, and drawing upon it selectively.
Dante is written out of *Romola* here, and his support for the Emperor
Henry VII as the deliverer of Italy is reduced to a single general
statement covering the whole of Italian history. Eliot slips into the
discourse of modern nationalism in the above passage, making an
implicit teleological link between the history of a '*nation* of divided
and jealous interests' (my italics) looking to Henry VII and Charles
VIII, and the 'strong feeling of national independence' already present in Eliot's British readers and presumably, in 1861–3, newly
acquired by the Italian nation whose interests were no longer
perceived as being divided and jealous, or at least much less so

than previously. Indeed, Eliot probably felt the final sentence to be inappropriate in the context of modern Italian nationalism and of the recent Unification of Italy. While Napoleon III had helped Victor Emmanuel and Piedmont against Austria, he was torn between support for national liberty and defence of the Pope, and his armies were to be a constant presence for the next ten years in Italy in the 'defence' of Rome. Eliot, as we have seen, was markedly anti-French in her support for Italian nationalism and, realizing the modern implications of her statement in the early 1860s, sought by expunging the passage quoted to avoid any suggestion that the continued presence of the modern Emperor Napoleon III in Rome could be sanctioned by Italian history.

Dante inherits his task of denouncing moral corruption and degeneracy from his ancestor Cacciaguida, and this is then taken up by Savonarola at the end of the fifteenth century. Both Dante and Savonarola believed in the separation of the powers of the Church and the State, with Dante championing the Holy Roman Empire against the power of the Pope, and Savonarola resisting the Pope's power in the interests of a spiritual regeneration. While Dante refused to be drawn into the party strife of the politics of his day and, in Cacciaguida's words, 'made a party of [him]self', Savonarola enters the political fray and by so doing exposes himself to compromise and ultimately the charge of being one of Dante's false prophets. Eliot's Machiavelli implicitly compares Savonarola with the Dante of the *Comedy*:

> [Savonarola] has got the ear of the people:...he gives them threats and promises, which they believe come straight from God, not only about hell, purgatory, and paradise, but about Pisa and our Great Council. But let events go against him, so as to shake the people's faith, and the cause of his power will be the cause of his fall. (pp.471–2)

Dante's prophecies were of course limited to threats and promises about hell, purgatory, and paradise, whereas Savonarola confuses religion and party politics to the extent that he can say to Romola 'The cause of my party *is* the cause of God's kingdom' (p.578). Machiavelli's prediction turns out to be true, and the comparison implicit here is to the detriment of Savonarola. The charge levelled against Savonarola of being a false prophet is made through reference to Dante. Francesco Cei says that Savonarola's 'proper place is among the false prophets of the Inferno, who walk with their heads turned hindforemost' (p.472).[7]

Dante also enters into Eliot's sense of structural unity in *Romola*, and particularly so in two areas, the characterization of Tito and in the novel's tripartite structure charting Romola's moral progress. Firstly, Eliot sketches out a Dantesque moral descent for Tito. Her allusions and imagery here often suggest *Inferno* rather than being explicitly associated with it, but there are sometimes specific references to the *Comedy* in the characterization of Tito, and there is a Dantesque feeling about his development which makes it possible to read him in the light of Dante's work. Tito is, of course, the character in the novel most associated with treachery, but Eliot is very precise in her portrayal of various kinds of treachery and of lesser sins which lead on to treachery. In the *Inferno*, each of these sins is precisely situated and has its own particular punishment, or *contrappasso*. Eliot, I think, had Dante's scheme for the lowest circles of Hell in mind in her portrayal of Tito and an examination of her use of Dante is therefore illuminating.

She was perhaps unsure as to the prominence to be given to Dante in a novel set in a particularly significant moment in fifteenth-century Florence, and Dante was sometimes written out of *Romola*. There are signs that originally a larger role in the book had been prepared for Dante in the 'mottoes' intended to head each chapter. Eliot had already chosen these for the first nine chapters, but they remained unused owing to the problems of serial publication in the *Cornhill Magazine*. One 'mottoe', that originally meant for Chapter 2, was to have been taken from Dante's *Purgatorio* XXXIII to serve as a comment on the impressionable nature of Tessa, the peasant girl whom Tito promises to marry: '...a gentle spirit that makes no excuse but makes its will of another's will as soon as it is disclosed by a sign'.[8] More can be read into this epigraph, however, for in the chapter for which it was intended Tito begs food and drink from Tessa on their first meeting, and this mirrors an episode in *Purgatorio* XXVIII in which Dante, guided by Matilda, the spirit of the perfected earthly life (described in the lines chosen for the epigraph), drinks the water of the river Eunoe which restores to him the memory of all the good which life has given him. In this reading, Tessa is not merely an impressionable girl but is associated with the symbolic action of drinking, which in Tito's case is highly ambiguous. Matilda explains that 'On this side [the water] flows down with virtue which takes from men the memory of sin; on the other it restores that of every good deed; here it is called Lethe and on the other side Eunoe and it does not operate here or there unless it is first tasted'.[9] Where Dante drinks twice, Tito drinks only once, and of the first draught which *removes* memories. Significantly, Tito 'would like [his] Romola, too, to see a new life. I should like to dip her a little in the soft waters of forgetfulness' (p.351). While, in the light of the Dante epigraph, Tessa with her 'baby face' and 'blue baby-eyes' embodies that innocence achieved by Dante at the end of *Purgatorio*, Tito's symbolic action is a portent of his moral decline, with his lack of any memory of sin apparently removing any checks against sinning in the future. The eroticism and sexual innuendo present in this first meeting between Tessa and Tito (his words 'I'm dying with hunger', 'muoio di fame' are repeated in both English and Italian! (p.69)) contrast markedly with Dante's *thirst* to drink in *Purgatorio* XXVIII and foreshadows Tito's sin of lust (Tessa will bear his children) early in the novel. This example of Eliot's early intention to give a certain prominence to Dante also gives an indication of the depth and complexity of the intertextuality at work. As it referred to Tessa, the epigraph was to be accepted at face value, but with Tito it was to provide an ironic commentary upon action and character which with hindsight was actually a parody of Dante, but one which acquired a predictive force. It seems reasonable to conclude that Eliot would have used the epigraph from Dante had the difficulties of providing 'mottoes' for each of the chapters not been too great given the method of publication chosen. Supporting the above interpretation is another moment echoing the meeting between Beatrice and Dante in the *Paradiso terrestre*, when Tito sees Romola again soon after the death of her brother Dino. To Tito's great relief, Dino has not revealed his treachery towards Baldassarre, thus sparing him certain disgrace: 'Romola was there. It was all like a flash of lightning: he felt, rather than saw, the glory about her head [...] "My Romola! My godess!"... He was in paradise: disgrace, shame, parting – there was no fear of them any longer....conceal-ment had been wisdom.' (pp.234–5). Here again, Eliot parodies Dante's *Purgatorio*, where Beatrice appears in the blinding sunlight from within a cloud of flowers and Dante is unable to raise his head, 'so great shame weighed on my brow'.[10] Dante has yet to drink of Eunoe but Tito, who has already drunk, instantly forgets his fear of shame. Tito, then, starts his own moral descent in the second circle of *Inferno*, the circle of the Lustful, though Eliot's choice of epigraph at the beginning of the novel was to have been deliberately ambiguous concerning the character of this fair youth whose drinking of the 'fragrant milk' appears purgatorial rather than infernal. As the novel progresses, it becomes clear that the deceit and lies in which Tito is involved in his relationship with Tessa are hallmarks of his behaviour and his engagement with Florentine society involves a moral descent through the lower regions of Dante's Hell via the eighth circle, 'Malebolge', to the lowest circle of the traitors.

Eliot's characterization of Tito occasionally draws upon images which either directly evoke or echo the Dantean punishments in the eighth circle and point up certain aspects of Tito's character. Indeed, Eliot specifically mentions Malebolge on one occasion. Nello talks of '... the incomparable Poliziano, not two months since, gone to – well, well, let us hope he is not gone to the eminent scholars in the Malebolge' (p.327) and very soon afterwards Tito, who has himself been called the 'new Poliziano', appears on the scene.[11] Tito appears to belong in the second ditch, that of the flatterers, at the beginning of the novel when he tries to ingratiate himself with Romola, Bardo and Florence in general, though he is associated with three lower bolgie, those of the Hypocrites (bolgia six), the Thieves (bolgia seven) and the Personators and Liars (bolgia ten) through Dantean allusion. As a hypocritical triple agent working for the Mediceans, Savonarola's party and the Compagnacci, Tito is afraid of exposure and particularly of Romola's judgement of him. When she laid her hand on his brow 'he felt... as unable to raise his head as if her hand had been a leaden cowl' (p.343) and he 'winced under her judgement, he felt uncertain how far the revulsion of feeling might go;... This was the leaden weight which had been too strong for his will, and kept him from raising his head to meet her eyes' (p.345). The detail here is based closely on Dante's *Inferno* XXIII:

> There below we found a painted people who were going round with very slow steps, weeping and looking weary and overcome. They had cloaks with cowls down over their eyes,... so gilded outside that they were dazzling, but within all lead and so heavy... O toilsome mantle for eternity![12]

Dante's sinners, unable to raise their heads, are forced to gaze sideways at Dante in *Inferno* XXIII, the canto of the hypocrites, and

Eliot's intention at this point is clearly to point up Tito's own hypocrisy.

In the next bolgia, Dante meets the thieves, whose *contrappasso* is to exchange their human forms for those of serpents for eternity. The incredulous Dante gives a detailed description of this transformation in *Inferno* XXV and Eliot probably had it in mind in the following description: '[Tito] felt as if a serpent had begun to coil round his limbs. Baldassarre living, and in Florence, was a living revenge, which would no more rest than a winding serpent would rest until it had crushed its prey' (p.286). The serpent image in a Dantean context, then, serves as a reminder of Tito's theft of Baldassarre's jewels, which could have been used to pay his ransom. Although there is no precise allusion to Dante, here and elsewhere the snake and viper are associated with the Tito–Baldassarre relationship in the traditional sense of the cunning and treachery of Satan, and reading through Dante does seem particularly appropriate at this point in the text.[13]

Tito would also appear to have strong affinities with the last bolgia of Malebolge, in which Dante placed the falsifiers of metals, of persons, of money and of the word. He is exposed as both an impersonator and a liar, though he escapes the particular punishments associated with these sins in Malebolge. On two occasions Tito impersonates messengers, and is able to bask in the glory that the bringer of good news enjoys. The artist Piero di Cosimo has an intuition of Tito's nature, and finds that his face would be a suitable one for a painting of 'Sinon deceiving old Priam'. Sinon is one of the great archetypes of deceit and Eliot may have had Dante in mind again here, as she had already made a note of a particularly striking image from *Inferno* XXX which was part of Dante's question as to the identity of the two 'wretches that smoke as wet hands do in winter'.[14] One of these wretches is 'false Sinon, the Greek from Troy'.[15] There are further parallels to be drawn between Sinon's treachery in the same canto (' "Remember, perjurer, the horse" ' (118)) and Tito's betrayal of Savonarola to the Compagnacci by persuading him to leave Florence.

In the lowest circle of Hell, holding the worst kinds of traitors, Dante places four categories of the fraudulent towards those who have trusted in them: those who betray their kindred; betrayers of country or cause; betrayers of guests or friends; and closest to the centre of Hell, those who have betrayed their benefactors. Tito falls into at least three of the four categories: he betrays his kindred, Romola and Bardo (in his adulterous relationship with Tessa and by selling Bardo's library); he informs against the Mediceans for Savonarola's party and then plots against Savonarola; finally, he betrays his adopted father and benefactor Baldassarre. An image from Dante's *Inferno* conveys Tito's momentary consciousness of his betrayal of Baldassarre: Francesco Cei reports seeing Tito's 'visage... "painted with fear", as our sour old Dante says' when Baldassarre had accosted him in public (p.474). In *Inferno* IV, Dante mistakes Virgil's expression for one of fear and Virgil explains that 'The anguish of the people who are down here paints my face with that pity thou takest for fear' (19–21). Tito's expression has been read aright however and, by contrast with Virgil's, points up the fact that he is unable to feel pity but only fear of discovery.

Eliot's treatment of the Tito–Baldassarre relationship and of their deaths towards the end of *Romola* is evocative of Dante's cantos XXXII and XXXIII of *Inferno*. Eliot parallels Dante's description of the sinners locked closely together in the ice of Cocytus for eternity with those they have betrayed so that only their heads protrude and the 'hair of their heads intermingle[s]' (XXXII, 42). There is no doubt that Eliot knew these canti well, for they include one of the best known 'Gothic' scenes from the *Comedy*, the episode in which Ugolino, reduced to bestial aggression, gnaws the head of Archbishop Ruggieri who had betrayed him.[16] Eliot's Baldassarre studies his revenge, which is prefigured in language echoing Dante's:

> His whole soul had been thrilled into immediate unreasoning belief in that eternity of vengeance where he, an undying hate, might clutch for ever an undying traitor, and hear that fair smiling hardness cry and moan with anguish. (p.339)

The description of Tito being swept down river and then cast violently up on the bank to meet his fate at the hands of Baldassarre echoes the fate of Dante's sinners, who are hurled below to their appointed place by Minos. There are reminders of the frozen lake of Cocytus ('Rigid – still rigid.... There was nothing to measure the time: it seemed long enough for hope to freeze into despair' (p.638)) as Tito becomes dimly aware of his *contrappasso*:

> ... he did not know whether it was life or death that had brought him into the presence of his injured father. It might be death – and

death might mean this chill gloom with the face of the hideous past hanging over him for ever. (p.638)

The vicious manner of Tito's death echoes Ugolino's revenge on Ruggieri. Baldassarre 'pressed his knuckles against the round throat [...] He would never lose his hold till someone came and found them [...] he would desire to die with his hold on this body, and follow the traitor to hell that he might clutch him there' (pp.638–9). Finally, Baldassare dies and 'his dead clutch was on the garment of the other. It was not possible to separate them' (p.639). In this close parallel of *Inferno* XXXIII, the dramatic visual image both points up Tito's essential inhumanity and provides a fitting final judgement on him within a Dantean scheme. Eliot alludes to Dante here without direct quotation or reference to the poet so that the *Comedy* remains a subtext. This technique, whereby Dante is assimilated and rewritten in her own text, recurs in Eliot's oeuvre after *Romola* and more examples of this kind of appropriation of Dante will be considered later.[17]

Tito has in fact been associated with Hell and with Satan from the beginnng of the novel. Nello makes a humorous reference to Dante's *Inferno* in Chapter 4: 'I have seen men whose beards have so invaded their cheeks, that one might have pitied them as the victims of a sad brutalizing chastisement befitting our Dante's Inferno' (p.81) and then likens Tito in his faded jerkin and hose to 'a fallen prince'; Tito in turn asks 'in what quarter I am to carry my princely air, so as to rise from the said fallen condition' p.82). Tito's character and the Dantean *contrappasso*, then, are already prefigured in Chapter 3, with its references to treachery, the Devil and Hell. In Dino's vision of Romola's future, Tito figures as the 'Great Tempter' (p.215), and he is repeatedly associated with diabolic forces and devils.[18] Moreover, Tito's physical beauty is linked with treachery by Piero di Cosimo: '... he has a face that would make him the more perfect traitor if he had the heart of one,...' (p.87) and this too finds an echo in Dante, who gives Geryon (the 'foul image of fraud' in *Inferno* XVII) 'the face of a just man, so gracious was its outward aspect, and all the rest was a serpent's trunk' (7, 10–12). This association of beauty and treachery can of course be traced to the lowest part of Hell, to Satan himself, 'the creature who was once so fair'.[19] In Eliot's creation of a web of 'diabolic' associations for Tito Melema, she, like Dante, draws upon Christian mythology, so that specific allusion to Dante helps reinforce the more general associations.

Although *Romola* was first published in the *Cornhill Magazine*
from July 1862 to August 1863, a slightly revised text was published
in three volumes by Smith, Elder & Co. in July 1863. Each volume
ends in a Dantesque manner as the final scene in each Book takes
stock of Romola's situation and marks the progress of her personal
pilgrimage. At the end of Book I, as Romola and Tito emerge onto
the steps of Santa Croce after their wedding, she is seized with a
cold horror as 'a strange dreary chant, as of a *Miserere*, met their
ears, and they saw . . . a stream of people impelled by something . . .'.
The procession is a Masque of Time and Death in which it appears
as though the figures come floating through the air 'and behind
them came what looked like a troop of the sheeted dead gliding
above blackness. And as they glided slowly, they chanted in a
wailing strain.' (pp.262–3). Here there are echoes of Dante's
entrance into Hell, when he is met by 'sighs, lamentations and
loud wailings resound[ing] through the starless air', and sees a
whirling banner behind which 'came so long a train of people
that I should never have believed death had undone so many'.[20]
Symbolically, the cross which Romola had accepted from Savonarola, representing the purgatorial way of suffering and renunciation,
is shut up in the casket (Tito has 'locked away all sadness from
[her]') as if to signal a Dantesque banishment from God. By the end
of Book II, however, Romola has achieved a new purgatorial spirit
as she returns to Florence: 'the whole bent of her mind now was
towards doing what was painful rather than what was easy' (p.438).

> She felt the dreariness, yet her courage was high, like that of a
> seeker who has come on new signs of gold. She was going to
> thread life by a fresh clue. She had thrown all the energy of her
> will into renunciation. The empty tabernacle remained locked
> and she placed Dino's crucifix outside it. (p.440)

The outward monotony of this return is broken only by the
coming of night 'like a white ghost at the windows'. This ghost,
however, like the angel pilot coming over the sea to Purgatory
who appears to Dante as 'a whiteness' (II, 23), is the harbinger of
a new life. Romola has accepted the Cross and Eliot, in true Dantean
fashion, marks this night as being the symbol of hope: it is Christmas Eve.[21]

Towards the end of the novel, the drama of infernal and purgatorial experience is played out again for Romola the second time she

leaves Florence after the execution of Bernardo del Nero and Savonarola's refusal to intervene. In drifiting away in the fishing boat
Romola wishes to free herself from the burden of choice:[22]

> ... with a great sob she wished that she might be gliding into
> death.
> She drew the cowl over her head again and covered her face,
> choosing darkness rather than the light of the stars, which seemed
> to her like the hard light of eyes that looked at her without seeing
> her. Presently she felt that she was in the grave, but not resting
> there: she was touching the hands of the beloved dead beside her,
> and trying to wake them. (p.590)

Though the drifting seems a descent into an infernal world,
Romola's waking is unmistakably purgatorial in tone. She finds
herself in the 'delicious sun-rays' of the morning in 'the presence
of peace and beauty'. The boat bearing her over the water has been a
'ship of souls', 'the gently lulling cradle of a new life', and not the
bark of Charon taking her to 'the unknown regions of death'
(pp.640–1) presaged in the passage above. The landscape which
presents itself to Romola is also suggestive of the geography of the
first cantos of *Purgatory*:

> ... a breadth of green land, curtained by gentle tree-shadowed
> slopes leaning towards the rocky heights. Up these slopes might
> be seen here and there, gleaming between the tree-tops, a path-
> way leading to a little irregular mass of building ... (p.640)

Like the souls transported to Purgatory, Romola arrives from the
sea and lands on a shore sloping up gently to the mountain proper
where the ascent is more arduous. Her horror on discovering the
plague-stricken village, however, suggests that the scene is about to
dissolve into the dream-like infernal vision she had imagined when
drifting ('Was she in a village of the unburied dead?' (p.643)), but
the burden of choice which she is here required to take up is really
part of her purgatorial ascent. Savonarola had earlier described
Romola's action, in leaving her responsibilities and quitting Florence, in the following way: 'The servants of God are struggling after
a law of justice, peace, and charity, ... but you think no more of this
than if you were a bird that may spread its wings and fly whither it
will in search of food to its liking' (p.431). This echoes the first part

of an image used by Dante in *Purgatorio* II to describe the souls –
newly arrived on the shore of Purgatory but momentarily distracted
by Dante's presence – on being reprimanded by the angel pilot: 'As
when doves collected at their feeding, picking up wheat or tares,
quiet, without their usual show of pride, if something appear to
frighten them suddenly leave their food lying, because they are
assailed with a greater care; so I saw that new troop leave the
song and go towards the slope,...' (124–31). As had happened
during the plague in Florence, Romola is again called back to duty
and accepts the presence of suffering and hardship in the village.
Like the souls in Purgatory she too is 'assailed with a greater care',
and 'the experience was like a new baptism to [her]' (p.650).[23]

The final scene in the Epilogue to *Romola* at the end of Book III
continues this purgatorial spirit, though Romola is clearly much
further on in her spiritual journey by now:

> Her hands were crossed on her lap and her eyes were fixed
> absently on the distant mountains:...An eager life had left its
> marks upon her: the finely moulded cheek had sunk a little, the
> golden crown was less massive; but there was a placidity in
> Romola's face which had never belonged to it in youth. (p.673)

Romola has now achieved a Beatrice-like serenity which makes her
capable of harsh judgements where these are appropriate (she tells
Lillo that Tito 'denied his father, and left him to misery; he betrayed
every trust that was reposed in him, that he might keep himself safe
and get rich and prosperous'), but also of extending compassion
and love to others ('[she] met Lillo's impatient gaze with a brighter
and brighter smile' (p.673)). The Romola of the Epilogue is an image
of achieved peace, independence and love. She has become a Beatrice, a nurturing 'Italia' figure looking after her children, and a
positive icon to set against so many despairing ones from Italian
literature.[24]

There is a strong sense that Eliot was experimenting with Dante
in *Romola* though, for there is evidence of some indecision as to the
prominence to be given to the Florentine poet in the novel, with
material being written in or out even quite late on. There is also a
slight forcing of Dante on occasion. In Chapter 6 there is a rare
instance of Eliot's wish to bring in Dante getting the better of her
aesthetic judgement. When Romola's blind father is interested in
some gems which Tito which is about to draw out from his wallet,

Romola, not wishing to involve Tito in a tedious lengthy description of the stones, stops him by 'placing her finger on her lips, "Con viso che tacendo dicea, Taci"' [With a look which said in silence, 'Be silent'] (p.117). The line from Dante's *Purgatorio* XXI (104) is given in Italian and inset as a single line quotation which gives it a prominence which would seem to indicate that it has some heightened importance at this point. This line was not in the original manuscript but was added to the *Cornhill* text, which indicates some late rethinking by Eliot. The Dantean context here is the moment when the Roman poet Statius, without recognizing Virgil, says that he would have consented to have stayed in Purgatory 'a sun more than [he] was due before coming forth from banishment' (101–2) if he could have lived at the time of Virgil. The latter then turns to Dante 'with a look which said in silence, "Be silent"' in a moment of mirthful complicity between Dante and Virgil before the latter's identity is revealed to the great joy of Statius. The scene is a rare touching moment of humour in the *Comedy* in which like-minded souls meet, and Statius is seen as a kind of Christian colleague of Virgil. Cortese argues that this line in *Romola* is intended as an example of true intellectual fellowship set against Tito's self-interest.[25] It is true that Tito's efforts to ingratiate himself with Bardo are dictated not by intellectual kinship but by his interest in Romola and in his career in Florence, but Cortese's argument is severely weakened by the fact that there is no direct parallel between the Virgil–Dante–Statius triangle in *Purgatorio* and Romola–Tito–Bardo in Eliot's novel. There is only a passing similarity based on Romola's wish for information to be concealed and on a moment of complicity between Tito and herself behind her father's back. No real teacher–pupil relationship between Bardo and Tito can be implied as it is Romola herself who acts the role of Virgil here, so that the attempt to find any deeper parallels between the two scenes merely leads to confusion. Eliot's use of the *Comedy* at this point seems rather superficial, or even superfluous, given that the same moment of complicity between Romola and Tito could as easily have been established without Dante, and is to my mind misjudged here: it impedes the flow of the text by being given such prominence, and this in a foreign language. The text invites us to look for deeper, more complex meanings but, based as it is on a merely passing resemblance, it is not well integrated into the whole and resists attempts to find any deeper moral significance.

6

Dante and Moral Choice in
Felix Holt, the Radical

In *Romola*, Eliot's use of Dante is limited in scope and consists mainly of a body of imagery characterizing Tito Melema, of precise allusion with local significance and of the poet's rather shadowy presence as a moral touchstone representing an earlier exemplary Florentine morality against which the decadence of the city at the end of the fifteenth century can be measured. Eliot's drafts for *Romola* occasionally suggest uncertainty over the role Dante was to play in the novel. Part of the reason for this may lie in a fear that too prominent a Dante might overshadow the figure of Savonarola and impair or even undermine moral clarity by blurring the meticulously created divisions of the structural dialectic (Pagan, Christian, Positive (?)) which Romola enacts.

In *Felix Holt, the Radical*, Dante is a more substantial presence and becomes central to the creation of the moral landscape of the novel. A number of critics have noticed Eliot's use of Dante in this novel, though their comments have, on the whole, been limited to pointing out general correspondences between Dante's and Eliot's texts.[1] Wiesenfarth draws attention to the 'substantial body of allusion' to the *Divine Comedy* of Dante in *Felix Holt, the Radical*, noting the allusions to *Inferno* canto XIII (the 'Wood of the Suicides') which Eliot uses to make Transome Court 'akin to a circle of Dante's Hell' and to create 'an atmosphere of hopeless suffering caused by Mrs Transome's sins' as she is tortured by her ex-lover Jermyn and her son Harold.[2] Wiesenfarth makes the further point that 'growth through suffering...seems peculiarly susceptible to presentation in terms of Dantean imagery' in the novel.[3] Taking these comments as a starting point, this chapter examines Eliot's absorption of material from Dante and shows how, through her thorough knowledge of the *Comedy*, she constructs a 'moral landscape' which sometimes closely parallels Dante's. Eliot greatly admired Dante for achieving a fine balance between judgement and pity in the *Comedy*, and this aspect of his humanism is of particular relevance to the moral universe of *Felix Holt*, where moments from the *Comedy* are carefully worked into the novel to elicit both judgement and compassion from the reader.

George Eliot makes specific reference to Dante on at least three occasions within *Felix Holt, the Radical*, uses lines from the *Divine Comedy* as epigraphs to two chapters, and makes numerous covert allusions during the course of the novel.[4] The first reference likens Sampson, the driver of the coach on which the author imagines us to be travelling through the English countryside, to Dante's Virgil: 'The coachman was an excellent travelling companion and commentator on the landscape; he could tell the names of sites and persons, and explained the meanings of groups, as well as the shade of Virgil in a more memorable journey' (p.81). The second reference to Dante, and the one Wiesenfarth gives in full, is that to canto XIII, the 'Wood of the Suicides':

The poets have told us of a dolorous enchanted forest in the under world. The thorn-bushes there, and the thick-barked stems, have human histories hidden in them; the power of unuttered cries dwells in the passionless-seeming branches, and the red warm blood is darkly feeding the quivering nerves of a sleepless memory that watches through all dreams. These things are a parable. (p.84)

Wiesenfarth's gloss on the above passage will serve as a starting point for further analysis:

The parable is evident in the novel when Eliot presents Mrs Transome as one of the 'passionless-seeming branches' living with the power of 'unuttered cries' in the hell of Transome Court; there she suffers the fate of a sinful queen who has failed to achieve happiness.... She took Jermyn as her lover, and he fathered Harold whom she loves. Now it is Jermyn and Harold who torture her most cruelly. Harold sits down beside her with 'the unmanageable strength of a great bird' (ch. I), and Jermyn turns 'tenderness into calculation'.[5]

Wiesenfarth notes the reference to the harpies as Harold sits beside his mother with the 'unmanageable strength of a great bird' and elsewhere the savage image of Jermyn's words to Mrs Transome which are 'as pleasant to her as if [they] had been cut into her bared arm', echoing both the harpies' destruction of the foliage of the trees and the injury Dante-character inflicts on Piero delle Vigne when, at the behest of Virgil, he snaps a twig from the tree in which Piero has been imprisoned for committing suicide. Transome Court, hidden behind a thick belt of trees, is intended to be strongly reminiscent of Dante's Hell in which a monotonous cycle of events repeats itself. Eliot uses the Wood of the Suicides as a metaphor for Mrs Transome's attenuated existence and for her imprisonment inside the wood surrounding Transome Court: 'she had contracted small rigid habits of thinking and acting' (p.99) and 'objects to changes' (p.119). Her husband spends his life in the fruitless occupation of repeatedly rearranging his collection of insects, and in a Dantean *contrappasso*, he is defined by his choice, and comes to resemble that which he has chosen: 'He will be like a distracted insect, and never know where to go, if you alter the track he has to walk in' (pp.94–5). Transome Court, then, may be likened to a private underworld of 'moral death' contrasting with the moral vitality of the eponymous hero Felix Holt and, as one critic has pointed out, it is between these two extremes that Esther must choose in the novel.[6]

Yet it would perhaps be too easy to equate the hell of Transome Court with Dante's Wood of the Suicides of *Inferno* XIII, and to assume that Eliot employs the Dantean imagery as an objective correlative for Mrs Transome's mental life, or merely to elicit pity for her. The references to Dante are very specific and function in various ways at different levels of the text to support Eliot's own moral universe. For as in the *Divine Comedy*, there is a strong element of judgement present in Eliot's novel. Piero delle Vigne, to whom Dante speaks in canto XIII, is a paradigm of intransigence. Unable to tolerate an image of himself created by those who accused him of treason, he commits suicide. Mrs Transome's oppressive dread is in part a fear of the altered image of herself which would be presented to the world on the revelation of the truth of her own past conduct, while her failure to give any meaning to her suffering, to make it a vehicle for repentance and forgiveness, makes her, like Piero, an 'imprisoned spirit'.[7]

The third direct reference to the *Divine Comedy* comes much later:

There is heroism even in the circles of hell for fellow-sinners who cling to each other in the fiery whirlwind and never recriminate. (p.520)

Jermyn and Mrs Transome, by contrast, do nothing but recriminate, though there is some justice in hers and none in his.[8] The above is a reference to canto V of *Inferno*, where in the circle of the lustful Dante meets the souls of Francesca da Rimini and Paolo Malatesta, who are evoked by Eliot as an ideal in comparison with Jermyn and Mrs Transome.[9] In the *Notebook 1854–1879*, there are two quotations in Italian from *Inferno* V.[10] The first of these is: '[she] was so corrupted by licentious vice that she made lust lawful in her law to take away the scandal into which she was brought' (55–7). These words, spoken by Virgil, refer to Semiramis, legendary queen of Assyria, and in *Felix Holt* we read of Mrs Transome that 'unlike the Semiramis who made laws to suit her practical licence, she lived, poor soul in the midst of desecrated sanctities, and of honours that looked tarnished in the light of monotonous and weary suns' (p.494). This comment prefigures the reference to the 'fellow-sinners who cling to each other' in Eliot's text in the same way that Semiramis comes before Paolo and Francesca, 'these two that go together' (74) in the procession of souls blown on the winds of passion of the 'bufera infernal'. *Inferno* V is of particular importance thematically in the novel, functioning as a subtext with direct bearing not only on the stories of Mrs Transome and Jermyn but also on those of each of the other major characters.

The most obvious parallel between the stories of Mrs Transome and Jermyn and Francesca and Paolo is that both pairs were lovers. Dante's lovers were discovered and killed in the very act of sinning, whereas the sins of Eliot's lovers emerge years after, and much of Mrs Transome's tragedy happens in the interval between the deed and its discovery. The parallels between Mrs Transome and Francesca are more specific, however. In the character of Francesca, Dante shows the power of literature to affect and influence the reader, and in particular the effect of the *Rime* of the *dolce stil novo*, which Dante had himself practised earlier in life. It becomes evident that Francesca is steeped in such romantic literature when she attempts to justify her actions using the erroneous ideologies embodied in this poetry, and in language which, in its obsession with *amor*, imitates the poetry of the Stilnovisti:

'Love, which is quickly kindled in the gentle heart, seized this man for the fair form that was taken from me, and the manner afflicts me still. Love, which absolves no one beloved from loving, seized me so strongly with his charm that, as thou seest, it does not leave me yet. Love brought us to one death.'[11]

Similarly, Mrs Transome has herself been the victim both of an inadequate education and of morally questionable literature which nurtures an inherent tendency in her character towards egoism:

> When she was young she had been thought wonderfully clever and accomplished, and had been rather ambitious of intellectual superiority – had secretly picked out for private reading the lighter parts of dangerous French authors – and in company had been able to talk of Mr. Burke's style, or of Chateaubriand's eloquence – had laughed at the *Lyrical Ballads* and admired Mr Southey's 'Thalaba'. She always thought that the dangerous French writers were wicked, and that her reading of them was a sin; but many sinful things were highly agreeable to her, and many things which she did not doubt to be good and true were dull and meaningless. She found ridicule of Biblical characters very amusing, and she was interested in stories of illicit passion...the notion that what is true and, in general, good for mankind, is stupid and drug-like, is not a safe theoretic basis in circumstances of temptation and difficulty. (pp.104–6)

One must be constantly vigilant with words, and neither Francesca nor Mrs Transome is. Each allows literature to provide a structure for her emotions, and to impose an order on her own experience.

Like Francesca, Mrs Transome lives in a state in which the past is for ever reasserting itself, or is eternally present. Both are irrevocably linked to the choices they have made ('he who never shall be parted from me' (*Inferno* V, 135)). In Mrs Transome there is no doubt that this choice stems ultimately from character. Throughout her life 'there had vibrated the maiden need to have her hand kissed and be the object of chivalry' (p.201), and Jermyn, with 'a selfishness which then took the form of homage to her', fulfilled this need (p.515). As Francesca is condemned to remain always with Paolo, so Mrs Transome is forever united with Jermyn through her son, Harold. Though they have been estranged as lovers for 20 years when the novel begins, there is a symbolic acknowledgement of their indivisibility when the past is suddenly made present:

After a few moments' silence she said, in a gentle and almost
tremulous voice –
'Let me take your arm.'
He gave it immediately, putting on his hat and wondering. For
more than twenty years Mrs. Transome had never chosen to take
his arm. (p.203)

Francesca's words apply again in the case of Mrs Transome: 'There
is no greater pain than to recall the happy time in misery'.[12]
Although she is bitter towards Jermyn in her misery, Mrs Transome's own 'happy time' is only indicated as the time before Harold
was born:

'Denner,' she said, in a low tone, 'if I could choose at this moment,
I would choose that Harold should never have been born.'
'Nay, my dear . . . it was a happiness to you then.'
'I don't believe I felt the happiness then as I feel the misery
now.' (p.490)[13]

Mrs Transome's words given here by George Eliot are a deliberate
echo of Dante's.
Canto XIII of the *Inferno*, with which Mrs Transome is strongly
associated, is especially bound up for Eliot with Dante's ability to
pity the sinners he meets and she refers to this specifically in her
Beinecke notebook:

To balance Dante's severity, there are many instances of tenderness and compassion: e.g. in the wood of suicides Canto XIII, 84,
he begs Virgil to ask questions for him of Pietro de' Vigni – 'Ch' io
non potrei: tanta pietà m'accora.' – Again, in C. XIV at the beginning, he cannot go away from the Florentine transfixed as a tree
without gathering up the scattered leaves & giving them back to
the poor trunk.[14]

and again: 'Throughout the Inferno I find only three instances of
what can be called cruelty in Dante. Everywhere else the sufferings
of the damned fill him with pity' (p.44).[15] In her own use of Dante in
Felix Holt, Eliot has been severe in her condemnation of Mrs Transome: the nature of her sin and the 'moral suicide' resulting from it
have been amply illustrated through allusion to, and the use of
images from, cantos XIII and V from *Inferno*. It is not surprising

therefore, that Eliot should seek to temper the severity of her portrayal of this 'poor soul' who lived 'in the midst of desecrated sanctities' (p.494), particularly as she has drawn heavily on the very episode (cantos XIII–XIV) in which pity is uppermost in her mind. One way in which Eliot elicits this sympathy for Mrs Transome is, as Cortese suggests, to allow the reader into her experience, to 'enter the tree, as it were, to feel how it feels to be inside looking out' so as to create a psychological depth and interest which is often felt to be lacking in the other characters. This is achieved by means of images of the restless Mrs Transome looking out from her lonely and dreary imprisonment at Transome Court onto a world which seems unheeding and indifferent.[16] Cortese, however, sees Eliot's strategies for eliciting pity for Mrs Transome as a fault in the novel in which 'the narrator's attitude toward Mrs Transome, severity tempered by pity, diverts the novel's ethical direction'.[17] In this view, the reader may lose sight of the moral dichotomies which the novel establishes and is torn between a human identification with Mrs Transome and the need to maintain a moral distance from her in order to accept Esther's rejection of Transome Court and all it represents at the end of the novel. This reading, however, fails to allow for the complexity of feeling and experience in the mixed reality which Eliot represents in *Felix Holt*: Mrs Transome is judged through the Dante allusions over the course of the novel, but Eliot also invites the reader to draw upon the same precious human compassion present in the Dantean texts underlying Mrs Transome's experience. One very reliable index of moral growth, which Eliot is at pains to register in her text, is Esther's increasing capacity for fellow-feeling, for compassion and pity towards others, and the reader is, as it were, guided along the same path by the novel's narrator.

George Eliot's concern to balance her own severity in assigning Mrs Transome to a Dantesque hell with tenderness and compassion is particularly clear from a highly Dantesque passage in the novel, which comes soon after the discovery of Mrs Transome's past relationship with Jermyn and of Harold's true parentage:

All had been stillness hitherto, except the fitful wind outside. But [Esther's] ears now caught a sound within – slight, but sudden. She moved near her door, and heard the sweep of something on the matting outside. It came closer, and paused. Then it began again, and seemed to sweep away from her. Then it approached, and paused as it had done before. Esther listened, wondering. The same thing happened again and again, till she could bear it no longer. She opened her door, and in the dim light of the corridor, where the glass above seemed to make a glimmering sky, she saw Mrs Transome's tall figure pacing slowly, with her cheek upon her hand. (pp.592–3)

The 'fitful wind', with its connotations of spent or curbed passion, the sound of the repeated sweeping past of Mrs Transome in the confined space of the corridor, together with the monotony and loneliness of her life are all strongly suggestive of Dante's vision in *Inferno* V. Mrs Transome is, in fact, coming to Esther for comfort in her sorrow. Her own isolating pride is beginning to melt, and she wishes for compassion and love from the younger woman. Yet, as in *Inferno* V, where the souls do not appear to be able to come of their own accord, Mrs Transome 'might have gone on pacing the corridor like an uneasy spirit without a goal, if Esther's thought, leaping towards her, had not saved her from the need to ask admission' (p.596). In *Inferno* V (82–7), Dante describes the effect of his call to the sinners in the following terms:

As doves, summoned by desire, come with wings poised and motionless to the sweet nest, borne by their will through the air, so these left the troop where Dido is, coming to us through the malignant air; such force had my loving call.

In the upper circles of Dante's *Inferno* (to which both cantos V and XIII belong) we still sense the essential humanity of the sinners. We are made aware of the common problems of the human condition, of the ties which link the damned to other human beings and often to Dante himself. In canto V, the image of Dante's call bridging the spatial distance between himself and the sinners is symbolic of this partial identification with them. Eliot uses a similar image when she describes Esther's 'thought leaping towards' Mrs Transome saving her 'from the need to ask admission'. Both authors are concerned to show the effect of pity in binding human beings together. This powerful, altruistic emotion is the converse of that selfish passion by means of which both Dante's and Eliot's characters were brought to the 'woeful pass'.[18] Esther has 'a passionate desire to soothe this suffering woman', but now the passion and desire are constructive, healing qualities, and the contrast serves to point up the Dantean precept that the sins of incontinence (those of the flesh) are essentially an excess or perversion of some good human quality.

Both the Dante-character in the *Inferno* and Esther in *Felix Holt* show extreme emotional reactions in the face of the suffering of the sinners. Dante says that 'for pity I swooned as if in death and dropped like a dead body' (*Inferno* V, 140).[19] The reason for Dante's reaction here may be the knowledge that he was himself implicated in the sin of Paolo and Francesca, through his writings in the *dolce stil novo*, which were similar in content to the literature of romance which contributed to their damnation:[20] it may also be the knowledge that he himself could so easily have shared the same fate in his own potentially adulterous relationship with his Beatrice. In a similar moment of realization, Esther 'found it difficult to speak. The dimly-suggested tragedy of this woman's life, the dreary waste of years empty of sweet trust and affection, afflicted her even to horror' (p.597). This extreme emotion is partly the result of her awareness of what the decision to accept Harold Transome would mean for her: she has her own 'dimly-suggested' future made present to her in the person of Mrs Transome. Her 'horror' also arises, I think, from a sudden overwhelming realization – the kind that made Dante '[drop] like a dead body' – of the strong similarities between herself and Mrs Transome. For like her, Esther has been fond of morally questionable literature. Felix acts as commentator on Esther's reading-matter: Byron's heroes are the 'most paltry puppets that were ever pulled by the strings of lust and pride' and *René* 'is idiotic immorality dressed up to look fine' (pp.151, 210). The reading (and writing) of such literature is associated with moral irresponsibility, and with the dissipation of intelligence. Esther is accused of giving her 'soul up to trifles' (p.210) and of being happy only when she can 'get rid of any judgment that must carry grave action after it' (p.211). It is in the context of moral choice that Esther is described in terms of the bird imagery, which, in Dante's fifth canto, is associated with the moral lightness of sin (*Inferno* V, 74–5). On her arrival at Transome Court Esther appears to little Harry like 'a new sort of bird' (p.491) and Felix tells her 'You don't care to be better than a bird trimming its feathers, and pecking about after what pleases it' (p.211). There is a deliberate note of ambiguity in Eliot's choice of image though. For while it is intended by Felix as a criticism of Esther's moral seriousness, it also has a predictive quality. Dante uses the same image (*Purgatorio* II) of 'doves collected at their feeding' which 'if something appears to frighten them suddenly leave their food lying, because they are assailed with a greater care'. Esther, too, will shortly be 'assailed with a greater care' and, like the souls who have been momentarily distracted by Dante's *dolce stil novo* poetry, she will 'leave the song' of rejected literature behind.[21] Eliot later links the bird image directly with Esther's moment of moral choice, in a deliberate echo of lines from Dante's *Inferno* V: 'That young presence, which had flitted like a white new-winged dove over all the saddening relics and new finery of Transome Court, could not find its home there. Harold heard... that she loved some one else, and that she resigned all claim to the Transome estates' (p.599). Esther is herself 'summoned by desire', but unlike the sinners in *Inferno* V, in Eliot's heroine the image is reinstated in a fitting context. Dante had placed the dove, Christian symbol of peace, love and gentleness, in the incongruous setting of the *Inferno* and this heightens the pathos of the sinners' plight once we realize that, although condemned for their sin, they too partake of those valuable qualities conveyed by the image.

Along with the allusions to and strong thematic and structural parallels with cantos V and XIII from *Inferno*, another powerful image from Dante – and one which was to become a favourite with Eliot in her two last novels – makes its first appearance in *Felix Holt*. While at Transome Court, Esther has a habit of sitting 'with a book on her knee and "making a bed for her cheek" with one little hand... or else standing in front of one of the full-length family portraits with an air of rumination' (pp.497–8): then at the end of the novel, Mrs Transome is portrayed 'pacing slowly, with her cheek upon her hand' (p.593). On this second occasion, there can be little doubt that this pose is an archetypal Dantean attitude of mental anguish and suffering, but Eliot is at pains to link Esther and Mrs Transome through this image from *Purgatorio* VII taken from an episode in which, in the Valley of the Princes, Philip III and Henry of Navarre mourn the corrupt life of their kinsman Philip the Fair ('the pest of France'), the former by beating his breast and 'the other... couches his cheek on his hand and sighs' (107–8). There are a number of parallels between *Purgatorio* VII and Eliot's text and the image serves to link a variety of themes common to both: firstly, the theme of 'woeful progeny' announced in the Introduction (p.83) – the two princes ('the father and father-in-law of the pest of France' [VII, 109]) are pierced with grief at the knowledge that their blood has become base and corrupted, while Mrs Transome grieves at the knowledge of her own son's indifference towards her; secondly, that of worthless genealogies – Sordello tells Virgil and Dante that 'rarely does human worth rise through the branches' (121–2) and Esther has learned this lesson when she rejects Mrs Transome's obsession with birth and family honour (with ancestral tales and her family lineage) for the true nobility of the individual; thirdly, the theme of cursed inheritance – as Philip the Fair is the 'tragic mark of kinship' of Philip III and Henry of Navarre, so Mrs Transome's adultery is 'cursed by its woeful progeny' through Harold's pitiless indifference, and it is this cursed inheritance (which turns out to be hers by rights) which Esther rejects (p.83); finally there is the theme of meaningful engagement in the world – the princes (most of whom had been engaged in sordid power struggles causing untold suffering during their lives) wait outside Purgatory to expiate the sin of moral laxity, for their preoccupation with earthly ambitions had long distracted them from looking to the care of their souls. The same dangers lie in wait for Esther should she choose to claim her inheritance and marry Harold. The close textual proximity of Esther's Dantean attitude of 'making a bed for her cheek' with her hand and her standing absorbed before the Transome family portrait bears out the view that a close parallel with the themes of *Purgatorio* VII is intended by Eliot, with Dante's text providing a commentary (albeit mutedly) on Esther's moral dilemma.[22] It is also significant in Esther's case, I think, that the image is a purgatorial one, hinting at upward movement and moral growth: the same image applied to Mrs Transome is fused with the Dantesque parallel of *Inferno* V in the passage discussed above (pp.104–5), in which it becomes clear that she, like Francesca, remains unredeemed. Thus, in addition to being 'the pathetic culmination of the theme of kinship turned into a curse',[23] it also contributes to a reiteration of the adultery theme and marks a final judgement on Mrs Transome who, however, is still entitled to claim our pity in Eliot's moral universe in the same way as is Francesca in Dante's.[24]

Eliot provides a further Dantean 'vision' of the hell from which Esther escapes in the scene where Jermyn betrays Mrs Transome and confronts Harold with the news that he is his true father:

... there was no sound between them, but only angry hatred gathering in the two faces. Harold felt himself going to crush this insolence: Jermyn felt that he had words within him that were fangs to clutch this obstinate strength, and wring forth the blood and compel submission.... He said, in a tone that was rather lower, but yet harder and more biting –

'You will repent else – for your mother's sake.' [...]

...the two men had got very near the long mirror. They were both white; both had anger and hatred in their faces; the hands of both were upraised. As Harold heard the last terrible words he started at a leaping throb that went through him, and in the start turned his eyes away from Jermyn's face. He turned them on the same face in the glass with his own beside it, and saw the hated fatherhood reasserted. (p.581)

This passage brings together allusions to and images from *Inferno* XXXII and XXXIII, those of the betrayers in Lake Cocytus. The description of hatred and rage in Jermyn's words, which become 'fangs to clutch' evokes Dante's description of Count Ugolino encased in the ice of the lake: 'That sinner lifted his mouth from the savage meal, wiping it on the hair of the head he had wasted behind'.[25] In Dante's account, Ugolino, who betrayed his own city of Pisa and was in turn betrayed by his accomplice Archbishop Ruggiero whose head he now gnaws in Cocytus, was imprisoned in a tower with his children and was driven by hunger to eat their flesh after their deaths. The Dantean echo in *Felix Holt* serves to point up, and to focus attention on, the nature of the 'crimes' of betrayal involved. The reference is even more specific, however, for Jermyn, too, has been feeding off the estate of his own child for years, and it is this which has induced Harold to '[set] the dogs on' him (p.286). Eliot's use of the mirror in the confrontation scene between father and son is an interesting reworking of elements from Dante's canto XXXII: 'I turned and saw before me and under my feet a lake which through frost had the appearance of glass and not of water'(22–4). The betrayers are compelled to look upon their own reflections, which expose to them the truth of their sins in the ice for all eternity. One of them asks Dante 'Why dost thou mirror thyself in us so long?' (XXXII, 54) and he breaks off staring at them and asks to know the names of the two sinners who are pressed so close together in the ice that the hair of their heads intermingles:

And they bent back their necks; and when they had raised their faces to me their eyes, which before were moist only within, gushed over at the lids, and the frost bound the tears between and locked them up again, never did clamp bind beam on beam so hard; whereupon they butted together like two goats, such fury mastered them.[26]

The two are unable to speak, but their rage finds expression in frozen tears and animal aggression towards each other. As with Ugolino, blood relations are involved, as these sons of a Tuscan nobleman had disputed their inheritance and subsequently killed each other. In the mirror scene, Eliot deliberately creates a Dantesque tableau of blood relatives locked in struggle as they clutch each other, in which Jermyn 'was suffering the torment of a compressed rage, which, if not impotent to inflict pain on another, was impotent to avert evil from himself' (p.579). Like the sinners in Cocytus, who cannot wait to betray each other to Dante, we are aware that Jermyn is himself something of a habitual betrayer, who has previously betrayed Bycliffe, Esther's true father. He has been condemned and imprisoned by his own actions, and is reduced to the brute state of the sinners in Cocytus.[27] Eliot uses the parallel with Dante to highlight the betrayal by Jermyn and to pronounce judgement on him at a moment of violent drama, and also perhaps to point to the betrayal by Harold who, in the Dantean scheme, is guilty of betraying a guest, Esther, in that he attempts to manipulate the human affections for his own advantage.

We turn now to a discussion of two quotations from Dante which Eliot modified and used as epigraphs to Chapters 15 and 22 of *Felix Holt*. These have local significance for the chapters to which they refer, but do not appear to have the same power to resonate over the novel as a whole. Nor is there an overtly judgemental content in these epigraphs.[28] The first of these modified quotations from Dante, 'And doubt shall be as lead upon the feet / Of thy most anxious will', is taken from *Paradiso* XIII, and although it is not a direct quotation, it does capture both the central image and the spirit of the words spoken by Thomas Aquinas: 'And let this always be lead on thy feet to make thee slow, like a weary man, in moving either to the yea or the nay where thou dost not see clearly' (112–14).[29] Aquinas' words concern the difficulty of making affirmative or negative pronouncements in ignorance of divine reason, and the consequent need for deliberation and for distinctions both in judgement and in speech. Part of the subject of this canto, then, is intellectual integrity; both Aquinas and Dante warn against the feelings binding the intellect either in the great questions of creation and

Providence or in practical human affairs. The importance of these lines for Chapter 15 is to announce the theme of self-doubt in both Rufus Lyon and in Esther. Rufus is 'inwardly torn by doubt and anxiety concerning his own private relations and the facts of his past life' (pp.259–60), by his transgression in allowing his affection for Annette to take precedence over the ministerial vocation. The epigraph, then, is a comment on two aspects of Rufus' nature, religious zeal alongside self-doubt. By the end of this chapter Esther too is beginning to question the certainties of her own romantic notions which she has hitherto taken for granted, and 'beginning to lose her complacency at her own wit and criticism; to lose the sense of superiority in an awakening need for reliance on one whose vision was wider, whose nature was purer and stronger than her own' (p.264). Eliot's particular interest in this canto of *Paradiso* is attested by the three quotations from it copied into her Beinecke notebook,[30] and Eliot had quoted from this canto as early as 1856.[31]

In the epigraph to Chapter 15, then, Eliot modifies Dante's original to some extent, though the central image of 'lead upon the feet' is taken directly from Dante. In the second epigraph, the one to Chapter 22, which Wiesenfarth traces back to its source in Dante, the lines are modified to a much greater degree so that they bear a less direct relationship to Dante's original and a more complex one to the chapter itself. The epigraph reads 'Her gentle looks shot arrows, piercing him / As gods are pierced, with poison of sweet pity' and the attributed source is two lines from *Inferno* XXIX.[32] Although the evidence from the Beinecke notebook supports the idea that Eliot had these lines strongly in mind, the way in which she changes them, and her reasons for doing so, add a further dimension to the direct correspondences between Dante's *Inferno* XXIX and the content of Eliot's Chapter 22. In Dante's lines it is the 'strange lamentations' which pierce, whereas in Eliot's it is 'gentle looks'; in Dante, the arrow carries 'pity', in Eliot it is 'poison of sweet pity'; Dante-character is pierced directly, whereas in Eliot both Felix ('him') and 'gods' are pierced. The effect of these changes is to generate associations other than those present in Dante's lines, to shift the emphasis from feelings of pain and pity for another's suffering and to activate the associations with courtly love poetry to which 'gentle looks', 'sweet pity' and 'gods...pierced with poison' belong. Through this framework, Eliot's epigraph is intended to suggest a relationship between Felix and Esther (where she is figured as mortal and he is associated with 'gods') in which his

'stronger nature' is struck with a pity so 'gentle' and 'sweet' that it is
in danger of turning into love. The extent to which Dante's lines
have been altered makes attempts to find correspondences and
parallels between Dante's canto and Eliot's chapter problematic.
Cortese argues for a broad correspondence between Dante's canto
of the alchemists, who attempt to turn base metal into gold, and this
chapter of *Felix Holt*, which marks the beginning of Esther's spiritual change whereby, from being 'a heap of fragments', her life
becomes a quest for the highest ideals. The epigraph prepares the
reader for Felix's change of feelings towards Esther in the rest of the
novel, but this emerges directly from the lines themselves and a
knowledge of the Dantean origin of the epigraph would only be
misleading. The alchemy practised by the counterfeiters of *Inferno*
XXIX, far from being the serious intellectual search of early modern
chemistry is, as Sinclair comments, 'a rascally quackery which
throve on men's ignorance and greed' and this 'pretended production of the precious metals by tricks and mystifications' is punished
in this canto.[33] This being the case, Cortese's argument in favour of
a connection between Dante's lines announcing the entry into the
alchemist's ditch and Eliot's epigraph announcing Esther's spiritual
change seems rather tenuous. Dante's lines have a wholly negative
force in context, whereas Esther's is a sincere transformation with
no counterfeiting. Rather than being concerned to establish analogies, Eliot was more interested in suppressing any hint of the
'infernal' source of the epigraph through modifications sufficient
to decontextualize the lines while preserving both the core image of
'arrows piercing with pity' and the Dantesque tone. More often than
not, Eliot does acknowledge her source where she uses an epigraph
from Dante and in this case the overriding aesthetic reasons for not
doing so have to do with privileging certain poetic associations over
others. Eliot probably also enjoyed the additional play of resonances
which occasionally not ascribing an epigraph allowed.[34] In the case
of the epigraph to Chapter 15 ('And doubt shall be as lead ... 'etc.),
which in manuscript was given in Italian and later translated without
ascribing a source, Cortese's censuring of Eliot for concealing her
source may be allowed.[35] Even here, however, had she ascribed the
epigraph to 'Dante – Paradiso', many readers would not have been
sufficiently familiar either with this part of the *Comedy* or this particular canto for the allusion to become meaningful, for it was probably
as true then as it is now that the *Paradiso* is the least accessible and
least well known part of the *Comedy*. To have ascribed the English

translation to Dante would have been inaccurate and misleading as it is not in fact a direct translation. Aquinas' injunction 'And let this always be lead on thy feet...' would not have served Eliot's purpose in this chapter for, as doubt is already the state prevailing in the minds of the characters, the line has been altered to 'And doubt *shall be* as lead upon th[e] feet...' (p.257). Cortese speculates that 'it is possible that the practice of adapting epigraphs from actual lines from Dante eventually turned to the practice of adapting more general ideas' and cites Eliot's use of the image of the hand as a bed for the cheek from *Purgatorio* VII as an example.[36] From *Romola* onwards we do indeed have a move in Eliot's fiction towards incorporating Dante's text at various levels, from the merest hint or echo, to a Dantean word or phrase, to whole scenes which are structurally and thematically parallel to ones in Dante. Within the body of her texts these sources of course usually remain unacknowledged as buried allusion contributing to the rich texture of Eliot's writing by allowing for the play of productive resonances.

Through her use of Dante, then, George Eliot creates a moral landscape in *Felix Holt* which sometimes closely parallels that of Dante in the *Divine Comedy*. Indeed, Esther's own journey echoes that of Dante-character. Towards the end of the novel several references to this journey support the opening characterization of Sampson the coachman as a Virgil-like guide. Esther 'had come to a new stage in her journey... and her young, untired spirit was full of curiosity' (p.484).[37] Her adoptive father tells her that she has been 'led by a peculiar path, and into experience which is not ordinarily the lot of those who are seated in high places' (p.505). Her stay at Transome Court becomes a 'moral descent' (p.551), and she comes to feel that 'in accepting Harold Transome she left the high mountain air, the passionate serenity of perfect love forever behind her' (p.547). She stood 'at the first and last parting of the ways' (an image reminiscent of the geography of Virgil's underworld in the *Aeneid*), facing the choice which would give unity and definition to her life, and her reflections at this point are once more strongly evocative of the seventh canto of Dante's *Purgatorio*, where the sinners are constrained to submit their own desire to progress upwards to a higher will, which rules that they may not move on by night, but must wait and watch in darkness:

A supreme love, a motive that gives a sublime rhythm to a woman's life, and exalts habit into partnership with the soul's highest needs, is not to be had where and how she wills: to know that high initiation, she must often tread where it is hard to tread, and feel the chill air, and watch through darkness. It is not true that love makes all things easy: it makes us choose what is difficult. (p.591)[38]

We get confirmation of her decision to renounce her inheritance for Felix only at the very end of the novel, but in terms of the Dantean moral landscape the choice has been made earlier. Esther's own journey echoes Dante's when he emerges from Hell and reaches the foot of Mount Purgatory. For Esther, Felix was 'like the return of morning' (p.555) after her stay at Transome Court. After breaking down in tears ('an unspeakable relief to her after all the pent-up stifling experience' (p.549)) at the thought that she might never see Felix again after his trial, she dries her own and then her father's eyes, in a gesture echoing Virgil's tenderness towards Dante in washing his tear-stained cheeks when they emerge from Hell.[39]

Felix himself takes on some of the characteristics of a Virgil figure and Eliot was, I believe, trying to parallel the Virgil–Dante relationship in her portrayal of the humble disciple Esther and the enlightened mentor Felix. The narrator comments that Esther 'went towards him with the swift movement of a frightened child towards its protector' (p.558) in a deliberate evocation of the attitude of Dante-character towards his own guide, teacher and protector, Virgil, in the lower regions of Hell. Several times indeed Dante relies on Virgil for protection in the *Inferno*. Eliot chooses a similar image to the one used by Dante in *Purgatorio* XXX: 'I turned to the left with the confidence of a little child that runs to his mother when he is afraid or in distress...'.[40] The relationship between Felix and Esther cannot always be fixed in this way however. At times, Esther assumes some of the qualities of Dante's Beatrice. She is associated with the Dantean symbols of light and the rose of *Paradiso*, albeit obliquely, even before she appears: 'There was a delicate scent of dried rose-leaves; the light...was a wax-candle in a white earthenware candlestick, and the table on the opposite side of the fireplace held a dainty work-basket frilled with blue satin' (p.139), and at the close of the novel, she 'mean[s] to go on teaching' Felix. Esther is shown as moving towards a 'difficult blessedness' (p.327) which for George Eliot consisted in an inner moral growth along with 'the mutual subjection of soul' between a man and a woman, and her progress is marked by an increasing physical beauty as she becomes transfigured by the knowledge and expression of truth.[41] Here, Eliot may be attempting to give physical embodiment to a moral vision in the same way that Beatrice becomes transfigured for Dante in the *Vita nuova*. As with Beatrice, Esther's humility, which is beyond doubt by the later stages of the novel, is given expression through her physical poise.

One of the ways in which Eliot underpins her moral landscape is by using Dante to provide paradigms of the 'sins' of which her characters are guilty. If we are sensitive to allusions which often remain buried, these serve to remind us of the issues and to clarify them in a world where, in its multiplicity and multiformity of relations, perspective and moral resolve can easily be eroded by currents of action. For, as Eliot's narrator warns us – with Dante's 'poetic story' very much in mind – 'these things, which are easy to discern when they are painted for us on the large canvas of poetic story, become confused and obscure even for well-read gentlemen when their affection for themselves is alarmed by pressing details of actual experience' (p.520). Eliot's reworking of elements from Dante's Cocytus at the end of the novel represents her own rejection of the sterile 'wasteland' of Transome Court. The theme cannot be pursued any further, and there is nowhere left for Esther to go, but to follow the road through to the other side: 'She resigned all claim to the Transome estates. She wished to go back to her father' (p.599).

Like Dante, George Eliot is a determinist, and this facilitates her integration of the Dantean elements into her novel. For Dante, it was the heavens which determined the character of a man, whereas for Eliot it was the sum of past experiences, actions, and reflections upon experience. Yet both acknowledge man's power to influence his own destiny: Dante through man's free will, and Eliot through the determinist position that a man is himself one of the causes of what he becomes.[42] Thus freedom becomes the freedom to obey a higher law: Divine Law for Dante, and a commonly agreed moral code, justifiable in purely human terms, for Eliot. The consequences of transgressing this code are made abundantly clear in the moral world of *Felix Holt*. Jermyn 'had sinned for the sake of particular concrete things, and particular concrete consequences were likely to follow' (p.205). This comment by Eliot might also be allowed to stand for the whole of Dante's *Inferno* and *Purgatorio*.

Both writers acknowledge that the will is often swayed by the passions and often extend their pity to those who fail in the struggle. Yet the full realization of man's humanity remains inextricably linked to the possession of freedom as they defined it, and upon knowledge of the higher laws. In *Felix Holt* this is the crux of the matter. Esther 'made a deliberate choice' (p.602): Mrs Transome and Jermyn, however, 'had seen no reason why they should not indulge their passion and their vanity' and 'the reasons had been unfolding themselves gradually ever since' (p.318). For both Dante and Eliot, the mind must be an active agent operating at the crucial moments of decision. The passivity of Dante's Francesca, whose special pleading consists of the assertion that she was powerless in the face of forces which were too strong for her, becomes merely a means of abdicating responsibility. This same passivity is present in Eliot's characters too. Mrs Transome 'must put up with all things as they are determined for me' (p.457) and believes herself to be 'too old to learn to call bitter sweet and sweet bitter' (p.204), while Jermyn reflects that 'perhaps if he had not allowed himself to be determined (chiefly, of course, by the feelings of others, for of what effect would his own feelings have been without them?) into the road he actually took, he might have done better for himself' (p.513). The two Dantean scenes in *Felix Holt*, the encounters between Esther and Mrs Transome (drawing on *Inferno* V) and Jermyn and Harold (*Inferno* XXXII and XXXIII), reflect Dante's division between the sins of the flesh (incontinence) and those of the fraudulent who abuse the intellect. In the lower region of *Inferno*, the emphasis is thrown upon the use and abuse of language, and the theme of the status of language itself (a recurrent one for Dante throughout the *Comedy*), is particularly clearly focused in the cantos of the betrayers, where there is a strong contrast between the use of language for the lowest moral purposes, and Dante's own insistence on truth: ' "Now," said I "I do not want thee to speak, vile traitor, for in spite of thee I shall carry of thee a true report." '[43] The same theme also runs through *Felix Holt*. Eliot comments that 'there is no private life which has not been determined by a wider public life' (p.129): language acts as a mediator between the private and public spheres in *Felix Holt* and, as the means whereby the individual may be judged by society, it tends to sanction the established moral code. Mrs Transome's dread is essentially fear of exposure through language, and the consequences of this. We repeatedly witness various degrees of the perversion of language. In the election campaign, Felix finds his 'own serious phrases, [his] own rooted beliefs, caricatured' by the political agent Johnson (p.226), who then accuses Felix of misrepresenting his words: 'I call it a poor-spirited thing to take up a man's straight-forward words and twist them. What I meant to say was plain enough' (p.227). Harold's language conceals his motives in courting Esther, and Jermyn betrays Mrs Transome to her son. Within the novel, those who transgress the moral code thereby choose alienation, become isolated from society, and as in the *Divine Comedy*, are shown regressing into an animal state. Language, for George Eliot, is an essential instrument in allowing access to accepted moral truths – in Felix's words, 'the ruling belief in society about what is right and what is wrong, what is honourable and what is shameful' (p.401). Felix insists that Mr Lyon should 'teach any truth you can, whether it's in the Testament or out of it. It's little enough anybody can get hold of, and still less what he can drive into the skulls of a pence-counting, parcel-tying generation, such as mostly fill your chapels' (p.146). In other words, the already fragile higher moral truths, which for Eliot were justifiable in purely human terms and upon which any truly 'human' organization must depend, were made more vulnerable by the fact that they must be filtered through the medium of language, which, as we see in the novel, easily distorts. For the author, as for her character Felix, language assumes even greater importance in a world in which morality is threatened by emerging economic, social, and political forces, by the breakdown of established religion and by the human implications of Darwin's theory. For Eliot, then, truthfulness in her own use of language becomes a moral imperative. As a novelist, mediating between her own private and the 'wider public life', it became incumbent on her to use language constructively to safeguard morality through sustained effort and continual striving to achieve clarity of expression in the representation of her own vision of truth without distortion. There was a constant need to guard against the possibility that fiction might become merely deceit. Eliot, like Dante, was fully aware of the difficulties involved in working with a distorting and fallible medium. 'Speech', she said, 'is but broken light upon the depth / Of the unspoken'.[44] Yet for Eliot this knowledge merely serves to underline her own moral imperative in the use of language.

We can look to George Eliot's *Theophrastus Such* for further evidence of her moral outlook and for the strong affinities which her moral vision had with that of Dante. In a 'godless' society, where the only sanctions are those of human morality 'our civilization, considered as a splendid material fabric, is helplessly in peril without the spiritual police of sentiments or ideal feelings. And it is this invisible police which we had need, as a community, strive to maintain in efficient force.'[45] It was with this sense of moral responsibility that Eliot wrote her novels, for she, like Dante, saw literature as a force either for truth or lies, good or evil.[46] She implicitly links her own activity in writing with Dante's:

> I respect the horsewhip when applied to the back of Cruelty, and think that he who applies it is a more perfect human being because his outleap of indignation is not checked by a too curious reflection on the nature of guilt – a more perfect human being because he more completely incorporates the best social life of the race, which can never be constituted by ideas that nullify action. This is the essence of Dante's sentiment (it is painful to think that he applies it very cruelly) –
> 'E cortesia fù, lui esser villano.'
> and it is undeniable that a too intense consciousness of one's kinship with all frailties and vices undermines the active heroism which battles against wrong.[47]

This comment may perhaps shed some further light on the attitude of severity tempered by pity of Eliot's narrator towards Mrs Transome in *Felix Holt*, which, argues Cortese, muddles the novel's ethical direction. Mrs Transome's sin is one of incontinence, and can in no way be associated with the 'cruelty' which Eliot talks of in *Theophrastus Such*. Yet Eliot, it seems to me, *does* apply the horsewhip by consigning her to the Hell of Transome Court. In the same way that Dante's cruelty is confined to the lower circles of the *Inferno*, Eliot's is associated with sins of the intellect, with the betrayals by Jermyn. In striving for a blend of judgement and compassion, she manifests a quintessentially Dantean attitude towards humanity, and the kind of discernment with which Aquinas had enjoined Dante in *Paradiso* XIII, one requiring a fine ability to distinguish between the gravity of the sins committed in *Felix Holt*. According to this kind of Dantean distinction, Mrs Transome cannot be wholly condemned, though Jermyn, like Tito Melema in *Romola*, is utterly banished.[48] We too are invited to exercise a Dantean discernment in judgement and, like Dante-character and Esther Lyon, to stop and look in awe and humility before moving on.

Eliot then, like Dante, passes judgement on her characters within her own moral framework, and her conception of character is very Dantean:

When we come to examine in detail what is the sane mind in the sane body, the final test of completeness seems to be a security of distinction between what we have professed and what we have done; what we have aimed at and what we have achieved; what we have invented and what we have witnessed or had evidenced to us; what we think and feel in the present and what we thought and felt in the past.[49]

Dante is used as a 'moral touchstone', providing parallels and contrasts with the text of *Felix Holt*, and the concrete, physical landscape of Dante's moral universe points and directs our judgements as well as our sympathies. Although we are asked to extend our pity to Mrs Transome, and perhaps, like Esther, to acknowledge our own 'kinship with all frailties and human vices', Eliot's final foreshortening of Mrs Transome's story ('The Transome family were absent for some time from Transome Court. . . . After a while the family came back, and Mrs Transome died there.' (p.605)) reinstates her in an 'infernal' setting and reasserts the judgemental aspect of Eliot's moral universe, suggesting that Dante is also present in this novel to counter any tendency towards 'a too curious reflection on the nature of guilt'.

In *Felix Holt*, Eliot attempts for the first time in her fiction to use Dante in a sustained fashion as a paradigm for her own moral world, drawing particularly on the first two cantiche of the *Comedy* but also to some extent upon the third. The Dantean version of the myth of the journey through the underworld to emerge into a 'difficult blessedness' (associated significantly with *Purgatorio* rather than with *Paradiso* where Eliot, like Dante's Virgil, is unable to follow) is present over the whole arc of the novel's development and is of structural importance. Eliot was to use a similar pattern in her last novel *Daniel Deronda*, where her use of Dante is more sustained and more fully assimilated into her text. But Dante was also to play an important role in *Middlemarch*.

7

Italian Culture and Influences in *Middlemarch*

This chapter examines the ways in which Italian life and culture repeatedly impinge upon the quotidian world of *Middlemarch*. Certain characters in the novel, in particular Dorothea, Ladislaw and some of the Middlemarchers, use, or attempt to use, aspects of Italian culture as hermeneutic devices in their readings of their fellow beings or the world around them. Italian life and culture enter the novel in a variety of ways, from vague prejudice to impassioned literary engagement and immediate sensory experience. There is an interlocking pattern of Italian references through which we observe the Middlemarchers as they interpret Ladislaw, Ladislaw as he sees Dorothea and Dorothea herself as she sees and attempts to understand Rome. The sections below touch upon the broad themes of British reactions to Italy and its culture, while the last section is a rather more extended discussion of Eliot's use of Dante in her novel. This arrangement creates an overall progression from Italy seen in a negative light in the first two sections to a rather more positive and constructive view of it in the third. I begin, though, with a discussion of Eliot's poem 'How Lisa Loved the King', written before she began work on *Middlemarch*, and which displays her continued interest in the past and recent history of Italy and contains the seeds of some of the Italian themes she was to develop in her last two novels.

'Invisible motion visible birth': 'How Lisa Loved the King'

In her journal for January 1st, 1869, George Eliot wrote: 'I have set myself many tasks for the year – I wonder how many will be accomplished? – A novel called Middlemarch, a long poem on Timoleon, and several minor poems.'[1] One of those 'minor poems' mentioned by Eliot is 'How Lisa Loved the King', which is often passed over in commentaries or, when it has been mentioned, it has been rather cursorily described as 'a rhymed story from Boccaccio'

120

or a 'slightly modified rendering of Boccaccio's Decameron X.7'.[2] Far from being a straightforward translation, it is, as Pinion says, 'freely rendered and amplified, [and] it displays originality throughout'.[3] When the poem was completed, she wrote to her publisher, Blackwood: 'I am glad that you liked Lisa's story which fascinated me. When I began to write it, it was simply with the longing to fulfil an old intention, and with no distinct thought of printing'.[4] Eliot was attracted by a number of elements in Lisa's story as it existed in Boccaccio, and in her rendering of it some of the themes treated at length in the novels are present in microcosm. In Lisa, Eliot found a heroine exceptional in the strength and power of her love, with the courage and imagination to think beyond social convention, and in this she in some ways anticipates Dorothea in *Middlemarch*. George Eliot's poem throws the emphasis on *how* Lisa loved the king. Eliot's Lisa is a girl striving towards an ideal, spiritual love, expressed in terms of 'some vision newly learnt'. Her story points beyond the individual and links the single life with that of society itself. King Pedro becomes the embodiment of the national 'idea and Eliot foregrounds Lisa's love of him as the expression of selfless altruistic love of wider humanity.

Eliot frames Lisa's story by referring to the political struggles and uprising (the 'Sicilian Vespers' of 1272) which made Pedro of Aragon king of Sicily: '... a deed of high renown, / A high revenge, had freed from it the yoke / Of hated Frenchmen, ...'. This is a departure from Boccaccio, who makes no specific reference to the political context of the story. Eliot returns again to the 'Sicilian Vespers' in the final line when 'Messina rose, with God, and with the dagger's thrust'. Within the main body of the poem, political strife and violence are relegated to the status of deeds of 'epic song', and Eliot emphasizes the cultural struggle as ultimately more significant.

> Six hundred years ago, in Dante's time,
> Before his cheek was furrowed by deep rhyme –
> When Europe, fed afresh from Eastern story,
> Was like a garden tangled with the glory
> Of flowers hand-planted and of flowers air-sown
>
> [...]
>
> ... springing blades, green troops in innocent wars,
> Crowd every shady spot of teeming earth,
> Making invisible motion visible birth.[5]

The political struggles in Italy are placed at a safe distance by Eliot, but they do appear to echo the changes within Lisa herself. The important movement is one from imprisonment ('...my dumb love-pang is lone, / Prisoned as topaz-beam within a rough-garbed stone'), to liberation and freedom of expression ('...she rose and walked, and, like a bird / With sweetly rippling throat, she made her spring joys heard'). The presence of Dante, the 'Sicilian Ves-pers', Boccaccio and the Stilnovista poet Mico di Siena, who Lisa engages to find the words to express her love to the king, are all there as reminders of the cultural inheritance of Italy and of the voices of a collective cultural and national memory. And Lisa her-self becomes a paradigm of how unhistoric acts can contribute to making 'invisible motion visible birth'.

In 'The Modern Hep! Hep! Hep!' (1878) these same themes of liberation and the finding of a voice are explicitly connected to the preservation of memory and to the creation of a national spirit during the Italian *Risorgimento*:

> ...the preservation of national memories is an element and a means of national greatness,...their revival is a sign of reviving nationality,...every heroic defender, every patriotic restorer, has been inspired by such memories....Half a century ago what... were the Italians? No people, no voice in European counsels, no massive power in European affairs: ...Thanks chiefly to the divine gift of a memory which inspires the moments with a past, a present, and a future, and gives the sense of corporate existence...all that, or most of it, is changed.[6]

Eliot is also concerned with political struggle in 'Lisa'. The closing lines of the poem return to the rising of the 'Sicilian Vespers', and the effect is to shatter the harmony achieved in Lisa's story:

> ...Frenchmen, who abused the Church's trust,
> Till, in a riteous vengeance on their lust,
> Messina rose, with God, and with the dagger's thrust.

Eliot is here declaring her own loyalties regarding contemporary events in Italy in the 1860s. The poem was intended to be both celebratory – the 'high holiday' following the first Unification of Italy in 1860–1 after the overthrow of the Bourbon monarchy in Naples and Sicily, and anticipatory or predictive – for the 'hated

Frenchmen' were, by 1869 when the poem was written, the only remaining obstacle to the Unification of Italy.[7] Napoleon III had occupied Rome intermittently for ten years, and Garibaldi had been defeated when he tried to enter the city in 1867.

The parallels between Eliot's poem and the Italian situation in the late 1860s would not have been lost on her readers. Support for the cause of Italian unification was never stronger than in the 1860s. Garibaldi, by now a hero of mythical proportions, had been given a rapturous welcome in England in 1864. Economic links between Piedmont and Britain were increasing and interest in the cause of Italian unity was strengthened by newspaper commentaries, letters, articles and poems in magazines like *Blackwood's*.[8] Eliot's King Pedro, in 'Lisa' elides easily into a Garibaldi, and the poem itself takes on an immediacy which it loses when divorced from the historical context of the 1860s. The 'Sicilian Vespers', evidence of nationalist sentiment directed against a foreign oppressor, was one of those 'national memories' which were so important in the mythology of the *Risorgimento*.[9]

Whether or not Eliot had any 'distinct thought of printing' before she began, 'Lisa' incorporates a strong hint of her position on Italy in the late 1860s and interestingly, on its publication in 1869, the usual rule of anonymity was waived and the poem appeared in Eliot's name, apparently at her particular request.[10] At a time when Swinburne was writing openly 'political' poetry in support of Italian unity and against Napoleon III, Eliot preferred to allow her own anti-Napoleonic sentiments to emerge in more muted tones from within the original story by Boccaccio transformed so that the final removal of 'the hated Frenchmen' and 'the dagger's thrust' figures as the necessary culmination of centuries of preparation. Her final 'prophecy' of Italian unity, though expressed in terms of political struggle, is ultimately seen as the outcome of the cumulative influences of tradition, love, vision and striving on both the individual and the collective consciousness.

Middlemarch: Dorothea in Rome

Whereas in 'How Lisa Loved the King' a coherent teleological vision of Italian history is allowed to emerge, in *Middlemarch* no such vision is forthcoming. The views expressed by the characters here reflect the historical setting of the novel in the 1820s and 1830s when British perceptions of Italy and Italians were very different from those in the more enlightened 1850s and 1860s. The ignorance and prejudices of English provincial life make for misunderstanding and failure of interpretation.

In 1829–32, the period in which *Middlemarch* is set, the Grand Tour, with Italy as its ultimate destination, was still at the height of its popularity. It is therefore natural that Casaubon and Dorothea should choose Rome as the location for their honeymoon. In the same way that Dorothea desires to take part in Casaubon's project of reading all past cultures so as to produce a 'Key to all Mythologies'[11] she is equally desirous of undertaking the mental reconstruction of the city she sees around her. She finds instead that she lacks any 'key', any 'binding theory' which will 'unite all contrasts', and becomes painfully aware of the inadequacy of 'her small allowance of knowledge' so that 'the weight of unintelligible Rome' lies heavily on her (p.225).

The 'glut of confused ideas' becomes an 'oppressive masquerade', 'a masque' in which she too seems to take part and where she wanders through galleries with 'long vistas of white forms whose marble eyes seemed to hold the monotonous light of an alien world'.[12] There are hints of Dante in the imagery at this point in the text, in which the dreamlike strangeness of Rome becomes akin to the alien 'blind world' of Limbo with its statuesque groups of 'spiriti magni',[13] and the hints are developed elsewhere in the light imagery through which Eliot characterizes Dorothea's relationships with Casaubon and Ladislaw, and in the image of Mr Casaubon 'lost among small closets and winding stairs' (p.229) and in 'anterooms and winding passages' (p.228). Dorothea's ardent nature transforms the commonly shared impressions of many tourists and travel writers ('Ruins and basilicas, palaces and colossi, set in the midst of a sordid present, where all that was living and warm-blooded seemed sunk in a deep degeneracy') into a Dantesque masquerade from which she must escape into the Campagna 'where she could feel alone with the earth and sky' (p.225) and – like Dante emerging from Hell – experience release from the weight of those 'broken revelations...thrust abruptly' on her. Dorothea's response to the degradation she sees around her is significantly different, however, from that of so many visitors on the 'brilliant picnic of Anglo-foreign society' who often accepted that the situation was in some degree fitting: 'in Rome' she says 'it seems as if there were so many things which are more wanted in the world than pictures'.[14] Characteristically, Dorothea's chief concern is with the 'quick', the here and now, and her comment merely underlines her inability to bridge the gap between the splendid past and the sordid present. This was the function of the myths of the *Risorgimento*, which 'breathed a growing soul into all historic shapes', connecting them and bringing them all within a teleological reading. Dorothea, of course, has no access to this form of knowledge and remains confused and disoriented by the spectacle of Rome. Without a guide, she is unable to embark upon her journey through this alien world.

Casaubon can bring no 'quickening power', and it is Will Ladislaw who is to guide Dorothea through the 'stupendous fragmentariness... the dreamlike strangeness' (p.224), and to 'quicken' the dead city for her. His own binding theory is the modern spirit of that German Romanticism which tests received opinion against emotional response. Ladislaw, an 'orphic messenger from the world of the arts', begins to open up the 'alien world' to Dorothea.[15] Through Will's instruction on how the work of his friend Naumann might be understood, 'Dorothea felt that she was getting quite new notions as to the significance of Madonnas seated under inexplicable canopied thrones... Some things which had seemed monstrous to her were gathering intelligibility and even a natural meaning;' (p.246) to the point at which the infernal quality of the city begins to be dispelled so that 'Rome, if she had been less ignorant, would have been full of beauty; its sadness would have been winged with hope' (p.247).

Rome is also a correlative of Casaubon's own endeavours to reconstruct a past world and of his failure to do so. He chases his 'Key' along winding passages and stairs 'which seem to lead nowhither' (p.228) and his capacity to place his researches in vital relation to living thought and feeling 'had long since shrunk to a sort of dried preparation, a lifeless embalmment of knowledge' (p.229). His lack of real engagement with or emotional response to his labours is underscored by his failure to commit himself to any personal opinion regarding the artefacts he sees in Rome. Ladislaw criticizes Casaubon for failing to take account of German scholarship in his researches: 'the Germans have taken the lead in historical enquiries, and they laugh at results which are got by groping about in the woods with a pocket-compass while they have made good roads'. Is there an echo of the famous opening of Dante's *Inferno* intended here perhaps? ('In the middle of the journey of our life I came to myself in a dark wood where the straight way was lost.') Casaubon characterizes his own mind as 'something like the ghost of an ancient, wandering about the world and trying mentally to construct it as it used to be, in spite of ruin and confusing changes' (p.40) and is associated with ghostly figures on more than one occasion: he 'liv[es] too much with the dead' and Naumann calls him 'the *Geistlicher*' (pp.220–1). In the face of Casaubon's deadening indifference, Dorothea's 'emotion roused to tumultuous activity' (p.228) leads her to respond negatively to Rome; her dismay at the petrified forms around her is also bound up with her growing intuition, with 'broken revelations', of her husband's true nature. The petrified masquerade is never brought to life for Dorothea and her vision embodies a pre-*Risorgimento* condition before the mythology of the Italian resurgence brought the present 'into strict connection with that amazing past' (p.112).In *Daniel Deronda*, however, George Eliot engages with that mythology to bridge the temporal gap and allows her Italian material to reassert a view of history in which past culture *is* placed in vital relation to the present and an order is imposed upon vast fragmentariness.

Rome does not, however, remain vast, alien and unintelligible to all the characters in the novel. Various attempts to link past and present through a binding theory are made in *Middlemarch*. Will Ladislaw makes himself the pupil of his friend, the painter Naumann, who belongs to the St Luke's Brotherhood (the 'Nazarenes'), a Romantic movement founded at the beginning of the nineteenth century and which was 'fermenting still as a distinguishable vigorous enthusiasm in certain long-haired German artists at Rome' (p.219). The Nazarenes imitated pre-Raphaelite and early German religious painting and, in the shape of Adolf Naumann in *Middlemarch*, are engaged in their own reading of the cultural artefacts in Rome. Will mentions Naumann as

> one of the chief renovators of Christian art, one of those who had not only revived but expanded that grand conception of supreme events as mysteries at which the successive ages were spectators, and in relation to which the great souls of all periods became as it were contemporaries. (p.245)

For Naumann, history is both alive and placed in a strict vital relation to the present through the binding theory of the Brotherhood: he has no difficulty in 'reading' Dorothea herself and placing her in relation to the Roman background of the Ariadne upon his first sight of her at Rome:

> There lies antique beauty, not corpse-like even in death, but arrested in the complete contentment of its sensuous perfection: and here stands beauty in its breathing life, with the consciousness of Christian centuries in its bosom. [...] ...antique form animated by Christian sentiment – a sort of Christian Antigone – sensuous force controlled by spiritual passion.' (pp.220–1)

For Naumann, Rome is no alien world of dead artefacts, its statues are not 'corpse-like' but simply arrested in the present alongside Dorothea. Indeed, in the description of Dorothea as a 'sort of Christian Antigone' she symbolically merges into the very past which for her is so unintelligible and herself becomes the locus of contemporaneity, a fusion of the ages into a living present. Will, however, repeatedly condemns Naumann's reading as false (or at best partial): 'I do *not* think that all the universe is straining towards the obscure significance of your pictures' (p.221), and he later tells Dorothea that 'the German artists here...are fine, even brilliant fellows – but I should not like to get into their way of looking at the world entirely from the studio point of view' (p.239). As we shall see, however, Ladislaw himself falls into the trap of looking at the world, or at least the part of it which concerns his relation with Dorothea, from a point of view which reveals itself to be just as restricting and partial as that of his Nazarene friends.

'Mr Orlando Ladislaw' or 'an Italian with white mice'

Will Ladislaw is an outsider in Middlemarch, 'a sort of gypsy, rather enjoying the sense of belonging to no class' (p.502). He exploits the freedom which this status gives him to move freely and to flout social decorum ('he was given to stretch himself at full length on the rug while he talked' (p.503)). His freedom from social constraints, allowing him the liberty to move among the poor in Rome is noted as a social oddity which 'did not quit him in Middlemarch' (p.503).[16] The effect of this behaviour on the Middlemarchers is merely to reinforce their own readings of Ladislaw, who repeatedly apply foreign stereotypes to him. He becomes a 'Polish emissary' (p.502), an 'adventurer' (p.651), the son of 'a rebellious Polish fiddler or dancing-master' (p.877) and 'Mr

Orlando Ladislaw' (p.676).[17] Ladislaw's foreignness, his dark complexion, physical appearance and 'preternatural quickness and glibness of his speech...which cast reflections on solid Englishmen generally' (p.502), merely confirm the Middlemarchers' pre-existing 'notions of his dangerously mixed blood and general laxity' (p.503). Ladislaw's presence and behaviour directly challenge the categories and social codes of the Middlemarchers and their defence is to defuse the threat by bringing him within the vague yet somehow comfortingly 'known' frame of reference of the 'foreigner', with all the negative connotations that idea implies.

The most damning of these readings which 'place' Ladislaw, and the one which worries and hurts Dorothea the most, seems to be Mrs Cadwallader's remark that Dorothea 'might as well marry an Italian with white mice' (p.532). Dorothea returns more than once to this comment: 'Why should he be compared with an Italian carrying white mice? That word quoted from Mrs Cadwallader seemed like a mocking travesty wrought in the dark by an impish finger' (p.535), and the chapter ends with Dorothea rejecting the statement entirely: 'An Italian with white mice! – on the contrary, he was a creature who entered into every one's feelings, and could take the pressure of their thought instead of urging his own with iron resistance' (p.539). It is evident from the vehemence with which Dorothea refutes the association of Ladislaw with 'an Italian with white mice' that she herself has a clear idea of the stereotype referred to and of just what is meant, or implied, by labelling Ladislaw in this way. Dorothea's question has been repeated on at least three different occasions by critics: why an Italian and why with white mice?[18] The best place to start in answering the two questions posed by Dorothea is Eliot's own 1865 essay 'A Word for the Germans' which deals with national stereotypes:

John Bull is open to instruction; slowly, by gentle degrees, he revises his opinions, his habits, and his laws. It is not to be expected that he will ever cease to regard himself as the supreme type of manhood, or to think that the most unmixed truth may always be known by the mark 'British', which prevents imposture. But he does modify his opinions about other nations. [...] The Italian of John Bull's imagination is no longer exclusively that dangerous jesuitical personage, with dark hair and darker intentions, who avails himself of momentary privacy to feel the edge of his stiletto; a personage adorned now with a false title, but in his earlier years nothing better than a small vagrant, who went about exhibiting his white mice and white teeth for casual halfpence.[19]

Sir James Chetham's condemnation of Ladislaw is illustrative of what Eliot called John Bull's former opinion of the foreigner and iterates the idea of the Italian character held by so many early nineteenth-century English travellers to Italy: Ladislaw, he says, 'has always had an objectionable position – a bad origin – and, I *believe*, is a man of little principle and light character' (p.874). Behind Mrs. Cadwallader's remark there is a whole range of associations which the Middlemarchers draw upon to 'place' the suspect Ladislaw. This same powerful stereotype, was also used by Dickens in *Little Dorrit* (1855–7) and by Wilkie Collins in *The Woman in White* (1860). Contemporary readers of *Middlemarch* could quite plausibly associate Ladislaw with Collins' Count Fosco, who keeps a white mouse in his pocket as a pet and who, in many respects, is 'the Italian of John Bull's imagination'. In Fosco, whose name means 'darkness' in Italian, there are sinister overtones of the 'cloak-and-dagger' Italian 'feel[ing] the edge of his stiletto', and he is, in fact, an *agent provocateur* keeping watch on the revolutionary secret societies of the Italian exiles in England.[20] This common image of Italian (particularly Mazzinian) revolutionaries was promoted, not without some justification, by the British press in the nineteenth century up until Unification. As late as 1856, Daniele Manin published a letter in *The Times* stating that the 'great enemy of Italy is the doctrine of political assassination, or, in other terms, the theory of the poniard'.[21] The possible association of Ladislaw with Fosco, then, lends added resonance to the Middlemarchers' phrases about Ladislaw being the son of a rebellious Polish fiddler (p.877) wanting to overturn institutions (p.502).

From Dickens in *Little Dorrit* we learn that the Italians in question were 'organ boys' brought to England (by Italians) as street entertainers who made mice or monkeys perform tricks while their masters played the organ. By comparing Will to an organ boy Mrs Cadwallader implies that he needs charity.[22] The organ is also of course linked to the musical stereotype of the Italian, though the street organ is a far cry from the more 'noble' image of the Italians as 'a race . . . chiefly adapted to the operatic stage'.[23] It may be that Mrs Cadwallader is also throwing out oblique references to Ladislaw's own musical activities in singing with Rosamond, for on a later occasion she makes a derogatory remark about 'Mr Orlando

Ladislaw', who is '. . . making a sad dark-blue scandal by warbling continually with your Mr Lydgate's wife . . . at the piano' (pp.676–7). There is also a further insinuation, in the association with vagrants with little skill to offer, of the dilettantism and amateurishness – 'a dislike to steady application' of which Mr Casaubon accuses Ladislaw on Dorothea's first meeting with him (p.107), and with which Naumann playfully charges him in Rome (p.221). This too was an important part of the Italian stereotype: 'Half a century ago, what was Italy? An idling-place of dilettantism'.[24]

Italians with white mice were already a familiar sight on the streets of London in the 1820s and had become synonymous with Italian poverty by 1830. A boost to the stereotype was undoubtedly given by the British press in 1839. The 'scandal' of the 'white slave trade' of the organ boys was denounced by the exiled Giuseppe Mazzini who was then living in London. Publicity in the press, which pointed out that it had taken this exile, who was neither rich nor powerful, to bring the situation to the attention of the British public, led to the involvement of Parliament and to the trial of those involved in importing the boys. This action won Mazzini the sympathy of the English and undoubtedly contributed to fixing the image of the organ boys in the public mind. Behind Mrs Cadwallader's remark, with its implications of Will's presumed dilettantism, need of charity, and its remoter association with John Bull's image of the dishonest Italian, there may also lie the suggestion that Will is to be pitied for the ill-treatment he has received from Casaubon and from Middlemarch.

Around the 'travesty' of Will's being compared to 'an Italian with white mice' there is a rich group of associations, not wholly negative, which could be brought into play by the reader. Eliot is consciously playing on the fact that the stereotype presented will be recognized by the reader of *Middlemarch* as an outdated prejudice. Ladislaw's true nature is hidden beneath his 'foreign' appearance and he therefore becomes suspect, a potentially villainous Fosco or an Italian urchin begging in the streets. The gap between appearance and reality revealed here also serves to expose the small-minded provincialism of Middlemarch and its acceptance of the outward shows of birth and heredity in place of the intrinsic virtues of loyalty, sincerity and selflessness which Ladislaw displays.[25]

As so often in Eliot, then, beyond the local significance of a phrase or image within the novel, there is a wider network of associations. Here these include the tangible evidence of the condition of Italy to be found on the streets of London and other cities and bring into play the changing perceptions of Italy and the Italians in Britain over 40 years of the century. The view of Italian culture in *Middlemarch* is rather a negative one overall. This is partly owing to the historical setting of the novel: British reactions to Italians in 1829–32 were on the whole less favourable than they were from the 1850s onwards. In *Middlemarch*, the characters either fail to read (Dorothea in Rome) or misread (the Middlemarchers' attempts to place Ladislaw) through Italian culture, which remains essentially alien and unassimilated, a composite of fragments, second-hand knowledge, opinions and prejudices. But time, Eliot believed, had changed the proportion of things, and she hoped her readers would recognize and reject the outdated, glibly superficial opinions concerning Italy. This negative picture of Italy does not, however, appear to touch the truly creative artists in the novel. Naumann easily moulds his world and has no difficulty in incorporating the 'vast fragmentariness' of Rome into his own binding theory. It is Will Ladislaw, to whom Italy is by no means 'an alien world', who makes the most sustained effort at bringing the Italian cultural inheritance into a vital relationship with his own existence in *Middlemarch*, for his relationship with Dorothea owes much to literature, and to Dante in particular.

'Love is encompassed in my Lady's eyes': Ladislaw and Dorothea

I now consider the two epigraphs which George Eliot chose from the *Divine Comedy* and the *Vita nuova*. The epigraph for Chapter 19 of *Middlemarch* (quoted in Italian) is from *Purgatorio* VII: 'See the other, who couches her cheek on her hand and sighs'.[26] that for Chapter 54 is Dante's Sonetto XVII ('Negli occhi porta la mia donna Amore') from Chapter XXI of the *Vita nuova*.

The image from *Purgatorio* is repeatedly used by Eliot as a striking static image of suffering.[27] In *Middlemarch*, Dante's lines form the epigraph to a chapter in which we meet Dorothea standing before the statue of Ariadne in the Vatican Museum in Rome, where she is seen by Will Ladislaw and his painter friend, Naumann:

They were just in time to see another figure standing against a pedestal near the reclining marble: a breathing blooming girl, whose form, not shamed by the Ariadne, was clad in Quakerish grey drapery; her long cloak, fastened at the neck, was thrown backward from her arms, and one beautiful ungloved hand

pillowed her cheek, pushing somewhat backward the white bea-
ver bonnet which made a sort of halo to her face around the
simply braided dark-brown hair. She was not looking at the
sculpture, probably not thinking of it: her large eyes were fixed
dreamily on a streak of sunlight which fell across the floor.
(p.220)[28]

The image of Dantean suffering prefigures her suffering in the
next chapter where we find her 'sobbing bitterly' when left alone
(p.224). George Eliot also employs her own light imagery (a further
reminder of Dante's *Purgatorio* VII) when talking of Dorothea's 'eyes
... fixed dreamily on a streak of sunlight'. In the following chapter,
Dorothea's 'view of Mr Casaubon, and her wifely relation, now that
she was married to him, was gradually changing [...] whatever else
remained the same, the light had changed, and you cannot find the
pearly dawn at noonday' (Chapter 20, pp.226–7). Though, as in this
case, Eliot often uses light imagery negatively to emphasize
moments of full realization of the consequences of actions 'in the
cold light of day', it is important that the epigraph is from the
Purgatorio. Eliot does not always give the sources of her epigraphs
in the chapters themselves, but in Chapter 19 she clearly indicates
the origin of the lines. The suggestion is being made, then, that
Dorothea's suffering is purgatorial, indicating hope and growth.

In *Purgatorio* VII, the Valley of the Princes who repent at the last
moment, Virgil tells the Christian poet Sordello 'Not for doing, but
for not doing, I have lost the sight of the sun above for which thou
longest and which was known by me too late' (25–6). The sun in the
Comedy represents the face, the promise of God. Virgil's words also
have a bearing on Dorothea's future in the novel. With her eyes
'fixed dreamily on a streak of sunlight', she is beginning to realize
the unhappy consequences of her marriage; she has entered into a
'static' relationship, with a person who 'had become indifferent to
the sunlight' (p.230), a relationship in which she is not allowed to
'do' so that, in an ironic reversal of the significance of Dante's 'sun
above for which thou longest', the change in the light to 'noonday'
for Dorothea is entirely negative, serving only to illuminate her
error more clearly to herself. The comparison with Virgil and the
light imagery associated with him in this canto bears further examination, for Dorothea's dilemma after Casaubon's death is that she
must 'do' – she must choose Ladislaw, whose first impression on
her 'was one of sunny brightness' (p.241) and whose smile was like

'a gush of inward light' (p.237) – in order to recover 'the pearly dawn' with its promise of the true 'sun above'. The light imagery at this point in the novel, then, provides both an echo of Virgil's condition, set against that of the penitents in Purgatory who move ever upwards towards the light, and foreshadows Dorothea's dilemma as to how to act at the end of the novel. The promise of redemption is present in the epigraph, to be fulfilled at the end of the novel when she renounces wealth and position to marry Ladislaw, and the strands of sun and light imagery are drawn together in the title of Book VIII, 'Sunset and Sunrise'. Thus, the image and the echoes (in the light imagery) from *Purgatorio* VII are allowed to bear a precise significance locally within the novel – Dorothea's realization of her mistake in marrying Casaubon – but also take on a wider significance through a web of connections stretching outwards from the initial image. I shall return to this first epigraph from Dante to illustrate this last point in a moment.

The second of Eliot's epigraphs also bears a close relationship to the one discussed above, and becomes part of the web of Dante connections in the novel. Much later in *Middlemarch* (in Book VI 'The Widow and the Wife') we find Dante's sonnet 'Love is encompassed in my Lady's eyes' from *The New Life*.[29] On one level, Eliot's choice of epigraph gives us a simple indication of the fact that Will is in love with Dorothea. The possessive pronoun 'mia' and the 'donna' of 'Negli occhi porta la mia donna Amore' are easily equated with Will and Dorothea who appear in the chapter which follows. The position of this sonnet in the *Vita nuova*, however, is such that it prefigures Dante's loss of Beatrice, for Dante has the shocking realization that she must die and will thus be unreachable. Thus, a further connection between Eliot's novel and Dante's poem is the 'new lives' embarked upon by Dorothea in being newly widowed, and Will in renouncing any claim to Dorothea, and the seemingly eternal separation of the two caused by the 'dead hand' of the jealous Casaubon, whose will states that in marrying Ladislaw Dorothea would be disinherited. In Chapter 54, Will comes to say good-bye to Dorothea, and for most of Book VI they are apart.

George Eliot gives us a long epigraph to this chapter. All 14 lines of the sonnet are quoted, and this of course suggests that the whole poem is relevant. I want now to link this epigraph back to Chapter 19, where Dorothea was portrayed in the Dantean attitude of suffering. In this earlier chapter there are a number of attempts by the male observers to portray Dorothea. The painter Naumann represents her as 'the most perfect young Madonna' and then as 'a sort of Christian Antigone – sensuous force controlled by spiritual passion'. Ladislaw however, refuses to accept the merely visual representation 'as if a woman were mere coloured superficies! You must wait for movement and tone.' To this the painter retorts 'I see, I see. You are jealous. No man must presume to think that he can paint your ideal' (p.222). By the end of the chapter, and after Naumann's joke that Dorothea, in being married to Will's second cousin (Casaubon), is in fact Will's great-aunt, Will was 'conscious of being irritated [...] he felt as if something had happened to him with regard to her' (pp.222–3).

Dante's sonnet dwells on the power of Beatrice's eyes to affect men:

> Love is encompassed in my Lady's eyes
> Whence she ennobles all she looks upon.
> Where e'er she walks, the gaze of everyone
> She draws; in him she greets, such tremors rise,
> All pale, he turns his face away, and sighs,

and on her voice:

> All gentleness and all humility
> When she is heard to speak in hearts unfold,[30]

In his commentary, Dante says:

> In the first I speak of her miraculous power of ennobling everything she sees, and this amounts to saying that she calls Love into potentiality where he is not; in the second I say how she actualizes Love in the hearts of all whom she sees;[31]

In the passage quoted earlier where Dorothea is standing against the background of the Ariadne statue, 'her large *eyes* were fixed dreamily on a streak of sunlight' and in the discussion about how she should be represented, Will says 'how would you paint her *voice*, pray?... her *voice* is much diviner than anything you have seen of her' (p.222 – my italics). In Will's irritation, and his feeling that 'something had happened to him with regard to her' there is already a hint that Dorothea, too, has this power to 'call Love into potentiality where he is not;' and to 'actualize Love in the hearts of all whom she sees'.

Dante's *Vita nuova* (and the Dante–Beatrice relationship) is also just below the surface in Chapter 19, then, though we only obtain confirmation of this 350 pages later in the book. There seems to be a replaying of Dante's experience in the character of Ladislaw, or possibly a structuring of his experience through Dante's in the *Vita nuova*. Literary readings, however, are not altogether to be trusted in *Middlemarch*. The appearance of the sonnet at the beginning of Book VI, and the promising opening line 'Love is encompassed in my Lady's eyes' lead us to expect some development in the Will–Dorothea relationship: we easily think of the poem as referring to the couple and accept it as an expression of Will's sentiments. But George Eliot is surely leading us on a false trail, for Book VI ends as it begins with Will (unable to stay away) coming back to take his leave of Dorothea again. Will has a tendency to read life through literature, and to allow literature to structure his emotions.[32] He had been 'educated in the passions by literature'[33] and

> was conscious of a generous movement, and of verifying in his own experience that higher love-poetry which had charmed his fancy. Dorothea, he said to himself, was for ever enthroned in his soul: no other woman could sit higher than her footstool; (p.510)

Barbara Hardy shows how Ladislaw is 'misguided and let down by literary expectation' in making 'joys of his own choosing' (p.509) in a rare and remote adoration of Dorothea.[34]

> It may seem strange, but it is the fact, that the ordinary vulgar vision of which Mr Casaubon suspected him – namely, that Dorothea might become a widow, and that the interest he had established in her mind might turn into acceptance of him as a husband – had no tempting, arresting power over him; [...] Will... could not bear the thought of any flaw appearing in his crystal:... and there was something so exquisite in thinking of her just as she was, that he could not long for a change which must somehow change her. (pp.509–10)

Will's courtly mode of loving and of controlling the passions is anachronistic and his 'worship, adoration, higher love-poetry, [enthroned] queens and footstools are inappropriate images for love in the quotidian world of Middlemarch'.[35] Hardy concludes: 'in a way, George Eliot seems to know this, or at least to glimpse the deficiency of those troubador images'.[36] I would go further and say that Eliot is fully aware of their inappropriateness, but that she actually encourages multiple interpretations even if her readers are, like Will, temporarily misled by the literary expectations arising from Dante's sonnet. The use of 'Negli occhi' as the epigraph to Chapter 54 is in some senses very ill-suited to the world of *Middlemarch* then. It both continues and undermines the courtly form of worship chosen by Ladislaw. Continues, in that it implies a final union of the two lovers, as Beatrice and Dante are united in the *Divine Comedy*, and undermines it, in that this love must unfold in the world of *Middlemarch*, in which motives are mixed, and expectations are thwarted.[37]

The parallels with the *Vita nuova* continue in the novel. Ladislaw, unable to worship Dorothea openly, employs the Dantean convention of the 'screen lady'.[38] Rosamond, of course, participates fully in the role and in the illusion that it is she who is the object of Ladislaw's desires. Once Dorothea discovers Ladislaw consoling Rosamond, however, the illusion dissolves and he reveals the true object of his adoration, and that he 'would rather touch [Dorothea's] hand if it were dead, than I would touch any other woman's living' (p.836). When it becomes clear that he must renounce Dorothea, Will takes his leave of her in terms highly suggestive of the *Vita nuova*:

> 'There are certain things which a man can only go through once in his life; and he must know some time or other that the best is over with him. This experience has happened to me while I am very young – that is all. What I care more for than I can ever care for anything else is absolutely forbidden to me – [...] Of course I shall go on living as a man might do who had seen heaven in a trance.' (p.681)

and admits to himself that his adoration from afar is 'a ghostly kind of wooing' (p.681). There is a strong parallel here with the life of Dante, with his loss of Beatrice and with his vision at the end of the *Vita nuova*, which points forward to the *Divine Comedy*: 'After this... there appeared to me a marvellous vision in which I saw things which made me decide to write no more of this blessed one until I could do so more worthily'.[39] Beatrice, of course reappears in the final cantos of the *Purgatorio* (XXX–XXXIII) to guide Dante through *Paradiso*. Once the codicil to Casaubon's will is known, Dorothea becomes an other-worldly presence for Will, who dwells on absence in images of physical death (touching her dead hand) and her removal to a non-terrestrial dimension.

The second time Will leaves Middlemarch he becomes one of the 'exiles [who] notoriously feed much on hopes, and are unlikely to stay in banishment unless they are obliged' (p.859). One such exile of course, was Dante himself, who in a well-known phrase 'tasted the bitter bread of exile' after leaving Florence. Will is only in voluntary exile (though he has been 'banished' by Casaubon's marriage to Dorothea and then by his will) and returns to Middlemarch 'very hungry for the *vision* of a certain form and the sound of a certain voice' (p.860 – my italics). Will has 'wrought himself into a state of doubt' (p.862) concerning Dorothea's opinion of his conduct and morals. Indeed, until the 'wretched yesterday' of Dorothea's discovery of him with Rosamond:

> all their vision, all their thought of each other, had been as in a world apart, where the sunshine fell on tall white lilies, where no evil lurked, and no other soul entered. But now – would Dorothea meet him in that world again? (p.862)

In this passage it is further evident that Will, ever the imaginative artist, has created a world drawing, in all probability, very largely upon his own knowledge of Dante, and in particular upon the 'Paradiso terrestre' of the *Purgatorio*. Will's 'world apart, where the sunshine fell on tall white lilies' may be read as an evocation of the dream of Leah ('I seemed to see in a dream a lady young and beautiful going through a meadow gathering flowers'[40]) and the appearance of Matilda:

> With feet I stopped and with eyes passed over beyond the streamlet to look at the great variety of fresh-flowering boughs, and there appeared to me there, as appears of a sudden a thing that for wonder drives away every other thought, a lady all alone, who went singing and culling flower from flower with which all her way was painted.[41]

The lilies of Will's world are twice mentioned specifically in *Purgatorio* XXIX (which foreshadows the appearance of Beatrice herself), in Dante's great allegorical pageant where the 24 elders of the Old Testament are wreathed with lilies symbolizing purity. The multiple significance of the lilies is carried over into Will's world from the world of art.[42]

Beyond this point, it is Eliot herself who continues the Dantean narrative scheme. Like Dante's, Will's 'new life' and his 'Earthly Paradise' hold out the promise of a meeting with the beloved, and when this meeting takes place in Chapter 83 of *Middlemarch* there are definite echoes of Dante's *Purgatorio* XXX. Both texts emphasize the strong fear of judgement and being shamed: 'great shame weighed on [Dante's] brow;' so that he was unable to look at his own reflection in the water (78). Ladislaw approaches Dorothea with the same apprehensiveness:

'Mr Ladislaw . . . fears he has offended you, and has begged me to ask if you will see him for a few minutes.'

. . . he came towards her with more doubt and timidity in his face than she had ever seen before. He was in a state of uncertainty which made him afraid lest some look or word of his should condemn him to a new distance from her; (pp.864–5)

But Dorothea *does* meet him in that world and, like Beatrice, accepts him in it. However, Eliot's mode of hinting at the still forbidden nature of their love in the moment when the couple kiss, is a rather troubling intrusion into Ladislaw's 'world apart . . . where no evil entered':

Her lips trembled, and so did his. It was never known which lips were the first to move towards the other lips; but they kissed tremblingly, and then they moved apart.

The rain was dashing against the window-panes as if an angry spirit were within it, and behind it was the great swoop of the wind; it was one of those moments in which both the busy and the idle pause with a certain awe. (p.869)

As Ladislaw is announced, Dorothea is thinking that 'she could not receive him in this library, where her husband's prohibition seemed to dwell' (pp.864–5). The nature of the language and the detail at this point in the novel are unmistakably evocative of Dante's famous scene between Paolo and Francesca in *Inferno* V: the sensuous quality of the language, with its concentration upon and repetition of 'lips' and of 'trembled/tremblingly' echoes Francesca's '(he) all trembling, kissed my mouth' (136); the rain and 'the great swoop of the wind' becomes 'the hellish storm, never resting, [which] seizes and drives the spirits before it; smiting and whirling them about, it torments them' (31–3). Will and Dorothea's kiss happens in a kind of suspension of time which seems to defy the natural laws of place as happens in *Inferno* V, where the condemned spirits are given a brief respite from the 'bufera infernal' in order to speak with Dante 'while the wind is quiet, as here it is' (96). The 'aweful' quality of the moment 'in which both the busy and the idle pause' is registered at the end of *Inferno* V by the extremity of Dante's reaction when he learns of the consequences for Paolo and Francesca of the forbidden kiss: 'I swooned as if in death and dropped like a dead body' (141–2). The scene is disconcerting at this point, for there is a sudden break with the Dantean narrative framework which Eliot has been following as there is a disjunction, a shift in location from the Earthly Paradise of the *Purgatorio* to a circle of *Inferno*. Casaubon's library, in which his 'prohibition seemed to dwell', throws back further echoes of Francesca's story ('We read one day for pastime . . .', 'Many times that reading drew our eyes together', 'A Galeotto was that book and he that wrote it; that day we read in it no farther'[43]) and thus reinforces those earlier suggestions of the dangers inherent for Will of 'misreading' while allowing one's emotions to be shaped through literature. The deliberate suppression of information by Eliot's narrator ('It was never known which lips were the first to move towards the other lips') gives the impression that memory has been erased in an irresistible impulse, a moment of overwhelming passion in which the power to will is suspended by both the actors. This again, is reminiscent of Francesca's attempt to justify her own helplessness in the face of forces too strong for her: 'Love, which absolves no one beloved from loving, seized me so strongly with his charm . . .' (103–4).

Incorporated into Chapter 83, then, is a subtle reworking of elements from the Paolo and Francesca episode in *Inferno* V which sets the scene between Dorothea and Will against Dante's scene. Eliot here displays a remarkable ability in transposing and recombining elements in the scene so as to make it her own while closely following Dante's episode, and in selecting precisely those elements necessary to set up faint resonances and echoes for the reader, suggestions of the *forbidden* quality of the moment and of shadowy consequences, which are yet contained beneath the surface of the text. The purposes for which Dante is invoked at this point in the story, however, are not perhaps immediately clear. We feel the 'rightness' of Dorothea and Will's union which the *Inferno* V passage seems to warn against. Dante's use of the *Dolce stil novo* in the Paolo and Francesca episode of *Inferno* V, is partly self-condemnatory, and registers both his feelings of complicity in the tragedy of the lovers by being himself a writer of a sensuous poetry which could lead the mind astray and also the knowledge that his own love for Beatrice had been potentially adulterous. There is, I think, also a hint of this condemnation, or at least mistrust, of the physical in Eliot's text at this point. It is as though she is momentarily unable to decide whether Dorothea is to be a spiritual, moral Beatrice or a physical, sensual Francesca. At the end of the chapter, Eliot does appear to reassert a physical dimension: 'In an instant Will was close to her and had his arms around her' though even here 'she drew her head back and held his away gently that she might go on speaking' (p.870) and the kiss is deferred – it is never narrated.

During the 1830s the English Romantic conception of the 'Promethean' Dante was replaced by an interest in the figure of Beatrice. It is not surprising, then, to find George Eliot making use of Beatrice in particular from the *Comedy*, for she was a specifically Victorian favourite.[44] Theodore Martin's translation of the *Vita nuova* turned it into 'something involving modern relations in social life between the sexes'[45] and worked against a vision of Beatrice as pure allegory. Dante's Beatrice could easily be associated with the Victorian conception of womanhood present in Coventry Patmore's 'The Angel in the House': 'Earth has many such [Beatrices] – pure, patient, gentle, wise and helpful spirits – who minister strength and guidance and consolation...'; and Carlyle talked of Dante's 'longings ...towards his Beatrice'.[46] There is an insistence on a very human Beatrice at the middle of the century which can be traced back to Gabriele Rossetti's *La Beatrice di Dante*. In what Ellis calls 'the cult of the *Vita nuova*', Dante Gabriel Rossetti (Gabriele's son) was one of the most prominent figures: his own translation of the *Vita nuova* on which he had been working since the late 1840s (and a copy of which George Eliot possessed) came out in 1861. Though the younger Rossetti was the most prominent of Beatrice's Victorian worshippers,[47] he was not the originator of the Beatrice cult and was himself building on an already established reading of Dante. Because of Will Ladislaw's connection with the German pre-Raphaelites (he apprentices himself to Naumann), his versatility (he sketches, paints and writes poetry) and his foreign blood, it is possible that George Eliot may have modelled him on Dante Gabriel Rossetti, who visited Eliot in 1869 before she began writing her Miss Brooke story.[48] There are indeed striking affinities between Rossetti and Ladislaw, not least of which is their shared interest in the writings of Rossetti's namesake, Dante Alighieri. For both men, Dante seems to be of central importance in their own lives. One of the ways in which Ladislaw defines himself by contrast with the provincial Middlemarchers, for example, is that 'the Middlemarch tribes... were in a state of brutal ignorance about Dante' (p.651).[49] It is interesting too to compare the selections from Dante made by Eliot's Ladislaw and by Rossetti. Such a comparison is instructive in placing Eliot's work within the context of a wider use of material from Dante, in particular of the figure of Beatrice, and of its significance for the Victorians.

If we look at Rossetti's paintings, the coincidence of his choice of subjects with Eliot/Ladislaw's in *Middlemarch* is striking. Rossetti painted only the Paolo and Francesca scene (canto V) from *Inferno* and nothing from *Paradiso*. From *Purgatorio*, he painted La Pia (canto V), Dante's vision of Rachael and Leah (XXVII), Dante's Vision of Matilda gathering flowers (XXVIII) and 'The Salutation of Beatrice' (*Vita Nuova* III and *Purgatorio* XXX). Steve Ellis points to Rossetti's tendency to paint the 'belle donne' from *Purgatorio* and makes the further point that for Rossetti 'all roads lead back to the *Vita Nuova*'.[50] In the choice of images from Dante, then, there would seem to be a strong similarity between Eliot in *Middlemarch* (drawing on the *Vita Nuova*, *Inferno* V, and the 'Paradiso terrestre', cantos XXVII–XXX of *Purgatorio*) and Rossetti's work, indicating perhaps that similar readings of Beatrice in particular are involved. Rossetti's view of Dante largely ignores Dante the philosopher and politician (the author of the *Monarchia* and the *Convivio*) and to a great extent the Dante of the *Comedy*. In his painting 'The Salutation of Beatrice' for example, Rossetti has made the 'Paradiso terrestre' meeting between Dante and Beatrice 'an exact continuation of the state of things "In Terra"'.[51] In Rossetti's painting, the great pageant procession and Beatrice's reproval of Dante in the *Divine Comedy* cantos XXIX–XXX are absent. Citing lines from the 'Blessed Damozel' as further evidence, Ellis concludes that for Dante Gabriel Rossetti, 'Paradise is precisely a trouble-free continuation of love on earth' and that Rossetti 'has cut out all the heavenly procession attending on Beatrice in accordance with his idea of what Love is, namely a private affair between man and woman with a minimum of unwelcome onlookers'. It is in this sense that for Rossetti, 'all roads lead back to the *Vita Nuova*', and to Beatrice as 'a woman once really living in Florence, and there really loved by Dante as woman is loved by man'.[52] There is a parallel here with the effect which Eliot herself seems to be trying to achieve in Chapter 83 where, in the meeting between Ladislaw and Dorothea (with its echoes of the 'Paradiso terrestre'), Love is finally allowed to become a private affair between man and woman without unwelcome onlookers ('a world apart, where... no other soul entered'). Indeed the scene in the library, for all that it contains a warning against transgression and all its attendant risks in terms of future social censure and isolation, is an assertion of Dorothea and Ladislaw's belief that this is precisely what Love should be. For neither Rossetti nor Ladislaw does Beatrice become an allegorical figure, such as we find for example in Shelley; she remains always a living, breathing, physical presence.

A recurrent theme in Rossetti's poetry is that of the suffering caused by enforced separation between a man and woman in love. There were perhaps parallels between Rossetti's own life and the Dante/Beatrice narrative of the *Vita Nuova*: much of the anguish in Rossetti's *The House of Life* (1870) for example, may arise from his enforced separation from Jane Morris. Clearly Dante's work provided Rossetti with material for the expression of an earthly vision of love in which the moment of meeting of separated lovers takes on a heightened intensity and significance. Similarly, the *Vita Nuova* provides a clear paradigm for Eliot's Dorothea–Ladislaw story, and in Eliot's Ladislaw there does seem to be something of a Rossettian quality about love and the imaging of it. Through Ladislaw, Eliot appropriates a Victorian version of Beatrice in which woman is idealized while at the same time being despiritualized and ultimately domesticated, as she is in the readings of Theodore Martin and Coventry Patmore. Ladislaw transforms Dorothea into a despiritualized, secular Beatrice with redemptive and judgemental powers over him in the private sphere of his 'world apart'. In the association of Dorothea with the lily, there is something of the Ruskinian transformation of the flower from being a symbol of Christian purity into one of a certain kind of secular female purity. In his *Sesame and Lilies (Of Queen's Gardens)* (1871), Ruskin cites Dante's Beatrice as an example of the way the woman watches over, teaches and guides her partner.[53] Will Ladislaw's world of lilies comes into focus at the end of the novel in terms of Ruskin's division into male and female spheres of activity, with Dorothea's support enabling Will to go out into the world of men as an MP while her energies are 'spent...in channels which had no great name on earth'.[54] The story of Dorothea and Will can be read as a secular nineteenth-century version of the Dante–Beatrice myth: except of course that *Paradiso* cannot be recounted directly, for Eliot, like Virgil who leaves Dante in the 'Paradiso terrestre', is unable to follow any further.

One aspect of the Victorian Beatrice, then, is the living girl worshipped by Dante in Florence ('Upon her path men turn to gaze at her').[55] For the Rossetti of *The House of Life*, woman (the Beatrice figure) is seen 'not as the vehicle of a divine force, but as the replacement for it, with love for her representing a complete abnegation of everything else'.[56] There is also something of this in Ladislaw's attitude at the end of *Middlemarch*: 'When I thought you doubted..., I didn't care about anything that was left. I thought it was all over with me, and there was nothing left to try for – only things to endure' (p.867). The other important aspect of the Victorian Beatrice, though, is the elevation of her into a redemptive temporal force for good ('He whom she greeteth feels his heart to rise, / And droops his troubled visage, full of sighs, / And of his evil heart is then aware: / Hate loves, and pride becomes a worshipper').[57] Eliot herself eschews the first version of Beatrice/Dorothea, and the scene in the library which transforms momentarily into the circle of the lustful in *Inferno* seems to warn against the passion and sensuality of too Rossettian a Beatrice, but her heroine does share the redemptive power of the Beatrice of the *Vita Nuova* and the 'Paradiso terrestre' (both Ladislaw and Lydgate are redeemed by Dorothea). Nor is Dorothea's redemptive function and influence as a force for good confined to the private sphere of much of Rossetti's poetry. Rather, Eliot chooses to highlight it as a public function and, as we know, 'the effect of her being on those around her was incalculably diffusive: for the growing good of the world is partly dependent on unhistoric acts' (p.896).

George Eliot's Beatrice, then, is the one whose public function in the *Vita Nuova* is foregrounded at the end of *Middlemarch* and whose sphere of influence is extended to the rest of society. Neither Rossetti nor Eliot, though for different reasons, was able to follow Dante and Beatrice beyond the 'Paradiso terrestre' into *Paradiso*: Rossetti had reduced Beatrice's significance to that of the *Vita Nuova* while for Eliot, human love had to replace the love of God which Beatrice represented for Dante. George Eliot's Beatrice, too, is ultimately a despiritualized one, though one invested with significance as a force for moral good in the public as well as the private sphere. Eliot's *Middlemarch* registers that Victorian shift in the focus of interest in Dante, and her narrative incorporates both the *Vita Nuova* and its fulfilment in the 'Paradiso terrestre', and lends something of the force of a Beatrice to Dorothea.

8

Gwendolen's 'Other Road': Dante in *Daniel Deronda*

In her last novel, George Eliot has echoes, allusions, parallel scenes and direct references to Dante running through the book, especially in the second half. Dante is used to illustrate the moral growth through suffering of the heroine, Gwendolen, and the world of the *Divine Comedy* is translated into the psychological world of the novel. The largest body of allusion to Dante refers principally to Gwendolen and her relationships with her husband Grandcourt, and with her mentor Daniel Deronda. Eliot uses Dante to create a moral framework for Gwendolen's journey and the Dante allusion in *Daniel Deronda* amounts to an overarching purgatorial metaphor.[1] Dante's influence can best be discussed by dividing Gwendolen's journey into four stages: firstly, when Gwendolen sins by marrying the rich Grandcourt for wealth and position, without love and in the knowledge that he has a mistress; secondly, as her developing relationship with Grandcourt leads to the onset of a Dantean *contrappasso*; thirdly, as she becomes increasingly dependent on Daniel Deronda as a spiritual guide and alternates between infernal and purgatorial states of mind; and finally, as she enters a purgatorial condition of 'difficult blessedness', despite being abandoned by Daniel.

1. Gwendolen's sin

In the gambling scene with which *Daniel Deronda* opens, Gwendolen's pawning of her necklace prefigures her later gambling away of her moral integrity in marrying Grandcourt after the loss of her own family fortunes. As she is playing, Gwendolen has 'the darting sense that [Daniel] was measuring her and looking down on her as an inferior, that he was of different quality from the human dross around her, that he felt himself in a region outside and above her, and was examining her as a specimen of a lower order...' (p.38). Gwendolen is soon afterwards said to bear '...too

145

close a resemblance to the serpent, ...' (p.47) and her *'darting* sense' of being observed gives a hint of the type of 'specimen of a lower order' involved. The whole scene can in fact be read as an evocation of the thieves ditch of *Inferno* XXV.[2] The spatial configuration of this canto, with Dante and Virgil looking down from above onto the . sinners, also signifying their moral superiority, is reproduced in this scene in which Daniel observes the 'human dross' from a higher vantage point. Through that 'darting sense', Gwendolen is, as it were, changed from human to serpent in the opening scene, a transformation which actually occurs in *Inferno* XXV and is to haunt Gwendolen throughout the novel. This Dantean reading also underscores the moral gulf which divides Gwendolen and Daniel and which will condition the Dantean roles each will play in the novel.

On returning from honeymoon, Gwendolen receives the diamonds which Grandcourt has asked his old mistress, Mrs Glasher, to return. With them is a letter containing both a Dantesque judgement of Gwendolen (who had previously promised Mrs Glasher that she would *not* marry Grandcourt) and a terrible prophecy of her future which is to be fulfilled in the novel:

You have broken your word to [Lydia Glasher], that you might possess what was hers. [...] The man you have married has a withered heart. His best young love was mine; you could not take that from me when you took the rest. It is dead; but I am the grave in which your chance of happiness is buried as well as mine. You had your warning. You have chosen to injure me and my children. [...] He would have married me at last, if you had not broken your word. You will have your punishment. I desire it with all my soul.

[...] Shall you like to stand before your husband with these diamonds on you, and these words of mine in his thoughts and in yours? Will he think you have any right to complain when he has made you miserable? You took him with your eyes open. The willing wrong you have done me will be your curse. (p.406)

These last words echo down the pages of the novel and hold out the prospect of a Dantean Inferno, for what distinguishes Dante's sinners who go to Hell from those who do not is that they actively will and continue to desire their sins. In the letter, Gwendolen's sins are identified as those of betrayal and theft ('You have broken your word to her, that you might possess what was hers'). George Eliot subtly works the Dantean imagery which characterizes these sins in *Inferno* (imagery which will recur in *Daniel Deronda*) into the text at this point: '... on opening the case, in the same instant that she saw [the diamonds] gleam she saw a letter lying above them. She knew the handwriting of the address. It was as if an adder had lain on them' (p.406). In a spasm of terror she consigns the letter to the flames of the fire in her mirror-filled dressing room before falling

> back in her chair again helpless. She could not see the reflections of herself then: they were like so many women petrified white; [...] She sat so for a long while, knowing little more than that she was feeling ill, and that those written words kept repeating themselves in her. (p.407)

Along with the flames of the fire in Gwendolen's dressing room (the archetypal symbol of the Christian Hell) and the adder (reinforcing the opening association of Gwendolen with Dante's Thieves' Ditch), multiple reflections of people petrified white (setting up echoes of the betrayers forced to look upon their own reflections in the frozen ice of Cocytus in Dante's cantos XXXII and XXXIII) provide the first fleeting indication of the punishments to come and these mark the onset of the Dantean *contrappasso*.[3]

2. Grandcourt and the 'contrappasso'

The relationship between Gwendolen and her husband Grandcourt is one of mastery and subjection. Grandcourt's manservant talks of him as a 'tyrannous patron', while Grandcourt himself thinks that 'to be worth his mastering it was proper that [his future wife] should have some spirit' (p.195) and only seven weeks into their marriage, Gwendolen

> had found a will like that of a crab or a boa-constrictor which goes on pinching or crushing without alarm at thunder.... [Grandcourt] had a surprising acuteness in detecting that situation of feeling in Gwendolen which made her proud and rebellious spirit dumb and helpless before him. (pp.477–8)

The serpent imagery returns again as Grandcourt is further described as 'a handsome lizard, of a hitherto unknown species, not of the lively darting kind' (pp.173–4) and as 'look[ing] as neutral as an alligator' (p.195). There are images of serpents crushing, of Gwendolen's hair being gathered up to make a coil (p.340), of strangling and throttling (p.651) and of being throttled: 'The thought of [Grandcourt's] dying would not subsist: it turned as with a dream-change into the terror that she should die with his throttling fingers on her neck avenging that thought' (p.669). At the end of the novel, Gwendolen comes to see her experience as

> a long Satanic masquerade, which she had entered on with an intoxicated belief in its disguises, and had seen the end of in shrieking fear lest she herself had become one of the evil spirits who were dropping their human mummery and hissing around her with serpent tongues. (p.831)

In this body of imagery there is a conscious evocation of *Inferno* XXV, in which Dante recounts with horror and disbelief the transformation of human forms into those of serpents winding around one another.[4] Gwendolen's world (and her relationship with her husband) becomes like that of the thieves in which all bonds of human honesty and trust are dissolved. Grandcourt prefers mastery to love, while Gwendolen, seemingly unable to love, betrays Lydia Glasher. With the inexorable progress of the *contrappasso*, the diamonds too become a coil around Gwendolen's neck when she is forced to have Grandcourt fasten them for her and to wear them in public (p.482), and her bitter comment, 'What a privilege this is, to have robbed another woman of!' (p.482) points up the connection between the gems and her sin of theft.

There are close parallels with Dante's *Inferno* XXV, and Dante's horror, disbelief and confusion at witnessing the transformation of human forms is shared by Gwendolen who, in far more immediate danger of being caught up in the scene herself than is Dante-character, vividly imagines her husband 'dropping [his] human mummery'. From the outset, Grandcourt is portrayed as having little or no personality. He is associated with an eternal boredom (p.147), having 'left off' doing most of the things that a gentleman of means usually does. Yet his apparent lethargy hides the serpent's traditional cunning, and Eliot's image of him as a 'lizard, [...] not of the lively, darting kind' (p.174) or a 'sleepy-eyed animal' (p.465) is reminiscent of Dante's description of the transforming serpents: 'The one transfixed stared at it, but said nothing, but only stood still and yawned, as if sleep or fever had come upon him' (88–90). Gwendolen herself remains passive in this process of transformation: she imagines herself being attacked by her husband – it is Grandcourt who is transformed through the imagery – as one serpent attacks another in Dante's scene. Grandcourt throttles and crushes and is imaged as a lizard, like Dante's serpents, with legs and claws. By having Mrs Glasher send Gwendolen the jewels, Grandcourt symbolically 'bites' his wife ('the poison had entered into this poor young creature' and she does not want to wear jewels which 'had horrible words clinging and crawling about them' (pp.407, 480)) as the serpent bites its victim in *Inferno* XXV ('[it] set its fangs in the one cheek and the other' (54)) as the first step in transforming the human form into that of a 'specimen of a lower order'. In the same way that Dante's serpents present an obscene parody of sexual union, the only union (indeed any kind of physical contact) between the husband and wife is this imagined throttling, coiling, crushing. During the transformation process in *Inferno* XXV, there is no sound other than the hissing of the serpents. Eliot registers the same breakdown of communication which accompanies the sinners' total absorption in their sins in the lower regions of Hell as Gwendolen realizes that her unnatural 'marriage had nullified all... interchange, and Grandcourt had become a blank uncertainty to her' (p.480). Though she is ultimately saved, Gwendolen imagines with horrific immediacy that she is participating fully in this obscene transformation and, by association with *Inferno* XXV, the imagery repeatedly reminds us of the sin of theft of which she is guilty and carries a damning judgement upon her.

Gwendolen undergoes a visible, dehumanizing transformation, and there are clear signs of a withering of the most valuable human qualities in her. 'Deronda now marked some hardening in a look and manner which were schooled daily to the suppression of feeling' (p.667) and 'there was an indescribable look of suppressed tears in her eyes' (p.624), reminiscent of the frozen tears of Cocytus.[5] Finally, there is the complete breakdown in communication between Gwendolen and her husband ('She was dumb' (p.667)), which is again reminiscent of Dante's sinners imprisoned in the ice of Cocytus. The Dantesque imagery helps create and characterize Gwendolen's psychological suffering and the relationship with Grandcourt in which he becomes her chief tormentor, and it impinges increasingly as the relationship develops. The second stage in Gwendolen's journey, the *contrappasso*, involves passing through Dante's Thieves' Ditch for her sin of theft, before descending lower still into silence and the freezing of all emotion. Dante's punishments for the crimes are also Eliot's.

3. Gwendolen and Daniel

Even when Gwendolen appears to be in the depths of her personal *Inferno*, there are signs that she is not truly lost, for though she has chosen her sin, after the letter from Lydia Glasher she no longer wishes for it, and herein lies the crucial difference between those of Dante's sinners who are eternally damned and those who are redeemed. Gwendolen is unable to give up the fruits of her sin, but does not actively desire it.[6] From the moment in which she pawns her jewels to pay for her last game Daniel Deronda is present to Gwendolen, 'measuring her and looking down on her' and his redemption of the necklace establishes a bond between them and prefigures his role as spiritual guide and mentor to Gwendolen. Daniel 'had a wonderful power of standing perfectly still, and in that position reminded one sometimes of Dante's *spiriti magni con occhi tardi e gravi*' (p.500). Eliot here conflates parts of two lines from *Inferno* IV (the first circle of. Hell, the Limbo of the virtuous heathens): 'Where were people with grave and slow-moving eyes' (112) and 'There . . . were shown to me the great spirits' (119). Foremost among these are Homer, Horace, Lucan, Ovid and Virgil, and Eliot establishes a connection between Daniel and the *spiriti magni* which soon becomes still more specific. Gwendolen, on a walk through the grounds of Sir Hugo Mallinger's manor with her husband and others, seeks an opportunity to talk with Deronda alone, '[taking] advantage of the winding road to linger a little out of sight, she then set off back to the house, almost running when she was safe from observation. [. . .] "I thought you were far on your walk," said Deronda. "I turned back," said Gwendolen' (pp.504–5).

Gwendolen turns back and meets Daniel as Dante had encountered Virgil in *Inferno* I, and in so doing actively chooses a more difficult way, the 'other road', in asking for Daniel's guidance. A similar parallel scene occurs later, when Gwendolen, by now in the depths of her infernal despair on Grandcourt's yacht in Genoa, 'was waked the next morning by the casting of the anchor in the port of Genoa – waked from a strangely-mixed dream in which she felt herself escaping over the Mont Cenis, . . . till suddenly she met Deronda, who told her to go back' (p.740). The strangely-mixed dream evokes the dreamlike opening of *Inferno* I where Dante, finding himself in a dark wood, rushes back the way he had come only to be stopped by Virgil in the 'strangely-mixed dream' which is the *Comedy*.[7] Dante's first words to Virgil on his headlong descent down the slope are ' "Have pity on me, whoever thou art," I cried to him "shade or real man"!' (65–6): Gwendolen's proud nature has refused 'to say to the world "Pity me" ' (p.482) but in these scenes paralleling the opening of *Inferno*, she is asking for pity and guidance from Daniel whose presence, like Virgil's, signifies that 'other road' passing through Hell to emerge, as Dante had done, to ascend Mount Purgatory. Gwendolen, like Dante-character with Virgil, becomes like a child dependent upon the support of Daniel for her actions during the infernal part of her journey and, like Dante, she too fears being forsaken.[8]

George Eliot is careful to mark the moment when Gwendolen's purgatorial ascent begins; at the point when she appears to be in her lowest spirits, there is an explicit comparison with Dante's La Pia, who appears very briefly in the *Comedy*.[9] Eliot's version is an imaginative expansion of the scanty details in Dante's original:

> Madonna Pia, whose husband, feeling himself injured by her, took her to his castle amid the swampy flats of the Maremma and got rid of her there, makes a pathetic figure in Dante's Purgatory, among the sinners who repented at the last and desire to be remembered compassionately by their fellow-countrymen. We know little about the grounds of mutual discontent between the Siennese couple, but we may infer with some confidence that the husband had never been a very delightful companion, and that on the flats of the Maremma his disagreeable manners had a background which threw them out remarkably; whence in his desire to punish his wife to the uttermost, the nature of things was so far against him that in relieving himself of her he could not avoid making the relief mutual. And thus, without any hardness to the poor Tuscan lady who had her deliverance long ago, one may feel warranted in thinking of her with a less sympathetic interest than of the better known Gwendolen who...is at the very height of her entanglement in those fatal meshes which are woven within more closely than without...(pp.731–2)

Dante's 'poor Tuscan lady' is offered as a type of the suffering that Gwendolen herself is undergoing. The story both foreshadows a violent event, Grandcourt's death, and introduces the theme of murder, and until the form of Gwendolen's 'deliverance' is revealed (it is the husband rather than the wife who dies, and by accident) the reader is left in suspense as to the significance of the Madonna Pia passage, given Gwendolen's murderous wishes towards Grand-court. The allusion is, however, reliable in predicting the beginning of Gwendolen's purgatorial life. Only a few paragraphs later, she too 'has her deliverance' and repents at last. The realization of the magnitude and the consequences of her actions is expressed with a clarity which reflects that of her mind in this moment of 'revelation':

> She had a root of conscience in her, and the process of purgatory had begun for her on the green earth: she knew that she had been wrong.
> [. . .] she found herself [in] the domain of her husband [. . .] – the husband to whom she had sold her truthfulness and sense of justice, so that he held them throttled into silence, collared and dragged behind him to witness what he would, without remon-strance. (p.733)

This passage is important in enabling the reader to disambiguate further allusions to Dante as Gwendolen returns to land after the accident: she is 'pale as one of the sheeted dead, shivering, with wet hair streaming, a wild amazed consciousness in her eyes, as if she had waked up in a world where some judgement was impending, and the beings she saw around were coming to seize her' (p.750). It is Daniel who meets her however, and she stretches out her arms to him saying 'It is come, it is come! He is dead!' (p.750). Gwendolen's murderous wishes towards her husband have taken on the force of action for her, as though her willing his death had been sufficient to cause it. Eliot's language at this point makes Gwendolen appear as one of the damned souls hurrying to the banks of Acheron to embrace their punishment. As Virgil explains, 'all those who die in the wrath of God assemble here from every land; and they are eager to cross the river, for divine justice so spurs them that fear turns to desire'.[10] Gwendolen, however, is not in Charon's boat and the Mediterranean is not Acheron: she is in fact returning to land and the scene, despite descriptions of the 'sheeted dead' and being seized, is perhaps more reminiscent of the very opening of *Purgatorio*: 'To course over better waters the little bark ... now lifts her sails, leaving behind her so cruel a sea, ...'[11] Gwendolen, like

Romola before her,[12] in 'leaving behind her so cruel a sea' is being
borne by the ship of souls to Mount Purgatory. Daniel's first words
of comfort to Gwendolen ('Hush, hush!...quiet yourself' (p.750))
have the 'tone of authority' of the guide and teacher Virgil, not that
of judgement and condemnation as Gwendolen fears. In appropriating Dante's narrative at this point, then, Eliot is consciously
rendering her own text ambiguous and disorienting, momentarily
mirroring the confusion over moral status (is she saved or
damned?) of Gwendolen herself. After Grandcourt's death, Gwendolen's infernal 'suppressed tears' melt and she is once more able to
weep, not for her husband but for her own past sins, and she feels
impelled (as does Dante to Beatrice) to confess to Daniel (p.757). She
comes to think of Deronda as 'a terrible-browed angel from whom
she could not think of concealing any deed so as to win an ignorant
regard from him: it belonged to the nature of their relation that she
should be truthful, for his power over her had begun in the raising
of a self-discontent which could be satisfied only by genuine
change' (p.737). Here, Gwendolen also appears to be projecting a
Beatrice role onto Deronda. As Dante undertakes his journey to
become worthy of Beatrice, so the impulse to confess, to be worthy
of Daniel, becomes stronger in Gwendolen as the novel progresses.

Eliot gives Daniel Deronda some of the large capacity for pity and
compassion which had so much impressed her in the *Comedy*,[13] and
appropriates the power of Dante's text to convey a sense of the
sensitivity, depth and power of sympathy in her hero.

> [Gwendolen's] words of insistence that he 'must remain near her
> – must not forsake her' – continually recurred to him with the
> clearness and importunity of imagined sounds, such as Dante has
> said pierce us like arrows whose points carry the sharpness of
> pity:
>
> > Lamenti saettaron me diversi
> > Che di pietà ferrati avean gli strali. (p.684)
> > ['strange lamentations assailed me that had their
> > shafts barbed with pity'][14]

The Italian epigraph to Chapter 55 is from *Inferno* VI: ' "Go back
to thy science, which requires that in the measure of a creature's
perfection it feels more both of pleasure and of pain." –
DANTE'.[15] It provides a commentary on Gwendolen's present

pain, it is true, but once we realize that she is not 'accursed', we can read the epigraph as an indication of hope. The 'science' to which Virgil appeals is itself an indication of hope, for it is a measure of Gwendolen's potential for perfection that she feels so much present pain. Through her suffering, Gwendolen is being perfected, and will have a greater capacity for future pleasure. Eliot does not reveal the precise source (*Inferno* VI) of her epigraph here (though elsewhere she does), perhaps from fear of misleading the reader as to the direction of Gwendolen's progress. Here, then, the theme of moral growth through suffering in the world finds expression in terms of Dante's moral universe, and is reiterated later:

> her remorse was the precious sign of a recoverable nature; it was the culmination of that self-disapproval which had been the awakening of a new life within her; it marked her off from the criminals whose only regret is failure in securing their evil wish. (p.762)

That crucial Dantean distinction between repentance and the continued desire for sin is articulated with regard to Gwendolen. Eliot has been working within and through Dante's moral framework in judging Gwendolen, though of course translating her Hell and Purgatory onto 'the green earth'.

4. 'But Virgil had left us bereft of him, Virgil sweetest father, Virgil to whom I gave myself for my salvation'[16]

In the final stage of Gwendolen's journey, there is a radical departure from Dante's scheme in the *Comedy*. For Daniel, who has played Virgil to Gwendolen's Dante-character, abandons her after her ordeal, marries Mirah Lapidoth and leaves England to promote Zionism by trying to raise a national consciousness in the Jews. Thus, Gwendolen is excluded (from the 'Paradise' of marriage) at the end of the novel. This has led some commentators to remark that Gwendolen's salvation seems a rather fragile affair and that there appears to be little hope that her resolve to be better will hold under pressure. Yet if we allow ourselves to read through the Dantean sub-text, there is indeed hope for Gwendolen. Eliot, I think, intended the body of allusion and the purgatorial metaphor over the course of the novel to sustain our hope for Gwendolen's future and to absorb the shock of Daniel's departure.

In terms of the Dantean narrative framework, Gwendolen is already saved when Daniel abandons her. She has entered her purgatorial journey, and the loss of Deronda is to form part of her testing. Daniel himself gives a Dantean interpretation of Gwendolen's experience and of his part in it as Virgil-guide:

What makes life dreary is the want of motive; but once beginning to act with that penitential, loving purpose you have in your mind, there will be unexpected satisfactions... You will find your life growing like a plant [...] Think that a severe angel, seeing you along the road of error, grasped you by the wrist, and showed you the horror of the life you must avoid. And it has come to you in your spring-time. Think of it as a preparation. (pp.839–40)

The image of Gwendolen's 'life growing like a plant' echoes a similar image from the very end of *Purgatorio*: 'From the most holy waters I came forth again remade, even as new plants renewed with new leaves, pure and ready to mount to the stars'. These lines, copied into her notebook, were deliberately marked as the 'End of Purgatorio'.[17] Thus, Dante's image of purification, pointing onwards and upwards on the journey, is subtly worked into Eliot's text, which has Dante very close to its surface at this point. A final Dante epigraph (in Italian in Chapter 64 where the source, *Purgatorio IV*, *is* given) is intended to reinforce our confidence in Gwendolen's ability to sustain motives for moral growth: '"This mountain is such / That it is always hard at the start below / And the higher one goes it is less toilsome." DANTE: Purgatory'.[18]

Where Eliot might have drawn on a large number of images from *Purgatorio*, she makes an interesting use of one from *Inferno* XIX at the beginning of Chapter 64 to describe Gwendolen's haste to get away from the beautiful city of Genoa and the sea: 'For what place, though it were the flowery vale of Enna, may not the inward sense turn into a circle of punishment where the flowers are no better than a crop of flame-tongues burning the soles of our feet?' (p.824). The last part of this is an allusion to Dante's

I saw ... the livid stone full of holes all of one size, and each was round.... From the mouth of each projected the feet of a sinner and the legs as far as the calf, and the rest was inside; all of them had both soles on fire, from which their joints writhed with such violence that they would have snapped withies or ropes.[19]

The vale of Enna is violently changed into a Dantean 'circle of punishment' in a way which reflects the cruelty of the tortures suffered by Gwendolen herself. The world is literally turned upside down, as she who has been walking among the flowers is upended and confined in the darkness of the holes, while the flowers themselves become burning flame tongues inflicting physical and mental tortures on the imprisoned being. Far from drawing on Dante merely to provide examples of types, Eliot, in a movement analogous to the incubus of Dante's serpents in *Inferno* XXV, here creates her own nightmare of violent physical transformation as a correlative for the mental suffering endured by Gwendolen, a nightmare which threatens her hard won yet fragile mental composure.

Towards the end of *Daniel Deronda*, Gwendolen's penitential state of mind is characterized:

the future which she turned her face to with a willing step was one where she would be continually assimilating herself to some type that [Deronda] would hold before her. (p.867)

The first part of the quotation is strongly reminiscent of lines from *Purgatorio* XXIII and XXIV, which were among Eliot's favourite cantos: 'I turned my face, and my steps not less quickly, after the sages, . . .' and 'all the people that were there, facing round, quickened their steps'.[20] The action of 'turn[ing] her face . . . with a willing step' is indicative of haste and the productive use of time as well as of acceptance of the role of penitent. Gwendolen sketches a purgatorial course in her mind analogous to Dante's system of examples of vice followed by examples of virtue upon which the purification of the souls in Purgatory is based. She imagines 'assimilating herself to some type that [Deronda] would hold before her' after the consequences of the sins of theft and betrayal have been made vividly clear to her. Daniel, however, ultimately refuses to carry through the Virgil role which he himself took on in redeeming the necklace at the beginning of the novel. Gwendolen's loss of Daniel at the end of the novel is a necessary part of her spiritual integration so that 'whatever residue is left in her of a "passionate egoism of imagination" (p.867) is displaced completely' in order that, through a mixture of sorrow and hope, she will arrive at fellow feeling.[21] True though this is, it is difficult to escape the feeling that Eliot is taking the judgemental aspect of the purgatorial metaphor, and her own Dantesque power of assigning punishment, to such a point that we may well doubt Gwendolen's power to resist.

In drawing on Dante's *Comedy* in *Daniel Deronda*, Eliot does not present a strictly chronological sequence. For a time she allows the two sets of allusion and imagery (infernal and purgatorial) to coexist, and this is indicative of Gwendolen's inner mental torment. But ultimately there is no doubt that the purgatorial metaphor points the direction for her development beyond the close of the novel. There is a double irony contained in Gwendolen's belief that marriage would be 'the gate into a larger freedom' (p.183). What she finds in fact, is the narrow entrance into a confining hell of her own choosing, but unbeknown to her it is of course the beginning of Dante's 'other road' and, passing through the infernal state of marriage, Gwendolen does eventually achieve 'her larger freedom', though the nature of this 'freedom' is one that she herself would have been unable to conceive at the beginning of her journey.[22]

The full force of George Eliot's disgust and Dantesque ire and judgement is reserved for one whose destiny has also been prefigured in the opening scene of the novel. Mirah's father, Lapidoth, provides an example of complete moral degeneracy and his willed actions repeatedly condemn him. He is seen, towards the end of the novel, stealing Daniel's ring in order to feed his vice of gambling. His thought *is* acted out, unlike Gwendolen's murderous wishes towards Grandcourt, and she and Lapidoth in fact embody the Dantean distinction which Eliot makes in 'False Testimonials' between 'what we have professed and what we have done' as the ultimate test of a human morality.[23] It is Mordecai who voices the Dantean judgement and scourges the vices which have led to his father's moral death.[24] The 'stronger visions of the night' (p.849) for Lapidoth are of his moves at *Roulette* in the past, 'reproducing the method of his play, and the chances that had frustrated it', and not 'his ireful son uttering a terrible judgement'. In Lapidoth's inverted morality, Mordecai does pass across his dreams of the gaming table, but 'like an insubstantial ghost, and his words had the heart eaten out of them by numbers and movements that seemed to make the very tissue of Lapidoth's consciousness' (p.849). Unlike Dante's gambler in *Purgatorio* VI who 'when the game of hazard breaks up ... is left disconsolate, going over his throws again, and sadly learns his lesson', Lapidoth clearly does not learn and his is an infernal condition in which there is no place for fellow feeling, for 'where shame and conscience were, there sits an insatiable desire'.[25] Within the moral framework of the novel, Lapidoth is linked to Gwendolen through the common gambling theme, but her 'difficult blessedness' is balanced by his banishment.

Dante is not only present in connection with the theme of Gwendolen's moral growth through suffering under the guidance of Daniel, however. Dante and the *Comedy* are also there to provide a touchstone against which to measure the worth of Eliot's characters, and Dante sets the standard of achieved moral and artistic excellence. Perhaps the clearest example of this is in the portrayal of the Rector of Lowick, whose complacent advice to Gwendolen to marry Grandcourt 'eventually turned the brilliant, self-confident Gwendolen Harleth of the Archery Meeting into the crushed penitent impelled to confess her unworthiness' (p.771), and Gwendolen's early confidence that she would win Grandcourt ('My arrow will pierce him before he has time for thought' (p.127)) is ironically contrasted with the pity Daniel feels for the crushed penitent, which was like arrows 'that had their shafts barbed with pity'.[26] The Rector does 'nothing solely with an eye to promotion except, perhaps, the writing of two ecclesiastical articles, which, having no signature, were attributed to some one else, except by the patrons who had a special copy sent them, . . .'

> Peaceful authorship! – living in the air of the fields and downs, and not in the thrice-breathed breath of criticism – bringing no Dantesque leanness; rather, assisting nutrition by complacency, and perhaps giving a more suffusive sense of achievement than the production of a whole *Divina Commedia*. (p.772)

Cortese explains the reference to this absence of 'Dantesque leanness' and the Rector's peaceful authorship 'rather, assisting nutrition by complacency' as an allusion to Cacciaguida's words to Dante in *Paradiso* XVII: 'For if thy voice is grievous at first taste, it will afterwards leave vital nourishment when it is digested'.[27] This allusion throws the insignificance of the Rector's literary voice into even greater relief when contrasted with the 'vital nourishment' of Dante's in the *Comedy*, and his complacency is exposed as part of the wider malaise of the English society to which he belongs. In creating the contrast between the Rector's 'suffusive sense of achievement' and the 'leanness' involved in writing the *Comedy*,

Eliot draws on the Romantic Promethean Dante who is conscious that the monumental task of producing 'a whole *Divina Commedia*' will only be accomplished through suffering. This is Carlyle's Byronic Dante, whose superhuman effort in writing the *Commedia* is no less a task than that of Dante-pilgrim who 'lives' the *Commedia*:

> Ah, yes, he had been in Hell; – in Hell enough, in long severe sorrow and struggle; as the like of him is pretty sure to have been. Commedias that come-out *divine* are not accomplished otherwise. Thought, true labour of any kind, highest virtue itself, is it not the daughter of Pain? Born as out of the black whirlwind; – true *effort*, in fact, as of a captive struggling to free himself: that is Thought. In all ways we are 'to become perfect through *suffering*.'[28]

This 'Dantesque leanness', unknown to the Rector, also applies to Gwendolen's sufferings, for she is required to live the *Comedy* in order to become more perfect through suffering, for she too has been 'a captive struggling to free [her]self' and thought for her has truly been 'the daughter of Pain'. Eliot's 'Dantesque leanness' is, in fact, a paraphrase of Dante's own words from *Paradiso* XXV, and Eliot may well have had Carlyle's Dante in mind here too: 'The labour of writing, we find ... was great and painful to him; he says, This Book, "which has made me lean for many years." Ah yes, it was won, all of it, with pain and sore toil, – not in sport, but in grim earnest.'[29] Where the Rector is calculating enough to have an eye to personal advantage and is conscious of the need to please his patrons, Dante's freedom from patronage, so the *Risorgimento* mythologizing of Alfieri maintained, was the very condition of his greatness and integrity.[30] Where the mediocrity of the Rector is exposed through allusion to Dante, a character who benefits from this allusion is Herr Klesmer, an artist striving for excellence, who is associated with Dante's Virgil as one of 'the masters of those who know', in a slightly modified translation of Dante's reference to Aristotle as 'the master of them that know' from *Inferno* IV.[31]

Dante is a strong presence in *Daniel Deronda*, then, with explicit references, parallel scenes, echoes or even single words or phrases resonating just below the surface of the text to create a sustained Dantean metaphor over the course of the novel. Eliot assimilates Dante's framework and his infernal and purgatorial scheme for human suffering as a means of charting Gwendolen's moral progress. Books III and IV of *Daniel Deronda* are entitled 'Maidens

Choosing' and 'Gwendolen gets her Choice': like the *Divine Comedy*, Eliot's last novel, which deals insistently with consequences, is concerned to emphasize that element of choice as being all-important.

9

Italian Poetry and Music in *Daniel Deronda*

In her last novel, George Eliot incorporates a number of musical settings of texts in Italian. The most important of these are three lines from Dante's *Inferno* V ('There is no greater pain than to recall the happy time in misery' (121–3)); '*Per pieta non dirmi addio*' ['For pity's sake say not Farewell'] by Metastasio and the patriotic ode *All'Italia* ['To Italy'] by Giacomo Leopardi.[1] The lines by Dante, particular favourites of Eliot's, have already been touched on in Chapters 6 and 7 but we shall return to them here. Pietro Metastasio (1698–1782) was well known as a poet and composer of libretti for operas. His work was familiar in England, was often included in anthologies of Italian literature and, particularly during the years of the Italianate fashion, was a favourite with those who wished to sing arias from his operas. Leopardi, on the other hand, was comparatively unknown in England. Between 1800 and 1850, there were at least 26 translations and editions of Dante published in England, 17 of Metastasio but none of Leopardi. In 1848, an article in *Frazer's Magazine* affirmed that the name of Giacomo Leopardi 'is a mere sound signifying nothing'.[2]

The writer of this article was G.H. Lewes, and it seems likely that George Eliot came to Leopardi through discussion with Lewes or through reading his 11-page article on his life and work. Lewes sympathized with the *Risorgimento* struggles and helped nurture the spread of its mythology in Britain, and his article throws light on what Leopardi and his work meant to the cultivated Englishman in the 1850s and beyond. For Lewes, Leopardi was first and foremost 'the poet of despair'[3] and the singer of 'the degradation of Italy' in his first two canzoni, *All'Italia* and *Sopra il Monumento di Dante* [On the monument to Dante]. 'Utter the name of Leopardi before any Italian', writes Lewes, 'and he instantly bursts forth with, – O patria mia, vedo le mura e gli archi / E le colonne e i simulacri e l'erme / Torri degli avi nostri,...'.[4] Lewes gives the first 17 lines in Italian and also provides his own musical indications for Leopardi's ode (as Eliot was herself later to do in *Daniel Deronda*) which amount to a musical setting of the work giving a key to the way in which it should be read:

> Often as her poets have reproached Italy – from Dante down-wards, there have been no more piercing, manly, vigorous strains, than those which vibrate in the organ-peal of patriotism sent forth by Leopardi...the irregular but rhythmic march... seizes hold of your soul and irresistibly hurries you along with it.[5]

The cause of Leopardi's despair over Italy's abasement was not that 'fatal gift of beauty' which had drawn the conqueror in Fili-caia's sonnet 'Italia',[6] but rather 'that her sons are no longer worthy of her: their ancient courage and manliness have deserted them'. Consequently, Leopardi 'turns from the degeneracy of his age to those happy antique times when men gloried in dying for their country' (p.661); indeed Rome is a continual source of inspiration to the poet. Leopardi's pessimistic vision, then, is aptly summarized in the very words from Dante ('There is no greater pain than to recall the happy time in misery') which Eliot incorporates into *Daniel Deronda*. Lewes himself puts it differently in his article, 'The distinctive characteristic of Leopardi's poetry is despair over the present, accompanied with a mournful regret for the past' (p.663).

In accordance with the *Risorgimento* tendency to read the indivi-dual life as symbolic of that of Italy as a whole, Lewes sees the suffering of the 'nation' mirrored in Leopardi's own: 'Suffering, deep and constant, was Leopardi's individual lot; and the condition of his nation seemed to him little better: for it was to the many one of cowardly submission, of galling servitude to the few, who felt their chains, and knew that liberty was hopeless' (p.664). Lewes emphasizes the way in which Leopardi, a follower in the great tradition of Dante, looked to literature as a means of national regeneration:

> In the first Revival of Letters, how great was Italy! Shall there be a second Revival, and no response be heard? The first produced a Dante, a Petrarch, an Ariosto, a Tasso, a Columbus; the second will produce a new race, of whom Alfieri is the chief.
> Nothing can be more natural than that a poet and scholar should look to literature as the regenerator of his country; and,

consequently, to a second Revival of Letters as the one thing needful. So long as the love of letters survives, [Leopardi] says, Italy will not be dead; (p.662)

Leopardi was also the poet of action: 'his great hope in literature was, that by means of it men would be stimulated to action.' Literature ' "... can have but one solid principle" [Leopardi] said, "and that is the regeneration of our country" ' (p.668). Thus, 'to do is more dignified than to meditate or to write', though (and Lewes quotes Leopardi) 'only those [like Alfieri] capable of executing great things are capable of writing them' (p.667). Writing, in Lewes' (*Risorgimento*) life of Leopardi, becomes 'a lower sphere of human activity' (p.667), a mere substitute for action and the radical Lewes, a supporter of Mazzinian 'thought and action', himself laments the tendency in more modern writers 'to overvalue thought and to undervalue action'.[7] The final picture of Leopardi which Lewes leaves his reader, however, is of the poet whose Muse 'when not roused to indignation...has but one low plaint – a yearning for release from life' (p.668), and he singles out Leopardi's *Amore e morte* [Love and death], a poem of suicidal despair which Lewes calls his 'appeal to death', for translation.[8]

This account firmly establishes Leopardi within the literary tradition of the *Risorgimento* for the British reader. Moreover, many of the themes which Lewes highlights (suicidal despair, thought and action, past greatness and present misery, regeneration through literature) have a direct bearing on *Daniel Deronda* where, writing 25 years later, well after the Unification of Italy, George Eliot tried to harness the energies vibrating in the great 'organ-peal of patriotism' which was *All'Italia*, to Daniel Deronda's Zionism.

Eliot quotes directly (in Italian) from Leopardi twice in *Daniel Deronda*. On both occasions, it is Mirah who sings a setting of the Ode by a fictitious nineteenth-century composer, Joseph Leo. On the first occasion, Mirah is auditioning for singing lessons before the musician/pianist Klesmer. Eliot quotes selectively from the 140-line poem, dramatizing her text by providing musical indications of tempo and mood to guide the reader through the musical experience and to heighten it as Lewes had done in his article:

> 'O patria mia, vedo le mura e gli archi
> E le colonne e i simulacri e l'erme
> Torri degli avi nostri' –

This was recitative: then followed –

> *'Ma la gloria non vedo'* –

a mournful melody, a rhythmic plaint. After this came a climax of devout triumph – passing from the subdued adoration of a happy Andante in the words –

> *'Beatissimi voi,*
> *Che offriste il petto alle nemiche lance*
> *Per amor di costei che al sol vi diede'* –

to the joyous outburst of an exultant Allegro in –

> *'Oh viva, oh viva:*
> *Beatissimi voi*
> *Mentre nel mondo si favelli o scriva.'* (pp.540–1)[9]

Eliot, like Lewes, emphasizes those aspects of the poem which make it a cry of despair in the present set against the idealized past of 'Italia'. The fictitious Joseph Leo's setting exalts those who have died for love of, or in defence of, 'La patria'. However, the hope for a 'rebirth' (or 'resurgence') is not in evidence here: past glory remains firmly *past*.

Yet Mirah sings *'O patria mia'* twice, and on the second occasion, to the mind of Daniel who is listening, the text is experienced differently.

> Daniel...knew well Leopardi's fine Ode to Italy (when Italy sat like a disconsolate mother in chains, hiding her face on her knees and weeping), and the few selected words were filled for him with the grandeur of the whole, which seemed to breathe as inspiration through the music....Certain words not included in the song nevertheless rang within Deronda as harmonies from one invisible–
>
> > *'Non ti difende*
> > *Nessun de'tuoi? L'armi, qua l'armi: io solo*
> > *Combatterò, procomberò sol io'**–
>
> they seemed the very voice of that heroic passion which is falsely said to devote itself in vain when it achieves the godlike end of manifesting unselfish love.

*Do none of thy children defend thee? Arms! bring me arms! alone I will fight, alone I will fall. (pp.619–20)[10]

Daniel, like so many of his generation, is familiar with the recent history of Italy, '(when [she] sat like a disconsolate mother in chains, hiding her face on her knees and weeping),' and in the present of the novel the 'prophecy' of Unification had all but been fulfilled. The focus in Daniel's experience of the musical setting, for which he supplies the Italian *con*text, is on battle and the need to take part in some great enterprise. The first time we hear Leopardi's Ode, it is a poem of despair which praises the fallen for the great and noble cause: the second time, it becomes a call to arms. Mirah is the vehicle for this 'awakening' in Daniel, and the whole experience depends upon, and is articulated through, the language of the Italian *Risorgimento*. Leopardi's Ode here takes on a predictive quality, for it is a presentiment of the forces which will have claimed Daniel by the end of the novel – those of hope for, and belief in, the possibility of national revival.

It is not immediately evident that the words '(when Italy sat like a disconsolate mother in chains, hiding her face on her knees and weeping),' are in fact a close paraphrase of the actual words of Leopardi's Ode:

> And this is worse,
> That both her arms are bound about with chains;
> So that with loosened locks and without veil
> She sits upon the ground disconsolate,
> Neglected hides her face
> Between her knees, and weeps. (12–17)

We move *back* 400 pages in the novel now, to the moment when Daniel rescues Mirah who, in her despair, is about to commit suicide. When he first notices her, 'her eyes were fixed on the river with a look of immovable, statue-like despair' (p.227). He rows on, but when he returns back along the river, Mirah has wet her cloak to use as a drowning-shroud: she 'sank down on the brink again, holding her cloak but half out of the water. She crouched and covered her face...' (p.230). For an instant, Eliot creates a Leopardian tableau of suicidal despair in which Mirah, her arms weighed down by the sodden cloak, herself appears a 'disconsolate mother in chains, hiding her face on her knees, and weeping'. Her 'statue-like despair' puts one in mind too of the 'images' of Leopardi's Ode and indeed the whole literary tradition of imaging the past greatness of Italy.

The Leopardian theme of suicide is strongly present in Chapter 17: 'I thought it was not wicked [to kill myself]. Death and life are one before the Eternal' (p.233). Mirah's despair over the loss of her mother and brother turns to an 'unmistakable' 'project of suicide' (p.233). Lewes had translated a similar passage from *Love and Death* (Leopardi's 'appeal to death'), in his 1848 article.[11] In Leopardi's later work, humanity is the victim of a cruel and indifferent fate and, though he ultimately rejects it, he allows the reasonableness of suicide when all hope had been lost.[12] On first seeing Mirah, Daniel is touched by this Leopardian sense of the universal tragedy of life: 'His mind glanced over the girl-tragedies that are going on in the world, hidden, unheeded, as if they were but tragedies of the copse or hedgerow, where the helpless drag wounded wings forsakenly, and streak the shadowed moss with the red moment-hand of their own death' (p.228). The initial impression made on Daniel by the 'image of helpless sorrow' becomes 'blent...with what seemed to him the strong array of reasons...why he should not draw strongly at any thread in the hopelessly-entangled scheme of things' (p.229).[13]

In *Daniel Deronda*, Gwendolen enacts a tableau of Hermione from the *Winter's Tale* in which, instead of coming to life, she freezes with fear as a wooden panel falls open. In the Leopardian tableau by the river bank, we have a scene which is a kind of mirror image of the Gwendolen/Hermione one. Mirah's infernal condition of despair and complete loss of hope enables her to receive a voice from another world, for while rowing along the river Daniel has been singing the famous words from Dante's *Inferno* V set to music by Rossini in *Otello*:

> Nessun maggior dolore
> Che ricordarsi del tempo felice
> Nella miseria: (p.227)

But the voice is also from *this* world:

> ...his voice had entered her inner world..., for when it suddenly ceased she changed her attitude slightly, and looking round with a frightened glance, met Deronda's face. (p.227)

Ironically, Gwendolen's Hermione refuses to come to life, and Dante's words from 'among the lost people'[14] have the power to awaken Mirah from her 'statuesque despair', to animate the statue. Mirah repeats the words

> I saw you before;... 'nella miseria'. [...] 'It was you singing?' she went on hesitatingly – 'Nessun maggior dolore.' ... (p.230)

> 'I cannot see how I shall be glad to live. The *maggior dolore* and the *miseria* have lasted longer than the *tempo felice*.' She paused and then went on dreamily, – '*Dolore – miseria –* I think those words are alive.' (p.233)

Those words are indeed alive. They neatly summarise the pre-*Risorgimento* condition of Italy itself in which Italians could only look back on a *tempo felice* in present *miseria*, and at the same time they give voice to Mirah's own personal suffering and to that of her people. Still unaware of his origins, Daniel has already acted out the drama of saving a Leopardian 'Italia' in his rescue of Mirah, in a kind of premonition of what his mission is to be. And this happens well before he receives his Leopardian call to arms, in the words 'Do none of thy children defend thee?' Drawing on her personal experience in Italy, George Eliot also blends her own voice with the many Italian voices (Dante, Francesca da Rimini, Rossini and Rossini's gondolier) present in this chapter:

> Of all dreamy delights that of floating in a gondola along the canals and out on the Lagoon is surely the greatest. We were out one night on the Lagoon when the sun was setting, and the wide waters were flushed with the reddened light. I should have liked it to last for hours; it is the sort of scene in which I could most readily forget my own existence and feel melted into the general life.[15]

Her own entrancing experience in Venice in 1860 is translated onto the Thames in *Daniel Deronda*:

> He used his oars little, satisfied to go with the tide and be taken back by it. It was his habit to indulge himself in that solemn passivity which easily comes with the lengthening shadows and mellowing light, when thinking and desiring melt together

imperceptibly [...] He was forgetting everything else in a half-speculative, half-involuntary identification of himself with the objects he was looking at, thinking how far it might be possible habitually to shift his centre till his own personality would be no less outside him than the landscape, – (p.229)

That evening, while meditating on his action of snatching Mirah from death

Deronda felt himself growing older... and entering on a new phase in finding a life to which his own had come – perhaps as a rescue?;... The moment of finding a fellow-creature is often as full of mingled doubt and exultation as the moment of finding an idea. (p.236)

As Daniel first encounters the idea of a Jewish nationalism, then, the yearning for an idyllic past in present despair, the search for the lost mother, the attempts to trace and reconstitute the family and the call to action are all mediated through the language, mythology and iconography of the Italian *Risorgimento*. The energies embodied in Leopardi and Dante's texts reach out and claim both Daniel and Mirah and place them in relation to a living *Risorgimento* tradition, and the body of literary allusion upon which Eliot draws constitutes 'a kind of remembering' which 'urge[s] on characters and readers alike the need to... respect the warnings and demands of the past, to absorb the succour and admonition of its precedents'.[16] We have, in Chapter 17 of *Daniel Deronda*, a re-enactment of some of the potent myths of Italian nationalism: Mirah/'Italia' is revived from a statuesque despair through the powerful voice of literature, and by a saviour who is himself to receive his call to arms from the poetry of Leopardi, heightened and intensified in the music of the fictitious composer Joseph Leo.

The scene of Mirah's attempted suicide is one of a number of highly melodramatic scenes in the novel which are Eliot's response to the problem of finding a suitable narrative idiom through which to express her characters' inner spiritual journeys.[17] The available idioms, the language of melodrama and the Gothic vocabulary of Gwendolen's journey, are rooted in English literary tradition, but Eliot is at the same time drawing heavily on a strong Italian one. The melodrama of Mirah's rescue is the more richly textured in that it owes much to Leopardi who, in *All'Italia*, consciously draws upon the ample rhetoric, lyrical eloquence and grandiloquence of the classical Italian tradition of Petrarch, Filicaia, Alfieri and Foscolo which was felt to be in keeping with themes of great heroism, generous impulses and the impassioned evocation of ancient and noble ages. In working through melodrama, then, Eliot was also aligning herself with the Italian literary tradition. Similarly, the Gothic vocabulary also belongs to the greatest Italian literature (*The Divine Comedy*) and takes on heightened significance when seen in relation to this.[18]

Musical settings of Leopardi's ode *All'Italia* existed by Verdi, Fanny Mendelssohn, and Ciro Pinsutti (a well-known singing master in England in the 1840s and 1850s), so why should Eliot invent her own composer? One critic felt convinced that Eliot's setting actually existed, but there is, I think, no real reason to suppose this to be the case.[19] Eliot had, I believe, a precise purpose in mind in attributing her piece to Joseph Leo. The composer's name throws out various associations which Eliot wished to resonate in her text, and one of these is undoubtedly *Leo*pardi. Joseph Leo had been Mirah's maestro at Vienna, yet it is strange that a setting of a patriotic ode urging resistance should be produced in the capital city of the Austrian oppressor of Italy. 'Leo' means *lion*, symbolizing courage, and the lion is also the symbol of the ancient Republic of Venice, still under Austrian domination at the time of the action in the novel (1865–6). Thus, 'Joseph' may readily be associated with resistance to the Austrian oppressor. The name and the music of Giuseppe (Joseph) Verdi embodied just such a resistance to the Austrians in Italy. In *Punch* (November 12th, 1859) for example, a 'telegram' on 'Verdi at Venice' reported that 'on the occasion of the reopening of the Opera, a noisy demonstration has taken place here.'

> ...the uproar which was made the other night at the Opera House at Venice was probably caused...by shouting the name of that composer. There is every reason to believe that the noisy demonstration consisted in cries of '*Viva* VERDI!' translated, if any Britons were included in the audience, by 'VICTOR EMMA-NUEL for ever! Hip hip hip – hooray.'

Verdi's own setting of Leopardi's '*O patria mia*' in *Aida* was also very popular in the early 1870s. Another Joseph who symbolized resistance to foreign oppression was Joseph (Giuseppe) Mazzini,

the 'prophet' of Italy, who was known to the British by the angli-
cized form of his name. The name of Eliot's invented composer,
then, throws out hints at themes of oppression and resistance and at
the as yet incomplete process of the Italian *Risorgimento*.[20]

Another setting of an Italian text which Mirah sings twice, though
unlike the Leopardi setting on neither occasion is the reader given
the words, is Beethoven's '*Per pietà non dirmi addio*'. On both occasions on which the piece is heard it makes claims upon Daniel's
affections and lays responsibilities on him. Shortly after her rescue,
Mirah sings '*Per pietà*' in the Meyrick's drawing room, and as the
song finishes, Daniel 'was ready to meet the look of mute appeal
which she turned towards him' and his comment ('I think I never
enjoyed a song more than that' (p.422)) indicates his receptiveness
towards these claims. The second time, although it is Mirah who
sings 'with that wonderful, searching quality of subdued song in
which the melody seems simply an effect of the emotion' (p.625),
Gwendolen unwittingly usurps the poignancy of Mirah's voice in
her own spoken appeal to Daniel just before the song begins:

> 'If you despair of me, I shall despair. Your saying that I should
> not go on being selfish and ignorant has been some strength to
> me. If you say you wish you had not meddled – that means, you
> despair of me and forsake me. [...]'
>   In Deronda's ear the strain (of *Per pietà*) was for the moment a
> continuance of Gwendolen's pleading... (pp.624–5)

There may be significance in the fact that Gwendolen is the more
closely associated with '*Per pietà*' on this second occasion. The text
set by Beethoven is by Pietro Metastasio, famous in *Risorgimento*
mythology as the poet who had sold his muse to the foreign tyrant.[21] Gwendolen had likewise sold herself to Grandcourt (who is
compared with the tyrant Cesare Borgia in this chapter (p.626)). It
may be significant in this sense that Eliot, who was dissatisfied with
her original choice of Schubert's *Adieu* and had asked Charles
Lewes for advice, rejected his first suggestion of Verdi's *Al piè
d'un salice* ['Beneath a Weeping Willow'] in favour of '*Per pietà*'.
Verdi would not have been a suitable choice here, as he was too
strongly linked with that *Risorgimento* spirit of resistance and liberation which Eliot wished Mirah and Daniel to embody. Metastasio,
on the other hand, was aligned with the tyranny and slavery into
which Gwendolen had sold herself.

In *Daniel Deronda*, then, Eliot translates a Jewish yearning for a national identity into the language and terms of the Italian *Risorgimento*. She was however faced with the greater problem of portraying the Jewish people and a culture essentially alien to British readers. Mirah and Daniel's singing of settings of Italian texts is part of a more sustained association of Jewish characters with Italy and its culture, in what amounts to a deliberate and carefully calculated hermeneutic strategy whereby the Jewish part of the novel is often mediated through Italian cultural references to provide 'a definite outline for our ignorance'.[22] Witemeyer notices how George Eliot uses a conscious and carefully controlled scale of artistic values, one which can be deduced from the 1860 Journal 'Recollections of Italy', and positively associates her Jewish characters with Italian, particularly Renaissance Venetian, painting.[23] Daniel puts Gwendolen's mother 'in mind of Italian paintings' (p.378), and is associated with two portraits by Titian, *The Young Man with a Glove* and *The Tribute Money*, the latter associating him with Titian's Christ and 'flesh[ing] out Daniel's portrait as a paragon, as a symbol, or personal saviour'.[24] *The Tribute Money* successfully achieves the ideal in the real, while the eighteenth-century English portrait tradition through which Gwendolen is depicted is, says Witemeyer, 'less than flattering'.[25] There is indeed a systematic and usually positive association of Jews with Italians, affecting both major and minor characters in *Daniel Deronda*. The pianist Klesmer 'draped in a loose garment with a Florentine *berretta* on his head, ... would have been fit to stand by the side of Leonardo da Vinci' (p.136); in the Frankfurt synagogue an elderly man has an 'ample white beard and old felt hat fram[ing] a profile of that fine contour which may as easily be Italian as Hebrew' (p. 416); Mirah Cohen, who performs Italian music and songs in Italian, is associated with Romans in Hans Meyrick's Titus and Berenice paintings, a series suggested by 'a splendid woman in the Trastevere – the grandest women there are half Jewesses – and she set me hunting for a fine situation of a Jewess at Rome' (p.514). Daniel discovers that his father had lived in Genoa and, in the synagogue there, sees 'keen dark faces of worshippers' who had a 'way of taking awful prayers and invocations with the easy familiarity which might be called Hebrew dyed Italian' (p.748). Eliot, then, hoped to circumvent British prejudices concerning Jews and to make them respectable as the Italians had become. By conferring dignity upon the Jews by association with the idealized and exalted physical descriptions in Titian's paintings, Anglo-Saxon readers might be 'induced almost subliminally' to accord the Jews the tolerance and respect they had learned to grant the Italians by 1876.[26]

Acutely aware of the difficulties involved in her Jewish project in *Daniel Deronda*, George Eliot attempted to mediate unfamiliar Jewish cultural experience through a more familiar Italian one. Nevertheless, the difficulties were considerable for the novel's first readers and remain so.[27] Daniel and Mirah are claimed as instruments by the powerful energies embodied in the Italian texts, but the particular images and ideas they contain are 'constantly ... fluctuating between death and re-birth. They are dependent on the active collaboration of other human imaginations to conspire in their withering or revival.'[28] A problem inherent in Eliot's technique, then, is that the fascination with nineteenth-century Italy and the urgent sense of engagement which George Eliot and many of her generation felt gradually became lost to readers as the *Risorgimento* faded into history. The force of reference and allusion diminishes and resonances and echoes fade and no longer have the power to move and to awaken sympathies as they had in 1876. For today's readers, who may be unfamiliar with Italian literature and yet are confronted with images and myths charged with meaning within the political and intellectual climate of the *Risorgimento*, the imaginative effort of recuperation is much greater if the energies once so powerful are to resurge productively in Eliot's last novel.

10

Daniel Deronda, Italian Prophecy, Dante and George Eliot

In her last novel, George Eliot invokes directly or makes allusion to some of the central myths and figures of the Italian *Risorgimento*. She pays tribute to the 'prophet' Mazzini, who is a direct inspiration for Daniel, and the arc of Italian *Risorgimento* history which is traced over the course of the novel provides a powerful analogue which renders Deronda's Zionist project both more concrete and more credible. Overall, Eliot's representation of the Italian experience as the achievement of a full and independent national identity is offered as the alternative to the harsh climate of European militarism and aggressive expansionism which intrudes into the world of *Daniel Deronda,* and thus it stands as her statement of faith in human possibilities despite her pessimistic vision of the Europe of the mid 1860s and 1870s.

The opening scene of the novel establishes a European perspective from the outset. We are presented with various types ('Livonian and Spanish, Graeco–Italian and miscellaneous German, English aristocratic and English plebeian' (p.36)) absorbed in play round a gaming table. One of these is 'a handsome Italian, calm, statuesque' constantly losing piles of Napoleons to 'an old bewigged woman with eye glasses pinching her nose' who acknowledges her winnings with 'a faint mumbling smile' while 'the statuesque Italian remained impassive' (p.37). On one level, we have a representation of the pre-*Risorgimento* condition of Italy, being plundered and exploited by foreign powers (with the old bewigged woman perhaps representing the Austro–Hungarian Empire?) and powerless to react. The gaming table also becomes an infernal battleground where isolated players, with 'bony yellow crab-like hands' and countenances which seem only 'a slight metamorphosis of the vulture' are 'compelled . . . to the same narrow monotony of action' and opponents are enemies to be conquered and bled dry (pp.36–7).

This vignette evokes the Italy of the pre-*Risorgimento* years. The Piedmontese Minister in Russia between 1811 and 1817, for example, reported a conversation with Nesselrode: 'I happened to speak of the *Italian spirit* which is active at this moment. He replied: *Yes, Monsieur; but this spirit is a great evil, for it may spoil the Italian arrangements*...It is not necessary to be very acute to see that Italy is a currency which must pay for other things...'; or again, a political cartoon in 1860 ('The Rub') showed the statuesque 'Italia' looking on while her fate is decided over a game of cards between Pope Pius IX, Victor Emmanuel, Ferdinand of Naples and Garibaldi.[1] From the outset of *Daniel Deronda*, the Italian experience is subtly woven in to Eliot's exploration of subjection and empire at both the social and individual levels. The pre-*Risorgimento* Italy represented here itself becomes one of the novel's many 'make-believe[s] of a beginning', a point of departure from which Eliot follows the thread of Italian history, through references and allusions which punctuate the novel.

Six hundred pages later, Daniel confidently asserts that 'we are sure soon to see [the unity of Italy] accomplished to the very last boundary' (p.595), and invokes the name of Giuseppe Mazzini to support the idea that a nation can be reborn. Eliot, as we know, admired and supported Mazzini.[2] As editor of the *Westminster Review*, she had read and published his article 'Europe: its Condition and Prospects' in 1852 and in 1865, although she refused to contribute to an Italian fund which she feared might be used for insurrection, she wrote that 'Mr Lewes and I have a real reverence for Mazzini'.[3] The kingdom of Italy had been in existence for four years by this time, and Eliot and Lewes both took the view that further conspiracy to incite revolution was hopeless, needless and unjustifiable. Indeed, Mazzini and his methods, which had never found widespread approval, had largely been discredited in British public opinion. Nevertheless, on the Italian's death in 1872 she wrote to one of Mazzini's closest supporters in England that 'Such a man leaves behind him a wider good than the loss of his personal presence can take away. [...] I enter thoroughly into your sense of wealth in having known him', and quotes her own words from *The Spanish Gypsy* that 'The greatest gift the hero leaves his race / Is to have been a hero'.[4] This support, however, was to draw heavy criticism from Lord Acton: 'Her tolerance for Mazzini' he said was 'a grave delinquency...a criminal matter, independent of the laws of states and churches'.[5] Many others had shared Acton's opinion of

Mazzini. Harriet Martineau had called him 'the most dangerous obstruction in the path of free Italy', and Elizabeth Barrett Browning's view was that 'Mazzini deserves what I should be sorry to inflict. He is a man without conscience',[6] and there had long been a potent cloak-and-dagger myth of Mazzini as a bloodthirsty revolutionary who would stop at nothing to achieve his ends.[7] The appearance of Mazzini in a George Eliot novel in 1876 is perhaps surprising then, given that after 1861 Eliot and Lewes, like many others, had effectively abandoned him, placing their faith instead in constitutional means as preferable to the misery caused by further insurrection in Italy. Eliot and Lewes' 'hero' was clearly not the raiser of insurrection, the diabolical cloak-and-dagger revolutionary despised by Acton and others, but rather the thinker, 'visionary' and 'prophet' of pro-Mazzini propaganda and of English liberal-intellectual perceptions of events in Italy. Eliot's admiration permeates wherever Mazzini is mentioned in her writings, though she consistently divorces him from any concrete political context.

There are, I think, a number of broad correspondences between the eponymous hero of *Daniel Deronda* and Mazzini which might lead one to believe that Deronda was in part inspired by, if not actually modelled on, the Italian revolutionary. Eliot has to work quite hard to establish a credible background for Daniel, to 'thread the hidden pathways of feeling and thought which lead up to... action' at the end of the novel.[8] Like Mazzini, Daniel has read Sismondi's *History of the Italian Republics*. Reading about the medieval Popes and their nephews heightens his consciousness of being himself a 'nephew' and not a 'son' and helps create in his own mind a sense of the mystery of his birth and the desire to discover his origins, so that his 'own face in the glass had during many years been associated for him with thoughts of someone whom he must be like' (p.226). These secrets, the 'new thoughts [which] seemed like falling flakes of fire to his imagination' (p.206),[9] help to 'intensify [the] inward experience' which is essential to his visionary make up. Sismondi also nurtures in Daniel a 'love of universal history, which made him want to be at home in foreign countries' (p.220). The *History of the Italian Republics*, tracing Italian history up to 1748 and arguing that the true Italian character had been weakened by specific historical factors including foreign oppression and the power of the Catholic Church, stands at the beginning of the *Risorgimento* quest for a national identity by justifying and giving focus to the agenda which many of the young revolutionaries of the early nineteenth century had set themselves. In the same way, it is also at the beginning of Daniel's quest, influencing him first on a personal, and then a wider social level, and helping to establish him as a highly sensitive and intelligent, if somewhat aloof and contemplative individual of wide sympathies, with a love of history and his fellow men and a feeling for justice and the excluded.

Deronda is like Mazzini in a number of ways. Eliot's tendency, in keeping with a *Risorgimento* spirit of heroism, to derive moral character from physical attributes, to read 'the grand meanings of faces' (p.226), is nowhere more pronounced than in *Daniel Deronda*.[10] She dwells on the 'consecrating power' of Daniel's face as a boy (p.205), 'the firm gravity of his face' and on 'the peculiarity of the gaze which Gwendolen chose to call "dreadful"', though it had really a very mild sort of scrutiny' (p.226).[11] Nobility of countenance and striking physical presence were among the ingredients Eliot required for her heroic type, and she has Mordecai search the portraits of the National Gallery for 'a face at once young, grand, and beautiful, where, if there is any melancholy, it is no feeble passivity, but enters into the foreshadowed capability of heroism' (p.529). Eliot's portrait is not unlike contemporary descriptions of Mazzini which, in their insistence on his gravity of face and penetrating yet sympathetic eyes, all tended to romanticize and mythologize him: 'His appearance was ... very striking; he had a high and prominent forehead, black, flashing eyes, fine olive features, set in a mass of thick black hair, a grave, serious face, that could look hard at times, but readily melted into the kindliest of smiles'.[12] It is quite possible, then, that Eliot had in mind her own memories of Mazzini or accounts of his appearance in creating Daniel.

Deronda has clearly read and been inspired by Mazzini: 'Look into Mazzini's account of his first yearning, when he was a boy, after a restored greatness and a new freedom to Italy, and of his first efforts as a young man to rouse the same feelings in other young men, and get them to work towards a united nationality' (p.595). Daniel refers to a *specific* text here, namely Mazzini's autobiographical account of 1861 which opens with the 'refugees of Italy' episode, famous in Italian *Risorgimento* mythology, in which after a chance encounter in Genoa with a man asking for money (actually one of the defeated revolutionists of the 1821 Piedmontese insurrection, 'a tall black-bearded man, with a severe countenance and fiery glance ... [who] held out a white handkerchief towards us saying "For the refugees of Italy"') the young Mazzini receives his mission when, haunted by the memory of that face, he began to realize that 'Italians *could* and therefore *ought* to struggle' for liberty.[13] This chance meeting, then, is charged with significance in signalling the beginning of Mazzini's quest. In *Daniel Deronda*, also full of chance meetings and coincidences, there is something of that same prophetic momentousness in Daniel's first meeting with Mordecai, who is himself associated with the great Italian *Risorgimento* prophet, Dante.[14] Mordecai's figure, too, is 'startling in its unusualness', a 'strange... blend of the unwonted with the common'. There is an uncanny moment of recognition when, as their eyes meet, the idea of some 'prophet of the Exile, or... some New Hebrew poet of the medieval time' flashes across Daniel's mind. As in Mazzini's account of *his* experience, Daniel is haunted by the memory of this meeting with Mordecai, whose figure had 'bitten itself into Deronda's mind as a new question' (p.528) in a way which echoes the 'refugees of Italy' episode, to which Eliot later alludes. Daniel receives *his* mission when he meets his mother, the singer Alchirisi, in Genoa and learns his true identity. While in Genoa he considers his new circumstances:

> That young energy and spirit of adventure which have helped to create the world-wide legends of youthful heroes going to seek the hidden tokens of their birth and its inheritance of tasks, gave him a certain quivering interest in the bare possibility that he was entering on a like track – all the more because the track was one of thought as well as action. (pp.573–4)

This generalized account of going forth to seek 'the hidden tokens of... birth and its inheritance of tasks' parallels the specific Mazzinian subtext to which Daniel refers, and there is even an echo of Mazzini's motto 'thought and action' in Daniel's speculation that his 'track [might be] one of thought as well as action'.[15] Genoa, then, becomes for Daniel, as it had been for Mazzini, a starting point, a place charged with possibilities, where old categories and identities are broken down and new ones established. There is, I believe, a tribute to Mazzini intended in Eliot's placing of the defining event in Daniel's life in *Genoa*, the birthplace of the *Risorgimento* 'prophet of Italy'. 'Almost everything seemed against [Mazzini]:' says Daniel: 'his countrymen were ignorant or indifferent, governments hostile, Europe incredulous. Of course the scorners often seemed wise. Yet you see the prophecy lay with him' (p.595). And Eliot of course intends that, by association with the name of Mazzini, Daniel's own Zionist project should appear the more credible, for Daniel takes up his mission at the place where Mazzini's may be said to have begun and at a time, 1866, when Italian unity was nearing completion.

Where initially Daniel questions 'whether it were worthwhile to take part in the battle of the world' (p.225), by the end of the book his innate altruism takes the form of personal sacrifice for a greater national cause. Eliot's narrator foreshadows this prospect for Daniel early on: 'It is possible (though not greatly believed in at present) to be fond of poverty and take it for a bride, to prefer scoured deal, red quarries, and whitewash for one's private surroundings, to delight in no splendour but what has open doors for the whole nation,...' (p.208). In this coupling of the spirit of self-sacrifice with 'the whole nation', one is again reminded of Mazzini, whose complete dedication to his cause, modest lifestyle and rigorous morality had earned him the respect and admiration of English liberals. As early as 1844, Carlyle had called him 'a man of genius and virtue, a man of sterling veracity, humanity, and nobleness of mind, one of those rare men numerable, unfortunately, but as units in this world, who are worthy to be called martyr souls, who in silence piously in their daily life, understand and practice what is meant by that'.[16] In the years immediately after the Roman Republic (1849) British liberals tended to see in Mazzini a symbol of the new Italy soon to be reborn and purified, and it was in the early 1850s, when Eliot was at the *Westminster*, that this particularly *English Risorgimento* myth took shape. Eliot was well aware of course of the sacrifice involved for Mazzini personally; Lewes had long been involved in fund-raising and Eliot herself was ready to contribute to a fund for Mazzini's personal use.[17] Without wishing to overemphasize this point, the existence of a number of broad parallels with a British liberal version of a noble, self-sacrificing and depoliticized Mazzini suggests that here, as elsewhere in the novel, there is a conscious attempt to harness the energies of the Italian *Risorgimento*, to re-evoke memories of a strong British sympathy and engagement with the Italian struggle and the protagonists of a generation earlier, in support of Eliot's own prophecy of a Jewish national revival.

The gambling scene which opens *Daniel Deronda*, discussed earlier in this chapter, is also a dark representation of the Europe of the late 1860s and early 1870s, and it sets the tone for the story which develops in a medium that is constantly being intruded on by reminders of a harsh British and European militarism: Nesslerode, the Russian soldier and diplomat is mentioned, as are 'the late Teutonic conquests' of Bismarck; a 'discussion of military man-oeuvres' (involving a clergyman) is interrupted; the narrator com-ments that 'The time-honoured British resource of "killing something" is no longer carried on with bow and quiver;... Arch-ery has no ugly smell of brimstone; breaks nobody's shins,...' (p.134); and again the narrator denounces 'the correct Englishman, drawing himself up from his bow into rigidity, assenting severely, and seeming to be in a state of internal drill' (p.145). The Gwendo-len/Grandcourt relationship, too, is characterized in terms of empire and subjection. Gwendolen 'was going to have indefinite power' over her husband, who would 'declare himself [her] slave'; his courtship of her is a 'war policy', a 'campaign' and, as the images become increasingly violent, he 'require[s]...that she should be as fully aware as she would have been of a locked hand-cuff, that her inclination was helpless to decide anything in contradiction with his resolve' (p.465); his 'speech was like a sharp knife-edge drawn across her skin' (p.662) and he gains 'an intense satisfaction in leading his wife captive' while enjoying 'the piquancy of despotism' (p.736). William Myers sees Grandcourt as the embodiment of a spirit of brutal faithlessness, based on political agnosticism and a will to violence, which, in the 1870s was 'a new and virulent threat to the humanism on which [Eliot] based her life.' In Grandcourt, 'perfect gentlemanly detachment is in secret alliance with "Blood and Iron"'.[18] Grandcourt's 'perfect gentlemanly detachment' is also in alliance with British colonialism for, as the ruthless governor of a difficult colony, 'with a little murdering he might get a title' (pp.128, 655).

Against this is ranged the rather more optimistic historical movement traced in the Italian material in *Daniel Deronda*. At the beginning of the novel there is passivity of the statuesque Italian constantly losing to the foreign oppressor, followed by despairing plaints from Dante and Leopardi.[19] Much later, Daniel states that 'we are sure soon to see [the unity of Italy] accomplished to the very last boundary' (p.595), in a nationalist discourse which reproduces the *Risorgimento* idea, stretching back to Dante, that there *were* 'natural' boundaries, so that his statement stands against the imperialist discourses found elsewhere in the novel. After Daniel's own Leopardian call to arms (pp.619–20),[20] the later stages of the *Risorgimento* obtrude upon the present of the novel in 1866:

'What on earth is the wonderful news?' said Mrs Meyrick,...
'Anything about Italy – anything about the Austrians giving up
Venice?'

'Nothing about Italy, but something from Italy,' said Hans,
with a peculiarity in his tone and manner which set his mother
interpreting. [...]

...'What *is* it that has happened?'

'[Grandcourt] is drowned, and [Gwendolen] is alive, that's all,'
said Hans,... (pp.793–4)

Eliot nicely juxtaposes the two sets of events here, to signal release
from oppression at both personal and national levels by linking the
news of Gwendolen's delivery from the despotic Grandcourt –
which also takes place in Genoa – to the struggles of the new nation
to complete its liberation. And readers of *Daniel Deronda* in 1876 and
after would of course have the certainty that the Italian prophecy
had indeed been fulfilled, with the inclusion of Venice in 1866 and
then Rome in 1870. Daniel's own statement of his life's work, which
echoes Mazzini's first halting steps in the account to which Daniel
had alluded, comes at the culmination of this arc of Italian history,
and draws force from the Italian analogue:

The idea that I am possessed with is that of restoring a political
existence to my people, making them a nation again, giving them
a national centre,... That is a task which presents itself to me as a
duty: I am resolved to begin it, however feebly. I am resolved to
devote my life to it. At the least, I may awaken a movement in
other minds, such as has been awakened in my own. (p. 875)

The project for a Jewish nation which Daniel inherits from his
grandfather Charisi and from Mordecai foresees the revival of the
'organic centre' and the achievement of a 'balance of separateness
and communication' (p.791). Although wholly decontextualized
and necessarily beyond the European context of the novel, this
task is aligned with the nationalism espoused by Mazzini, in
which the State, representing the general will, and the Nation,
representing a homogeneous people, should be co-extensive, and
physical and ethnological boundaries were seen as the 'natural'
confines of states. This 'continental' nationalism provided an alternative model to both pre-*Risorgimento* continental notions of empire
in which the state might itself include different races and national-

ities, and to the climate of expansionism which prevailed in the 1860s and 1870s and which Eliot felt the need to warn against. In the midst of her dark vision of European militarism and an arrogant expansionism, the Italian material in *Daniel Deronda*, evoking memories of the heady days of the *Risorgimento* successes, generates hope for Daniel's project of restoring a political existence to his people. Picking up on this Italian theme in a review in 1876, a sympathetic reviewer puts it succinctly:

> The transformation of...Deronda, [and his] readiness...to undertake a national mission of the most improbable realisation, only proves an amount of belief in possibilities which all great men who have achieved difficult enterprises must have shared. The unity of Italy half a century since appeared as idle a dream as may now seem the reassembling of Israel in its own kingdom. Garibaldi and Mazzini were regarded as fanatics and visionaries, yet the leader of the thousand of Marsala has sat in the Parliament of United Italy which holds its meetings in the Eternal City.[21]

Daniel Deronda, then, is the locus of a conflict between, on the one hand, the aggressive nationalism and arrogant imperialism which Eliot saw emerging in Britain and Europe in the 1870s and, on the other, a moral humanist, though essentially depoliticized, vision of the possibility of a Jewish nationalism, which is born in Deronda by the end of the novel and owes some of its inspiration to the Italian *Risorgimento*.

Mazzini's nationalism was part of a wider world view based on a belief in the infinite progress of mankind towards the 'Great Society of Man' which transcended national boundaries. To this end, Mazzini had promoted an outward-looking European literature[22] which would reach forward towards Europeanism and a universal humanity. Although working in the very different context of the 1870s, Eliot is, I believe, consciously writing in this humanist tradition in incorporating other literatures, European and non- (often in the original languages), into *Daniel Deronda*, where she appears to be testing that formula of 'separateness and communication'. Eliot venerates both her own national past and that of other countries and consistently, and with varying degrees of explicitness, condemns manifestations of prejudice and ignorance associated with the insularity of the English characters, few of whom actually escape her irony. Literature in *Daniel Deronda* becomes a way of moving beyond insular discourse and affirming 'other' ways of perceiving universal human experience, of 'discern[ing] likeness amidst diversity'.[23] Eliot herself sets up, and then breaks down, national identities for her characters: Daniel and Mirah are at the same time English, European and Jewish, and Klesmer 'looks forward to a fusion of races', but significantly, even abroad, Milord Grandcourt and his wife remain firmly 'English'. The English, with their increasingly insular discourse and the prejudices, misconceptions and arrogance to which this gives rise, are repeatedly exposed and condemned for their separateness *without* communication. In her text, Eliot self-consciously enacts both the creation of separate national identities and the fusion of these identities into a wider humanity. Her vision reflects her essential humanism, her 'religion of humanity', and is boldly stated despite the direction in which European, and particularly British, politics were moving.

* * * * *

Eliot and Lewes returned to Italy on two more occasions after their 1861 trip to research *Romola*. In 1864, after Eliot had finished this novel, they went in the company of the painter Frederick Leighton, stopping in Turin and Milan before moving to Venice where they stayed three weeks and where Eliot conceived the idea for *The Spanish Gypsy*. They took a further three weeks on the homeward journey via Padua, Verona and Milan reaching London on June 20th. Five years later, the couple returned to Florence, staying once more with the Trollopes, before going on to Naples by train, and from there to Rome. They returned this time via Florence, Ravenna and Verona. Both Eliot and Lewes were ill during this 1869 trip and were glad to be home after an exhausting journey spoiled, as Eliot told Henry James, by the 'evil faces: oh the evil faces'.[24] In 1880, over a year after the death of Lewes, Eliot returned to Italy in what was to be her only continental trip in her new life with John Cross. The couple retraced the steps of Eliot's earlier journeys with Lewes, travelling slowly through the north of Italy, spending a week in Milan on their way to Venice. Eliot's love for this 'enchanting city' remained undiminished, though she was forced to admit that 'man is somewhat vile'. Liberation from the Austrian yoke had apparently done nothing for the aspect of the Venetian populace, who 'even physically ... look[ed] less endowed than I thought them when we were here under the Austrian dominion. We have hardly seen a sweet or noble woman's face since we arrived, but the men are not so ill-looking as the women.'[25] During the second week in Venice, Cross had 'a sharp but brief attack',[26] and jumped from his hotel balcony into the Grand Canal, probably suffering from some form of mental depression. Cross himself glossed over the incident as an illness resulting from the effects of too much sun, lack of physical exercise and the bad air at night from the Grand Canal,[27] but whatever its cause, it shook Eliot greatly and the Italian honeymoon ended rather abruptly. After their return from Italy, although the relationship with Cross was good, Eliot realized that it was not like that with Lewes and, as Jennifer Uglow says, one detects a determined cheerfulness in her letters which 'fights against an emptiness beneath'.[28]

In the years after the publication of *Daniel Deronda*, Eliot returned to Dante, and there is evidence of her interest in the Florentine and in Italy in *Impressions of Theophrastus Such*, published in 1878. The picture which emerges here confirms Eliot's vision of an Italy where the *Risorgimento* was the culmination of a history which, through 'invisible motion' had been preparing a 'visible birth' over the centuries and in which the elements of memory and cultural transmission are ultimately more important than any particular configuration of political, social or economic forces. Consequently, Eliot did not need to examine the political vicissitudes of the *Risorgimento* in any great detail or test what sometimes appear to be rather naïve statements against contemporary events, and she merely hints that the Italian nation had not yet been perfected:

… the pathos of his country's lot pierced the youthful soul of Mazzini, because, like Dante's, his blood was fraught with the kinship of Italian greatness, his imagination filled with a majestic past that wrought itself into a majestic future. Half a century ago, what was Italy? An idling-place of dilettanteism or of itinerant motiveless wealth, a territory parcelled out for papal sustenance, dynastic convenience, and the profit of an alien Government. What were the Italians? No people, no voice in European counsels, no massive power in European affairs: a race thought of in English and French society as chiefly adapted to the operatic stage, or to serve as models for painters; disposed to smile gratefully at the reception of halfpence; and by the more historical remembered to be rather polite than truthful, in all probability a combination of Machiavelli, Rubini, and

Masaniello. Thanks chiefly to the divine gift of a memory which inspires the moments with a past, a present, and a future, and gives the sense of corporate existence that raises man above the otherwise more respectable and innocent brute, all that, or most of it, is changed.[29]

As in *Daniel Deronda*, so in 'The Modern Hep! Hep! Hep!', the *Risorgimento* is simply allowed to stand as the great historical achievement of the nineteenth century and as an inspiration in the battle against what Eliot calls British 'historic rapacity and arrogant notions of our own superiority'.[30]

In the last months of her life with Lewes, who died after a brief illness on November 30th, 1878, Eliot reread Dante. In July Lewes wrote: 'I get up at 6, and before breakfast take a solitary ramble... which I can't get Madonna to share. Instead of this, she sits up in bed and buries herself in Dante or Homer.'[31] Eliot's own correspondence reflects her reading and, increasingly in her letters, she filters her own feelings and experience through Dante quotation and allusion. On the subject of Charles Bray's health she wrote to Cara that

> He is sure to make the most of each good, and will not be punished in the Dantesque circle of mud, as one who 'piange là dove esser dei giocondo,' or even in the fog, with those who say 'Tristi fummo nell'aer dolce che'l sol rilume.' I fear that I have often deserved those severe ways of being 'made to know better.'[32]

Edith Simcox remembers Eliot quoting from Dante on October 13th, 1878: 'In the afternoon they went for a long lovely drive; they had never had a happier day and she quoted from Dante (a passage she asked me to find) that they would never see the Dawn of such a day again...'.[33] Eliot herself playfully points out her own paraphrase of Dante in a letter to Mrs Burne-Jones: '... Let me know this good and satisfy the thirsty sponge of my affection. If you object to my phrase please observe that it is Dantesque – which will oblige you to find it admirable.'[34]

After Lewes' death, Eliot's interest in Dante is sustained and the poet is quoted (and sometimes misquoted) in her letters more frequently than at any other time in her life. By coincidence, the development of her relationship with John Cross was also closely bound up with Dante. Deeply affected by the loss of Lewes, Eliot had for a while remained shut up with her grief, seeing no one. She slowly returned to life, writing to Barbara Bodichon in January 1879, and to Cross, who she began seeing often. He, too, was trying to overcome grief at the loss of his mother who had died only a week after Lewes, and had begun reading Dante's *Inferno* with John Carlyle's translation. Cross reports that, on hearing of his new pursuit, Eliot's immediate reaction was 'Oh, I must read that with you':

> In the following twelve months we read through the 'Inferno' and the 'Purgatorio' together – not in a *dilettante* way, but with the minute and careful examination of the construction of every sentence. The prodigious stimulus of such a teacher (*cotanto maestro*) made the reading a real labour of love. Her sympathetic delight in stimulating my newly awakened enthusiasm for Dante, did something to distract her mind from sorrowful memories. The divine poet took us into a new world. It was a renovation of life.[35]

They probably began reading Dante together in April or May of 1879 and this 'labour of love', something she might also have done with Lewes, was instrumental in bringing them closer together.

The Dante included in her letters in the year following Lewes' death tends to reflect her deep underlying sorrow. It is surely not simply coincidence that she refers only to the *Inferno* at this time. She draws once again, poignantly, on the lines from *Inferno* VII (121–2) which she reserved for the state of melancholy against which she felt it her duty to struggle:

> As for me, I try to make life as interesting as I can, and everybody is good to me. But I am of course more uninterruptedly alone here, and friendship comes to me chiefly in letters. The silence and beauty of this spot would be bliss to me but for – what I cannot write about. I have simply to live, and I must live as well as I can, making myself as little as possible a burthen on the earth and trying not to be one of that crowd whom Dante puts in the chill mud, making them confess,
> > ... Tristi fummo
> > nell'aer dolce che'l Sol rallume.
> There is no virtue in gloom which is the easiest hiding-place for languid idleness.[36]

As Gordon Haight comments, 'the luxury of grief was an indul-gence her intellect had long rejected', though after Lewes' death 'her own works scourged her'.[37]

In October, 'ugly London' seemed to her to be 'something of a Dante limbo, a preliminary circle of the Inferno'. Four days later, wishing to excuse herself for sending a 'little doggish whimper asking for attention' and to dispel Georgie Burne-Jones' remorse at not writing earlier, Eliot quotes the words with which Virgil softens his earlier reproach to Dante, who has been overcurious at the noisy squabble of the sinners in the Malebolge: ' "Maggior difetto men vergogna lava" as says Virgil to the blushing Dante'.[38] In December 1879, in replying to Elma Stuart's letter sent from Florence, she alludes to the cantos of the betrayers in *Inferno*:

> I comfort my mind with thinking that you have found comfort-able rooms and a comfortable host. Otherwise, this cold time in Florence would make one think of Dante's frozen tears. We were one spring at the Victoria Hotel on the Arno, so that I can imagine your view – just as I can imagine your beds and pillows. The pillows were the worst torture.[39]

Eliot agreed to marry John Cross on April 9th, 1880, the wedding took place on May 6th, and the couple immediately set off for Italy to evade the shocked reactions of friends who had been given scant warning of Eliot's intentions. Their itinerary was very similar to those of earlier trips with Lewes, and Eliot's letters display a renewed excitement and enthusiasm about being in Italy again:

> Dearest Florence,
>   Our life since we wrote to you has been a chapter of delights, worthy of paragraphs with sensational headings of American enthusiasm – Grenoble, unsurpassable position! Grande Char-treuse, inexpressible sublimity and beauty! Chambéry, paradisi-acal walk to Les Charmettes! Roses gathered in Jean Jacques' garden! Modane, illustrative of Dante's Purgatorio! Souls in penance eating an infant chicken, the size of a lark! Mont Cenis tunnel and emergence into Italian sunshine![40]

Cross too, full of Dante and Italian culture, writes from Verona:

> This is *the* most delicious town you can conceive – molto molto pittoresquo e sympatico – a very proper place for Romeo and

Juliet. The Capulets palace is within a few doors of this hotel and one can see the balcony cette chère creature leaned out of. Also the stairs of Can Grande's palace where poor Dante found how salt was the bread of another as you will no doubt remember in your Purgatorio...
[...]
...this beautiful city...in a great bend of the swiftly flowing Adige, over which there are 5 very picturesque bridges and the sense that our dear Dante might have been there, and no doubt often was – musing on the hardness of his lot as an exile.[41]

'Mia Donna continues in excellent form' he reports: 'We have not talked to another soul since we left England and if I don't become very wise with Cotanta Amante, guide, philosopher, and friend – well I ought to!' The tone of this letter is light-hearted, but Cross casts himself implicitly in the roles of stilnovista poet and Dante-pilgrim to Eliot's 'Donna' and Virgil, thus pointing up his own awareness of the unequal nature of the relationship. It is perhaps inevitable that George Eliot who was 20 years Cross' senior should have become the 'guide' and Cross, aware that he was (almost literally) following in Lewes' footsteps in Italy, the pupil. Their reading of Dante would only highlight this difference and thus played a part in 'fixing' these roles and, what is more, they seem to have enjoyed this game: Eliot signs herself 'Beatrice' in a letter to Cross[42] and he, like Dorothea in Rome who 'felt that she was getting quite new notions as to the significance of Madonnas seated under inexplicable canopied thrones', finds that, under *cotanto maestro*, 'My knowledge of early art is becoming surprising to myself! Imbued with the spirit of Cimabue and Giotto I come to my Mantegna and find him adequate'.[43] Cross took care to present their relationship as one of guide–pupil in his *Life*, and he and Eliot create a romanticized and rather sentimentalized Dante ('we read our dear old Cantos of the Inferno that we were reading a year ago')[44] with great redemptive powers. Eliot herself, in a reversing of roles, felt she had been rescued by Cross from a Dantesque Inferno of withering solitude akin to Gwendolen's in *Daniel Deronda*: 'I was getting hard, and...I think I should have become very selfish', and again, 'I had thought that my life was ended, and that, so to speak, my coffin was ready for me in the next room'.[45] She now found that 'I am able to enjoy my newly reopened life', and that 'I seem to have recovered the loving sympathy that I was in danger of losing. I mean that I had been conscious of a certain drying up of tenderness in me, and that the spring seems to have risen again.'[46] Eliot herself had struggled with the darkness of grief, solitude and depression and Edith Simcox believed that this goes some way to explaining her union with Cross for, writes Simcox, Eliot's knowledge of his precarious state of mental health 'throws a flood of light upon the relation and on Her previous enthusiasm of admiration for one who led so cheerily a busy, useful life in spite of such impending cloud'.[47]

Gordon Haight takes up the comparison, offered by Cross himself in referring to Eliot as 'Cotanta Amante' (sic), between the couple and the great love of Paolo and Francesca in *Inferno* V:

> In a new *solitude à deux* in the summer house at Witley she and Johnny studied the *Divine Comedy*. With her soft, low voice, *soave e piane*, Marian read him those wonderful words,
>
> Nessun maggior dolore,
> Che ricordarsi del tempo felice
> Nella miseria.
>
> In August there came a day when in that book they read no more.[48]

This biographical fleshing out of the details of the Eliot–Cross relationship acknowledges the power of the words from *Inferno* V from a scene which Eliot had incorporated into *Felix Holt, Middlemarch* and *Daniel Deronda*, and which took on such personal significance for her once she had lost her own happiness with Lewes' death. Daniel Waley, probably following Haight, comments that 'reading Dante together played a part in transmuting friendship with J. W. Cross into romance. Was the Paolo and Francesca episode an influence? If so, they were too shy to record it.'[49] It *is* recorded of course, albeit indirectly, in Cross' (perhaps rather insensitive) 'Cotanta Amante' (sic) from *Inferno* V in his letter (see above). Haight also picks up on Eliot's own identification of herself with Beatrice, comparing the quality of Eliot's voice with the 'angelica voce' of Beatrice as reported by Virgil in *Inferno* II,[50] to further mythologize what to some appeared a ludicrous and embarrassing relationship by 'explaining' it as a 'great love'. Haight's comparison only works, however, if we suppress the strong overtones of transgression in the Paolo and Francesca episode, aspects to which Eliot had herself been sensitive in *Middlemarch*.[51] For indeed, the whole relationship and the subsequent marriage had an air of transgression: Eliot was 20 years older than Cross, which in itself flouted social convention and, fearing the judgements of friends of hers and Lewes', she had kept silent about the relationship until it could no longer be hidden.[52]

Friends and observers seemed drawn to compare Dante's physiognomy with Eliot's, and in addition to the obvious compliment to her in being associated with the great Florentine poet, the comparison was another way of casting George Eliot as Victorian sage. Eliot also possessed likenesses of both Dante and Savonarola and had more than a passing interest in Dante's physiognomy, as the lengthy note on 'Dante's Skull and mask' her Folger Notebook for *Middlemarch* testifies.[53] Thomas Adolphus Trollope, for example, writes:

> She had been compared to the portraits of Savonarola (who was frightful) and of Dante (who though stern and bitter-looking, was handsome). *Something* there was of both faces in George Eliot's physiognomy. Lewes told us in her presence, of the exclamation uttered suddenly by someone to whom she was pointed out at a place of public entertainment – I believe it was at a Monday Popular Concert in St. James's Hall. 'That,' said a bystander 'is George Eliot.' The gentleman to whom she was thus indicated gave one swift, searching look and exclaimed *sotto voce*, 'Dante's aunt!' Lewes thought this happy, and he recognised the kind of likeness that was meant to the great singer of the *Divine Comedy*.[54]

Eliot does not resist such comparisons and indeed, writing to Mrs Elma Stuart of F.W. Burton's portrait of her, uses Dante to correct what she saw as a poor likeness of her: 'As to the portrait, I am not one bit like it – besides it was taken eight years ago. Imagine a first cousin of the old Dante's – rather smoke-dried – a face with lines in it that seem a map of sorrows'.[55] Eliot's own readiness to identify with Dante, then, seems also to have extended to courting a physical resemblance. Brett Harte, who visited Eliot in January 1880, wrote to a friend

> I was very pleasantly disappointed in her appearance, having heard so much of the plainness of her features. And I found

them only strong, intellectual, and *noble* – indeed, I have seldom seen a grander face! I have read somewhere that she looked like a horse – a great mistake, as, although her face is long and narrow, it is only as Dante's was. It expresses elevation of thought, kindness, power, and *humour*.[56]

What people saw in portraits of Dante changed over the course of the nineteenth century as views of his work changed as serious scholarship gradually replaced fragmented and anecdotal evidence, and as the two main sources for Dante's physiognomy (the Tofanelli and the Stothard portraits, neither of which can have been genuine) showing the poet as 'a crabbed old man'[57] were supplemented after 1840 by the Bargello portrait. Here, Dante appears as a young man in his late twenties, 'not the mask of a corpse of 56 – a ruin – but a fine, noble image of the Hero of Campaldino, the Lover of Beatrice …A parchment book under his arm – perhaps the *Vita Nuova*'.[58] Both the Tofanelli and the Stothard portraits had been gloomy, emphasizing the 'grim Dante' of the Romantics. To these were added the description by Boccaccio (of a retired individual wrapped up in his studies and with a face melancholy and pensive) and a number of reported incidents from Dante's life which showed him to be a sullen, misanthropic and humourless individual.[59] Thus, Macaulay's Dante had '[stood] amidst those smiling and radiant spirits with that scowl of unutterable misery on his brow, and that curl of bitter disdain on his lips, which all his portraits have preserved,…' and Carlyle saw a Dante hardened and 'ruined' by experience:

> I think it is the mournfulest face that ever was painted from reality; an altogether tragic, heart-affecting face. There is in it, as foundation of it, the softness, tenderness, gentle affection as of a child; but all this is as if congealed into sharp contradiction, into abnegation, isolation, proud hopeless pain.[60]

From mid century onwards, though, the influence of the Bargello Dante came to be felt. Thus Henry Clark Barlow in 1864, criticizing Frederick Leighton's picture *Dante in Exile* which pictures a melancholy humourless Dante in Can Grande's court in Verona aloof from the lovers on one side of him and the jester on the other, quotes the same line later chosen by Eliot in her letter to Cara Bray in 1878 as a way of staving off melancholy[61]

[Dante] would not have gone with a sour face to a feast. He, who had doomed, along with suicides, the ungrateful wretch who is sad when he ought to rejoice,

> 'E piange là dov'esser dee giocondo' (*Inf.* XI.45)

would not have condemned himself by wearing the aspect of melancholy at a public festival.[62]

Ruskin, though, comments of the Bargello Dante that it is, 'in its quiet, earnest, determined, gentle sadness, the very type of the spirit of the good men of his time... you cannot conceive a smile on such a face'.[63] The 'grim' Dante of the Romantics is replaced by a more 'human' figure and, while the superficial facial features are retained, they are now associated with a different range of character traits. Brett Harte's impression of Eliot's features also reflects the change in perceptions of Dante: although 'her face is long and narrow, it is only as Dante's was. It expresses elevation of thought, kindness, power, and *humour*' (Brett Harte's emphasis).

Eliot herself, fully aware of various Dantes, likens herself to 'the old' Dante, but softens the hardness of the Stothard portrait: 'Imagine *a first cousin* of the old Dante's' (my italics). She aligns herself with the tradition of 'grim' Dante ('rather smoke-dried') though the fierceness is gone while the sorrow remains, and she draws hers as 'a face with lines in it that seem a map of sorrows'. She becomes the world-weary Dante marked by experience: 'Deep down below there is a hidden river of sadness but this must always be with those who have lived long'.[64] Far from the bitter, scornful, disdainful Dante, Eliot's is the knowing, compassionate poet who fights against the melancholy within himself, empathizes strongly with suffering in others, and is himself perfected through suffering. She could not but have been flattered by being likened to a poet whose works she admired so greatly and whose achievement reflected so many of her own artistic aspirations, a poet who was 'at once the most precise and homely in his reproductions of actual objects, and the most soaringly at large in his imaginative combinations',[65] the poet of vision who, with a quintessentially moral conception of art and within a powerful moral framework, achieved that balance between judgement and compassion which Eliot herself came to see as essential to the future of civilization.

* * * * *

George Eliot's engagement with Italy and with its culture was deep and sustained over almost the whole of her life, and this remains true in spite of the fact that in three of her novels, *Adam Bede*, *The Mill on the Floss* and *Silas Marner*, there is little or no evidence of any Italian interest. These three novels were written within a period of less than five years between 1857 (soon after 'Mr Gilfil's Love Story') and 1861 when *Silas Marner*, which had 'thrust itself between' Eliot and her Italian novel *Romola*, was published.[66] The writing of the story of the weaver of Raveloe, however, was itself framed by the two visits to Italy in 1860 and 1861 with Lewes to gather the fresh ideas and new inspiration which were to permeate all her fiction from 1861 onwards.

Eliot's whole career as a novelist owes much to G.H. Lewes, and his importance in the context of Eliot's contact with Italy and its literature cannot be overstated. Long before the couple met, Lewes already knew the language, history and literature of the country well, had promulgated *Risorgimento* readings of Italian literature in his writings, actively supported European nationalisms, and was in contact with exiles and revolutionists, including Mazzini. Lewes brought this rich experience to the relationship with George Eliot, who shared his enthusiasm and interest. Together they read and discussed Italian literature from Dante to Alfieri and Leopardi and together they discovered the country whose culture they admired and with whose struggles for liberation they had long sympathized, giving a local habitation and a name to the places which had fired their imaginations.

The later novels reveal a deep knowledge of and close engagement with the work of Dante Alighieri. Eliot admired the power of his writing, his homely images and soaring conceptions, and respected his moral rigour and the internal coherence and beauty of his vision. Many of the qualities which she singled out for praise in the Florentine not surprisingly reflected her own aspirations and intentions as an artist. Eliot drew increasingly and ever more assuredly upon Dante, establishing and reinforcing her moral vision by appropriating the authority of his within her novels. The intertextuality at work in these borrowings almost always repays detailed examination and consistently reveals a play of analogy, metaphor and ironic comment operating at various levels of complexity, with significance locally and also resonating outwards over the whole. Dante underpins Eliot's own moral universe, functioning as a touchstone against which character is tested and pointing up the direction of moral change, whether this be progression or regression. In *Romola*, *Felix Holt, the Radical* and *Daniel Deronda* Eliot deals insistently with choice and the consequences which follow as determining the destiny of the individual. However, the Dante with which she comes to identify is not the grim, scornful and severe figure of Romantic tradition, but rather the poet who manifests immense fellow-feeling, whose severity of judgement is tempered by compassion, and whose face is lined with the sorrow of his own suffering and that of humanity generally. This Dante was well suited to Eliot's own moral outlook, and his 'sacred poem' could provide the overarching metaphors for moral growth through suffering and help establish the framework in which this might take place. Thus, much of Eliot's allusion is to the first two cantiche, which are more congenial to her particular brand of meliorism. Moreover, in Eliot's godless universe, morality had to be justifiable in purely human terms so that there could be no place in her work for the suggestion of other-worldly reward for present suffering which Dante's *Paradiso* might imply. Eliot's Hell and Purgatory were here 'on the green Earth', and though with Will Ladislaw in *Middlemarch*, she might occasionally ascend as far as the Earthly Paradise, even here there could only be a 'difficult blessedness', after which, like Dante's Virgil in the *Comedy*, Eliot could follow no further. That blessedness might occasionally be achieved in the encounter with a Beatrice/Dorothea 'the effect of [whose] being on those around her [is] incalculably diffusive', who has redemptive powers over individuals and is a force for moral good in the world. Yet that encounter is withheld from Gwendolen at the end of *Daniel Deronda*, and can only be conceived as a hazy and far-off goal requiring an arduous and perilous ascent in the uncertain future beyond the close of the novel.

In Eliot's assimilation of the Italian *Risorgimento*, a clear division emerges between those works which portray a pre-*Risorgimento* condition of subjection and stasis, and those in which the Italian prophecy of liberation has been or is about to be fulfilled. 'Mr Gilfil's Love Story' reflects the historical condition of Italy until the time of writing (1857), when there was no real sign that Unification was imminent. The interwoven narratives of the subjection of women and of Italy itself share a common language and imagery and both end in defeat. The silencing and finding of a voice (recurring themes in Eliot's work belonging to discourses of both sexual and national oppression) are explored in the Italian context of

Eliot's earliest fiction, and Caterina's story, narrated as a cycle of oppression and exploitation – anger – rebellion – exile – surrender and death, can be read as an allegory both of the as yet unresolved struggles in Italy to achieve a national identity and of the condition of women oppressed by patriarchy. Eliot's text resists earlier nineteenth-century British prejudices against Italians, though I have suggested that it relies heavily upon the very stereotyping it purports to eschew. Like 'Mr Gilfil's Love Story', *Middlemarch* registers the often negative attitudes towards Italians prevailing in the 1820s and 1830s around the time when the novel is set and, like 'Mr Gilfil', exposes many of these as outdated prejudices which the discerning reader of Eliot's fiction from the late 1850s onwards would be expected to reject. In neither 'Mr Gilfil's Love Story' nor *Middlemarch*, however, can Italian history be perceived as leading towards the ultimate goal of national Unification.

In *Romola* and *Daniel Deronda*, by contrast, Eliot sketches out the great *Risorgimento* epic and brings a teleological reading of Italian history to bear. In *Romola*, the heroine draws together past and present in the tableau which closes the novel, to emerge as a positive icon, a symbol of the achievement of true independence and full maturity. In the present of *Daniel Deronda*, the completion of the *Risorgimento* with the inclusion of Rome into a regenerated Italy was only four years off. In the plot, in the delineation of character, and in the use of Italian locations and musical settings of Italian texts from Dante and Leopardi, I have argued, Eliot's text alludes to or replicates *Risorgimento* mythology, and creates parallels between the character of Daniel and Mazzini. Over the course of the whole novel, this body of allusion constitutes an analogue for Jewish national aspirations. Moreover, in true Dantean fashion, Eliot (in 1876) was able to 'prophecy' the Unification of 1870 in a novel set in 1866, in the certain knowledge that the prophecy *would* be fulfilled. The purposes which Eliot makes her Italian material serve in her last novel, however, are more complex. Unfamiliar Jewish culture is frequently mediated through the more familiar Italian one, which Eliot now consistently presents in a wholly positive light by contrast with her earlier representations of it in 'Mr Gilfil's Love Story' and *Middlemarch*. In the immediate historical context of the 1870s, after the publication of *Daniel Deronda*, the *Risorgimento* and the Unification of Italy stand as a critique of the aggressive militarism of contemporary Europe and act as a paradigm which takes on a prescriptive function, pointing the way in which, through 'separateness and communication', there might be peaceful coexistence between the nations. On a wider level, in *Romola* and in *Daniel Deronda* the Italian *Risorgimento* is allowed to stand as a susbstantive metaphor for the progress of humanity itself, and as a significant stage on that slow journey from egoism to altruism.

Notes

Introduction

1. 'The Intellectual Background of the Novel: Casaubon and Lydgate' reprinted in Watt, I. (ed.) *The Victorian Novel*, (London: OUP 1971) p.313.

Chapter 1

1. GE wrote in 1861, 'Mr Trollope has returned and seduced us into prolonging our stay for another week, in order that we may witness the great national festival of *regenerated* Italy on Sunday;' (my italics). (*Letters* III, p.421).
2. Derek Beales in *The Risorgimento and the Unification of Italy* (London: Longman [1971] 1981, p.14) talks of a 'generalized myth'; Lucy Riall in *The Italian Risorgimento: state, society and national unification*, (London: Routledge 1994, p.2) refers to a 'mythology of national unification'.
3. G. Candeloro defines the *Risorgimento* as 'a movement which led to the formation of the Italian national unitary state' in *Storia dell'Italia moderna*, Vol. I (Milan: Feltrinelli 1956) p.14, cit. Beales, *op. cit.*, p.14; N. Rodolico writes: 'The *Risorgimento* was the spirit of sacrifice, it was the suffering in the ways of exile and in the galleys, it was the blood of Italian youth on the battlefields... it was the passion of a people for its Italian identity.' *Archivio storico italiano* 1960, p.299, cit. Beales, *op. cit.*, p.19.
4. Riall, L., *op. cit.*, pp.5, 9.
5. *Ibid.*, p.9.
6. On this, see Wiesenfarth, J., *George Eliot's Mythmaking* (Heidelberg: Carl Winter Universitätsverlag 1977), which argues that George Eliot's novels present a 'mythology of fellow-feeling' which subsumes specific Hebrew, Christian and pagan myths into its structure; see also Bonaparte, F., *The Tryptich and the Cross: the Central Myths of George Eliot's Poetic Imagination* (New York: New York University Press 1979) which discusses *Romola* as a symbolic structure employing a complex series of mythological images to transform the realistic historical novel into an epic poem.
7. The British Prime Minister Lord Palmerston described the unification as 'miraculous as no one in his senses or in his dreams could have anticipated such continuous success'; 10th November, 1860, Clarendon to Cowley (P.R.O. F.O. 519/178), cit. Beales, *op. cit.*, p.13.
8. Felice Orsini, an ex-Mazzinian patriot, travelled to Paris where he threw three bombs at Napoleon, which, however, left the destroyer of the Roman Republic and the Empress unscathed. Sentenced to death for the assassination attempt, he repented and asked Napoleon

to listen to the appeal of 'a patriot on the steps of the scaffold'. George
Eliot reviewed Felice Orsini's *The Austrian Dungeons in Italy*, in *The
Leader*, August 30th, 1856, p.835. (See Chapter 2.)

9. Beales, D., *England and Italy 1859–60* (London: Nelson 1961) p.8.
10. Piranesi, M., *Reminiscenze* (1852) cit. Trevelyan, G.M., 'Englishmen
    and Italians' in *Recreations of an Historian*, (London: Thomas Nelson
    and Sons Ltd 1919) p.218.
11. Beolchi, *Reminiscenze dell'esilio* (Turin 1852) cit. Brand, C.P., *Italy and
    the English Romantics: the Italianate Fashion in early nineteenth-century
    England*, (Cambridge: CUP 1957) pp.33–4.
12. This impression of Italian dishonesty was strengthened by 'the
    Queen's Affair' (1820) in which Queen Caroline, wife of George IV,
    was tried for adultery. Public opinion was strongly behind the Queen
    when Italian witnesses were called to testify against her: it was
    widely believed that they had been bribed, their testimony was
    revealed to be unreliable and they were lampooned in the press.
13. *Edinburgh Review*, October 1840, LXXII, p.161, cit. Brand, *op. cit.*, p.22.
14. Russell had also translated the *Paolo and Francesca* episode from
    Dante's *Comedy* (*Inferno* V); Gladstone contributed a long article
    on Leopardi to the *Quarterly Review* (Vol. LXXXVI, No. CLXXII,
    pp.294–336) in March 1850.
15. A second edition appeared in 1819, and further editions were pub-
    lished in 1831 and 1844.
16. *Monthly Review*, February 1828, n.s. VII p.258, cit., Brand, *op. cit.*,
    p.211.
17. Trevelyan, *op. cit.*, p.217.
18. For an extended list of works see Rudman, H.W., *Italian Nationalism
    and English Letters*, (London: George Allen & Unwin 1940) pp.419–32.
19. G.M. Young in *Early Victorian England*, Young, G.M., (ed.), p.248, cit.
    Beales *op. cit.*, p.9.
20. Beales, *op. cit.*, p.20.
21. Trevelyan, *op. cit.*, p.213.
22. *Saggio sulla filosofia delle lingue* [1785], ed. M. Puppo, Milan 1969,
    p.105, cit. Caesar, M. (ed.), *Dante: the Critical Heritage 1314(?) – 1870*
    (London: Routledge 1989) p.48.
23. Alfieri wrote: 'Dante wrote without any form of princely protection
    and he is supreme, he lives and will always live; but no protection
    has ever given birth, nor would it be able or worthy to do so, to a
    Dante. On the contrary, where such a man were born, princely
    protection would unfortunately only be a hindrance to him.' Cit.
    Mazzoni, G., 'Dante nell'inizio e nel vigore del risorgimento' in
    Almae luces malae cruces: studii danteschi (Bologna: Nicola Zanichelli
    Editore 1941), p.63 [My translation].
24. Caesar, *op. cit.*, pp.68, 56.
25. Cesare Balbo sets his *Vita* (*Life of Dante*) within a rhetorical frame
    aimed at heightening the importance of his subject. The biography is
    prefaced by the rhetorical statement that, unable to 'portray the life of
    the whole nation, [he] will attempt to portray at least that of the
    Italian who more than any other gathered in himself the talents,

virtues, vices and fortunes of the country'. Moreover, Dante 'is the most Italian Italian there has ever been.' (p. 3). The same rhetoric reappears at the end of the book: 'We began by saying that Dante was the most Italian of the Italians: but now that we know the doings of his life ... we can further conclude that he was the best of Italians. If I am mistaken it is merely the rude error of the biographer; but how or why could the whole of our generation be mistaken?' (*Vita di Dante Alighieri*, Unione Tipografico – Editore Torinese, 1857 p.444). [My translation.] There is a copy of Balbo's *Vita di Dante Alighieri* in the GE/GHL Library. Eliot likens Daniel in *Daniel Deronda* to the 'spiriti magni' (see Chapter 8).

26. Published in Paris 1839, (revised edn. 1845). George Eliot possessed a copy of Ozanam.
27. Caesar, M. (ed.) *op. cit.*, p.60.
28. Toffanin, G., 'Ciò che Dante rappresentò nel risorgimento italiano' in *Perchè l'umanesimo comincia con Dante* (Bologna: Zanichelli editore 1967), pp.186–7.
29. *De Monarchia*, Bk. II, Ch. 5.
30. For Gioberti in his *Primato*, Dante 'was the condition necessary for the resurgence of Italian thought and genius' which was to bring the country into the modern age. Part of Dante's importance was to discover the political function in the laity and identify this with the national function. Thus, Gioberti says: 'When a people comes of age and realizes its own strength, a highly gifted layman often appears in the ordinary world who, through some great work, makes clear the meaning of the change which has occurred, lays the foundation of a new literature and begins an intellectual movement which is destined to last for many centuries. Such a man may be identified as the embodiment of that national consciousness and personality which is already burning in the breasts of the many. ... From the inspired lips of this man come those hitherto unheard notes which will soon be repeated and echoed on thousands of lips. [...] The Italy of the thirteenth century was happier still in giving to the world the founder of the lay Catholic civilization of the modern age who began for his class that which the greatest medieval pope had done three hundred years earlier for the clerical orders.' (cit. Toffanin, *op. cit.*, pp.196–7); it was in this sense that, for Gioberti, 'Dante created the Italian nation'. (cit. Mazzoni, *op. cit.*, p.64). [All translations from the essays by Toffanin and Mazzoni are mine.]
31. This image of Dante derives largely from the writings of Foscolo and was popularized in particular by Byron's poem *The Prophecy of Dante* (written 1819, translated into Italian the same year, and published in 1821).
32. Toffanin, *op. cit,*. p.191, refers to a 'religion of Dante'.
33. *Scritti di Giuseppe Mazzini*, Vol. 1 (Letteratura Vol. 1) (Imola: Cooperativa Tipografico-editrice Paolo Galeati 1906) pp.3–23; the image of 'Italia' as a statue was also a common topos in *Risorgimento* iconography.
34. *Ibid.*, p.21.

35. In Cacciaguida's long speech, he tells Dante that 'it shall be to thine honour to have made a party by thyself' (*Paradiso* XVII, 68–9). All translations are from *The Divine Comedy of Dante Alighieri*, with Translation and Comment by J.D. Sinclair, 3 vols (New York: Oxford University Press 1961) except where otherwise indicated.

36. *Purgatorio* VI, 76–8; in 1849, for example, when Daniele Manin was defending the newly created Venetian Republic, a medallion was minted bearing the winged lion of Venice and the inscription 'Here must all cowardice be ended' (*Inferno* III, 15). Caesar (*op. cit.*, p.64) cites a Danish journalist's account of a conversation with a Roman waiter who had fought with Garibaldi in 1847 and who produced a copy of the *Comedy* in which he had underscored the 'Come, see your weeping Rome' passage (ll. 112 ff) from *Purgatorio* VI.

37. Mazzoni, *op. cit.*, p.68.

38. *Ibid.*

39. cit. *ibid.*, p.70.

40. cit. *ibid.*, p.71.

41. cit. *ibid.* Balbo makes a similar comparison between Dante and Alfieri, thus mythologizing Alfieri in the same way as Mameli had Mazzini, and drawing him into that magic circle of 'spiriti magni' of the *Risorgimento*. Alfieri 'restored the worship of Dante. He had a truly Dantesque spirit. Love, anger, pride, themes of moderation, exaggeration and changes of side, everything is similar in the two of them. Thus Alfieri's was an unsought imitation, unintentional, effortless and inherent.' (*Vita*, p.440).

42. GE, *Theophrastus*, p.168.

43. Mazzoni, *op. cit.*, p.88.

44. Shelley acknowledged his debt to Dante in the Preface to *Prometheus Unbound* (1820).

45. Medwin, T., *Journal of the Conversations of Lord Byron* (1814) p.160, cit. Brand, *op. cit.*, pp.59–60. For a discussion of Dante as the Byronic hero, see Ellis, S., *Dante and English Poetry: Shelley to T.S. Eliot* (Cambridge: CUP 1983) pp.36–65.

46. See, for example, Mazzini's Tract *Non-Intervention*, published in 1851 by the 'Friends of Italy' in England: 'But what is a nation? According to any possible definition of this word, a nation is a larger or smaller aggregate of human beings bound together into an organic whole by agreement in a certain number of real particulars, such as race, language, physiognomy, historic tradition, intellectual peculiarities, or active tendencies. Thus the *Russians* are a nation [...]. So also *the French* are a nation; *the English* are a nation; *the Spaniards* are a nation – these names implying in each case a certain number of real characteristic differences impressed by nature herself on the fragments of the human race to which the names refer.' *Life and Writings of Mazzini (Vol VI, Critical and Literary)* (London: Smith, Elder and Co. 1891) Appendix, p.302.

47. Carlyle, T., Lecture III 'The Hero as Poet. Dante; Shakespeare' from *On Heroes and Hero Worship* in *Sartor Resartus / On Heroes and Hero*

Worship Introduced by W.H. Hudson (London: Dent Everyman's Library [1908] 1965), pp.346, 323.

48. See Beer, G., *George Eliot*, (Brighton:The Harvester Press 1986) p.202 ff.

49. Thomas Medwin (together with Shelley) wrote a version of the *Ugolino* passage, and *Ugolino* inspired Shelley's poem *The Tower of Famine* and Edward Wilmot's *Ugolino of the Tower of Famine* (1828). It may also have inspired Byron's *Prisoner of Chillon*. Byron translated *Paolo and Francesca* in *terza rima*, Leigh Hunt's *Story of Rimini* and Keat's sonnet *A Dream after reading Dante's episode of Paolo and Francesca* were based on this passage; Shelley translated the 'Matilda gathering flowers' episode; *Pia dei Tolomei* (*Purgatorio* V) inspired a number of poems and was a favourite passage of Byron's.

50. See Ellis, *op. cit.*, pp.101–2.

51. Sainte-Beuve, cit. Caesar, *op cit.*, p.65.

52. Ellis, *op. cit.*, p.103.

Chapter 2

1. *Letters* I, pp. 51–2.

2. *Ibid.* p.69.

3. *Ibid.* p.53.

4. The full title of the work is *The Austrian Dungeons in Italy: Narrative of Fifteen Months' Imprisonment and Final Escape from the Fortress of S. Giorgio* by Felice Orsini. Translated from the unpublished manuscript by J. Meriton White (Routledge and Co.) 1856. It was reviewed in *The Leader* on August 30th, p.835.

5. *Letters* I, pp.253–5.

6. In her journal, 'Recollections of Italy', written after the 1860 trip, she wrote: 'In Genoa again on a bright, warm spring morning! I was here eleven years ago, and the image that visit had left in my mind was surprisingly faithful, though fragmentary.' (cit., Cross, p.123). (See also *Letters* III, p.285.)

7. *Letters* I, p.294.

8. Without actually stating it, G.S. Haight's *Biography* (p.99) strongly implies that Eliot did meet Mazzini in the early 1850s. Though I have not found any direct evidence to this effect, or to support Haight's statement that, by 1852, Eliot 'had long admired [Mazzini's] efforts to unite Italy,' both seem to be fairly safe suppositions.

9. Mazzini, it seems, was initially led to believe that *The Leader* was to be a mouthpiece for *him*. See *Mazzini's Letters to an English Family* E.F. Richards, (ed.), 3 Vols., (London: John Lane, The Bodley Head 1920–22) Vol i, p.144.

10. Ashton, R., *George Henry Lewes: a Life* (Oxford: Clarendon Press 1991) p.107.

11. 'Alfieri and the Italian Drama', *The British and Foreign Quarterly Review*, July 1844, pp.357–90; 'The Life and Works of Giacomo Leopardi', *Fraser's Magazine*, 38, (December 1848) pp.659–69.

12. Richards, E.F. (ed.), *op.cit.*, pp.191–2, 193.

13. *Letters* II, p.5.
14. Quotations from the article are from Mazzini, G., 'Europe: its Condition and Prospects.', *WR*, April 1852, pp.442–67.
15. One thinks, however, of Felix Holt's words at his trial that he refuses to say that he would *never* fight against authority. 'I hold it blasphemy to say that a man ought never to fight against authority: there is no great freedom and no great religion that has not done it, in the beginning.' He would not fight, however, unless 'urged to it by what I hold to be sacred feelings, making a sacred duty either to my own manhood or to my fellow-man'. (George Eliot, *Felix Holt, the Radical*, London: Penguin [1972] 1988, p.565)
16. Letter to Charles Bray, April 17th, 1852 (*Letters*, II, p.18).
17. See 'D'una letteratura Europea' [On a European Literature] in *Scritti di Giuseppe Mazzini*, (Letteratura Vol. 1), pp.177–222.
18. *Letters* II, p.15.
19. *The Examiner*, March 27th, 1852, p.207.
20. Dr Edward Vehse, *History of the Austrian Court and Aristocracy, and of the Austrian Diplomacy (Geschichte des östreichischen hofs und Adels und der östreichischen Diplomatie)*, *WR*, April 1st, 1855, pp.303–35.
21. *WR*, July 1856, pp.299–300. Giovanni Ruffini was the author of these works. He and his brother Iacopo were close friends of Mazzini's for many years and lodged with him in London. *Lorenzo Benoni* (written in English in 1853) is autobiographical and includes a character, Fantasio, who is clearly intended to be Mazzini. (See Rudman, *op. cit.*, pp.108–9)
22. Much later, in 1863 or 1864, Eliot copied a long passage from Colletta's *History of the Kingdom of Naples* into her notebook in which, in the scourging of a member of the *Carbonari*, the suffering of Christ's passion is recalled. (See *Notebook, 1854–1879*, pp.84–5, 194)
23. *Leader*, August 30th, 1856, p.835.
24. *WR*, January 1857, pp.297–310.
25. *Leader* VII, May 17th, 1856, p.475.
26. *WR*, July 1856, p.271.
27. *WR*, July 1856, p.307. The quotation, ('working like the artist / who has the skill of his art and a hand that trembles.') is from *The Divine Comedy* (Paradiso XIII, 77–8). The same lines were copied into her Beinecke Notebook (*Notebook, 1854–1879*, p.46).
28. The 1860 trip is listed as her first in Haight's Index to the *Letters* (Vol. IX). Eliot had of course been to Genoa and Lombardy in 1849.
29. GE Journal, 'Recollections of Italy' 1860, cit. Cross, ii, p.120.
30. See Witemeyer, H., *George Eliot and the Visual Arts* (New Haven and London: Yale University Press 1979) and Witemeyer, H., 'George Eliot and Italian Portraiture in *Daniel Deronda*', *Nineteenth-Century Fiction* 30 (1975–76), pp.477–94.
31. *Letters* III, p.279.
32. Cross, ii, p.122.
33. Eliot described the Prince as 'a notability with a thick waist, bound in by a golden belt, and with a fat face, predominated over by a large mustache– "non ragionam di lui" ' (Journal cit., Cross, ii, p.122). Eliot

adapts a line from Dante's *Inferno*. The original is 'non ragioniam di lor, ma guarda e passa' ('Let us not talk of them; but look thou and pass.' [III, 51]), which is Virgil's comment on the Neutrals, those who embraced no cause but always sought their own safety. Eliot would also have had in mind Virgil's earlier comment, 'The world suffers no report of them to live' (49). Eliot's choice from Dante then is, literally, a damning comment on the Prince.

34.   *Letters* III, p.287. A slightly different account is also given in the Journal (cit. Cross, ii, p.122).

35.   *Ibid.*

36.   GHL Journal (26–28 March 1860), cit. *Biography* p.322.

37.   *Letters* III, p.285.

38.   cit. Cross, ii, p.123.

39.   GE Journal (1860) cit. Cross, ii, pp.126–7.

40.   GE, *Letters*, III, p.287.

41.   GE Journal (1860) cit. Cross, ii, p.127.

42.   *Letters* III, p.286.

43.   GHL Journal (April 18th, 1860) cit. Ashton, R., *op. cit.*, p.207.

44.   GE Journal (1860) cit. Cross, ii, p.132. Eliot incorporated this detail into the picture of St Peter's given in *Middlemarch*, with its 'red drapery which was being hung for Christmas spreading itself everywhere like a disease of the retina'. Haight points out that this use of a detail from the 1860 trip is one of George Eliot's rare factual mistakes, since the liturgical colour of Christmas is white (*Biography*, p.324).

45.   GE, *Letters* III, p.288; GHL Journal, cit. Ashton, R., *op. cit.*, p.207.

46.   *Letters* III, p.288.

47.   *Ibid*. The phases of Italy's struggle for independence and in particular the part played in that struggle by Napoleon III was 'a subject which sat very near to [Elizabeth Barrett Browning's] heart' (Trollope, T.A., *What I Remember*, Van Thal, H, ed., London: William Kimber 1973, p.179). Unlike many of her compatriots in Italy, she trusted and believed in Napoleon III.

48.   GE, May 18th. *Letters* III, p.294.

49.   *Ibid.*

50.   'Honour the glorious poet'. cit. Cross, ii, p.159.

51.   There is only one explicit reference to Dante in *The Mill on the Floss*: 'Does not the Hunger Tower stand as the type of the utmost trial to what is human in us?' (pp.430–1), a reference to Dante's account of Ugolino's sufferings in watching his children die and then eating their flesh in *Inferno* XXXIII. (*The Mill on the Floss*, Byatt, A.S., (ed.), Harmondsworth: Penguin 1985).

52.   *Letters* III, p.295.

53.   *Ibid.*, p.300.

54.   *Ibid.* p.307.

55.   cit. Cross, ii, p.171.

56.   *Ibid.*, p.172.

57.   *Ibid.*

58.   *Ibid.*, p.174. The prison of San Marco, a symbol of Austrian oppression, would already have been known to Eliot through, for example,

Byron's *Childe Harold's Pilgrimage,* Canto IV of which begins: 'I stood in Venice on the Bridge of Sighs, / A palace and a prison on each hand:'; it also figures in Silvio Pellico's *Le mie prigioni* (Milano: Biblioteca Universale Rizzoli [1953] 1988) p.155.

59.   cit. Cross, ii, p.177.
60.   *Letters* III, p.307.
61.   cit. Cross, ii, p.180.
62.   *Ibid.*, p.182. Eliot's Journal entry recalls the Epilogue to 'Mr Gilfil's Love Story': '... the bright Italian plains, with the sweet *Addio* of their beckoning maidens, are part of the same day's travel that brings us to the other side of the mountain, between the sombre rocky walls and among the guttural voices of the Vallais.' (*Scenes of Clerical Life,* Lodge, D., (ed.), Harmondsworth: Penguin 1973) p.243.
63.   *Letters* III, p.311.
64.   *Ibid.* In another letter Eliot wrote: 'We both feel immensely enriched with new ideas and new veins of interest.' (*Letters* III, p.307)
65.   GE to John Blackwood (March 23rd, 1861): 'We are meditating (do you know it?) another visit to Florence with grave purposes, and I suppose we shall set out by the end of April, ...' (*Letters* III, pp.392–3).
66.   May 5th, 1861 (*Letters* VIII, p.283).
67.   *Ibid.*, p.283; among the volumes they bought were Varchi's *Istoria Fiorentina* and an unnamed novel about Savonarola. (See *Biography,* p.344)
68.   GHL Journal (April 29th, 1861), cit. *Letters* VIII, p.283.
69.   *Letters* VIII, p.283.
70.   See also my discussion in Chapter 10 of Eliot's reading of moral greatness in noble features in *Daniel Deronda.*
71.   Trevelyan, G. M., 'The War Journals of Garibaldi's Englishman', *Cornhill Magazine,* January 1908, pp.96–110; Trevelyan, G. M., *Garibaldi and the Thousand,* Longmans, Green and Co., London 1910, p.89.
72.   Trevelyan, G. M. *Garibaldi,* p.97.
73.   Viotti, A., *Garibaldi: The Revolutionary and his Men,* Blandford Press, Poole, Dorset, UK, 1979, p.109.
74.   *Letters* III, p.420.
75.   *Ibid.*, p.418.
76.   *Letters* III, p.421.
77.   GHL, *Letters* III, p.422.
78.   *Ibid.*
79.   *Biography,* p.346.
80.   cit. *Letters* III, pp.423–5.
81.   Trollope, T. A., *op. cit.*, pp.208–9.
82.   *Athaeneum* (June 29th, 1861) pp.851–5; GE to Mrs T.A. Trollope, *Letters* III, p.436.

Chapter 3

1.   *WR* (January 1857) p.307.

2. Introduction to *Scenes of Clerical Life* (Harmondsworth: Penguin 1973), p.24. For Jennifer Uglow, 'Caterina, the heroine of "Mr Gilfil's Love Story" is less successful [than 'Amos Barton'], because she is conceived almost entirely in cultural terms and remains stereotypical... To this artificial plastic world of art and architecture (Cheverel Manor has been remodelled on Italian lines), Caterina brings the mobility and emotion of the theatre; the passion of Gothic melodrama is contrasted with aristocratic rigidity.' (*George Eliot*, London: Virago 1987, pp.86–7); for John Purkis the story is only redeemed by its occasional humour:' "Mr Gilfil's Love Story" seems impossibly melodramatic and might, with its romantic love and tragic coincidence, be the work of a different writer; the climax...made even Blackwood demur.' (*A Preface to George Eliot*, London: Longman 1985, p.95).

3. She quotes from memory from the novel in a letter to Maria Lewis of October 27th, 1840. (*Letters* I, p.71) and asked to borrow an English edition of the novel from Sara Hennell in 1852 (*Letters* II, p.31). Mme de Staël's *Corinne*, which achieved immense success in its day (written in 1807 and translated into English the same year) and went through some 40 editions between 1807 and 1872.

4. Gutwirth, M., *Mme de Staël Novelist: the emergence of the artist as woman* (Urbana, Chicago, London: University of Illinois Press 1978), p.248.

5. Vincenzo Monti (1754–1828). This is one of the great patriotic songs of Italy. Eliot also includes a patriotic Italian sonnet, Filicaia's 'Italia', in her own story, echoing Mme de Staël's technique. (See discussion below).

6. Gutwirth, M., *op. cit.*, p.248.
7. Gutwirth, M., *ibid.* and *Corinne* II,ii, cit. Gutwirth p.242.
8. cit. Gutwirth, *op. cit.*, p.212.
9. See, for example, J.C.L. Sismondo Sismondi, in his *Storia Delle Repubbliche Italiane dei secoli di mezzo*, (1809–18).
10. Kaplan, C., Introduction to Barrett Browning, Elizabeth *Aurora Leigh: with Other Poems* (London: The Women's Press 1978), pp.16, 20. The passage which Kaplan has in mind at this point is from *Aurora Leigh* I, 617–39.
11. Kaplan, C., *ibid.*, p.21.
12. *Ibid.*, p.19.
13. Barrett Browning, E., *Aurora Leigh*, I, 626–7. It is interesting in this context to note that Eliot selected a passage from Book VII (ll.453–89), which narrates Aurora's return to Italy (to Genoa) with Marian, for quotation in her *WR* review (January 1857, pp.309–10).
14. DeCuir, A., 'Italy, England, and the female artist in George Eliot's "Mr. Gilfil's Love Story"' in *Studies in Short Fiction*, Vol. 29, No.1. Winter 1992, pp.69, 153.
15. The narrator remarks on her 'speaking good English too, and joining in Protestant prayers' (p.147).
16. *Biography*, pp.210–11.
17. The same prejudice is voiced more explicitly when Mrs Bellamy says: 'we shall...hev the house full o' [Italian] workmen colloguing wi' the maids, an' makin' no end o' mischief'. (p.155).

18. Caterina's pallor, her being dressed in white and her association with moonlight clearly foreshadow her death. Eliot's text here echoes *Aurora Leigh*: ' "The Italian child, / Thrives ill in England: she is paler yet / Than when we came the last time; she will die." ' (I, 495–8). U.C. Knoepflmacher, in *George Eliot's Early Novels: The Limits of Realism* (Berkeley and Los Angeles: University of California Press 1968) p.63, describes Caterina as 'an exotic bride'.

19. 'Jackanapes' is Blackwood's description. (Letter to GE February 16th, 1857, in *Letters* II, p.297).

20. Brand, C. P., *op. cit.*, p.189.

21. A. Manning, *Stories from the History of Italy* (1831), cit. Brand, *op. cit.*, pp.189–90.

22. *Aurora Leigh*, I, 361–4.

23. That contrast between the English and Italian character and the power of Italy to release emotions is reiterated in Mrs Sharp's reaction on seeing the infant Caterina with her dead father in Italy: 'Even Mrs Sharp had been so smitten with pity by the scene she had witnessed ... as to shed a small tear, though she was not at all subject to that weakness;' (p.151). *Only* the 'magic circle' of Italy (*Aurora Leigh*, I, 622) one feels, could draw forth such a reaction as this in the Cheverels' servant.

24. 'poveraccio' is an expression of pity here, but the suffix 'accio' can also be pejorative; 'padroncello' is a diminutive epithet, with affectionate overtones.

25. In addition to the presence of Italian workmen, an Italian singing master is engaged to spend a number of months at Cheverel Manor, so that the house appears in fact to be filled with Italians who, however, are effectively written out of the text. It is not true, as DeCuir says (*op. cit.* p.68) that Caterina is denied her own culture altogether. Italians are present at Cheverel Manor periodically throughout her childhood, one of them, the singing master, with the express purpose of giving Caterina access to part of her culture. Sir Christopher is engaged in transplanting 'that marble miracle', Milan Cathedral, to Cheverel Manor and this implies that Caterina had opportunities for contact with Italian. It is difficult to see how (in the light of contemporary views of Italy as the land of art, music and sublime landscapes) Caterina could have been given much greater access short of actually visiting the country. What is important here is the diminished significance attributed to that culture when transplanted into England. This is a fact doubly indicated precisely by Eliot's signalling its presence yet choosing to write it out of the text.

26. Knoepflmacher points to the 'strain of maternal tenderness' in Gilfil and comments: 'it is noteworthy that the clergyman's surname should be matronymic, "gille fil" or "fil gille" being the equivalent of "son of Jill" [...] George Eliot balances the "feminine" surname with a virile Christian name, the Germanic Maynard ("mein-hart") carries connotations of bravery and firmness.' (*op. cit.*, pp.61–2 [fn.])

27. Myers, W., *The Teaching of George Eliot* (Leicester: Leicester University Press 1984), p.90.

28. Beer, G., *op. cit.*, p.206.
29. The words are in fact misquoted by Eliot; the original is 'Dono infelice di bellezza'.
30. Byron's closely rendered translation of Filicaia's sonnet appears as stanzas xlii and xliii of *Childe Harold*. Filicaia's sonnet is reprinted in *The Oxford Book of Italian Verse*, 2nd edition, Dionisotti, C. ed., (Oxford: OUP 1952), pp.266–7.
31. G.H. Lewes mentions the poet in his 1848 article on Leopardi: 'Filicaia mourned over the fatal gift of Beauty in a passionate music which has stirred all hearts; but his sonnet is many degrees below the ode by Leopardi,...' (p.661); see also the following opening to an article from *The Times* (May 28th, 1856, p.9): 'Italy has indeed a title to the name of an unfortunate country. The fatal gift of beauty and the still more fatal gift of genius in her people, disunited from political wisdom and moral firmness, have laid her at the feet of foreign despots,...'
32. See GE to John Sibree, March 8th, 1848, (*Letters* I, pp.253–5) – 'we English are slow crawlers'.
33. However, Sir Christopher's hubris is exposed in a dramatic reversal, where his boast is interrupted in the next instant by the news of his heir's death. There is a parallel here with Eliot's more sinister domestic tyrant, Grandcourt who, in *his* hubris, is associated with Cesare Borgia and the tyranny of Renaissance Italy: 'Tis a hard and ill-paid task to order all things beforehand by the rule of our own security, as is well hinted by Machiavelli concerning Cesare Borgia, who, saith he, had thought of all that might occur on his father's death, and had provided against every evil chance save one: it had never come into his mind that his own death would quickly follow' (GE, Epigraph to Chapter 48 of *Daniel Deronda*, p.644).
34. Matthias, T. J., *The Pursuit of Literature* (1796), cit. Botting, F., *Gothic* (London and New York: Routledge 1996), p.80.
35. Brontë, C., *Jane Eyre* (Harmondsworth: Penguin Popular Classics 1994), pp.107, 111.
36. DeCuir, *op. cit.*, p.74.
37. On this, see the discussion of Leopardi in Chapter 9. The analogy with slavery is, as Gillian Beer (*op. cit.*, pp.17–18) points out, a 'metaphor that recurs over and over again in feminist writing of the period.'
38. Uglow (*op. cit.*, p.89) argues that Caterina's death is one of 'fruitful sacrifice' insofar as it generates a 'hallowed', 'consecrated' and 'sacred' love in Mr Gilfil's response to her suffering.
39. Knoepflmacher, U.K., *op. cit.*, p.71.
40. Eliot's concern for historical realism would also of course have prevented her from ending her story with any form of independence or fully achieved identity: neither at the end of the eighteenth century nor by 1857 was there any guarantee that Italian independence would be achieved. Knoepflmacher sees the expending of Romance to affirm the 'harsh realities of a time-bound world' as the central movement in the story, in which the fragile world of romance is pressed upon and eventually crushed by the pressure of contact with temporal experi-

ence. Part of the argument of this chapter has been, however, that Eliot's text probes and questions some of the very bases of ordinary experience (sexual, class and national divisions) and exposes these as social constructs and not absolute values in themselves. Caterina's rebellion, then, becomes a direct challenge to the very codes which define the limits of ordinary experience.

Chapter 4

1. *Letters* IV, p.96, cit. Bonaparte, F., *op. cit.*, p.14. References to the novel are to *Romola*, edited with an Introduction by A. Sanders (Harmondsworth: Penguin [1980] 1986).
2. Bonaparte, *ibid.*, p.29.
3. *Ibid.* pp.1–33.
4. Eliot herself calls Romola an 'ideal' heroine. *Letters* IV, pp.103–4.
5. *Middlemarch*, Chapter 20 (p.224); Gordon Haight (*Biography*, p.351) states that the title for the novel was taken from the name of a mountain outside Florence: 'Romola is not a Christian but a place name. South-west of Florence towards Certosa there is a little hamlet on a hill called Romola, which appears in a list of nine mountains that Lewes scribbled down for her in his travel notebook.' Yet Eliot herself wrote to Alexander Main in 1871: 'You have been right in pronouncing Romŏla, and in conceiving Romŏlo as the Italian equivalent of Romŏlus. I can assure you that the Italians say Romŏlo, and consequently Romŏla. The music of the name is quite lost in the painful quantity Romōla.' (*Letters* V, p.173). Felicia Bonaparte points to the connection with the mythical founder of Rome, and hence to the history of Western civilization (*op. cit.*, p.20).
6. GHL Journal, (May 21st, 1860) in *Letters* III, p.295. Lewes had been reading a guide-book about Savonarola. On the same day as Lewes made his suggestion, Eliot began looking for material and bought a book of Savonarola's poems and F.T. Perrens' *Jérôme Savonarole, sa vie, ses prédications, ses écrits* (1853) which they probably began reading the same evening (*Letters* III, p.296). On Eliot's 'sympathies' see my Chapter 2.
7. Bonaparte notes how Lewes and Eliot often exchange insights and how Eliot is familiar with material that, as far as we know, only Lewes appears to have studied. (*op. cit.*, p.22).
8. G. Ferrari (*Corso sugli scrittori politic italiani*, Milano: Tipografia di F. Manini 1862, p.184), for example, reiterates Cei's accusation (*Romola*, p.472) that Savonarola was a 'false prophet' who belonged in the fourth bolgia of *Inferno* (canto XX), saying that Savonarola deceived the people, that the art of prophecy was unknown to him and that 'he deserves only the place of a Phaeton among the Italian prophets,' – Phaeton being a classic story of hubris followed by nemesis.
9. See my discussion in Chapter 5.
10. Tosello, M., *Le Fonti Italiane della 'Romola' di George Eliot* (Torino: G. Giappichelli editore 1956), p.48; *Romola* p.670.

11. *Dictionary of Modern Italian History*, F.J. Coppa (Editor-in-chief), (Westport Connecticut and London: Greenwood Press 1985), p.438; *La Storia di Girolamo Savonarola e de'suoi tempi* (1861) by Pasquale Villari. Eliot read Villari's *Savonarola* in the summer and autumn of 1861 and made careful notes from it.

12. Villari, P., *Life and Times of Girolamo Savonarola*, [Trans. Linda Villari] (London: T. Fisher Unwin 1897), p.770.

13. Villari, P., *Machiavelli e i suoi tempi* (3 vols.) (Firenze: successori le Monnier, 1877), I, p.299.

14. See also my Chapter 3.

15. Myers, W., 'George Eliot: Politics and Personality' in *Literature and Politics in the Nineteenth Century*, Lucas, J., (ed.), (London: Methuen & Co. 1971), p.116.

16. Villari, *Savonarola*, pp.171–2; 772.

17. p.666 (Eliot's italics).

18. Salvadori, C. (ed.), *Lorenzo de'Medici: Selected Writings*, Belfield Italian Library, (Dublin: University College Dublin 1992), p.11; Villari, P. *Machiavelli*, p.200; Eliot also copied lines from Lorenzo's *La Nencia da Barbarino* into her notebook (*Notebook 1854–1879*, p.57).

19. George Eliot provided the English translation. The Italian quoted in the text is 'Quant'è bella giovinezza, / Che si fugge tuttavia! / Chi vuol esser lieto, sia, / Di domani non c'è certezza.' (*Romola*, pp.184, 707)

20. 'Quest'è Bacco e Arianna / belli, e l'un l'altro ardenti; / perché 'l tempo fugge e inganna / sempre insieme stan contenti.' (ll. 5–8)

21. The second unused epigraph, that to Chapter 5, was to have been a passage from Pulci's *Morgante maggiore* XV: 'She was most courteous, she was gentle, / Honest, wise, chaste and modest, / Like a man she always kept promises, / Sometimes she was haughty / With an attitude that was great and noble / For she was generous from her heart and blood.' (*Romola*, p.685)

22. I do not therefore share Felicia Bonaparte's view (*op. cit.*, pp.140–1) that George Eliot had a low opinion of Pulci.

23. GE to Alexander Main, August 1871. (*Letters* V, p.174). She refers in her letter to *Romola* Chapter 16, 'A Florentine Joke.'

24. Machiavelli, *Istorie fiorentine* VIII, 36, cit. Salvadori, *op. cit.*, p.20.

25. *Decameron*, Day V, Novel 2. *Romola*, p.588.

26. 'Machiavelli' (*The Edinburgh Review*, March 1827), reprinted in Macaulay, T.B., *Critical and Historical Essays*, (London: Longman, Brown, Green, and Longmans 1850), pp.28–9.

27. J.C.L. Sismonde de Sismondi, *On the Literature of the South of Europe*, translated from the original, with notes and a life of the author, by Thomas Roscoe, third edn., Vol I., (London: Henry G. Bohn 1850), p.429.

28. Eliot was familiar with a number of Machiavelli's writings and often paraphrases the ideas expressed in them in *Romola*. There are three Machiavelli items in the GE/GHL collection at Dr Williams' Library (*Catalogue*, Items 1352–4). See *Romola* p.683, for the unused Epigraph to Chapter 1. See also: Eliot's *Quarry* for *Romola* (numbered pages 26,

42–3); *Notebook 1854–1879*, pp.56, 181; *Some George Eliot Notebooks*, Vol. II MS 708, Baker, W., ed., pp.7, 122. Eliot returned to Machiavelli between 1868 and 1871, and an entry in the Folger Notebook shows that she read (or perhaps reread) Macaulay's essay on Machiavelli between 1868 and 1870, and in the Berg Notebook she took down several pages of quotations, mostly concerned with means and ends and the application of principles, from *The Prince* and the *Discourses* (*George Eliot's* Middlemarch *Notebooks*, Pratt J.C. & Neufeld, V.A. (eds.) pp.46, 133; 216–17, 268–9). Eliot's later interest in Machiavelli is shown by an epigraph in Chapter 48 of *Daniel Deronda*.

29. Villari, *Machiavelli*, p.234. Villari's image of the 'petrifying' of the national spirit is a common one in *Risorgimento* mythology.

30. Sismondi calls him a man 'whose name is in no danger of being buried in oblivion. This celebrity is his due, as a man of profound thought, and as the most eloquent historian, and most skilful politician that Italy has produced' (*Literature of the South of Europe*, p.429); Macaulay (*op. cit.*, p.29) writes '...we are acquainted with few writings which exhibit so much elevation of sentiment, so pure and warm a zeal for the public good, or so just a view of the duties and rights of citizens, as those of Machiavelli.'

31. 'The people, the people. Death to the tyrants!' Macaulay, *op. cit.*, p.50.

32. Ferrari, G., *op. cit.*, p.225.

33. 'Let your illustrious house undertake this task, therefore, with the courage and hope which belong to just enterprises, so that, under your standard, our country may be ennobled, and under your auspices what Petrarch said may come to pass:

> Vertue 'gainst fury shall advance the fight,
> And it i' th' combat soone shall put to flight:
> For th' old Romane valour is not dead,
> Nor in th' Italian brests extinguished.'

Machiavelli, N., *The Prince*, translated by George Bull, (Harmondsworth: Penguin Classics (1961) 1972), p.138. The lines quoted are from Petrarch's 'Italia mia (Ai Signori d'Italia)' (Canzone CXXVIII of the *Rime*, ll. 93–6) and Bull offers Edward Dacres' 1640 rendering of these lines in his translation.

34. cit. Tosello, *op. cit.*, p.68.

35. Eliot's Bardo says that Petrarch is 'the modern who is least unworthy to be named after the ancients' (p.97) and later talks of 'the divine Petrarch' (p.101).

36. Petrarch, 'Spirito gentil' (*Rime* LIII): the translation is from *Petrarch's Lyric Poems*, translated and edited by Robert M. Durling, (Cambridge: Harvard University Press 1976) pp.124–5.

37. Sanders, A., note on 'Spirito gentil' in *Romola*, p.736.

38. Though in the 'Proem' Eliot's Florentine mentions Lucretius as 'an ancient, and a great poet' and Pulci as 'only a poet in the vulgar tongue' (p.48), both Marullo and Poliziano, in their visits to Nello's shop have railed 'against the Roman scholars who want us all to talk

Latin again' (p.78). Eliot portrays the life of the Florentine Mercato Vecchio through quotation in Italian from the popular burlesquing poet Antonio Pucci (p.58). (She transcribed a long poem from Pucci into her *Quarry* for *Romola*); Nello quotes from Pulci on the language question ('Forgive me if I am wrong: let him who hears me speak understand my common tongue with the help of his latin.' ['Perdonimi s'io fallo: chi m'ascolta / Intenda il mio volgar col suo latino'] *Morgante*, II, 57, 2–3) and then reflects that 'I find myself knowing so many things in good Tuscan before I have time to think of the Latin for them; and Messer Luigi's rhymes are always slipping off the lips of my customers: – that is what corrupts me' (p.109). Eliot also noted down a similar sentiment from Doni's *I Marmi* (Venice, 1609) (no. 606 in the GE/GHL Catalogue): 'If you know things in Greek and in Latin, we know them in the vernacular' ['Se voi sapete le cose in Greco, e in Latino, noi le sappiamo in vulgare'] (*Some George Eliot Notebooks*, Baker, W., ed.,Volume II, MS 708, p.11). Eliot writes of the 'modern language being in an unorganised and scrambled condition for the mass of people who could read and write' (*Romola*, p.599) and gives an example from Boccaccio's *Decameron* (Day III, Novel 8): 'The old diarists throw in their consonants with regard rather to quantity than position, well typified by the Ragnolo Braghiello (Agnolo Gabriello) of Boccaccio's Ferondo' (*Romola*, p.731).

Chapter 5

1. In the 'Proem', the spirit of a fifteenth-century Florentine asks 'what fiery philosopher is lecturing on Dante in the Duomo?', and the first chapter focuses on 'il divino poèta' by imagining a 'stranger...in a dubious search for a certain severely simple door-place, bearing this inscription: QUI NACQUE IL DIVINO POETA'. Later, there is a conversation in a barber's shop about the death of Lorenzo de' Medici: ' "It appears the Magnifico is dead – rest his soul! – and the price of wax will rise?" [...] "Ah! a great man – a great politician – a greater poet than Dante." ' (60–1). A comic paraphrase of Dante is used by Nello to ask what brings Tito to his barber's shop: ' "Let me see the very needle's eye of your desire, as the sublime poet says, that I may thread it." "That is but a tailor's image of your sublime poet's" said Tito' (pp.184–5). Dante comments on a question put by Virgil in *Purgatorio* XXI: 'By this question he so threaded the needle of my desire' (37–8).

2. Eliot took the quotation from Farinata which she puts into the mouth of Bernardo from the historian Villani. The passage appears in *Some George Eliot Notebooks* Baker, W., ed., MS 708 p.18, and is immediately preceded (p.17) by a 'quotation' from Dante: 'Dante says of Florence "Che quel che d'ottobre filava non giungeva mai a riveder l'Agosto" ' ['What Florence was spinning in October never managed to reach August']. Eliot seems to have been quoting from memory here, however, for in the *Comedy* (*Purgatorio* VI, 143–4) Dante says of Florence:

'ch'a mezzo novembre / non giugne quel che tu d'ottobre fili.' ['the threads thou spinnest in October do not last to mid-November'].

3. Dante's line reads: 'the cruelty that bars me from the fair sheepfold where I slept as a lamb' (*Paradiso* XXV, 4–5).

4. *Paradiso* XV, 131–2; 97–100; Eliot noted down five quotations from the long Cacciaguida passage in *Paradiso* XVI and XVII in *Notebook 1854–1879*, p.46 and Extracts, p.44.

5. Eliot noted a 'peacock boiled with the feathers on' in her *Quarry* for *Romola*. Machiavelli reminds Tito of the supper in the Rucellai Gardens: 'we are to eat a peacock ... there are to be the choicest spirits in Florence' (p.221). Among these 'choicest spirits' Eliot includes 'Dante's pattern old Florentine', Machiavelli, and perhaps Dante himself, as there may be an oblique reference to the poet in the detail of the peacock. She noted a passage from Boccaccio's *Life of Dante* in which his *Divine Comedy* is likened to a peacock: 'Its quill is angelic and has a hundred eyes; its feet are filthy, and its gait stately; moreover, its voice is sour and loud and horrible. And so in Dante's place we have his poem the Divine Comedy, which can very well be compared to a peacock.' (*Notebook 1854–1879*, pp.52; 179 [trans. Cortese]).

6. British Museum Add. MS 34,028, p.12; cit. Cortese, R., *George Eliot and Dante*, (University of Winsconsin-Madison, unpublished PhD., 1981), p.50.

7. A reference to *Inferno* XX, 13, where the diviners of the fourth bolgia walk with their 'face ... turned towards the loins'. The accusation of being a false prophet was one repeated by some *Risorgimento* commentators on Savonarola. (See Chapter 4, fn. 8.)

8. *Purgatorio* XXXIII, 130–2.

9. *Purgatorio* XXVIII, 127–32.

10. *Purgatorio* XXX, 78.

11. There are no scholars in the Malebolge. Cortese suggests that Eliot may have made a deliberate mistake in the interest of associating Tito with Malebolge (*op. cit.*, pp.72, 81). It is more likely I think that she misremembered certain details and confused Poliziano with Luigi Pulci. Ambrogini di Monte *Pulci*ano (my italics), later known as Poliziano, is less easily associated with Hell than Luigi Pulci, who was buried in an unconsecrated grave and who, in a famous letter, had promised to send Lorenzo the Magnificent some verses from Hell when he arrived! (*cit.* Villari in *Machiavelli*, p.229).

12. *Inferno* XXIII, 58–67.

13. Eliot knew *Inferno* XXV well and copied lines 79–81 into Extracts (p.202) and she was to return to it in *Daniel Deronda* (see Chapter 8, p.146ff).

14. *Inferno* XXX, 91–2; Extracts, p.43.

15. *Inferno* XXX, 98.

16. Eliot had referred briefly to the scene in *The Mill on the Floss*, pp.430–1; see my Chapter 2, fn.51.

17. Eliot returns to the Ugolino episode in *Felix Holt, the Radical* (See my Chapter 6, pp.108–10).

18. See, for example, pp.252, 333, 342, 387, 506.

19. *Inferno* XXXIV, 18. I am indebted to Cortese (*op cit.*, pp.59–64) in the above discussion of Tito Melema.

20. *Inferno* III, 22–3, 55–7.

21. The wedding takes place just before Easter (p.263), symbolically the death of Christ and of hope, and Romola's rebirth occurs at Christmas. Similarly, Dante is careful to give precise time references to mark the stages of his journey: he begins his descent into Hell on Good Friday 1300, and emerges on the evening of the next day; he arrives at the summit of Purgatory at noon on Easter Wednesday.

22. Romola's drifiting away (p.588) was inspired by the story of Gonzaga from Boccaccio's *Decameron*.

23. The same image is used again in *Felix Holt* (See my Chapter 6, pp.106–7).

24. In Dante, Filicaia and Leopardi all include the despairing 'Italia': see my Chapters 3 and 8. Also relevant are more recent 'Italia' figures like Elizabeth Barrett Browning's 'Mother and Poet (*Turin, After News from Gaeta, 1861*)' in which the patriot and poet Laura Savio (whose two sons were killed in the struggle for the unification of Italy) mourns: 'Dead! One of them shot by the sea in the east, / And one of them shot in the west by the sea. / Dead! both my boys! When you sit at the feast / And are wanting a great song for Italy free, / Let none look at *me!*'.

25. *op. cit.*, p.42.

Chapter 6

1. Tye, J.R., 'George Eliot's Unascribed mottoes', *NCF*, 22 (1967–68) pp.235–49; Levine, G., 'Introduction' to *Felix Holt* (New York: W.W. Norton 1970), p.xv; Coveney, P., Introduction to *Felix Holt* (Harmondsworth: Penguin 1972), pp.7–64; Wiesenfarth, J., *George Eliot's Mythmaking*, pp.180, 182–3, and *Notebook 1854–1879*, p.xxxi; Cortese, R., *op. cit.* gives a much fuller account. However, in concentrating on the unascribed epigraphs to the novel, she misses some of the richness of the allusion within the text and this, in my view, leads to a failure to appreciate Eliot's Dantean balance of judgement and compassion fully. In the present chapter, although I do not always agree with her conclusions, I am particularly indebted to Cortese's work; the reader is also referred to my 'George Eliot, Dante and Moral Choice in Felix Holt, the Radical' (*The Modern Language Review*, Vol. 86, Part 3 (July 1991), pp.553–66).

2. *Notebook 1854–1879* p.xxxi.

3. *Ibid.*, p.xxxviii.

4. Eliot loosely translates lines from Dante as the epigraphs to Chapters 15 and 22 of *Felix Holt*. The first reads: 'And doubt shall be as lead upon the feet / Of thy most anxious will.' The source is *Paradiso*, XIII, 112–14; the epigraph to Chapter 22 reads: 'Her gentle looks shot arrows, piercing him / As gods are pierced, with poison of sweet pity.' Here, the source given by Tye, Wiesenfarth (*Notebook 1854–*

1879, pp.43, 46, 171 and 173) and Cortese is *Inferno* XXIX, 43–4, but see my discussion in this chapter.

5. *Notebook 1854–1879*, pp.xxxi-xxxii.
6. Coveney, P. (ed.) *op. cit.*, pp.40–1.
7. *Inferno* XIII, 87.
8. *Notebook 1854–1879*, p.xxxii; Cortese, R., *op. cit.*, p.90.
9. *Notebook 1854–1879*, p.170.
10. *Ibid.* pp.42–3.
11. V, 100–6.
12. *Inferno* V, 121–3.
13. See my discussion of Eliot's use of *Inferno* V (112–23) in *Daniel Deronda* (my Chapter 9).
14. *Notebook 1854–1879*, p.43.
15. The translation of *Inferno* XIII, 84 is 'for I cannot, such pity fills my heart'. Eliot refutes the romantic idea of the 'grim Dante' and of the *Comedy* as a gallery of gothic horrors. On this, see Wiesenfarth in *Notebook 1854–1879*, p.171. Eliot does not specify *which* are the three instances of 'what can be called cruelty' in the *Inferno* so that these can only be conjectured: (i) she does specifically mention his cruelty to Fra Alberigo in Canto XXXIII (see later discussion and Note 47 below); (ii) in canto XXVIII when Mosca de' Lamberti reminds Dante of his name, the poet's reply '– and death to thy stock!', increases that sinner's suffering, so that he 'went away like a man crazed with grief' (109–11); (iii) after inadvertently kicking the head of Bocca degli Abati on the ice of Cocytus (canto XXXII), Dante tries to force him to name himself by wrenching his hair (98–9). There is one other example of cruelty much earlier in *Inferno*, though Eliot is less likely to have included it in her 'three instances': in canto VIII, on encountering Filippo Argenti who rises from the muddy waters of the Styx, Dante wishes to 'see him soused in this broth before we leave the lake' (52–4). Eliot's reading of Dante-character's cruelty is therefore confined to the lower circles of Hell, those of the fraudulent (Circle VII) and the traitors (Circle IX).
16. Cortese gives two such examples from the novel: ' "I am not at rest." ... the far-off unheeding stars' (pp. 489–90) and 'God had no pity, ... monotony of her life' (pp.595–6) (*op. cit.* pp.86–7).
17. *op. cit.*, p.84.
18. Eliot transcribed Dante's comment on the sinners in canto V, 112–14 (*Notebook 1854–1879*, p.43).
19. See also note 4, on Eliot's epigraph to Chapter 22 of *Felix Holt*.
20. Dante, of course, has Francesca tell her story in the very language of the *dolce stil novo*. See note 11 and my discussion of Eliot's use of the same episode in Chapter 7.
21. *Purgatorio* II, 124–31.
22. I have largely reproduced Cortese's argument (*op. cit.*, pp.94–9) in this paragraph.
23. Cortese, *op. cit.* p.99.
24. Cortese also draws attention to the 'Dantean stamp' of the epigraph (composed by Eliot herself) to this chapter (Chapter 49) of *Felix Holt*:

here, the narrative voice, raised to 'the level of Dante's mentor and guide, Vergil' (sic) (*op. cit.*, p.111) urges Esther to renounce 'all meaner choice for evermore' and to 'seek the noblest [good]' (p. 585). Cortese comments: 'Esther's choice...is triggered by the sight of Mrs Transome, who, striking the Dantesque pose of sorrow, stands for moral lethargy and spiritual death.' (*op. cit.*, p.112) It may be that Esther's vision of this suffering triggers her decision, but here Mrs Transome stands for much more than moral lethargy and spiritual death: Esther's pity and compassion ('"O why didn't you call me before?"'(p. 596)) and her succouring of the suffering woman, show that Esther is already far on the journey 'to seek...for that higher vision' (Epigraph to Chapter 49, p.585). Her rejection of Transome Court and the moral death it represents is not an utter rejection of Mrs Transome: Esther's symbolic action in undressing and putting her to bed is analogous to the tender gesture of Dante in *Inferno* XIV to which Eliot draws attention in her Beinecke notebook where: '[Dante] cannot go away from the Florentine transfixed as a tree without gathering up the scattered leaves & giving them back to the poor trunk' (*Notebook 1854–1879*, p.43).

25. XXXIII, 1–3.
26. XXXII, 44–51.
27. 'And a man may reach a point in his life in which his impulses are not distinguished from those of a hunted brute by any capability of scruples' (p. 579). Given the presence of this parallel scene from *Inferno* XXXII and XXXIII in *Felix Holt*, Levine's statement that Jermyn's 'moral vulgarity' makes him fit for 'the vestibule of Dante's Hell rather than...its lower depth' is clearly mistaken (Levine, G., 'Introduction' to *Felix Holt*, W.W. Norton, New York 1970, p.xv).
28. I am again indebted Cortese in the following discussion.
29. The origin of this epigraph was first traced by J.R. Tye, *op. cit.*, p.240.
30. *Notebook 1854–1879* p.46.
31. Lines 77–8 quoted in the *Belles Lettres* section of the *WR* (July 1856, p.307) (See Chapter 2, fn. 27).
32. Dante's lines read 'strange lamentations assailed me that had their shafts barbed with pity' (*Notebook 1854–1879* p.43).
33. Sinclair, J. D., *The Divine Comedy* (vol. 1), p.367.
34. There are other examples of Eliot's failure to acknowledge Dante as a source, or to acknowledge the part of the *Comedy* from which the quotation is taken. Where Eliot does this, however, it is consistently the result of conscious decision for aesthetic purposes which require this type of suppression within her text. See my discussion of this in Chapter 8 on Dante in *Daniel Deronda*.
35. *op. cit.*, p.106.
36. The image first appears within the text in quotations (Chapter 40) but the second time it appears without (Chapter 49); *op cit.*, p.99.
37. Esther's 'untired spirit' is in clear contrast to the 'wearied', the 'tired souls' and the 'weary people' of the *Inferno* (V, 80; VII, 65; XXIII, 70): the word 'tired' occurs ten times in *Inferno* and only once in *Purgatorio*. Esther is now associated with the 'swift spirits' (XXII, 9) of

Purgatorio: speed, haste and making the best use of time are defining characteristics of *Purgatorio*.

38. The relevant passage is *Purgatorio* VII (40–60) in which the poet Sordello explains the self-imposed rule of the penitents to Virgil: 'See, not even this line shouldst thou cross after the sun is gone, not that anything else hinders the going up but the darkness of night; that baffles the will with helplessness. One might indeed return downward in the dark and go wandering round the hillside while the horizon holds the day shut off' (53–60).

39. *Purgatorio* I, 124–7.

40. XXX, 43–6; see also *Inferno*, VIII, 97–102; X, 29–30; XVII, 85–99, and *Purgatorio* VIII, 40–2.

41. *Letters* IV, p.468; Eliot refers to Esther's physical poise on pp.468, 537 and 572.

42. Levine, G., 'Determinism and Responsibility', *PMLA*, 77 (1962), 268–79.

43. *Inferno* XXXII, 109–11.

44. GE, *The Spanish Gypsy* in *Works of George Eliot*, XI (Blackwood and Sons, Edinburgh and London, 1901), p.82.

45. GE, 'Debasing the Moral Currency', in *Theophrastus*, p.100.

46. Eliot's interest in this aspect of Dante is shown in her transcription of the following: 'and if I am a timid friend to truth I fear to lose my life among those who will call these times ancient' (*Paradiso* XVII (118–20)) spoken by Dante-character before Cacciaguida charges him to 'put away every falsehood and make plain all thy vision' (127–8) when he comes to write the *Commedia* (*Notebook 1854–1879*, p.46). Eliot herself saw in much contemporary literature a lowering of 'the value of every inspiring fact and tradition so that it will command less and less of the spiritual products, the generous motives which sustain the charm and elevation of our social existence'. This, she thought, was often achieved through a 'greedy buffoonery' which 'debase[s] all historic beauty, majesty, and pathos' ('Debasing the Moral Currency', *Theophrastus*, pp.97–8).

47. 'And it was courtesy to be a churl to him' (*Inferno* XXXIII, 150, in 'False Testimonials', *Theophrastus*, pp.122–3). After promising the traitor Fra Alberigo that he would remove the ice which sealed up his eyes and open them in return for Alberigo's story, Dante-character callously deceives him: 'And I did not open them for him; and it was courtesy to be a churl to him' (148–50) See also fn. 15.

48. 'Mr Jermyn's establishment was broken up, and he was understood to have gone to reside at a great distance: some said "abroad," that large home of ruined reputations' (p. 605). Eliot herself uses the 'horsewhip' on Jermyn, in the passage where he betrays Mrs Transome to her son: 'At that sound, quick as a leaping flame, Harold had struck Jermyn across the face with his whip' (p. 581). In *Romola*, too, the eponymous heroine scourges her husband for selling her father's library: '[She] had been driven to utter the words as men are driven to use the lash of the horsewhip' (p. 357).

49. 'False Testimonials', *Theophrastus*, p.125.

Chapter 7

1. *Letters* V, p.3.
2. *Biography*, p.413; Secor, C.A., *The Poems of George Eliot: a Critical Edition* Unpub. ed. Cornell Univ. PhD. 1969, cit. Baker, W., *Some George Eliot Notebooks*, Salzburg Studies in English Literature 1984. Vol. II MS 708, pp.128–9.
3. Pinion, F.B., *A George Eliot Miscellany* (New Jersey: Barnes & Noble 1982). pp.132–3.
4. *Letters* V, p.16.
5. 'How Lisa Loved the King' in Pinion, F.B., *op. cit.*, p.133. The mention of Dante, the setting of the story and image of the garden are all suggestive of Dante's image in *Purgatorio* VI of Italy as 'the garden of the Empire' ['l giardino dello 'mperio] (105)]. Dante's image, by contrast with George Eliot's, is used in the context of the bloodshed and factional strife which was rife in Dante's Italy in 1300.
6. Eliot, G., 'The Modern Hep! Hep! Hep!' in *Theophrastus*, pp.169–70.
7. British public opinion had been well prepared for the overthrow of the Bourbon monarchy by Garibaldi and the Thousand ('...the flower of heroes...he / Who drove those tyrants from dear Sicily,' – 'How Lisa Loved the King' in Pinion, *op.cit.*, p.135), and by the publication of Gladstone's *Two Letters* (1851).
8. Notable among the poets publishing in the periodicals in the 1860s was Swinburne, whose poems 'Ode on the Insurrection in Candia', 'The Halt before Rome, September 1867', and 'Super Flumina Babylonis', were all published in the *Fortnightly Review* between March 1867 and October 1869.
9. Garibaldi himself returned to Sicily in 1882 to celebrate the 600th anniversary of the Sicilian Vespers (and presumably the 22nd of his own achievement).
10. GE to Blackwood, *Letters* V, p.15. Blackwood's reason for departing from his rule does not appear to have been for any gain in sales or prestige for the *Magazine* (see Blackwood to GE, February 18th, 1869 in *Ibid.*), but rather a strong desire to accommodate Eliot.
11. GE, *Middlemarch*, Harvey, W.J. (ed.), London: Penguin 1971, p.313.
12. *Ibid.*, p.225.
13. *Inferno* IV, 13; 119.
14. *Middlemarch*, p.239.
15. Argyle, G., *German Elements in the Fiction of George Eliot, Gissing and Meredith*, (Frankfurt: Peter Lang 1979) p.56.
16. *Middlemarch*, see also p.244.
17. There are connotations both of 'the adventurer' (perhaps after Dorothea's money) and madness (Ladislaw's unconventionality) in the allusion to Ariosto's *Orlando Furioso*. The original Sicilian story was often told as a puppet show, and Ladislaw himself puts on a puppet show for the children of Middlemarch (p.503).
18. Skelton Grant, J., 'Italians with White Mice in *Middlemarch* and *Little Dorrit*', in *English Language Notes*, Vol. XVI, No.3 (March 1979),

pp.232–4; Bates, R., 'The Italian with White Mice in *Middlemarch*' in *Notes and Queries*, December 1984, p.497; Kurata, M.J., 'Italians with White Mice again: *Middlemarch* and *The Woman in White*', in *English Language Notes*, Vol. XXII, No.4 (June 1985), pp.45–7.

19. *Pall Mall Gazette* (March 7th, 1865) in *Essays of George Eliot*, Pinney, T. (ed.) pp.386–7. Surprisingly, this source is not mentioned by the three critics I have cited. Pinney adds a note 'Cf. Mrs. Cadwallader's characterisation of Ladislaw in *Middlemarch*, Ch. 50: "an Italian with white mice" '.

20. Rudman, H.W., *op. cit.*, p.126.

21. *The Times'* rather sententious comment on Manin's letter is that 'The Italians have been so long oppressed that it is not wonderful they should have contracted some of the vices of slaves.... But now that a fairer day is dawning for Italy it is time that the accursed practice should cease altogether.... [Italians] will, we trust, know better than to resort to practices which can only prolong their misfortunes.' (May 28th, 1856, p.9). (Mazzini's reply to Manin was published in *The Times* on August 11th, 1856.)

22. Skelton Grant, J., *op. cit.*, p.234.

23. GE, 'The Modern Hep! Hep! Hep!' in *Theophrastus*, p.170.

24. *Ibid.*, p.169.

25. Kurata, *op. cit.*, p.47.

26. Lines 107–8. Eliot changes the Italian in her quotation from the masculine 'l'altro' to 'l'altra' to fit her heroine, Dorothea: the original is 'L'altro vedete che ha fatto alla gauncia...'

27. Twice in *Middlemarch* (the epigraph to Chapter 19, and Chapter 55, pp.592–3), twice in *Felix Holt, the Radical* (pp. 497–8, 593), and in *Daniel Deronda* (Penguin, 1967) of Gwendolen (p.335).

28. The same image occurs at least twice more during the novel: the painter Naumann has her pose in the same position later on in the novel: 'It is as Santa Clara that I want you to stand – leaning so, with your cheek against your hand – so – looking at that stool, please, so!' (p.249); in Chapter 55, Dorothea holds a miniature portrait of Ladislaw's grandmother, which she had noticed earlier, to her cheek. It marks, then, an increase in Dorothea's understanding of herself, of Ladislaw and an expansion of feeling for his grandmother 'who had been too hardly judged' (*Middlemarch*, p.591).

29. Sonetto XVII 'Negli occhi porta la mia donna Amore' (Chapter XXI) *Dante Alighieri, Vita Nuova – Rime* a cura di F. Chiappelli, (Milano: Mursia 1965). The English translations given are from *Vita Nuova (Poems of Youth)* translated by Barbara Reynolds, (London: Penguin 1969).

30. *Vita nuova (Poems of Youth)*, pp.60–1.

31. *Ibid.*, p.61.

32. Hardy, B., '*Middlemarch* and the Passions' in *Particularities: Readings in George Eliot* (London: Peter Owen, 1982) pp.86–103.

33. *Ibid.*, p.96.

34. *Ibid.*, p.88.

35. *Ibid.*, p.98.

36. *Ibid.*
37. *Ibid.*, pp.96–103.
38. Cortese, *op. cit.*, p.145. The 'screen lady' is another woman, who appears to be the object of the poet's attention, but through whom he hopes to gain access to the true beloved.
39. Dante in Reynolds, B., *op. cit.*, p.99.
40. *Purgatorio* XXVII 97–9.
41. *Purgatorio* XXVIII 34–42. Eliot noted down quotations from *Purgatorio* XXVII, XXIX, XXX and XXXIII in her notebooks – evidence that she knew these cantos particularly well. Eliot made a note of the lines which immediately precede these in the canto.
42. The lily mobilizes a range of associations, including the biblical 'lilies of the field' (Matt. VI, 28) representing the inner beauty of God's creation revealed. It is also the symbol of Dante's Florence itself, a further reminder of the possible origins of Will's imagined world. See John Ruskin, *The Queen of the Air*, Lecture II, Athena Keramitis (Athena in the Earth), George Allen (1869) 1906, pp.112–13.
43. *Inferno* V, 127, 130–1, 137–8.
44. Ellis, S., *op. cit.*, p.103.
45. Matthew Arnold, cit. Ellis, *op. cit.*, p.105.
46. cit. Ellis, *op. cit.*, pp.106, 107.
47. Ellis, S., *op. cit.*, p.107.
48. Argyle also makes this suggestion in *op. cit.*, p.48. Dante Gabriel Rossetti studied with Ford Madox Brown, who himself went to Rome and was influenced by the Nazarenes.
49. Rossetti himself suffered from some of the same prejudices which affected Ladislaw: thus John Everett Millais' mother writing to Holman Hunt after the formation of the Pre-Raphaelite Brotherhood 'I wish you had never had anything to do with *that* Rossetti...I don't like the look of him; he's a sly Italian...' (W.H. Hunt: *The PreRaphaelites and the PreRaphaelite Brotherhood*, Vol. I, p.219, cit. Dobbs, B. and Dobbs, J., in *Dante Gabriel Rossetti: an Alien Victorian*, London: MacDonald and Jane's Publishers, 1977, p.71).
50. *op. cit.*, p.112.
51. *Ibid.*, p.113.
52. *Ibid.*, p.112; William Michael Rossetti, 'Notes on Rossetti and his Works', *Art Journal* 43 (July 1884), p.205, cit. Ellis, *op. cit.*, p.114.
53. 'Lilies of queen's gardens' Lecture II from *Sesame and Lilies* in *The Literary Criticism of John Ruskin*, Bloom, H. (ed.) Da Capo Paperback, NY, 1965, p.188.
54. In *Sesame and Lilies*, says Elaine Showalter (*A Literature of Their Own*, Virago, London 1978 [New revised edition 1988], p.184), Ruskin outlines 'a theory of the compensation of the sex-roles' and sets the physical and psychological boundaries of 'woman's true place': the home, rather than being a concrete place is 'a mystical projection of the female psyche, something a woman generates through her femaleness alone' (Showalter, *op. cit.*, p.184). Ruskin, says Showalter, also 'projected national redemption onto the spiritual virginity of women who were unravaged by the power drives of a rapacious

commercial society' (*Ibid.*). We have, then, the fusion of the Dantean myth of Beatrice with the powerful contemporary one of the compensation of the sex-roles, and this is articulated, though in different ways, by both Ruskin and Eliot.

55. 'Negli occhi...' D.G. Rossetti's translation from *Poems and Translations by Dante Gabriel Rossetti*, OUP, London 1959, (1913), p.351.
56. Ellis, S., *op. cit.*, p.122.
57. Rossetti's translation (*op. cit.* p.351) does not follow Dante faithfully, but renders the sentiment being discussed here well.

Chapter 8

1. See Moldstad, D. 'The Dantean Purgatorial metaphor in "*Daniel Deronda*", *Papers on Language and Literature* 19, i (Winter 1983), pp.183–98.
2. Cortese (*op. cit.*, pp.172, 191–2) reads the scene in this way, and also points up the connection in Eliot's mind between gambling and Hell, quoting two letters written to Mrs William Cross in 1872, 'I am not fond of denouncing my fellow-sinners, but gambling being a vice I have no mind to, it stirs my disgust even more than my pity...Hell is the only right name for such places,' (*Letters* V, 312); 'The Kursaal is to me a Hell not only for the gambling, but for the light and heat of the gas, and we have seen enough of its monotonous hideousness' (*Letters* V 314).
3. See also my discussion of the great betrayers Tito Melema in *Romola* and Jermyn in *Felix Holt* in Chapters 5 and 6.
4. Eliot copied lines 79-81 from *Inferno* XXV into Extracts p.41.
5. See Chapter 6, fns. 26, 47.
6. Moldstad, D., *op. cit.*, p.188. I am indebted to Moldstad for stimulating a number of the ideas in the present work.
7. In *Inferno* I, 91, Virgil tells Dante 'Thou must take another road...'.
8. 'If she cried towards [Daniel], what then? She cried as the child cries whose little feet have fallen backward – cried to be taken by the hand, lest she should lose herself' (p. 842). References in the *Comedy* to the father/child relationship are *Inferno* VIII, 97–102; X, 29–30; XVII, 85–99; XXX, 43–6 and *Purgatorio* VIII, 40–2.
9. '...remember me, who am la Pia. Siena gave me birth, Maremma death. He knows of it who, first plighting troth, wedded me with his gem.' (*Purgatorio* V, 130–6). These words are particularly fitting for Gwendolen, who has also been wedded with Grandcourt's jewels.
10. *Inferno* III, 122–6.
11. *Purgatorio* I, 1–3.
12. See my discussion in Chapter 5, pp.95–6.
13. *Notebook 1854–1879*, pp.43–4; see Chapter 6, pp.103-4.
14. *Inferno* XXIX, 43–4. The same image is used to later characterize Daniel's feeling towards Gwendolen: 'The sight pierced him with pity' (p.753). Dante's lines, copied into *Notebook 1854–1879*, (p.43), were also used as the epigraph to Chapter 22 of *Felix Holt*.

15. *Inferno* VI, 107–9. The name 'Gwen*dolen*' itself has Dantean resonances in the 'doglienza' (pain) of Dante's lines. Does it also perhaps contain the idea of the journey in 'wend' ('to wend one's way')?
16. *Purgatorio* XXX, 49–51.
17. *Purgatorio* XXXIII, 142–5; *Notebook 1854– 1879*, p.45.
18. Eliot quotes in Italian. *Purgatorio* IV, 88–90.
19. *Inferno* XIX, 13–15; 22–7.
20. *Purgatorio* XXIII, 7–8; XXIV, 68–9.
21. Cortese, *op. cit.* p.185.
22. *Inferno* I, 91.
23. GE, *Theophrastus*, p.125. (See Chapter 6).
24. *Daniel Deronda* p.847.
25. *Purgatorio* VI, 1–3; *Daniel Deronda* p.847. Lines 64–6 and 72 of *Purgatorio* VI are in *Notebook 1854–1879* (pp.44, 48) and a paraphrase of lines 143–4 is noted in Baker, W. (ed.), *op. cit.* MS 708, p.17 (see Chapter 5, fn.2).
26. *Daniel Deronda* p.684; *Inferno* XXIX, 44. See Note 14 above.
27. *Paradiso* XVII, 130–2; Cortese, R., *op. cit.*, p.192 (fn.15).
28. Carlyle, T., *Sartor Resartus / On Heroes and Hero Worship*, Dent, London (1908) 1965. Lecture III, 'The Hero as Poet: Dante, Shakespeare, (1840). p.324.
29. Carlyle, T., *op. cit.*, pp.322–3; Carlyle repeats 'it had made him lean for many years' (pp.324–5), quoting from *Paradiso* XXV, 1–3. Eliot knew this canto well, and had already used part of line 5 in *Romola* (see Chapter 4, fn.3). The contrast with the Rector of Lowick can also be seen in Dante's own account of his exile, when he chose poverty and hunger rather than the 'nourishment' of returning to Florence with a pardon: 'I have gone through almost all the parts to which this tongue extends, a pilgrim, almost a beggar, showing against my will the wound of fortune,...I have been, in truth, a ship without sail or rudder, borne to diverse ports and narrows and shores by the dry wind that rises from wretched poverty,...' (*Convito*, cit. Sinclair, ed., *Paradiso*, p.254).
30. See Chapter 1, p.21, and fn. 23.
31. *Inferno* IV, 131; Eliot's version is '(the "masters of those who know" are happily altogether human)' (p.295); cit. Cortese *op. cit.*, p.164.

Chapter 9

1. Mirah also sings Händel's *'Lascia ch'io pianga'* ['Let me Weep'] (p.423), which might be one of several vocal pieces by Händel, but it is probably Rinaldo's air from *Rinaldo* (1711) with a libretto by Giordigiani.
2. Lewes, G.H., 'Life and Works of Leopardi', *Frazer's Magazine* (December 1848) pp.659–9. The only person to have written on Leopardi in England prior to Lewes was Giuseppe Mazzini (*WR*, 28, 1837). In 1850, W.E. Gladstone wrote his 'The Life and Works of Giacomo Leopardi' in the *Quarterly Review* 86, pp.295–336. See Williams, P.,

'Leopardi in the English-speaking World: a Bibliography', *Italian Studies*, Vol. XLIII, 1988, pp.41–59.

3. Lewes, G.H., *op. cit.*, p.659.
4. 'I see the walls and arches, o my Italy, / The columns and the images, the lone / Towers of our ancestors, . . .' (All translations of Leopardi's *All'Italia* in this chapter are by J.H. Whitfield, *Leopardi's* Canti: *Translated into English Verse*, G. Scalabrini Editore, Napoli 1962, pp.26–33).
5. Lewes, G.H., *op. cit.*, pp.660–1.
6. George Eliot refers to this sonnet in 'Mr Gilfil's Love Story'. See my discussion in Chapter 3.
7. See my discussion of Lewes' radicalism in Chapter 2 pp.33–4.
8. Lewes provides his own translation of the 124–line poem.
9. 'I see the walls and arches, o my Italy, / The columns and the images, the lone / Towers of our ancestors, / But [the glory] I do not see, [. . .] – Oh how most blessed are you, / Who to the hostile spears offered your breast / For love of her who gave you to the light; [. . .] And yet / Most blessed shall you be / While speech or writing lasts within the world.' (ll. 1–4; 84–6; 118–20).
10. Eliot herself provides a translation of these lines.
11. 'Often the inward trouble grows so fierce, / That mortal strength, unable to endure it, / Either the body yields, and thus Death / Through her brother's power prevails, / Or else so vehemently love incites them, / That the rustic clown / Or the tender maiden / End their own lives with violent hands;' (G.H. Lewes, 'Life and Works of Leopardi' *Frazer's Magazine*, p.669); Leopardi had written that '. . . since human life is a constant war in which we are attacked by things from outside (by Nature and Fortune), our brothers, parents, and relatives are given to us as allies and helpers, etc.' (cit., P. Williams, *An Introduction to Leopardi's* Canti., University of Hull, Department of Italian, 1987, p.8). The young Leopardi expressed this same desire for death by drowning: 'Already in the first youthful turmoil / of happiness, anxiety and desire, / I often called upon Death / and sat long by the fountain / Thinking to end all my hopes and suffering / in those waters.' 'Le Ricordanze' XXII, 104–9.
12. Williams, P., *op. cit.*, pp.9–10.
13. In the reference to the 'girl-tragedies', in Daniel's fear that 'perhaps my mother was like this one' (p.231) and in Francesca's words from *Inferno* V which Daniel has been singing, there is also the muted yet insistent suggestion of adultery.
14. *Inferno* III, 3.
15. George Eliot, Journal (1860), cit. Cross, p.177.
16. Poole, A. ' "Hidden Affinities" in *Daniel Deronda*', *Essays in Criticism*, Vol. 33, 1983 (pp.294–311) p.294.
17. Sudrann, J. '*Daniel Deronda* and the Landscape of Exile', *ELH* 37 (1970), p.446. Other similar scenes are the recognition between Mordecai and Deronda on Blackfriars Bridge, the curse on the Grandcourt diamonds, and the panel and the dead face in Gwendolen's Hermione tableau.
18. See my discussion of Dante in Chapter 8.

19. Laski, M., 'The music of *Daniel Deronda*' in *The Listener*, September 23rd, 1976, p.374.

20. 'Joseph Leo' thus contributes to the urgent concern with the completion of the process of the Italian *Risorgimento* which is present in *Daniel Deronda* (pp.793–4). See my discussion in Chapter 10, pp.179–82.

21. Alfieri refused to stop on his journey to visit the poet and reported this in his *Autobiography*: '[In 1796] I might easily, during my stay at Vienna, have been introduced to the celebrated poet Metastasio... But I declined [...] I had seen Metastasio... perform the customary genuflection to Maria Theresa in such a servile and adulatory manner that I...could not think of binding myself either by the ties of familiarity or friendship with a poet who had sold himself to a despotism which I so cordially detested...' (Alfieri, cit. Beales, D., in *The Risorgimento and the Unification of Italy*, Longman, London [1971] 1981, pp.97–8). George Eliot had read Alfieri's *Vita* (*Autobiography*) with Lewes while in Italy in 1860 (*Biography*, p.325) and reread it with Cross in Italy in 1880 (*Letters* VII, p.295). Metastasio is often contrasted with Dante, who refused to prostitute his Muse (see, for example, Mazzini, G., 'Dell'amor patrio di Dante' in *Edizione nazionale degli scritti di Giuseppe Mazzini*, VI (Letteratura) Vol.1, Galeati, Imola 1906, p.21).

22. George Eliot, epigraph to Chapter 11 of *Daniel Deronda*: 'The beginning of an acquaintance whether with persons or things is to get a definite outline for our ignorance' (p.145).

23. Witemeyer, H., 'Portraiture in *Daniel Deronda*', *Nineteenth-Century Fiction* 30 (1975–76), pp.489–90.

24. Cirillo, A. cit. Witemeyer, *Ibid.*, p.493.

25. Witemeyer, *op. cit.*, pp.493, 478.

26. Witemeyer, *ibid.*, pp.478, 487; Rivkah Zim discusses Eliot's conscious use of strategies, intended to enable the reader to approach forms of experience which would have been remote from the Anglo-Saxon reader through representing 'the remote and unknown...in terms of a common denominator' (p.223). 'Awakened Perceptions in *Daniel Deronda*' in *Essays in Criticism* 36, (1986), pp.210–34.

27. One reviewer wrote of 'the utter want of sympathy [between the author and her readers] with the motive and leading idea of her story....The author is ever driving at something foreign to [readers'] habits of thought,' while for another the novel's ending creates 'a sense of bewilderment and affront' in the reader. (*The Academy*, September 9th, 1876 and *The Saturday Review* September 16th, 1876, cit. Zim, *op. cit.*, p.231).

28. Poole, *op. cit.*, p.309.

Chapter 10

1. J. de Maistre *Correspondance diplomatique, 1811–1817*, Paris 1860, cit. Beales, D. in *op. cit.*, p.117; *Punch*, October 27th, 1860,

reproduced in Morrogh, M., *The Unification of Italy*, (Documents and Debates), Macmillan, Basingstoke and London, 1991, p.97.

2. See Chapter 2 pp.35ff.
3. *Letters IV*, pp.199–200 (August 1st, 1865).
4. Eliot, Letter to Mrs Peter Taylor, March 17th, 1872, *Letters V*, p.258; *The Spanish Gypsy* (End of Book I).
5. Paul, H., ed., *Letters of Lord Acton to Mary Gladstone* New York, 1904, p.326. Lord Acton (Historian and Professor of Modern History at Cambridge), cooperated with John Cross on *George Eliot's Life as Related in Her Letters and Journals* (1885).
6. Harriet Martineau, 'Political Agitators' in *Once a Week* V December 1861, p.698; Elizabeth Barrett Browning, *Letters*, (2 Vols) ed. F.G. Kenyon (London: Smith Elder 1897), Vol.II p.442.
7. The Catholic Alphonse Balleydier describes him in 1851 as 'the greatest enemy of Italy... Like a bird of ill-omen, his presence is a sign of evil. With every step he provokes catastrophe, with every word he brings a storm; his heart is a revolutionary volcano, his glance a demagogic lava. For him, mankind is nothing, the idea everything...' (*Historie de la Révolution de Rome*, Tome II, Libraire européenne, Genève, 1851, pp.35–6: cit., Bracalini, *Mazzini* (Milano: Mondadori 1994), pp.227–8.
8. *Daniel Deronda*, Epigraph to Chapter 16, p.202.
9. Dante *Inferno* XV (37–9). The falling flakes of fire, imaging mental torment as physical pain, suggest Daniel's feelings of shame. The flakes of fire form part of the *contrappasso* of the sodomites in the seventh circle of Hell, where Dante encounters his teacher and mentor Brunetto Latini.
10. c.f. Lewes' description of Col. Peard in Genoa (see Chapter 2, p.47).
11. c.f. the 'occhi tardi e gravi' from Dante which characterize Daniel (p.500), and the comparison with portraits by Titian (p.226).
12. Bolton King, H., *Life of Mazzini*, p.6. Though not a contemporary, Bolton King's account conveys well the impression Mazzini made on observers; Giovanni Ruffini's *Lorenzo Benoni* (written in English in 1853) includes a character, Fantasio, who is clearly intended to be Mazzini. Rudman in *Italian Nationalism and English Letters* (pp.108–9) quotes Ruffini's description of Fantasio/Mazzini.
13. See *Life and Writings of Joseph Mazzini* London: Smith, Elder and co., Vol. I, Autobiographical and Political, (1870) 1890, pp.1–3. Eliot may have read Mazzini's account in *Life and Writings*, though it was published in Italian in 1861. The same passage from Mazzini is alluded to again in 'The Moden Hep! Hep! Hep!': 'The pathos of his country's lot pierced the *youthful soul* of Mazzini, because, like Dante's, his blood was fraught with the kinship of Italian greatness, his imagination filled with the majestic past that wrought itself into a majestic future' (my italics) (*Theophrastus*, pp.169–70).
14. Like Dante, the 'Father of Italy', Mordecai is imaged as a visionary who transmits his own poetry to future generations ('My words may rule him some day....It is so with a nation – after many days' (p.533)). He, too, is a 'father', for his passionate vision 'is something

more than a grandiose transfiguration of the parental love that toils, renounces, endures, resists the suicidal promptings of despair – all because of the little ones, whose future becomes present to the yearning gaze of anxiety' (593). He is also explicitly linked to Dante, when Daniel furnishes lodgings for him with 'bas-reliefs of Milton and Dante' (p.606); Cortese (*op. cit.*, pp.17–18) suggests Dante's *Purgatorio* XVII, (29–30), which Eliot knew particularly well, as a possible source in Dante for Mordecai: 'the just Mordecai who was in speech and deed so blameless'.

15. Mazzini's frequently quoted motto ('Pensiero ed azione') indicated the means by which he hoped to achieve Italian unity. The principles and precise political programme upon which Mazzini had founded 'Young Italy' were to be translated into action through constant efforts to educate the people to receive his ideas and through insurrectionary actions.

16. *The Times* Wednesday, June 19th, 1844, cit. Jack, I., *Browning's Major Poetry*, (Oxford Clarendon, 1973) p.89; Robert Browning's poem 'The Italian in England' (1845) may well have been inspired by Mazzini, the 'Italian in England' *par excellence*.

17. GE to Mrs Peter Taylor, August 1st, 1865, *Letters* IV, p.199.

18. Myers, W., *op. cit.*, p.214.

19. See Chapter 9, pp.161ff.

20. *Ibid.*, pp.164–5.

21. James Picciotto in the *Gentleman's Magazine*, November 1876, xvii, pp.593–603, cit. *George Eliot: the Critical Heritage*, D. Carrol (ed.), (London: Routledge and Kegan Paul 1971), p.410.

22. In his essay 'On a European Literature' in which he quotes Goethe as an epigraph: 'I glimpse the dawn of a EUROPEAN LITERATURE: it will belong to no single people; each will have contributed to its making. GOETHE' (*Scritti di Giuseppe Mazzini*, Vol.1 (Letteratura Vol. 1), pp.177–222).

23. GE, *Theophrastus*, p.168.

24. *Biography*, p.416.

25. To Charles Lee Lewes from Venice on June 9th (*Letters* VII, p.293). While in Venice they read, Alfieri's *Autobiography* (see Chapter 9, fn.21).

26. Eliot Letter to Barbara Bodichon, August 1st, 1880, cit. Cross, iii, p.295.

27. Cross, iii, pp.293–4.

28. Uglow, J., *op. cit.*, p.248.

29. *Theophrastus*, pp.169–70.

30. *Ibid.*, p.172.

31. GHL to Elma Stuart (July 10th, 1878) *Letters* VII, p.39; see also *Letters* IX, p.234.

32. July 8th, 1878, *Letters* VII, p.37; Eliot is quoting *Inferno* XI, 45 ('lamenting where he should rejoice') from memory; it should read 'dee giocondo'. The second line from Dante is a *mis*quotation from *Inferno* VII, 121–2: 'We were sullen in the sweet air that is gladdened by the sun.' ['Tristi fummo / nell'aere dolce che dal sol s'allegra']. Eliot

writes 'rilume' (= rilucere – shine) instead of 's'allegra' (= gladdens). She had used the same lines (again slightly misremembered) to describe her own 'disposition to melancholy' in a letter to Barbara Bodichon four years earlier (July 16th, 1874): 'I ought to have said then, but did not, that I am no longer one of those whom Dante found in a Hell-border because they had been sad under the blessed daylight. I am uniformly cheerful now – feeling the preciousness of these moments in which I still possess love and thought' (*Letters* VI, p.70).

33. Simcox, E. *Autobiography*, cit. *Letters* IX, p.258. The passage Eliot quoted was Virgil's words to Dante from *Purgatorio* XII, 84: 'Remember that to-day never dawns again.'

34. August 26th, 1878, *Letters* VII, p.64; the source is *Purgatorio* XX, 3 – 'I drew the sponge unfilled from the water' – where Dante's curiosity is not satisfied by his exchange with Pope Adrian V.

35. Cross, iii, pp.359–60, cit., *Letters* VII, pp.139–40.

36. Letter to Mrs Elma Stuart, June 18th, 1879, *Letters* VII, p.169 (see also *Letters* VII, p.210). Eliot, again misquotes the line (see note 32). In discussing the same lines in *The Stones of Venice* (1853), John Ruskin had expressed a similar sentiment to Eliot's and commented on 'the profound truth couched under the attachment of so terrible a penalty to sadness or sorrow', and concluded 'I do not know words that might with more benefit be borne with us, and set in our hearts momentarily against the minor regrets and rebelliousnesses of life, than these simple ones' (*The Stones of Venice*, Vol II (Illustrated Edition), George Allen , London 1905, p.325). Ruskin quotes the same words again in *Modern Painters*, Vol. III, cit., *The Literary Criticism of John Ruskin*, Doubleday, NY, 1965 (reprinted by Da Capo Press, New York,), p.104. One wonders whether Eliot's attention might first have been drawn to these lines by Ruskin.

37. *Biography*, p.517.

38. 'Less shame washes away a greater fault than thine has been' *Inferno* XXX, 142; Letter to Mrs Burne-Jones, October 18th, 1879, *Letters* VII, p.212.

39. *Letters* VII, p.232.

40. Eliot to Florence Nightingale Cross, Milan, May 25th, 1880 (*Letters* VII, p.285). The reference to the souls in penance is to the Sixth Terrace of *Purgatorio* XXIII (64–6) on which Gluttony is purged.

41. *Letters* IX pp.310–11; Cross is referring to *Paradiso* XVII, 58.

42. October 16th, 1879, *Letters* VII, p.212.

43. *Middlemarch*, p.246; *Letters* IX, p.311.

44. George Eliot to Eleanor Cross, *Letters* VII, p.273.

45. GE to Charles L. Lewes, May 21st, 1880, cit. Cross, iii, pp.285–6; GE to Barbara Bodichon, June 1st, 1880, cit. Cross, iii, p.290

46. *Ibid.*, pp.290, 296.

47. Simcox, E. *Autobiography*, cit. *Biography*, pp.544–5.

48. *Biography*, p.528.

49. *George Eliot's Blotter: A Commonplace-Book*, The British Library, London 1980, p.18.

50. *Inferno* II, 56–7: Haight misspells 'piana' as 'piane'.

51. See my discussion in Chapter 7, pp.138–40.
52. Eliot wrote to Mrs Burne-Jones: 'If [the marriage] alters your conception of me so thoroughly that you must henceforth regard me as a new person, a stranger to you, I shall not take it hardly,... Always, in all changes either with you or me, I shall be your deeply attached friend' (*Letters* VII, pp.269–70). A Mrs Jebb, who met Eliot in 1880 believed, for example, that 'such a marriage is against nature' (cit. *Biography*, p.545).
53. The portraits (or busts) of Savonarola and Dante were probably given to her by Mrs Elma Stuart. (See *Letters* p.233.) Eliot read and summarized Professor H. Welcker's 'Der Schädel Dante's,' in *Jahrbuch der Deutschen Dante-Gesellschaft*, I, (1867), 35–6. (*George Eliot's Middlemarch Notebooks: A Transcription* Edited with and Introduction by John Clark Pratt and Victor A. Neufeld. University of California Press, Berkeley 1979, pp.17–18, 111).
54. Trollope, T.A., *op. cit.*, p.223.
55. GE to Mrs Elma Stuart, September 17th, 1873, *Letters* V, p.437.
56. January 4th, 1880, *Letters* VII, p.241, fn. 2.
57. Ellis, S., *op. cit.*, p.65.
58. Seymour Kirkup, letter to Gabrielle Rossetti, cit., Ellis *ibid.*, p.104.
59. See Ellis *op. cit.*, pp.51–2.
60. cit., Ellis *op. cit.*, p.49: 'The Hero as Poet' (1840) cit, Ellis, *op. cit.*, p.63.
61. *Letters* VII, p.37 (see also fn. 32 above).
62. cit., Ellis, *op. cit.*, p.56.
63. cit., Ellis, *op. cit.*, p.112.
64. To Barbara Bodichon May 29th and June 1st, 1880, cit. Cross, iii, p.290.
65. GE, 'How We Come to Give Ourselves False Testimonials and Believe in Them' in *Theophrastus*, p.127.
66. GE, *Letters* III, p.339.

Bibliography

Adams, I., (ed.) *This Particular Web: Essays on Middlemarch*, Toronto University Press, Toronto 1975

Argyle, G., *German Elements in the Fiction of George Eliot, Gissing and Meredith*, Peter Lang, Frankfurt 1979

Ashton, R., *George Eliot*, OUP, Oxford and New York 1983

—— *George Henry Lewes: a Life*, Clarendon Press, Oxford 1991

Baker, W., *The George Eliot and George Henry Lewes Library. An Annotated Catalogue of their Books at Dr. Williams's Library, London*, Garland, New York and London 1977

—— *Some George Eliot Notebooks: an edition of the Carl H. Pforzheimer Library's George Eliot holograph notebooks MMS 707–711*, (4 vols), Salzburg Studies in English Literature, Romantic Reassessment 46, Salzburg 1976–85

Balbo, C., *Vita di Dante Alighieri* (Nuova edizione – con correzioni e giunte inedite lasciate dall'Autore) Unione Tipografico – Editore Torinese 1857

Barrett Browning, E., *Letters*, F.G. Kenyon (ed.), (2 Vols), Smith Elder, London 1897

—— *Aurora Leigh: with Other Poems*, (Introduced by Cora Kaplan), The Women's Press, London 1978

Bates, R., 'The Italian with White Mice in *Middlemarch*' in *Notes and Queries*, December 1984, 497

Beales, D., *The Risorgimento and the Unification of Italy*, Longman, London (1971) 1981

—— *England and Italy 1859–60*, Nelson, London 1961

Beaty, J., 'The Forgotten Past of Will Ladislaw', *Nineteenth-Century Fiction* 13 (1958–59), 159–63

Beer, G., *George Eliot*, The Harvester Press, Brighton 1986

Bennett, J., *George Eliot: Her Mind and Her Art*, CUP, Cambridge 1954

Bertone, G. e Surdich, L., *La letteratura italiana*, Minerva Italica, Bergamo 1990

Blake, K., '*Armgart* – George Eliot on the Woman Artist', *Victorian Poetry*, 18, (1980), 75–80

Bloom, H. (ed.), *The Literary Criticism of John Ruskin*, Da Capo Paperback, New York 1965

Bolton King, H., *Life of Mazzini*, Dent, London 1912

Bonaparte, F., *The Tryptich and the Cross: the Central Myths of George Eliot's Poetic Imagination*, New York University Press, New York 1979

Botting, F., *Gothic*, Routledge, London and New York 1996

Bracalini, R., *Mazzini*, Oscar Mondadori, Milano 1994,

Brand, C.P., *Italy and the English Romantics: the Italianate Fashion in early nineteenth-century England*, CUP, Cambridge 1957

—— 'Dante and the English Poets', in Limentani, U. (ed.) *The Mind of Dante*, CUP 1965, 163–200

—— 'Byron and the Italians', *Byron Journal* I, (1973) 14–21

Brontë, C., *Jane Eyre*, Penguin Popular Classics, Harmondsworth 1994

Burgan, W., 'Little Dorrit in Italy', *Nineteenth-Century Fiction* 29, (1975), 393–411

Caesar, M. (ed.), *Dante: the Critical Heritage 1314(?) – 1870*, Routledge, London 1989

Candeloro, G., *Storia dell'Italia moderna*, (10 Vols.), Feltrinelli, Milano 1956

Carlyle, T., *Sartor Resartus / On Heroes and Hero Worship* Introduced by W.H. Hudson, Everyman's Library, Dent, London (1908) 1965

Carroll, D. (ed.), *George Eliot: the Critical Heritage*, Routledge and Kegan Paul, London 1971

Chadwick, O., 'Young Gladstone in Italy', *Journal of Ecclesiastical History*, (1979), 243–59

Churchill, K., *Italy and English Literature 1764–1930*, Macmillan, London and Basingstoke 1980

Cooksey, T.L., 'Dante's England, 1818: The Contribution of Cary, Coleridge, and Foscolo to the British Reception of Dante', *Papers on Language & Literature*, XX, No. 4 (Fall 1984), 355–81.

Cortese, R., *George Eliot and Dante*, (unpublished Ph.D.) University of Winsconsin-Madison 1981

Coveney, P., Introduction to *Felix Holt, the Radical*, Penguin, Harmondsworth 1972

Cross, J., *George Eliot's Life as Related in Her Letters and Journals. Arranged and Edited by Her Husband, J.W. Cross*, (3 Vols.), Blackwood & Sons, Edinburgh and London 1885

Dale, P., 'Symbolic Representation and The Means of Revolution in *Daniel Deronda*', *The Victorian Newsletter* 59, Spring 1981

Dante Alighieri, *Vita Nuova (Poems of Youth)* translated by Barbara Reynolds, Penguin, London 1969

—— *Vita Nuova – Rime* a cura di F. Chiappelli, Mursia, Milano 1965

—— *De Monarchia*; traduzione italiana moderna e commento di E. Albino, Federico & Arcadia, Napoli 1965

—— *The Divine Comedy of Dante Alighieri*, Italian text with translation and comment by Sinclair, J.D. (3 vols.), OUP, London (1939) 1971

Dean, W. and Knapp J.M., *Handel's Operas 1704–1726*, Clarendon Press, Oxford 1987

DeCuir, A.L., 'Italy, England, and the female artist in George Eliot's "Mr. Gilfil's Love Story" ', *Studies in Short Fiction*, Vol. 29, No.1, Winter 1992, 67–75

Dictionary of Modern Italian History, F.J. Coppa (Editor-in-chief), Greenwood Press, Westport Connecticut, London England 1985

Dionisotti, C. (ed.), *The Oxford Book of Italian Verse* (2nd edn), OUP, Oxford 1952

Dobbs, B. and Dobbs, J., *Dante Gabriel Rossetti: an Alien Victorian*, Macdonald and Jane's Publishers, London 1977

Eliot, G., 'Memoirs of the Court of Austria', *WR* LXIII, April 1855, 303–35

—— 'German Wit: Heinrich Heine', *WR* LXV, January 1856, 1–33

—— 'Belles Lettres', *WR* LXV, January 1856, 290–312

—— 'The Court of Austria', *Leader* VII, April 12th, 1856, 352–3

—— 'Margaret Fuller's Letters from Italy', *Leader* VII, May 17th, 1856, 475

Eliot, G., 'Belles Lettres and Art', *WR* LXVI, July 1856, 257–8

—— 'Felice Orsini', *Leader* VII, August 30th, 1856, 835

—— 'Belles Lettres', *WR* LXVII, January 1857, 306–26

—— 'A Word for the Germans', *Pall Mall Gazette* I, March 7th, 1865, 201

—— *Scenes of Clerical Life*, Lodge, D. (ed.), Penguin, Harmondsworth 1973

—— *The Mill on the Floss*, Byatt, A.S. (ed.), Penguin, Harmondsworth 1985

—— *Romola*, Sanders, A. (ed.), Penguin, Harmondsworth 1980

—— *Felix Holt, the Radical*, Coveney, P. (ed.), Penguin, Harmondsworth 1987

—— *The Spanish Gypsy* in *Works of George Eliot* XI, (Library Edition) (12 vols.) Blackwood and Sons, Edinburgh and London 1901

—— *Middlemarch*, Harvey, W.J. (ed.), Penguin, London 1971

—— *Daniel Deronda*, Hardy, B. (ed.), Penguin, Harmondsworth 1967

—— *Impressions of Theophrastus Such; Essays and Leaves from a Note-book* in (*Works of George Eliot* X, Library Edition), Blackwood and Sons, Edinburgh and London 1901

—— *George Eliot's Blotter: A Commonplace-Book*, Whaley, D. (ed.), The British Library, London 1980

—— *Quarry for Romola.* Manuscript notebook containing notes concerning Savonarola and Florence (1861), British Library, London (Additional Manuscript no. 40768)

Ellis, S., *Dante and English Poetry: Shelley to T.S. Eliot*, CUP, Cambridge 1983

Ermarth, E., 'Incarnations: George Eliot's conception of "Undeviating Law" ', *Nineteenth-Century Fiction* 29 (1974) 273–86

Ferrari, G., *Corso sugli scrittori politic italiani*, Tipografia di F. Manini, Milano 1862

Galimberti, A., *Dante nel pensiero inglese*, Felice Le Monnier, Firenze 1921

Gilbert, S., 'From Patria to Matria; Elizabeth Barrett Browning's Risorgimento', *PMLA* 99, (1984) 194–211

Gladstone, W.E., 'The Life and Works of Giacomo Leopardi', *Quarterly Review* 86, 1850, 295–336

Gutwirth, M., *Mme de Staël Novelist: the emergence of the artist as woman*, University of Illinois Press, Urbana, Chicago, London 1978

Haight. G.S. (ed.), *The George Eliot Letters* (9 Vols.), Yale University Press and OUP, New Haven and London 1954–78

—— *George Eliot: a Biography*, Penguin, Harmondsworth (1968) 1985

—— (ed.), *A Century of George Eliot Criticism*, Methuen, London 1986

Hardy. B., *The Novels of George Eliot: A Study in Form*, Athlone Press, London 1959

—— (ed.) *Critical Essays on George Eliot*, Routledge and Kegan Paul, London 1970

—— *Particularities: Readings in George Eliot*, Peter Owen, London 1982

Harvey, W.J., *The Art of George Eliot*, Chatto & Windus, London 1961

—— 'The intellectual Background of the Novel: Casaubon and Lydgate' reprinted in Watt, I. (ed.), *The Victorian Novel*, OUP, London 1971

Hearder, H., *Europe in the Nineteenth Century 1830–1880*, Longman, London (1966) 1988

—— *Italy in the Age of the Risorgimento 1790–1870*, Longman, London 1983

Hester, E., 'George Eliot's Use of Historical Events in *Daniel Deronda*, *English Language Notes* 4 (December 1966), 115–18

Hillis Miller, J., 'Narrative and History', *ELH* 41 (1974) 455–73

Himmelfarb, G., *Lord Acton: a Study in Conscience and Politics*, Routledge and Kegan Paul, London 1952

Hirshberg, E.W., *George Henry Lewes*, Twayne Publishers, New York 1970

Jack, I., *Browning's Major Poetry*, Clarendon Press, Oxford 1973

Kimbell, D.R.B., *Verdi in the Age of Italian Romanticism*, CUP, Cambridge 1981

Kitchell, A.T., *George Lewes and George Eliot: A Review of Records*, The John Day Company, New York 1933

Knoepflmacher, U.K., *George Eliot's Early Novels: the Limits of Realism*, University of California Press, Berkeley and Los Angeles 1968

Kurata, M.J., 'Italians with White Mice again: *Middlemarch* and *The Woman in White*', *English Language Notes*, Vol. XXII, No.4 (June 1985), 45–7

Laski, M., 'The music of *Daniel Deronda*', *The Listener*, September 23rd, 1976, 373–4

Leavis, F.R., *The Great Tradition*, Chatto & Windus, London 1948
—— Introduction to *Felix Holt, the Radical*, Everyman's Library, Dent, London (1966) 1983

Lenkeith, N., *Dante and the Legend of Rome*, Mediaeval and Renaissance Studies Supplement II, The Warburg Institute, University of London 1952

Levine, G., 'Determinism and Responsibility', *PMLA*, 77 (1962), 268–79
—— (ed.), *Felix Holt*, W.W. Norton, New York 1970
—— *An Annotated Bibliography of George Eliot*, Harvester Press, Brighton 1988

Levinson, S., 'The Use of Music in *Daniel Deronda*', *Nineteenth-Century Fiction* 34 (1969), 317–34

Lewes, G.H., 'Leigh Hunt on the Italian Poets', *Foreign Quarterly Review* 36 (1846), 179–90
—— 'Life and Works of Leopardi', *Frazer's Magazine*, (December 1848), 659–69

Lineham, K.B., 'Mixed Politics: The Critique of Imperialism in *Daniel Deronda*', *Texas Studies in Literature and Language* 34, (1992) 323–46

Macaulay, T.B., 'Machiavelli' in *Critical and Historical Essays*, Longman, Brown, Green, and Longmans, London 1850, 28–50

Machiavelli, N., *The Prince*, translated by George Bull, Penguin Classics, Harmondsworth (1961) 1972

Mack Smith, D. *Italy: a Modern History*, University of Michigan Press, Michigan 1959

Manin, D., Letter in *The Times*, May 28th, 1856, 9

Mario (White) J., *Della Vita di Giuseppe Mazzini*, Edoardo Sanzogno Editore, Milano 1886

Martineau, H., 'Political Agitators', *Once a Week* V, December 1861

Mazzini, G., 'Europe: its Condition and Prospects', *WR*, April 2nd, 1852, 442–67
—— Letter in *The Times*, August 11th, 1856
—— *Life and Writings of Mazzini* (6 vols), Smith, Elder and Co., London (1870) 1891

Mazzini, G., *Edizione nazionale degli scritti di Giuseppe Mazzini*, (98 vols) Cooperativa Tipografico-editrice Paolo Galeati, Imola 1906–40

Mazzoni, G., 'Dante nell'inizio e nel vigore del Risorgimento' in *Almae luces malae cruces*, Zanichelli editore, Bologna, 1941

McCobb, A., *George Eliot's Knowledge of German Life and Letters*, Salzburg Universitat: Institut für Anglistik und Amerikanistik, Salzburg, Austria 1982

Melchiori, G., 'Byron and Italy', Byron Foundation Lecture, University of Nottingham Press, 1959

Moers, E., *Literary Women*, The Women's Press, London 1978

Moldstad, D., 'The Dantean Purgatorial metaphor in *Daniel Deronda*', *Papers on Language and Literature* 19, i, (Winter 1983), 183–98

Moore Putzell, S., 'George Eliot's Location of Value in History' in *Renascence*, Vol XXXII, No. 3, Spring 1980, 167–77

Morley, J., *Life of Gladstone*, (3 vols) Macmillan and Co., London 1903

Morrogh, M., *The Unification of Italy*, (Documents and Debates), Macmillan, Basingstoke and London 1991

Myers, W., 'George Eliot: Politics and Personality' in *Literature and Politics in the Nineteenth Century*, Lucas, J., (ed.), Methuen & Co., London 1971

—— *The Teaching of George Eliot*, Leicester University Press, Leicester 1984

Newman, F.H., *The Francesca da Rimini Episode in English Literature*, CUP, Cambridge 1942

Paul, H. (ed.), *Letters of Lord Acton to Mary Gladstone*, George Allen, New York (1904) 1906

Pell, N., 'The Fathers' Daughters in *Daniel Deronda*', *Nineteenth-Century Fiction* 36, (1982), 424–51

Pellico, S., *Le mie prigioni* (1832), Biblioteca Universale Rizzoli, Milano (1953) 1988

Petrarch, F., *Petrarch's Lyric Poems*, translated and edited by R.M. Durling, Harvard University Press, Cambridge 1976

Pinion, F.B. (ed.), *A George Eliot Miscellany*, edited with commentary and Notes, Barnes & Noble, Totowa, New Jersey 1982

Pinney, T. (ed.), *Essays of George Eliot*, Routledge and Kegan Paul, London 1963

—— 'The Authority of the Past in George Eliot's Novels', *Nineteenth-Century Fiction* 21 (1966), 131–47

Poole, A. ' "Hidden Affinities" in *Daniel Deronda*', Essays in Criticism, Vol. 33, 1983, 294–311

Pratt, J. C. and Neufeld, V. A. (eds.), *George Eliot's 'Middlemarch' Notebooks: a Transcription*, edited with an Introduction, University of California Press, Berkeley, Los Angeles and London 1979

Praz, M., 'Dante in Inghilterra (e in America)', in *Maestro Dante*, Vettori, V. (ed.), Marzorati, Milano 1962

Praz, M., *Machiavelli in Inghilterra ed altri saggi sui rapporti letterari anglo-italiani*, Sansoni, Firenze 1962

Purkis, J., *A Preface to George Eliot*, Longman, London 1985

Putzell-Korab, S.M., 'The Role of the Prophet: The Rationality of Daniel Deronda's Idealist Mission', *Nineteenth-Century Fiction* 37, (1982) 170–87

Raina, B., 'Daniel Deronda: A View of Grandcourt', Studies in the Novel 17 No. 4, Winter 1985, 271–82

Reilly, J., Shadowtime: History and Representation in Hardy, Conrad and George Eliot, Routledge, London and New York 1993

Riall, L., The Italian Risorgimento: state, society and national unification, Routledge, London 1994

Richards, E.F. (ed), Mazzini's Letters to an English Family (3 vols) John Lane, The Bodley Head, London 1920–22

Roscoe, W., The Life of Lorenzo de'Medici, (2 vols.), London 1795
—— The Life and Pontificate of Leo the Tenth, (6 vols.), London 1805

Rosenberg, B., 'George Eliot and the Victorian "Historic Imagination" ', The Victorian Newsletter 61, Spring 1982, 1–5

Rossetti, D.G., Poems and Translations by Dante Gabriel Rossetti, OUP, London (1913) 1959

Rudman, H.W., Italian Nationalism and English Letters, George Allen & Unwin, London 1940

Ruskin, J., The Stones of Venice, (3 vols), George Allen, London 1905
—— The Queen of the Air, George Allen, London 1906

Salvadori, C. (ed.), Lorenzo de'Medici: Selected Writings, Belfield Italian Library, University College Dublin 1992

Salvatorelli, L., Pensiero ed azione del risorgimento, Einaudi editore, Torino 1943

Sanders, A., The Victorian Historical Novel 1840–1880, Macmillan, London and Basingstoke 1979

Secor, C.A. , The Poems of George Eliot: a Critical Edition Unpub. ed., Cornell University Ph.D. 1969

Shannon, R., Gladstone, (Vol. 1, 1809–65), Hamish Hamilton, London 1982

Showalter, E., A Literature of Their Own British Women Novelists from Brontë to Lessing, Virago, London (1978) 1988

Sismondi, J.C.L.S., Storia Delle Republiche Italiane dei secoli di mezzo, (16 vols) Capolago presso Mendrisio, Tipografia Elvetica (1809–18) 1831
—— On the Literature of the South of Europe, translated from the original, with notes and a life of the author, by Thomas Roscoe, (2 vols), (third edn.), Henry G. Bohn, London 1850

Skelton Grant, J., 'Italians with White Mice in Middlemarch and Little Dorrit', English Language Notes, Vol. XVI, No.3 (March 1979), 232–4

Sudrann, J., 'Daniel Deronda and the Landscape of Exile', ELH 37 (1970), 433–55

Talmon, J.L., Political Messianism: The Romantic Phase, Secker and Warburg, London 1960
—— Romanticism and Revolt: Europe 1815–1848, Thames and Hudson, London 1967

Thompson, A.N., 'George Eliot, Dante and Moral Choice in Felix Holt, the Radical', The Modern Language Review, Vol. 86 Part 3, July 1991, 553–66

Times, The, 'The Italian occupation of Rome', September 28, 1870

Toffanin, G., 'Ciò che Dante rappresentò nel risorgimento italiano' in Perchè l'umanesimo comincia con Dante, Zanichelli editore, Bologna 1967, 183–207

Tosello, M., *Le Fonti Italiane della 'Romola' di George Eliot*, G. Giappichelli editore, Torino 1956

Trevelyan, G.M., 'The War Journals of Garibaldi's Englishman', *Cornhill Magazine*, January 1908, 96–110

—— *Garibaldi and the Thousand*, Longmans, Green and Co., London 1910

—— 'Englishmen and Italians' in *Recreations of an Historian*, Thomas Nelson and Sons, London 1919

Trollope, T.A., *What I Remember*, Herbert Van Thal (ed.), William Kimber, London 1973

Tye, J.R., 'George Eliot's Unascribed mottoes', *NCF* 22 (1967–68), 235–49

Uglow, J., *George Eliot*, Virago, London 1987

Vassallo, P., *Byron: The Italian Literary Influence*, Macmillan, London 1984

Viglione, F., *L'Italia nel pensiero degli scrittori inglesi*, Bocca Editore, Milano 1946

Villari, P., *La Storia di Girolamo Savonarola e de'suoi tempi* (1861), translated by Linda Villari as *Life and Times of Girolamo Savonarola*, T. Fisher Unwin, London 1897

—— *Machiavelli e i suoi tempi* (3 vols) Successori le Monnier, Firenze 1877

Viotti, A., *Garibaldi: the revoutionary and his men*, Blandford Press, Poole 1979

Watt, I. (ed.), *The Victorian Novel*, OUP, London 1971

Whitfield, J. H., *Leopardi's Canti: Translated into English Verse*, G. Scalabrini Editore, Napoli 1962

Wiesenfarth, J., *George Eliot's Mythmaking*, Carl Winter Universitätsverlag, Heidelberg 1977

—— (ed.), *George Eliot: A Writer's Notebook 1854–1879*, University of Virginia, Charlottesville Virginia 1981

Williams, D., *Mr George Eliot: A Biography of George Henry Lewes*, Hodder & Stoughton, London 1983

Williams, P., *An Introduction to Leopardi's Canti*, University of Hull, Department of Italian, Hull 1987

—— 'Leopardi in the English-speaking World: a Bibliography', *Italian Studies*, Vol. XLIII, 1988, 41–59

Witemeyer, H., 'English and Italian Portraiture in *Daniel Deronda*', *Nineteenth-Century Fiction* 30 (1975–76), 477–94

—— *George Eliot and the Visual Arts*, Yale University Press, New Haven and London 1979

Woolf, S., *A History of Italy 1700–1860: the Social Constraints of Political Change*, Methuen, London 1979

Wright, H.G., *Boccaccio in England from Chaucer to Tennyson*, Athlone Press, London 1957

Young, G.M. (ed.), *Early Victorian England 1830–1865*, OUP, Humphrey Milford, London 1934

Zim, R., 'Awakened Perceptions in *Daniel Deronda*', *Essays in Criticism* 36/3 (1986), 210–34

Zimmermann, B., '*Felix Holt* and the True Power of Womanhood', *ELH* 46 (1979), 432–51

Zuccato, E., *Coleridge in Italy*, Cork University Press, Cork 1996

Index